Mr. Darcy Came to Dinner

A PRIDE & PREJUDICE FARCE

JACK CALDWELL

WHITE SOUP PRESS

MR. DARCY CAME TO DINNER – A Pride & Prejudice farce

For information, address Jack Caldwell, P.O. Box 592, DeForest, WI, 53532.

http://webpages.charter.net/jvcla25/
http://whitesouppress.com/
http://austenauthors.net/

ISBN: 978-0-9891080-0-3

Layout & design by Ellen Pickels
Cartoon design by Elaine Eigel

Dedication

**To Barbara,
the joy of my life.**

In Appreciation

To **Debbie Styne**, **Ellen Pickels**, and **Mary Anne Mushatt**,
for their endless hours editing this work.

To **Moss Hart** and **George S. Kaufman**,
for showing me the way.

To **Jane Austen**,
for her genius.

I could not have done it without all of you.

Chapter 1

Elizabeth Bennet was not having a good day. Her sister Lydia's intention of walking to Meryton had not been forgotten even though there was company for dinner. Every sister except Mary agreed to go, and their cousin Mr. Collins was to attend them at the request of Mr. Bennet, who was most anxious to be rid of him for an hour or so. Elizabeth would much rather *not* go, but she obeyed her mother's entreaties and set off on the excursion with the others, discontentment filling her mind.

At twenty years of age, Elizabeth was the second of five daughters born to an obscure country gentleman from Hertfordshire. She was of middling height with a light and pleasing figure and was complimented frequently on her rich brown curly hair, sparkling eyes, and excellent teeth. She would be considered the beauty of her family if not for her eldest and youngest sisters.

Jane, the eldest, possessed all that a lovely English rose could possibly want — save fortune and connections — and Lydia, while very young and very silly, was vivacious, usually in good spirits, and womanly for her age. The middle two sisters — poor Mary and Catherine, who went by the name of Kitty — were overlooked in comparison to their siblings. Mary took refuge in her books while Kitty parroted Lydia's antics.

Elizabeth overcame her shortcomings in appearance by sharpening her mind. She prided herself on her discernment and wit, and many a pretentious person was the unknowing subject of her condescension. This was an occupation she shared with her father, who was as misanthropic as his favorite daughter was otherwise sociable and friendly. From Mrs. Bennet, Lizzy, as she was known to her family, inherited little save good looks and a jolly countenance.

Alas for our heroine — for Elizabeth Bennet is the heroine of our tale — she had no brothers, and her father's modest estate of Longbourn was entailed upon the son of a cousin. Because of this state of affairs, Mrs. Bennet's failure to produce a male heir resulted in that lady's obsession with making fine marriages for all her girls. While it would be well that the Miss Bennets find happiness in the matrimonial state, the primary motivation for their mother was her own house and board should she survive her good husband. A vision of starving in the hedgerows was her constant nightmare.

Therefore, when said cousin arrived to repair the breach between the Collins and Bennet families, Mrs. Bennet was determined that the young man would marry one of her girls. In that way, Mrs. Bennet could realistically expect to remain mistress of Longbourn until the time came for her to receive her heavenly reward.

You, gentle reader, knowledgeable in the ways of the world, might wonder at Mrs. Bennet's reasoning. Surely upon Mr. Bennet's demise, her son and daughter would establish the mourning widow in the dowager cottage. Such an idea never occurred to Mrs. Bennet. A daughter of hers, tossing her mother out of Longbourn? Unthinkable! This denial only fueled the good lady's fixation.

The Reverend William Collins of Hunsford was a tall, heavy look-ing young man of five and twenty with a grave and stately air, formal manners, and a rather empty head. He could read and write — useful talents for someone in his profession — but he lacked the intellectual capacity to understand fully what he read or wrote. He learned as little as possible at university, and it was only due to a fortunate chance that he enjoyed a somewhat prosperous living in Hunsford rather than earning his bread as a missionary in some faraway place such as Africa or India. Lady Catherine de Bourgh was his patroness, and such was the man's gratitude that others might wonder whether he had exchanged worship of the Almighty for glorification of the mistress of Rosings Park, Kent.

Now established as a vicar, Mr. Collins was determined that, since he was the heir to Longbourn, it was only right that the next lady of that estate should be chosen from the daughters of Mr. Bennet. Such was his generous object in visiting Hertfordshire, and his plan did not vary on seeing the ladies. His first choice was the eldest, but a quarter-hour's *tête-à-tête* with Mrs. Bennet before breakfast disabused him of that notion as the general expectation was that the lady would soon receive an offer from a very respectable gentleman of five thousand pounds per annum! Mr. Collins had only to change his favor from Jane to Elizabeth — equal next to Jane in birth and beauty — and it was soon done, even while Mrs. Bennet was stirring the fire.

Lizzy, as one might imagine from reading the earlier description of the lady, was not at all happy about this turn of events. Dutiful daughter she might be, but loyalty had its limits. Nothing could be further from her notions of an agreeable companion for her future life than this vainglorious, simple-minded, fool of a minister, but her veiled protests to her mother went unheard and unheeded.

This situation was but one ingredient in Lizzy's stew of discontent. Company was invited to dinner that evening: the agreeable tenant of neighboring Netherfield Manor, his disagreeable relations, and his haughty guest. Mr. Bingley was by all accounts a complying and pleasant man with happy manners and generous conversation. He also had the excellent taste apparently to be enchanted by Miss Bennet, a situation that had much to recommend it.

His sister, Mrs. Hurst, was condescending and ill informed, while the other sister, Miss Bingley, was obnoxiously superior. What was especially insufferable about these two ladies was their hypocrisy. They believed their brother's income of five thousand pounds from the Funds entitled them to look down upon the family of Mr. Bennet and his modest two thousand a year even though the Bingleys' roots were in trade. Old Mr. Bingley worked himself to death on the docks of London to make the money that would ensure his progeny became part of the gentry. Of Mr. Hurst, little could be said; he was more interested in cards and brandy than in partaking of the other delights of country society.

Mr. Darcy was another matter altogether. It was whispered he was the owner of a fine estate in Derbyshire, which brought him ten thousand a year, and counted among his relations earls, bishops, and judges. A darkly handsome man of eight and twenty, he was tall and well-formed and surely would be in the dreams of every maiden in Meryton if he had proven to be as open and friendly as he was rich. Unfortunately, it was not two days after his arrival at Netherfield that the whole of Meryton declared the gentleman to be proud and disagreeable, well above the common folk of Hertfordshire.

It was enough that Lizzy had to share dinner with her unctuous cousin, but three hours at table with the Superior Sisters and Mr. Tolerable — for she had overhead an ungracious remark from the gentleman at the last assembly dance — was almost more than she could endure.

A third vexation was Mrs. Bennet's nerves. The lady of the house was in an uproar, dashing about as if the Prince Regent were due at the door any moment. To be fair, Mrs. Bennet might be a pickle short of a peck, but there was no better table set in Hertfordshire than at Longbourn. She soon decided that the presence of her darling daughters and hateful cousin — she would not forgive the man his existence until he was her son — was a distraction that could no longer be borne. She must have peace and quiet if she was to prepare a masterpiece that would cause Mr. Bingley to fall upon his knee and claim Jane for his own.

Thus was Lizzy's state of mind as the party rambled the miles to Meryton on a fine November day. In pompous nothings on Mr. Collins's side and civil assents on that of his cousins, their time passed till they entered the village. The attention of the younger ones was then no longer to be gained by him, and their eyes immediately wandered up the street in quest of officers; nothing less than a smart bonnet or new muslin in a shop window could recall them.

However, the attention of every lady was soon caught by a young man of most gentlemanlike appearance whom they had never seen before, walking on the other side of the way with an officer of their acquaintance, a Mr. Denny by name. The civilian's appearance was greatly in his favor. He had all the best part of beauty — a fine countenance, a good figure, and very pleasing address. All wondered who he could be, and an introduction was soon entreated. The gentleman was a Mr. Wickham, a native of Derbyshire, lately from London, who had accepted a commission in the militia that very week.

The whole party was still standing and talking together very agreeably when the sound of horses drew their notice, and Mr. Darcy and Mr. Bingley were seen riding down the street. On distinguishing the ladies of the group, the two gentlemen came directly towards them and began the usual civilities. Mr. Bingley was the principal spokesman.

"Miss Bennet!" cried he from horseback. "We were just on our way to Longbourn to inquire after you. Were we not, Darcy?" he said as he reluctantly tore his eyes from the lady.

Mr. Darcy corroborated the truth of Bingley's account with a bow and had just fixed his eyes on Elizabeth when he was suddenly distracted by the sight of the stranger. Both changed color; one looked white, the other red. Mr. Wickham, after a few moments, touched his hat — a salutation that Mr. Darcy barely deigned to return.

Elizabeth happened to see the reaction of both as they looked at each other and was all astonishment at the effect of the meeting. What could be the meaning of it? It was impossible to imagine; it was impossible not to long to know.

Jane seemed not to notice anything remarkable about the meeting. "We are just collecting a few items for our mother. She is so looking forward to our dinner tonight. May I introduce you to our cousin? This gentleman is Mr. Collins from Hunsford."

Mr. Darcy tore his furious gaze from a slightly quaking Mr. Wickham. "Hunsford, did you say?" he enquired more pointed than polite.

"Indeed," injected the clergyman. "I have the very good fortune to have earned the Hunsford living thanks to the condescension of my very great patroness, Lady Catherine de Bourgh of Rosings Park." The tall, fat man bowed deeply. A chuckle could be heard from Mr. Wickham.

"I say, Darcy," said Mr. Bingley, "that is your aunt, is it not?"

Mr. Darcy acknowledged it was so, an intelligence that sent Mr. Collins into raptures.

"Of course! Mr. Darcy — the nephew of the esteemed Lady Catherine de Bourgh!" The gentleman took off his hat, placed his free hand over his heart, and executed a full bow from the waist. "What an honor for me! Forgive me not knowing you on sight. Such a noble visage can only belong to the family Fitzwilliam. You see, Lady Catherine has kindly acquainted me with her splendid heritage. I can assure you, sir, of Lady Catherine's good health and that of Miss Anne de Bourgh, too. Your intended is surely the finest flower in Kent — nay, all England! It will be a great day in Hunsford when you take her away from us."

Elizabeth was surprised to hear that Mr. Darcy was an engaged man. No one in Hertfordshire had any notion of it, and for some reason, the information troubled her.

For his part, Mr. Darcy's crimson countenance did not fade, but his chin rose and his eyes narrowed. "*Who* did you say you were, sir?" he demanded, his voice as cold as a strong winter's breeze.

The vacuous vicar smiled. "William Collins at your service, your lordship."

"I have no title. Keep your aggrandizements to yourself." Mr. Darcy's teeth hardly moved as he hissed, "By what right do you bandy about my family's business?"

Mr. Collins did not take offence. "Lady Catherine does confide in me, my good sir. I might be looked upon as her most important counselor."

"But you are not mine!" Mr. Darcy snapped. "You would do well to remember that and that you are in Hertfordshire, not Kent. Come, Bingley!"

Mr. Bingley had witnessed the entire exchange, as had many in Meryton. He blushed and nodded from his saddle to Jane. "Miss Bennet, ladies, gentlemen — until this evening." In another minute, Mr. Bingley rode on with his friend.

Mr. Denny and Mr. Wickham walked with the young ladies to the door of Mr. Philips's house and then made their bows in spite of Miss Lydia's pressing entreaties that they would come in and even despite Mrs. Philips's throwing open the parlor window and loudly seconding the invitation.

Mrs. Philips was always glad to see her nieces. The two eldest were particularly welcome, and she was eagerly expressing her pleasure for their company when her civility was claimed towards Mr. Collins by

Jane's introduction of him. She received him with her very best polite-ness, which he returned with much more, apologizing for his intrusion without any previous acquaintance with her.

Mrs. Philips was quite awed by such an excess of good breeding, but her contemplation of one stranger was soon put to an end by exclama-tions and inquiries about another, of whom, however, she could only tell her nieces what they already knew. Mr. Denny had brought Mr. Wickham from London, and he was to have a lieutenant's commission in the ——shire. She had been watching him the last hour, she said, as he walked up and down the street.

Lydia and Kitty thought that an excellent occupation and were soon at their chosen station, but unluckily for them, no one passed the window now except a few of the officers, who, in comparison with Mr. Wickham, were proclaimed "stupid, disagreeable fellows."

This judgment did not sway the girls once they learned of a party to be hosted the next day by Mr. and Mrs. Philips for those officers or from demanding that their aunt invite her nieces too. This was agreed to, and Mrs. Philips added that they would have a nice comfortable noisy game of lottery tickets and a little bit of hot supper afterwards. The prospect of such delights was very cheering, and they parted in mutual good spirits.

As they walked home, Elizabeth related to Jane what she had seen pass between the two gentlemen. Elizabeth could not make any sense of the altercation, and though Jane would have defended either or both had they appeared to be wrong, she could no more explain such behavior than her sister.

Interspersed in Elizabeth's new sentiments about the gentleman was an unsettling feeling of disappointment. She knew no earthly reason why she should have such a feeling, but she could not rid herself of it. She made a silent vow to learn more on the morrow about the mysteri-ous Mr. Darcy from the agreeable Mr. Wickham.

FITZWILLIAM DARCY WAS NOT HAVING a good day, and he left Netherfield early for the dinner appointment at Longbourn in a dark mood. He knew his demeanor was too cross for company, and the in-tensive simpering offered by Miss Bingley only made things worse. He needed to follow his usual practice of riding his troubles away on the back of a favored horse. Unfortunately, all his mounts were in London or Pemberley, and Bingley had neglected to bring more than one. Darcy had to make do with a rented beast from Meryton.

Since coming to Hertfordshire as guest and advisor to his great friend, Mr. Bingley, Darcy found he had to deal with a pair of consternations — one expected and one not. Mr. Bingley's sister, Caroline, had long labored to attach herself to the master of Pemberley. Darcy could be a one-legged midget with a humpback, and still Miss Bingley would shower the man with compliments and flirtations. She had her cap set on Pemberley and what the estate would bring to her — full acceptance by the First Circles — but Darcy was clever and had successfully kept her at arms' length for some years. This visit would be no different.

What *was* different was Elizabeth Bennet. Darcy could not for the life of him determine what the girl was about. Since setting eyes on her at a crowded and rowdy assembly — just the sort of gathering that always set his teeth on edge — he could not get the impertinent girl out of his head. Miss Elizabeth seemed lovelier each time they met, and it almost ignited a suspicion that the lady was primping herself for his benefit, but that conjecture was dismissed by any knowledge of her character.

Did she not walk three miles in mud just to visit an ill sister? Was not her complexion the healthy glow earned by long walks in the countryside, not the smooth ivory favored by young ladies of fashion? Did she not read the works of Aristotle and poetry by Wordsworth, rather than the dreadful novels found in the sitting rooms in Town? Did Miss Elizabeth not tease and challenge him at every turn, rather than sit and simper and make tiresome conversation in the manner of Miss Bingley?

Darcy had tried to keep his distance. It would not do to raise expectations. As lovely and interesting as Miss Elizabeth was, she was not of his circle. He was expected to do right by his Darcy and Fitzwilliam heritage and bring honor and money into the family by his marriage. It was what he was raised to do. Surely he could find an agreeable companion of his future life amongst the denizens of the *ton* as his father had before him. Somewhere in England was a woman of beauty, breeding, benevolence, and fortune who could carry on an intelligent conversation. It was a mighty challenge, but Darcy was not discouraged. *Fortune Favors the Bold* was the family motto.

His dilemma was that this standard was met in almost every particular by Miss Elizabeth. If only she were the secret child of a viscount!

Instead, the object of his admiration was the second of five daughters born to a modest, country gentleman and the ill-tempered, silly daughter of a tradesman. Miss Elizabeth's condition in life was bad enough, but the behavior of her siblings, parents, and relations was intolerable. They were either bookish snobs who apparently lacked the wit to comprehend what they were reading, vainglorious gossips who forever disparaged their neighbors without tending to their own faults, or empty-headed fools. How did two superior ladies — Miss Bennet and Miss Elizabeth — emerge from this unfortunate situation?

Perhaps they were foundlings from a dead baron? If only Darcy and Bingley could be so lucky!

Bingley's recent preference was another problem. If Miss Elizabeth was unsuitable for him, Miss Bennet was almost as unpalatable for his friend. Bingley was trying to establish himself as a gentleman. For all of Jane Bennet's loveliness, she could do nothing for Bingley in that matter.

True, Bingley's quest for acceptance by the *ton* was half-hearted at best. Darcy knew his friend would be happy living as an obscure, country squire but only if he was happy in his marriage. Bingley was a generous, cheerful, and trusting man, just the sort to attach himself to a pretty face that hid a cold heart. If Miss Bennet was genuine in her admiration of Bingley, Darcy would raise no complaint, save to make sure Bingley knew what he was about. He had seen his friend in love before. Miss Bennet was an enigma, however. She accepted Bingley's attentions with pleasure, but Darcy could see no special regard in her interactions with him. Would Darcy have to save his friend *again*?

Tonight Darcy was to suffer the company of Miss Elizabeth and her family. To bear the pain of intercourse with the foolish Bennets while trying to withstand the allure of Miss Elizabeth's charms and attempting to digest what was sure to be an unappetizing meal was certain to be shear torture. Mr. Collins's attendance would surely only add to his misery. Darcy expected his rebuke was sufficient and that the fool would not again mention Lady Catherine's fantasy of an engagement, but Darcy was certain that there was no end to the parson's insipid conversation; Darcy's aunt would have no other type of man as her vicar. Furthermore, there would be no escape once the Netherfield party returned home. Miss Bingley was certain to rail incessantly about the unsuitability of the Bennets.

If things were not bad enough, Wickham was in town! *What is that reprobate doing here?* Was Wickham following him? Oh, Darcy knew he should have listened to his cousin Colonel Fitzwilliam and let Georgiana's other guardian deal with his sister's erstwhile suitor. If he had, Wickham would have been fortunate to survive, but he would have to deal with being so disfigured that cows would scream at his approach.

A headache was to be his reward that night; he was sure of it. He would tell his valet, Bartholomew, to prepare some white willow bark for a nightcap.

His musings were broken by the realization that it was growing dark. Blast! He had ridden too long. He needed to hurry to Longbourn, or he would be behind his time. He was justifiably proud of his attention to promptness; it would not do to be late.

Darcy looked about, got his bearings, and spurred the hired horse towards Longbourn.

ELIZABETH WALKED OUT OF THE garden of her home, her cat, Cassandra, in her arms, and wondered whether wishing her mother ill was a sign that she was a bad daughter.

Normally, Mrs. Bennet would be nervous about a dinner party. For all of her defects, the mistress of Longbourn was celebrated as a gracious hostess. It was a reputation difficult to achieve and one she was jealous to maintain, particularly as Mr. Bingley was to come to dine. Therefore, Mrs. Bennet's efforts and exclamations of calamity were redoubled, for Mr. Collins was to be impressed, as well. According to Elizabeth's mother, this dinner might mean the difference between having two daughters comfortably married and starving in the hedgerows.

Elizabeth sought quiet and received permission from a relieved Mrs. Bennet to step outside. Her mother would not have been as happy to know her daughter had retrieved her pet. The ginger-colored cat was tolerated because the girls loved her, and Mr. Bennet loved peace — peace that would be broken by the wails of the girls should the furry beast be sent away. Cassandra was an agreeable creature, at least for the girls, Mr. Bennet knew, and Elizabeth was his favorite daughter. So Mrs. Bennet's protests fell on unhearing ears, and Cassandra was firmly established at Longbourn.

Elizabeth strolled about the lane in front of the house in a thoughtful haze, her mind wondering over the events in Meryton while her hand stroked the purring feline. Mr. Wickham was declaimed by all of the Bennet girls as a handsome and agreeable man, and even Mr. Collins said some words of praise for the new lieutenant — three times as many words as necessary for the compliment. Mr. Darcy was known to be a prideful and disagreeable man, but the look on his face when he encountered Mr. Wickham was far above the disdain she would expect from the haughty gentleman. It seemed more akin to rage, disgust, and even hatred. Fear marked Mr. Wickham's countenance, as well as something else — something Elizabeth could not quite identify. She hoped to learn more from Mr. Wickham on the morrow at the Philipses'. She felt she would learn nothing that night from the silent and taciturn Mr. Darcy.

She wondered why Mr. Darcy was so angry at Mr. Collins's declaration of his engagement to Miss de Bourgh. While the gentleman gave no indication he was betrothed, that was not an unusual occurrence. Certainly it was nobody's business in Meryton as to Mr. Darcy's eligibility. But his disapproval of the words of Lizzy's foolish cousin seemed disproportionate to the offence. Did Lady Catherine de Bourgh disapprove of the match? Certainly, if Miss de Bourgh was anything like Mr. Collins's flowery description, Elizabeth could understand a loving mother's reluctance to unite a daughter for life with as unpleasant a man as Mr. Darcy, no matter what his income.

Elizabeth allowed a small chuckle to escape her lips. Mr. Darcy's set-down of Mr. Collins was very apt even if the recipient was ignorant of it. Only the manners drilled into her from birth prevented Elizabeth from saying the same to her oblivious cousin.

Elizabeth shuddered, an action that disrupted Cassandra's contentment. She knew that her mother was set on her becoming Mrs. Collins and the next mistress of Longbourn. While confident that her father would support her certain refusal of any proposal from Mr. Collins, she knew the lamentations from Mrs. Bennet would be great indeed and painful to hear. She would much rather not deal with the issue at all, but nothing Elizabeth did discouraged Mr. Collins in any meaningful way. She feared that the man's stupidity would lead inevitably to scenes unpleasant to more than one person.

Elizabeth's fine, plump lips tightened. There must be a way to put Mr. Collins off! She set her mind on the problem at the cost of her comprehension of all else. That was why she did not hear the beat of hooves until the horse was around the bend of the road.

Startled, she loosened her grip on Cassandra, and to her horror, the cat ran towards the path of the large brown stallion as its rider cried out, pulling hard on the reins. Stopping in the middle of the road, the cat arched its back and hissed before jumping away. This action was enough to cause the horse to turn and rear, and the next thing Elizabeth knew, the rider was on the ground, flat on his back, gripping his leg and screaming in pain, the horse dashing through the meadow.

Elizabeth's heart was in her mouth. "MR. DARCY!"

Mr. Darcy turned his agonized face to her, and Elizabeth was frightened to see that he had gashed his forehead in the fall. "Miss...Miss Elizabeth," he gasped, "I am afraid I require assistance." He winced and cursed, his head falling back into the dirt and dust.

Instantly, Elizabeth took to her heels and dashed inside Longbourn. Within moments, she had raised the house and returned with her parents, sisters, and Mrs. Hill, bearing cloths. Mr. Hill was dispatched without delay to Meryton to fetch Mr. Jones, the apothecary. The older ladies comforted Mr. Darcy and saw to his head wound while the others stood about in degrees of shock or amusement. Never before had Elizabeth dearly wanted to throttle her two youngest sisters.

Elizabeth was proud of her mother, however. Silly she might be, but Frances Bennet knew her remedies and, in the face of this calamity, showed great fortitude. The last time influenza visited Meryton proved that. Elizabeth expected this sensibility was only temporary, and once the immediate crisis was handled, her mother would give free rein to her baser particulars, and her nerves would run wild.

Her father, however, was a disappointment. Concerned as he was over the accident, he did little to correct Lydia or Kitty besides a weak admonishment. It fell to steady Jane to quietly scold the youngest Bennets. Mary did little more than stare.

Mr. Collins was a trial. He stood, wringing his hands, intermittently praying to the Almighty to save his worthy servant, Mr. Darcy, when he was not agonizing over what this disaster would do to the affectionate feelings of Lady Catherine de Bourgh. Elizabeth could see that Mr. Darcy was aware of his surroundings, for when not grimacing in pain, he was glaring at Mr. Collins.

"Would someone please silence that imbecile?" Mr. Darcy finally managed.

Lydia and Kitty laughed aloud, and Lizzy almost joined them. It was a shame she did not like Mr. Darcy, otherwise she would have admired him for saying what they were all thinking.

Mr. Bennet finally took it upon himself to speak to his cousin, and just then, the carriage from Netherfield came into view. Mr. Bingley was out of the vehicle before it came to a stop and dashed to his houseguest's side, Miss Bingley and the Hursts close behind.

"My God!" cried Mr. Bingley. "What has happened? Darcy — Darcy, are you well?"

Mr. Darcy pushed away Mrs. Bennet's attentions to his forehead. "Must you yell, Bingley?"

Miss Bingley was quite overcome. "Oh, Mr. Darcy! Good lord! Someone fetch a physician — this instant! Mr. Darcy, I — "

Elizabeth saw Miss Bingley's eyes go wide, and she turned to see what had paled the lady's complexion so completely. All she could see was Mr. Darcy, trying to prop himself up by one elbow, the wound on his forehead once again bleeding freely, as such injuries are wont to do.

The next instant there was the sound of a body crumpling to the road as Miss Bingley fainted dead away.

"Oh, bother! Now I have *two* people to care for," grumbled Mr. Bennet. "Come, gentlemen, let us bring them inside."

It was not a good day for Mr. Bennet.

Chapter 2

Miss Bingley was brought into the house by her brothers, and as Mr. Bennet was considered too old and Mr. Collins too nervous to perform the same service for Darcy, two coachmen were commandeered for the task. Mrs. Bennet pointed at the parlor as she led the way upstairs to a room for Miss Bingley.

"Put Mr. Darcy in there. The room is quite warm as the windows are full west."

Mrs. Hurst followed the parade upstairs, and Miss Elizabeth and Miss Bennet accompanied their father into the parlor. The other Miss Bennets gathered at the door while Mr. Collins volunteered to stand watch outside for the apothecary.

The men laid the gentleman on the couch as gently as they could. Darcy endeavored to act the gentleman; he had not uttered a sound during his transport save a grunt that escaped his lips when first lifted. By the time the party reached its destination, Darcy's face was damp with pain and aggravation. Mrs. Hill shooed the men away as she again tended to Darcy's injured forehead.

"There, there, dearie," the housekeeper said in the same soft tone that she had used years ago when caring for the girls when ill. "All will be right soon. Mr. Jones will be here in two shakes."

Darcy thought himself a man and such ministrations childish. He tried to halt Mrs. Hill's attentions. "I...I thank you, but that is not necessary." The weakness in his voice belied his words.

Mrs. Hill looked to Mr. Bennet. "I expect he could use something for the pain, sir," she said with a nod of her head towards the door. The action roused her employer from a bemused observance.

"Jane," he said, "please fetch a bottle of brandy from my book room." The lady turned, made her way through a gaggle of sisters, and was only a minute in returning with a bottle.

Mr. Bennet groaned softly. "Not my good Cognac! Another bottle, my dear." His words were soft, meant only for his daughter, but in the quiet of the room, every syllable was overhead by all, including Darcy. Lydia and Kitty found this hilarious, and Darcy saw that Miss Elizabeth blushed in mortification.

An acceptable brandy was soon acquired, and Darcy consumed the first glass quickly. Mr. Bennet poured a refill and enquired how the accident happened. Darcy glanced at a beet-red Miss Elizabeth.

"I was riding to Longbourn, and as I was slightly behind my time, I took the turn in the road rather quickly. I must have startled some animal. I had a glimpse of something furry in the road. Whatever it was, it frightened the horse, and I was thrown."

"You fell off your horse?" Mr. Bennet said in a voice that could have been kinder. "How extraordinary! Elizabeth, did you see what terrifying animal caused Mr. Darcy to be unhorsed?"

Darcy was taken aback at the older man's sarcasm. For her part, Miss Elizabeth seemed embarrassed as she said, "It was Cassandra."

"Indeed?" cried Mr. Bennet to the sound of Miss Lydia's and Miss Kitty's renewed giggles. "It seems the family cat almost did you in, Mr. Darcy!"

Darcy was angry. What sort of gentleman mocks another's misfortune? He wanted to lash out at the old fool but refrained in deference to Miss Bennet and Miss Elizabeth and settled for a dry, "How amusing," before drinking his brandy, his intense stare fully on Miss Elizabeth.

"Cassandra is very gentle. I am sure she was frightened out of her wits!" was Miss Elizabeth's defensive reply. "Such a big horse you ride, sir!"

Mr. Darcy winced as he shifted on the couch. "My apologies, Miss Elizabeth, for frightening your cat." He tried his best to keep sarcasm from creeping into his voice. He did not blame Miss Elizabeth for the mishap and hoped the girl would understand and have pity on him.

Miss Bennet, ever the peacemaker, now broke in. "We are so sorry for your misfortune, sir. Are you in very great discomfort?"

Finally some kindness! "Thank you, Miss Bennet. Do not concern yourself. The pain is *tolerable*." Mr. Darcy's eyes darted to Elizabeth's at the last word, his mouth twitched into a painful grin. Surely the lady would understand the apology in his joke. The target of his attention and admiration did widen her eyes, and Darcy thought himself clever.

During this time, Mrs. Hill gently lowered the stocking on Darcy's left leg. "The skin is not broken, sir, and there's no blood, but I cannot like the coloring. It'll be black-and-blue by morning, sure as I'm born."

Just then there was a noise from the front of the house. "Make way! Make way, I say! The apothecary is here! Gentle cousins, make way!" The girls parted, and Mr. Collins burst into the room, followed by Mr. Hill and a third man, carrying a black bag.

"Oh, my esteemed Mr. Darcy, here is deliverance! Here is care!" cried Mr. Collins, who turned to the third man. "Make haste, sir! Make haste!"

The gentleman, middle-aged and rather portly, walked directly up to Darcy. "Mr. Jones, the apothecary of Meryton, at your service. May I know your name, sir?"

"I am Mr. Darcy. Thank you for coming so quickly." Darcy hoped the man knew his business but held no real hope. He knew he had to get word to his personal physician in Town.

"No trouble at all," said the apothecary. "I understand you suffered a fall from a horse?" He glanced backward as the young Bennet girls snickered again.

"It is my leg, sir." Darcy knew the niceties had to be followed. "Tell me, is Miss Bingley well?"

Mr. Jones had begun to examine his leg and glanced up at the question. "I beg your pardon, sir?"

Mr. Darcy sighed. Was the man witless? "Miss *Bingley* — the lady who swooned. Is she well?"

Mr. Jones stood. "I know nothing of any lady. Is someone else ill?"

Darcy gaped. Did no one tell the apothecary that a lady was in distress?

Darcy had learned well many lessons from his father and family, and chief among those was that a lady's comfort *always* came first. His earliest memories were those of his honored father taking the gentlest care of his beloved mother, who often suffered from some malady or another. Mr. Darcy had hardly left his wife's side during her last decline and grieved her until the day he joined her in heaven. An indelible impact had been made on Darcy. Miss Bingley might be the disagreeable sister of a dear friend, but she deserved all the respect and deference due a lady of quality.

Miss Bennet stepped forward. "Yes. Another of our guests, Miss Bingley, fainted. She is upstairs."

"Oh, do not concern yourself about that!" Mr. Collins cried. "This is *Mr. Darcy of Pemberley* in Derbyshire!"

"Oh, I see." Mr. Jones turned to Darcy. "Am I supposed to know you, sir?"

Mr. Collins bristled. "My good man, this is the honored nephew of the esteemed *Lady Catherine de Bourgh*!"

Darcy stirred himself to growl, "Enough! Mr. Jones, please see to Miss Bingley. I can wait."

"Mr. Darcy, I must protest!"

"You may do so, Collins, so long as it is outside this room. Be gone with you." Darcy sipped from his refilled brandy glass, allowing the alcohol to loosen his tongue. He had had enough of the pompous parson. For his part, Collins blanched before fleeing the room.

"Sir," Mr. Jones objected, "your leg looks to be seriously injured, and you have a gash on your — "

"And I have full use of my wits," Darcy cut in roughly. Was anyone in Hertfordshire capable of taking instruction? "I am a gentleman, sir. You *will* see to Miss Bingley first! Do I make myself clear?"

Mr. Jones shrugged. "As you wish. Will someone show me the way?" Miss Bennet volunteered to do the service, and the two left.

Darcy turned to Mr. Hill. "I believe you are called Hill. Thank you for retrieving the apothecary. Please be so kind as to rush to Netherfield and inform my man, Bartholomew, what has befallen me. He is to send an express to London for my physician, Mr. Macmillan. Do you have that name, man? Good. Have Bartholomew bring my necessities as quickly as may be. Off with you."

Mr. Hill nodded and took to his heels without so much as a glance at Mr. Bennet. It was then Darcy remembered that Mr. Bennet was still in the room.

"My apologies, sir. I should have asked for your leave. I meant no offense."

"None taken, Mr. Darcy," Mr. Bennet quipped. "I am certain that a man of your station is used to having your own way."

Darcy turned his attentions to Miss Elizabeth. If Mr. Bennet was going to be difficult, he would waste no more time on him. Instead, he would entertain himself with a study of the lady's fine eyes, which were gazing at him in a rather peculiar and fascinating manner.

A young maid entered through another door. "Mr. Bennet, Mrs. Hill, the cook's compliments, an' she says the dinner's ready."

"Ah," said Mr. Bennet. "I do not suppose you can join us, Mr. Darcy."

Apparently, this was too much for Miss Elizabeth. "Father!"

"What? Forgive me for stating the obvious, but I do not think Mr. Darcy will be moving from my couch."

"He is quite right, Miss Elizabeth," Darcy allowed. "Thanks to this injury, I must remain." Darcy's only reason for speaking up was to give relief to the dismay written clearly across Miss Elizabeth's lovely face. As for Mr. Bennet, he could go to the devil.

Mrs. Hill turned to Darcy. "Are you hungry at all, sir? Stomach's not too upset? 'Tis usual in these cases."

Darcy thought about that. "I think I could manage something."

"Cook's white soup is very good. How's 'bout a wee bit of chicken in it? Does that sound tempting?"

"Perhaps with bread and wine?"

"Well-watered wine, sir," said Mr. Jones as he reentered the room with Bingley close at his heels. "I can report that Miss Bingley is well and resting. She suffered no injury as a result of her loss of consciousness."

Bingley was all apologies. "You know how queasy Caroline gets at the sight of blood, Darcy. How is your leg?"

"That is for Mr. Jones to determine. Please, do not forgo your dinner on my account. Go on and eat." He waved his hand imperiously.

"If you say so," said Bingley dubiously. He extended his arm to Miss Elizabeth. "Shall we?"

Miss Elizabeth took Bingley's arm, gave Darcy one more unreadable look, and left the room. Meanwhile, Mr. Bennet, erstwhile master of Longbourn, stood silent — annoyed and impotent. Finally, he nodded at his guest and followed.

Darcy felt no pity for the man. If he chose to be only an observer in life rather than a participant, then Darcy would leave him to stew in his own juices.

Mrs. Hill gestured at the young maid. "I must see to dinner service, Mr. Darcy. But here's Sally, and her responsibility is your comfort." To Sally, she continued, "Mind none of your other duties, girl, until you hear my say-so."

"Aye, ma'am." The girl beheld her charge with wide, fearful eyes. Darcy, half in his cups from the brandy, could only shake his head.

"Never mind, Mrs. Hill. I am comforted that I am in the good hands of Mr. Jones and Sally." Darcy did not really believe it, but it was in his character to treat servants kindly. "I thank you for your attentions, but leave Mr. Jones to his work." He smiled at the apothecary. "I am at your disposal, sir!"

Elizabeth found Jane and Mr. Hurst at the foot of the stairs, Mrs. Hurst remaining above with her sister. Before Elizabeth could have more than a word with Jane, Mr. Bennet bade them into the dining room in a brusque manner. An anxious Mrs. Bennet awaited them. Now that the true crisis was past, she gave free rein to her nerves.

The party that took seats about the table was not a happy one. Mrs. Bennet, when not predicting that the dinner was ruined, expressed her fears that Mr. Darcy, should he not die, would seek redress through the courts, and the Bennets would certainly end their days in the poorhouse. Mr. Bennet said little; he only glowered into his soup. Jane discussed her concerns over Miss Bingley's health with the lady's brothers. A far-from-chastised Mr. Collins held court, pontificating. The subject of his monologue was his most respected patroness — how she must suffer should she know of her dear nephew's misfortune, how attached she was to her family and village, and how astute the grand dame's opinions. This extraordinary speech held small attention about the table, save to fuel the ill-bred amusement of Kitty and Lydia. Even Mary, who had shown some interest in the parson, simply sat, bored with the whole exercise. The three empty seats were a glaring reminder of those without.

And as for Elizabeth? Hers was a mind amazed at its own discomposure. She suffered from culpability, concern, and confusion.

Certainly blame for this entire incident could be fairly laid at her door. Hers were the hands that held Cassandra. Hers was the mind that was allowed to partake in selfish introspection and, therefore, took no heed of her surroundings. Oh, if she had but remained in the garden! Now Miss Bingley was shut up in the bedroom she shared with Jane, and Mr. Darcy was ensconced on the couch in the sitting room.

Elizabeth disliked Mr. Darcy — disliked him exceedingly — but she wished no harm to anyone, even such an unpleasant man. The accident caused a jolt of pain in Elizabeth's breast of such intensity that she was astonished. Seeing the tall, handsome gentleman writhing on the ground in agony was the great shock of her young life. She told herself it was her Christian upbringing that gave her the ability to pity Mr. Darcy.

The episode in the sitting room was most disturbing. Her father she knew to be a sardonic observer of the human condition, always ready to laugh at the follies of others. Before today, she thought this wit was a sign of his intelligence. But his performance with the injured Mr. Darcy seemed that of a confirmed misanthrope. Why had she not seen this before?

Elizabeth could not help but notice Mr. Darcy's commanding personality. Injured, prone on a couch, he had taken full control of the room with a few words and a glare, while her father did little more than chuckle or sulk. Certainly, Mr. Darcy was wrong to send Hill to Netherfield without her father's leave, but in all honesty, that request should have been unnecessary. Mr. Bennet should have directly offered his people's assistance out of simple courtesy. Elizabeth toyed with the concept that Mr. Darcy, for all his other faults, was a man of action and cool thinking, while her father, jealous of his peace of mind, was not.

She could hardly believe she was giving more than a moment's attention to the matter, but she could not turn from the introspection. What did Mr. Darcy think of her? Did the man hold her accountable for his injury? Perhaps he did; his dark scrutiny was as intense as it had been at Netherfield during Jane's late illness when he looked to find fault with her. However, he graciously took the responsibility for his fall onto himself. Was this simply due to the strict training of a proud gentleman, or was there something else — and if so, what?

The comment about his *tolerable* pain — Elizabeth could almost believe Mr. Darcy was making a joke at his own expense, but she dismissed the thought instantly. Everyone knew Mr. Darcy had no sense of humor. She wondered if the man knew how funny — and just — was his set-down of Mr. Collins.

This brought to mind another mystery. When Mr. Darcy heard that Miss Bingley had been left unattended, he was almost beside himself. What could it mean? In spite of all evidence to the contrary, was Mr. Darcy favorably disposed toward Miss Bingley?

Elizabeth considered what she knew. Mr. Collins had reported that Mr. Darcy was the betrothed of Lady Catherine's daughter, and Mr. Darcy was not happy that he had announced such news. Perhaps there was a clandestine attachment between Mr. Darcy and Miss Bingley! That could account for Mr. Darcy's keeping his engagement secret. Elizabeth had thought Mr. Darcy had treated Miss Bingley with barely disguised disdain while she was in residence at Netherfield. Could that be a clever performance to deceive onlookers? Did the two laugh together behind closed doors at the people of Hertfordshire? If so, Mr. Darcy was a man without scruples.

Then, Elizabeth remembered how deferential Mr. Darcy had been with Mrs. Hill. Would a man without scruples treat another man's servant with such respect? Confusing, confusing man! She would think of him no more.

The soup was taken away, and just as the party began to partake of the next course, Mr. Jones came into the room. Mr. Bennet immediately invited the apothecary to join them to dine. This earned a comment from Mr. Collins about inappropriate condescension of a country squire — what was perhaps acceptable in Hertfordshire would not be tolerated in Kent. Mr. Bennet allowed this insult to pass without comment, and Mr. Jones took his seat — in Mr. Darcy's chair, Elizabeth noticed.

With quiet efficiency, a plate appeared before the gentleman while he gave his report. "As you know, Miss Bingley is well. She suffered no ill effects from her swoon. I understand she dines upstairs with her sister?" Assured that his information was correct, Mr. Jones continued. "I advised her to rest once she returns to Netherfield this evening. As for Mr. Darcy, he was not as fortunate. I suspect a fracture of the lower leg, the fibula, to be exact. The discoloration reveals the location of the injury, you see. Very painful, I am sorry to say."

"Oh, Mr. Jones, how dreadful!" Mrs. Bennet cried. "Shall you be able to save the leg?"

The apothecary was astonished. "Save it? Oh, most certainly, Mrs. Bennet! There are two bones in the lower leg, you see, and the fibula is the minor of the two. I have slapped a splint on it, and given quiet rest, the gentleman shall be as right as rain in a couple of months. Madam, this chicken is excellent!"

"I am glad to hear that the gentleman is on the road to recovery," said Mr. Bennet. "Mr. Bingley, would your carriage be sufficient to transport your friend back to Netherfield, or shall we use one of my wagons?"

"Transport?" cried the apothecary. "Oh, no, Mr. Bennet! The patient cannot be moved." This pronouncement was like a thunderbolt in the room.

"What? What do you mean, he cannot be moved? Certainly you are not saying he must remain here!" returned Mr. Bennet.

"We cannot take any chances. Moving Mr. Darcy may exacerbate the injury; the bone may shift, endangering the leg! No, Mr. Darcy certainly cannot be moved. It is unthinkable."

"Oh, my goodness, my nerves!" Mrs. Bennet placed a hand on her heart. "I...I must prepare a room for —"

"Madam," Mr. Jones cut in, "Mr. Darcy must not be moved at all, even upstairs. He must stay where he is."

"*In my parlor?*" the good lady cried. The apothecary nodded. Mrs. Bennet bristled. "I never heard of such a thing!"

"Mama, at least Mr. Darcy will be comfortable. It is the warmest room in the house, you always said," offered Jane.

"True, very true," Mrs. Bennet reluctantly agreed.

"Warmth is important in recovery," Mr. Jones pointed out. "Would someone please pass the potatoes?"

"This is stuff and nonsense!" Mr. Bennet proclaimed. "Mr. Darcy is not going to spend two months in my parlor!"

"Of course not," said the apothecary patiently. "He should be able to tolerate a carriage ride in four weeks or so — no longer than six weeks, certainly."

"F-four to six weeks!" cried Mr. Bennet.

"I agree with you, dear cousin. This humble abode, which sadly will one day decline to my ownership, is not fine enough for a relation of my generous patroness. Other arrangements must be made," Mr. Collins interjected.

"If you wish to endanger Mr. Darcy's leg and, therefore, his life," warned Mr. Jones, "then by all means move him. I will take no responsibility for it."

"Oh, Mr. Bennet! Think of Mr. Darcy's relations! They will have us transported to Australia!"

"Mama, please!" cried Elizabeth. "No one is going to Australia! Mr. Jones, are you quite satisfied with your diagnosis?"

"I am. As I told his valet, who arrived during my examination, Mr. Darcy should be kept quiet and warm for the next — "

The gentleman was interrupted by an extraordinary sound from without:

"Farewell and adieu to you, Spanish ladies,
Farewell and adieu to you, ladies of Spain;
For we've received orders for to sail for ole England,
But we hope in a short time to see you again!"

The table as one started at the singing — a loud baritone, slightly slurred. Everyone rose to their feet, the sound of chairs being moved all but drowned out the singing, and dashed to the sitting room, where upon opening door, they beheld Mr. Darcy, a glass of brandy in his hand bellowing:

"We will rant and we'll roar like true British sailors,
We'll rant and we'll roar all on the salt sea!
Until we strike soundings in the channel of ole England;
From Ushant to Scilly is thirty-five leagues!"

The gentleman took notice of his impromptu audience and called out to a tall, thin, white-haired man in the room, "Ah, Bartholomew, we have guests! Come in, come in!"

"I gave him laudanum," said Mr. Jones in *sotto voce*. "One cannot predict how the patient will react, especially in combination with sprits."

Shockingly, Mr. Darcy was laughing! "Come, Bingley, do not stand about in that stupid manner — fill a glass! We must sing to the ladies! I know you will not decline a glass, Hurst! Mr. Bennet, your brandy might be only adequate, but at least it is plentiful. Pour for us all, will you? Mr. Jones, too! We must sing! Sing to your good wife and fair daughters!

"Now let ev'ry man drink off his full bumper,
And let ev'ry man drink off his full glass;
We'll drink and be jolly and drown melancholy,
And here's to the health of each true-hearted lass!"

Mr. Darcy drained his glass before returning to the refrain. *"We will rant and we'll roar like true British sailors…"* Meanwhile, the other gentlemen stood in various stages of amazement, joined by most of the ladies. Kitty and Lydia were almost doubled over in laughter.

Once Mr. Darcy had finished his song, the man referred to as Bartholomew removed the glass. "Well done, sir," he said in the dry, unemotional voice of a senior servant of a rich man. "It is time to retire."

"Is it?" cried Mr. Darcy.

"Yes, sir. There is much to do tomorrow. You informed me to make certain that you get your rest."

"Did I? Well then, I suppose I must say good night to my friends."

Mr. Darcy turned to the door. "Good night, all!"

Bartholomew crossed over to the open door, his long, lanky, almost frail body blocking the view of the room to the observers without. Without preamble, he addressed the apothecary, his voice dripping with condescension. "Are there any other instructions for tonight, Mr. Jones?" He looked down the long, narrow beak of a nose, not for a moment hiding his disdain, proving the maxim there was no snob like the personal valet of a member of the Quality.

Mr. Jones only suggested a very small amount of laudanum if the patient had any difficulty sleeping. The valet gave the man a hard look. "Be aware, sir, that I have sent an express to Mr. Darcy's personal physician, the distinguished Mr. Macmillan of Park Place. He will most certainly be here in the morning."

Instead of taking insult at the servant's pronouncement, Mr. Jones seemed delighted. "Mr. Macmillan, you say? I have heard of the gentleman! Very high up in the Academy! I should be pleased to hear his diagnosis!" He turned to Mr. Bennet. "I shall stop by in the morning, then." He turned back to Bartholomew. "What time did you say he would be here?"

"I expect him no later than ten o'clock. We will not wait for you." Bartholomew then turned to Mrs. Bennet. "I take it you are Mrs. Bennet? The girl, Sally, is adequate. Please see that she is here first thing tomorrow to see to Mr. Darcy's breakfast."

Mrs. Bennet was flustered. "Of... of course. I shall tell Mrs. Hill and have her arrange quarters for you."

"That will not be necessary, madam," the valet said with only the barest civility. "I shall make do with an armchair in this room, but you may have a couple of blankets brought by. The rest of you, I would ask that you remain as quiet as possible for my master's sake."

Mr. Bennet finally roused himself to respond to the outrageous servant. "Now, see here! I am Mr. Bennet, and Longbourn is my house. Who are you to make such demands of my family?"

Bartholomew narrowed his eyes as he stared, not at Mr. Bennet's face but at his cravat. "It has been a long time since you visited Town, I see. That knot has been out of fashion for ten years." Mr. Bennet blanched, but the valet continued. "This may be your house, sir, but this room is reserved for the use and care of *my* master. I have served the Darcy family all my life, father and son both, and I will have no one trouble Mr. Darcy whilst he is incapacitated. You can have no business here. Therefore, I wish you all a good night."

With that, he closed the door in the crowd's collective faces. The assembled looked at each other in astonishment.

Mr. Bingley shrugged. "My apologies, Mr. Bennet. Bartholomew is somewhat...protective of Darcy, I have learned through experience."

"Too right there," agreed Mr. Hurst, his first words of the evening save a couple of grunts.

Mrs. Bennet, white with anxiety, wrung her hands. "Well, let us return to dinner before it is spoiled!" She spun on one heel and made for the dining room, the others in her wake.

Two lingered — her husband and second daughter — who stared at the closed door incredulously. Then, with a sigh, Mr. Bennet put his head down and followed the others.

Elizabeth remained flat-footed and flabbergasted in the hallway.

Chapter 3

ELIZABETH AROSE EARLY AND made an abbreviated *toilette*. She had retired right after Mr. and Miss Bingley and the Hursts returned to Netherfield and wanted to be downstairs in good time to witness the arrival of Mr. Darcy's physician, the paragon from Park Place, Mr. Macmillan.

Alas, just as the maid finished her hair, she glanced through the bedroom window to see that a carriage and a curricle were being attended to by the groom. As she recognized Mr. Jones's curricle, she supposed the other must be that of the famous physician. She was too late.

Elizabeth was not made for gloom and made her way into the dining room in good humor. Only those who knew her intimately could perceive a slight air of disappointment in her mood. One of those people was her father who, to Elizabeth's surprise, had arrived at the breakfast table before her.

They greeted each other affectionately and, save for informing Mr. Bennet that Jane would soon be coming down, they ate in agreeable silence. Not long after that, Mr. Jones came into the room accompanied by a distinguished gentleman introduced as Mr. Macmillan. Elizabeth was impressed with his serous mien yet gentle manner of speaking. At Mr. Bennet's invitation, given reluctantly to Elizabeth's dismay, the two men of medicine helped themselves to the offerings at the side table. By that time, Jane had joined the party, and Mr. Macmillan gave his report as he ate.

"I must concur with the diagnosis of my colleague." He indicated Mr. Jones. "It is my belief that Mr. Darcy has suffered a simple fracture of the fibula. There seems to be no damage to either the knee or ankle, and from what one can judge by the aspect of the leg, the bone has not shifted out of place. With time, Mr. Darcy should have a full recovery."

"How much time?" was Mr. Bennet's question.

"The leg must be immobilized for at least two months before we can chance placing weight on it."

Mr. Bennet dropped his face into a hand. "And can he be moved?"

"I should not think Mr. Darcy will be fit for travel for at least four weeks, sir. These things take time."

Mr. Bennet groaned, earning a sharp look from his favorite daughter.

"I am certain that they do," said Jane to Mr. Macmillan. "Is Mr. Darcy in any discomfort?"

Mr. Macmillan's countenance brightened at Jane's concern. "There is pain, to be sure, but it can be managed with quiet and laudanum." He turned to Mr. Jones. "*Careful* administration of laudanum. I understand there was an unfortunate incident yesterday."

The color rose in Mr. Jones's face. "Yes…well, the determination of the proper dosage is often a matter of trial and error."

The London physician immediately set the other man at ease. "Very true. I meant no disparagement of your abilities. Rather, I am impressed with your knowledge. If you will pardon me for saying so, you are very learned for a country apothecary."

Mr. Jones preened. "I thank you, sir. After finishing my apprentice-ship and beginning my practice, I began reading any medical text that became available to me. I have an uncle who is a solicitor at Chancery Court, and he taught me Latin. I have had the honor of reading several treatises by you, Mr. Macmillan, and have learned a great deal. Your views on phlebotomy and its substitutes were very enlightening."

"You are very kind. But why remain a mere apothecary? Surely you have the training to be a surgeon."

Mr. Jones shrugged. "While there is no surgeon in Meryton, one from Hertford can always be gotten when such services are required. The distance is not too great. To own the truth, I dislike the saw; I much prefer my potions and elixirs. I leave the bloody work to others."

Mr. Macmillan chuckled. "You have all the makings of a physician! There are many of my brothers who will not soil their hands on a patient. I do not hold to that and am considered a bit of a radical."

"Your splint was a revelation, sir," said the apothecary. "You immobilize the knee and ankle?"

"Yes — a French invention. They do make things besides wine and trouble."

This impromptu meeting of the mutual admiration society was interrupted by the arrival of Mr. Bingley. The pleasant young man greeted everyone happily, particularly Jane, which earned a blush from the lady. For Elizabeth's part, she was happy that the Superior Sisters had not accompanied him. Mr. Bingley was introduced to Mr. Macmillan, and after refusing a plate — he had eaten before leaving Netherfield — he reported that his sister was much recovered from her swoon the day before and asked about his friend. Given the same intelligence as the Bennets, Mr. Bingley thanked the physician for his quick response to Bartholomew's summons.

"Do you now return to London, sir?"

"No," replied Mr. Macmillan. "I intend to spend the night and readjust the splint tomorrow. There may be some swelling. Mr. Darcy's man, Bartholomew, will attend me, and I shall show him how it is done."

"If you do not mind, I should like to observe," offered the apothecary. "I am always looking to improve my technique." Mr. Macmillan assured him that his presence would be welcomed.

"You cannot stay here!" Mr. Bennet said ungraciously.

The reader can be assured that this pronouncement was met with astonishment by all assembled.

Seeing his error, Mr. Bennet softened his objection. "We are rather full up, Mr. Macmillan, with Mr. Collins in residence. I am sorry we cannot accommodate you." As much as he tried, his tone left the company convinced that Mr. Bennet's regrets were at best half-hearted. Elizabeth could not believe her father could show such ill-breeding.

"I certainly understand your predicament, Mr. Bennet," said the physician with the grace Elizabeth's father should have shown, "but there is no harm done. I had already fixed my mind to stay at an inn in Meryton."

"Nonsense!" cried Mr. Bingley. "We have rooms enough at Nether-field, and we are less than three miles away. You shall stay as my guest. I insist upon it!"

Elizabeth was pleased by Mr. Bingley's generosity and was happy that the usually reserved Jane allowed herself to smile fully at her erst-while suitor. Mr. Macmillan demurred, of course, but Mr. Bingley was persistent, and soon the physician agreed to the scheme. As the rest of the Bennet family remained above stairs in the embrace of Morpheus, the remainder of the breakfast passed in a quiet and agreeable manner before Mr. Bingley and the two men of medicine took their leave.

As was their settled routine, Mr. Bennet retreated to his book room, Jane took up her embroidery in the sitting room, and Elizabeth indulged in a walk in the garden. The flower beds were mostly barren, prepared for the coming winter's sleep, and Elizabeth had to be content with the crunching of the leaves beneath her feet while she turned her thoughts once again to their unexpected guest.

Every moment in Mr. Darcy's company seemed designed to throw her into more confusion as to his character. Never in all her life did Elizabeth expect to see anything like the exhibition of the previous evening, and that Mr. Darcy was the performer…well, she had no words to fully express her astonishment.

She knew that the gentleman was under the influence of laudanum and brandy and therefore had no control over and bore no responsibil-ity for his actions. But to sing a drinking song — in honor of the ladies of Longbourn, he claimed! His disheveled, smiling countenance was undeniably handsome, she had to admit. And that voice! That deep baritone sent shivers down her spine! Elizabeth's traitorous heart was at war against her reason. How could she admire and despise a man in the same instant?

Never had Elizabeth longed for a day to pass as quickly as she did that day. The Philipses' party that evening would bring her in contact with Mr. Wickham and perhaps the answer to a growing mystery.

"ARE YOU DONE WITH YOUR breakfast, sir?" asked Sally.

Darcy, half-sitting up on the couch, handed the maid his nearly empty plate. "Yes. My compliments to Cook. The chicken was very fine." It was no false compliment; for all of Longbourn's shortcomings, there was nothing wrong with the quality of the food served there.

Sally smiled prettily and set the plate aside. "Are you comfortable, sir? Shall I fluff the pillow? A blanket — shall I fetch you one? You mustn't catch your death."

Darcy heard Bartholomew's huff of exasperation, and Darcy himself barely stopped rolling his eyes. He had experienced this phenomenon before — a young maid's flirtations while he was a guest at a friend's estate. There were those of his acquaintance who would not hesitate to take advantage of the situation, but they were not Fitzwilliam Darcy. He would never lower himself to bed a servant; he would never act as had Wickham.

The thought of his former childhood playmate darkened his expression. Wickham in Meryton! Nothing good could come of that! Thank goodness he had not brought Georgiana to Netherfield. It had been many months since Ramsgate, but his sweet sister still suffered from mortification and had withdrawn from society. How much worse would it be for her to be but a few miles from that reprobate!

Apparently, his morose thoughts were transparent, for Sally grew worried and concerned. "Oh, sir, are you in any pain? Mr. Bartholomew, more laudanum, if you please!"

"No, no," Darcy labored to reassure the girl, "I am quite comfortable."

Actually, he was not. A few hours on the Bennet's couch might be agreeable, but a full night's sleep had done away with the sofa's appeal. The light dose of laudanum administered that morning had done little to relieve his discomfort. What made matters worse was that Darcy could not move very much; he was limited to placing both legs on the sofa or his right foot on the floor. In either position, he was flat on his back, his left leg immobilized. And now Macmillan said he was not to be moved for a month, except for the necessities? A month on this couch? In what level of hell had Darcy landed?

Bartholomew answered a knock on the door; it was Miss Jane Bennet. "Mr. Darcy, are you up to having visitors?" the lady asked kindly.

Darcy set aside his self-pity. "I should like it of all things, Miss Bennet. Please…" He gestured to a chair near the couch. Once she was seated, Bartholomew begged to be excused, saying he had a few things to discuss with Mrs. Hill. The valet left, leaving the door slightly ajar, while Sally in the role of chaperone busied herself by puttering about, dusting the room.

Miss Bennet worked on her embroidery while sharing small talk with Darcy. After only a few minutes, he found himself almost as much at ease talking to her as he had been in conversing with Miss Elizabeth at Netherfield weeks before — easier in some ways, for he was not fighting the attraction he felt for her sister. They spoke of family and horses, two subjects Darcy enjoyed. He was surprised to learn that Miss Elizabeth did not ride; a childhood fright had quite put her off the occupation. Darcy found himself speaking of the joy he found in riding with Georgiana when they were interrupted.

"Oh, go away, you furry thing!" cried Sally.

Darcy glanced at the door and saw a ginger cat slowly walking in.

"No, no, Cassandra, you are not welcome here." Jane put aside her embroidery and rose to expel the cat, but it was too quick for either lady and, with a bound, planted itself on Darcy's chest. The cat was not light, and Darcy gave a *whoof*. Not discouraged in the least, the feline settled down upon the prone man.

"Oh, Mr. Darcy, I am so sorry!" Miss Bennet made to remove the beast, but Darcy forestalled her.

"No, no, I am not troubled. After all, this is her house, not mine." He glanced at the purring cat. "I believe we have met before although we have not been properly introduced."

Jane turned bright red. "This is our cat, Cassandra. I am afraid you met yesterday."

"I thought I recognized the color." Darcy gently rubbed the animal behind the ears, and the cat accepted his attention with rumbling delight. "Come to apologize, eh? Very well, I suppose the blame must be shared with the horse and its rider. You are welcome here, Miss Cassandra."

"She is very sweet to us but not usually accepting of strangers." Miss Bennet smiled. "You have made a conquest."

Darcy chanced a quick glance at Sally, who was watching the scene with adulation. *There* was one conquest he would eschew even if his life depended on it.

"Your sister must be very worried about you," Jane observed.

Darcy absently stroked the cat. "She would be if she knew of this."

"She does not?" Jane said with some emotion. "Has no one written her?"

"I would, but the laudanum — it is difficult to concentrate."

Miss Bennet firmed her lips, an act Darcy heretofore thought the lady of incapable of performing. "Then allow me to assist you. We together shall pen a quick note to her." Before Darcy could protest, the lady marched to a desk opposite, sat herself down, and gathered ink and paper. She turned her head, brandishing a pen. "Tell me what you wish to say, sir, and I shall write it down."

It took a while and several drafts, but in the end, Darcy signed a letter written by Miss Bennet that informed Georgiana that an accident would necessitate his remaining in Hertfordshire until Christmastide. He claimed that he was in no danger or pain and only regretted this time away from his dear sister. He charged her to attend to her lessons, not to worry, and soon he would join her in London. Miss Bennet rose with the now-sealed letter in her hands.

"I shall have my father post it directly."

Darcy tried to dissuade her from that action — he could certainly pay for the postage — but Jane would not hear of it. She was almost at the door when it was opened by Mrs. Hill, a beaming Mr. Bingley close behind. The reason for Bingley's quick return to Longbourn was instantly revealed.

"Cheer up, Darce!" cried Bingley. "I have brought you a bed!"

He had brought more than a bed. The entire Netherfield party was now in attendance, including Mr. Hurst and Mr. Macmillan. The ruckus raised the house, and soon the hallway was filled with Bennets, Bingleys, and other persons as Mr. Hill and a few other servants moved the furniture about the parlor and assembled the bed.

The crush of people convinced Cassandra to flee the scene. Mrs. Bennet, once she recovered from her initial astonishment at the scheme, joined the work of redecorating whole-heartedly, assisted by Miss Bennet and Miss Elizabeth. Miss Bingley contented herself with making a few suggestions, all of which were ignored. The younger Miss Bennets did little but stare. As for the master of Longbourn, he simply threw up his hands and retreated to his book room in a huff.

Once the bed was established, Mr. Macmillan requested a few minutes privacy, and under his direction, Bartholomew and Mr. Hill helped Darcy into his new accommodations.

Darcy sighed as he lay back on the mattress, Mrs. Hill and Sally tucking the covers about him. Never had a bed felt so welcomed than after his forced occupation of the Bennet's couch. The ladies returned and completed the re-orientation of the parlor.

"There, Mr. Darcy!" cried Mrs. Bennet when the labors were completed. "This is as fine a room as may be found in Hertfordshire, I declare! Warm and cozy — certainly better than Purvis Lodge. The attics there are dreadful!"

"Harrumph!" Mr. Collins turned up his nose. "Good enough for Hertfordshire, I suppose, but nothing to Rosings Park! I say that these accommodations are unfit for my patroness's nephew, and he should be moved to better quarters."

"Mr. Collins," said Darcy wearily. "Please. Leave. My. Presence. *Now.*" The fastidious parson flushed and fled while Darcy turned his attention to Mrs. Bennet. "Madam, this room is perfectly acceptable. I thank you and your staff for your kind attentions."

A wide smile grew on the matron's face. "I am told by Hill that you fancied Cook's white soup. I knew you would. It is the best in the district." She leaned in and continued, "It is ten times what you will find on Lady Lucas's table!"

"Mother!" cried Miss Elizabeth.

"What?" Mrs. Bennet replied. "I speak nothing but the truth. Ask Mr. Darcy; he is the *connoisseur.*" She turned back to her guest. "I suppose you have three French cooks at your Pemberley, at least!"

For once, Darcy found amusement in the foolish lady's boasting but said in all honesty, "Mrs. Bennet, your white soup is as fine as I have ever had the pleasure of enjoying."

"There, you see?" Mrs. Bennet cried triumphantly before her eye fell on the clock. "Oh, but we must get ready for the Philipses' party! Pray excuse us, Mr. Darcy. I am certain you appreciate the responsibilities we have, being one of the most distinguished families in the district!" She sighed. "We are always dealing with invitations, and we must honor them. It would not do for us to so disparage society. Surely, *you* understand these things!"

Darcy did not know whether it was an aftereffect of the laudanum, but he was quite diverted by Mrs. Bennet. "I would by no means suspend any pleasure of yours. I hope you will enjoy yourselves."

THE PARTY AT THE PHILIPSES' was tolerable only because of the inclusion of the militia. The officers of the ——hire were in general a very creditable, gentlemanlike set, and the best of them were of the present party. Mr. Wickham was as far beyond them all in person, countenance, air, and walk, as *they* were superior to the broad-faced, stuffy Uncle Philips, breathing port wine, who held court in a corner of the room.

Almost every female eye in the room was on Mr. Wickham, but it was Elizabeth and Lydia with whom he seated himself. At first, there was danger of Lydia monopolizing the conversation with idle talk of ribbons and red coats, but fortunately for Elizabeth, the gentleman seemed predisposed toward the topic closest to *her* heart — namely, the history of his acquaintance with Mr. Darcy. He enquired how long Mr. Darcy had been staying in the neighborhood.

"About a month, almost all of that time at Netherfield until his accident," said Elizabeth.

"Now we are stuck with him in our parlor!" added Lydia.

"I do understand your feelings," said the officer. "Even a pleasant man in pain can be a difficult guest."

Lydia laughed. "There is nothing pleasant about Mr. Darcy, I can tell you."

"The story about town is that he was thrown from his horse because he was overtaken by drink. I hope that is not true. It would be very shocking if it were," Mr. Wickham said carefully.

"Oh no, it was not drink but our cat!" Lydia explained.

Elizabeth, wanting to get back to the subject of interest, said, "He is a man of very large property in Derbyshire, I understand."

"Yes," replied Wickham, "his estate there is a noble one. A clear ten thousand per annum. You could not have met with a person more capable of giving you certain information than myself, for I have been connected with his family from my infancy." He sighed. "You may well be surprised at such an assertion after seeing the very cold manner of our meeting yesterday. Are you much acquainted with Mr. Darcy?"

"As much as I ever wish to be," cried Elizabeth heatedly. "I spent four days at Netherfield with him prior to his accident, and I think him very disagreeable."

"*I* think him not at all handsome!" Lydia declared.

"I have no right to give *my* opinion," said Wickham, "as to his being agreeable or handsome or otherwise. I am not qualified to form one. I have known him too long and too well to be a fair judge. It is impossible for *me* to be impartial."

Lydia laughed again. "He is not at all liked in Hertfordshire. Everybody is disgusted with his pride. You will not find him more favorably spoken of by anyone."

"I wonder," said Mr. Wickham, "whether he is likely to be in this county much longer."

"That is up to his physician, I am afraid," said Elizabeth. "I hope your plans in favor of the ——shire will not be affected by his being in the neighborhood."

"Oh, no! It is not for *me* to be driven away by Mr. Darcy. If *he* wishes to avoid seeing *me*, he must stay away." He smiled. "Which should not be difficult, given the present circumstances."

Mr. Wickham then spoke of Derbyshire. "His father was one of the best men that ever breathed and the truest friend I ever had. I could forgive Mr. Darcy anything and everything but disappointing the hopes and disgracing the memory of his father.

"You see, the church *ought* to have been my profession. I was brought up for the church, and I should by this time have been in possession of a most valuable living had it pleased the gentleman we were speaking of just now. The late Mr. Darcy bequeathed to me the next presentation of the best living in his gift. He was my godfather and excessively attached to me, but when the living fell, it was given elsewhere."

"Good heavens!" cried Lydia. "While a red coat suits you *exceedingly* well and I should hate to see you in black, I am sorry you lost the living!"

Elizabeth asked, "But how could that be? How could the late Mr. Darcy's will be disregarded? Why did not you seek legal redress?"

Mr. Wickham shrugged his shoulders. "There was an informality in the terms of the bequest as to give me no hope from the law. The living became vacant two years ago, exactly as I was of an age to hold it, and it was given to another man. I cannot accuse myself of having done anything untoward to deserve to lose it, but I have a warm, unguarded temper, and I may perhaps have sometimes spoken my opinion *of* him and *to* him too freely. I can recall nothing worse. But the fact is that we are very different sorts of men, and he hates me."

"This is quite shocking!" said Elizabeth

"He deserves to be publicly disgraced!" was Lydia's opinion.

Mr. Wickham shook his head slowly. "Some time or other he will be, but it shall not be by *me*. Until I can forget his father, I can never defy or expose him."

"But what," said Elizabeth, "could have been his motive? What can have induced him to behave so cruelly?"

"A thorough, determined dislike of me," said Mr. Wickham in a matter-of-fact manner. "A dislike which I cannot but attribute in some measure to jealousy. Had the late Mr. Darcy liked me less, his son might have borne with me better, but his father's uncommon attachment to me irritated him, I believe, very early in life. He had not a temper to bear the sort of competition in which we stood — the sort of preference that was often given me."

"I had not thought Mr. Darcy so bad as this," Elizabeth reflected, "but I *do* remember his boasting one day at Netherfield of the implacability of his resentments, of his having an unforgiving temper. His disposition must be dreadful."

"Even though his singing voice is quite nice," Lydia allowed.

"I will not trust myself on either subject," replied Wickham, "I can hardly be just to him. But I can state that almost all his actions may be traced to pride, and pride has often been his best friend. It has connected him nearer with virtue than any other feeling. But we are none of us consistent, and in his behavior to me, there were stronger impulses even than pride."

"Can such abominable pride as his have ever done him good?" demanded Elizabeth.

"Yes, it has often led him to be liberal and generous — to give his money freely, to display hospitality, to assist his tenants, relieve the poor, and mind his singing master. Filial pride has done this. Not to appear to disgrace his family, to degenerate from the popular qualities, or lose the influence of the Pemberley House — these are a powerful motive. Why, when I was a boy, I lost the principal part in the annual Christmas pageant to Darcy, even though my voice was universally hailed as excellent. I am sure to this day there was skullduggery about.

"He has also *brotherly* pride, and *some* brotherly affection makes him a very kind and careful guardian of his sister. You will hear him generally cried as the most attentive and best of brothers."

"What sort of a girl is Miss Darcy?" asked Lydia.

He shook his head. "I wish I could call her amiable. It gives me pain to speak ill of a Darcy, but she is too much like her brother — very, very proud. As a child, she was affectionate and pleasing and extremely fond of me. I have devoted hours and hours to her amusement. But she is nothing to me now. She is a handsome girl, about fifteen or sixteen, and I understand, highly accomplished. Since her father's death, her home has been London, where a lady lives with her and oversees her education."

Elizabeth frowned. "I am astonished at Mr. Darcy's intimacy with Mr. Bingley! How can Mr. Bingley, who seems to be good humor itself, and is, I believe, truly amiable, be in friendship with such a man? How can they suit each other? Do you know Mr. Bingley?"

"Not at all."

"He is a sweet-tempered, amiable, charming man," said Elizabeth, but Lydia had another opinion.

"He is a bore, but he loves Jane, so we tolerate him."

"Lydia!" cried her sister.

Meanwhile, Mr. Collins was loudly describing to Mrs. Philips the very grand chimneypieces to be found at Rosings Park. Mr. Wickham's attention was caught, and after observing Mr. Collins for a few moments, he asked Elizabeth in a low voice whether her relation was very intimately acquainted with the family of de Bourgh.

"Lady Catherine de Bourgh," she replied, "has very lately given him a living. I hardly know how Mr. Collins was first introduced to her notice, but he certainly has not known her long."

"You know, of course, that Lady Catherine de Bourgh and Lady Anne Darcy were sisters, consequently, that she is aunt to your houseguest."

"Yes, that is our understanding."

Lydia said, "But we never heard of her existence until the day before yesterday."

"Her daughter, Miss de Bourgh," said Wickham, "will have a very large fortune, and it is believed that she and her cousin will unite the two estates."

The verification of Mr. Collins's information made Elizabeth smile as she thought of poor Miss Bingley. Vain indeed must be all her attentions, vain and useless her affection for his sister and her praise of Mr. Darcy if he were already destined for another.

"Mr. Collins speaks highly both of Lady Catherine and her daughter, but from some particulars that he has related of her ladyship, I have lately come to suspect his gratitude misleads him, and that in spite of her being his patroness, she is an arrogant, conceited woman."

"I believe her to be both in a great degree," replied Wickham. "I have not seen her for many years, but I very well remember that I never liked her and that her manners were dictatorial and insolent. She has the reputation of being remarkably sensible and clever, but I rather believe she derives part of her abilities from her rank and fortune — part from her authoritative manner and the rest from the pride of her nephew, who chooses that everyone connected with him should have an understanding of the first class."

Elizabeth allowed that he had given a very rational account, and she and Lydia continued talking with Mr. Wickham with mutual satisfaction until supper gave the rest of the ladies their share of the officer's attentions.

When the party was done, Elizabeth went away with her head full of thoughts of Mr. Wickham. She could think of nothing all the way home but the gentleman and what he had told her, but there was no time for her even to mention his name as they went, for neither Lydia nor Mr. Collins was ever silent. Lydia talked incessantly of Mr. Wickham. Mr. Collins described the civility of Mr. and Mrs. Philips, protested that he did not in the least regard his losses at whist, enumerated all the dishes at supper, and repeatedly expressed his fear that he crowded his cousins before the carriage stopped at Longbourn House.

All quietly departed above stairs, and Elizabeth did not know whether she was relieved or disappointed that there was no repeat of the concert from the night before.

Chapter 4

RAIN BEGAN FALLING THE day after the Philipses' party, an unfortunate circumstance for Elizabeth as she had much to ponder, and nothing was more appropriate for contemplation than a long walk in the countryside. Dispirited, she trudged downstairs and had her breakfast, one eye on the window. Her vigil had no effect on the weather; the cold November rain would stop and start but would not cease long enough to suit Elizabeth's purposes.

If she could not deliberate, she would discuss, and after breakfast, she made her way into her father's book room. There she found Mr. Bennet engrossed in a biography of Julius Caesar. He put aside his study of Caesar's Gallic campaign — he was planning his own "rout of a barbarian or two," he said with a twinkle in his eye — and gave over his full attention to Elizabeth. Before she was fully settled in her favorite chair, they were joined by Jane. She, too, sought a discussion with her father.

Elizabeth frowned. The night before, after her return from the party, she had tried to talk with her dearest sister about Mr. Wickham's revelations, but to her surprise, Jane would not believe a word of it. She had spent time with Mr. Darcy, Jane said sharply — sharply for *her* — and "no friend of Mr. Bingley could act in so callous a manner," she declared. She allowed that there might be some misunderstanding between the two gentlemen, but if given the choice of believing the testimony of either man, she would stand by Mr. Darcy. With that, she ended the conversation and remained adamant, regardless of Elizabeth's protests.

Now the rare argument was to start again. It pained Elizabeth to disagree with Jane, but she felt her father should know Mr. Wickham's tale. She gave a brief accounting of Mr. Wickham's grievances, and Mr. Bennet listening attentively.

"Interesting," was his comment before turning to Jane. "You do not seem to agree with Lizzy."

Jane continued her uncharacteristic behavior. "I cannot, Father. I am sure that Mr. Wickham truly believes that he has been harmed by Mr. Darcy, but in my dealings with the gentleman, I have found Mr. Darcy to be honorable and thoughtful."

"Thoughtful?" cried Elizabeth.

"Yes," said Jane. "Just yesterday, I helped Mr. Darcy write a very kind letter to his sister. It was apparent to me that he is much attached to her."

Elizabeth almost sighed. She had known for years that Jane was the most tenderhearted person, always thinking the best of everyone, but this was a bit much. Of course, Mr. Darcy would send a letter to his sister! But that did not speak to Mr. Darcy's sensibilities at all. Besides, Mr. Wickham had names, proofs — there was truth to his looks.

Mr. Bennet grunted. "Yes, and I posted it. I hope this will not lead to a flood of letters from London; my pocketbook may not survive. This circumstance will cost me more than I feared."

"Father!" cried Jane. "You must not jest so! I am certain that Miss Darcy would be concerned over her brother's health."

"Of course, of course. I can afford a few letters. It seems this Mr. Wickham has called our guest's character into question. Now we all know that Mr. Darcy is a proud, unpleasant sort of man, used to getting his own way" — Mr. Bennet uttered this last with a trace of bitterness — "but this indictment is very serious. We should keep it in mind. However, true or not, it does not change the present circumstances. The fact of the matter is that Mr. Darcy will be in residence at Longbourn for some time. It would be best to keep this intelligence to ourselves and refrain from inviting Mr. Wickham to Longbourn whilst Mr. Darcy is here. Are we agreed?"

Elizabeth colored. "Lydia was with me when I spoke to Mr. Wickham."

Mr. Bennet groaned. "Then the story will be all over Hertfordshire by week's end. Well, there is nothing for it."

"There is," said Jane. "We could hear Mr. Darcy's side of the story."

"What? Walk right in and demand to know whether Mr. Darcy disregarded the terms of his father's will? Jane, you know better than that!"

Jane was not chastised by her father's reprimand. "There are other, more proper ways. For example, we could let Mr. Darcy know that Mr. Wickham is airing grievances against him. I think it would be a kindness, and it would give Mr. Darcy the chance to defend himself before his reputation is ruined with all our neighbors."

Elizabeth thought it was too late for that. Her father had a different objection.

"Well, we cannot do it now. Mr. Macmillan and Mr. Jones are with him at present. They arrived just as I sat down for breakfast." He darkened. "I suppose I ought to warn Cook to put out more food."

Suddenly, there came a commotion at Longbourn's front door. Mr. Bennet arose in annoyance. "Who could be coming here in such weather? I had best see to it." However, before another step could be taken, Mrs. Hill threw open the door to the book room.

"Colonel Fitzwilliam and Miss Darcy to see Mr. Darcy, sir."

Elizabeth flew to her feet. Colonel Fitzwilliam's identity was a mystery, but Miss Darcy could only be Mr. Darcy's proud sister! Her eyes darted to Jane, but she appeared as astonished as the rest.

"I do not understand," Jane said. "Mr. Darcy's letter could not have reached her yet."

The three left the book room instantly and beheld the visitors in the hall. Colonel Fitzwilliam, wearing civilian clothes, was a man of about thirty years of age with a grim countenance but, in person and address, was most truly a gentleman, particularly in the manner with which he assisted the young lady beside him. This had to be Miss Darcy. Tall and larger proportioned than Elizabeth, her figure was one of womanly grace. She was less handsome than her brother and obviously agitated. The colonel espied them and walked forward with a respectful, yet earnest manner.

"Colonel Fitzwilliam at your service, sir," he said to Mr. Bennet.

"Allow me to present my cousin and ward, Miss Darcy. We are relations of Mr. Darcy. We are sorry to burst upon you like this, with no warning or introduction, but we have received the most distressing express and hurried to Hertfordshire to see with our own eyes Mr. Darcy's condition. I trust you will forgive us."

Mr. Bennet assured the colonel of their welcome while Elizabeth watched Miss Darcy closely. The lady had said not a word. Her eyes were red, and her body was shaking. Elizabeth's heart went out to the girl, and she and Jane moved quickly to comfort her.

After a hurried introduction, Miss Darcy finally managed, "Tell me, is my brother well? Please say that he is!"

The raw pain and fear in that simple statement almost overwhelmed Elizabeth. On close inspection of her face and voice, Miss Darcy proved to be younger than her figure suggested, and there was good sense reflected in her face. Elizabeth would have thought the girl's manners perfectly unassuming and gentle were she not so concerned over her brother.

"He is being well cared for, Miss Darcy, never fear. Father, let us take our guests to Mr. Darcy without delay."

Mr. Bennet agreed, and in short order, the little party was at the parlor door. Elizabeth espied a grimace come over her father's face as he suffered to knock on a door in his own house. It went unnoticed by the others, however, and all other thoughts disappeared as Bartholomew opened the door, and Mr. Darcy's relations rushed to enter before the valet could announce them. The Bennets followed at a more sedate pace, and Elizabeth's tender heart was captivated at the sight of a sobbing Miss Darcy half on the bed, embracing her brother, and an ashen-faced Colonel Fitzwilliam standing close by.

The sound of her father's voice alerted Elizabeth that the physician and the apothecary were still in attendance. The noise had attracted others, and Mrs. Bennet, the remaining Bennet girls, and Mr. Collins soon crowded about the open doorway. Mr. Macmillan voiced his concerned over the growing spectacle and requested Mr. Bennet's assistance in clearing the hallway. The opinion was shared by another gentleman in the sickroom.

"Miss Bennet, Miss Elizabeth — your assistance, please," said Mr.

Darcy. To his sister he gently requested, "Please, sweeting, go with these ladies and rest. You must not overdo. I shall be here when you have recovered."

"But, I would not leave you!" she cried pitifully.

Lovingly yet firmly, he replied, "I am going nowhere, Georgiana. Please do as I ask. These ladies will see to your comfort."

She glanced at Elizabeth and Jane, her tear-filled eyes wide with question and anxiety. "Are these the kind ladies you wrote of from Netherfield?"

That Mr. Darcy wrote to his sister of the ladies of Longbourn did not surprise Elizabeth, but that he had apparently done so with praise was astonishing, and her confusion was increased by the gentleman's smiling acknowledgement of the fact. With reluctance, Miss Darcy rose and walked over to Elizabeth and Jane, eyes downcast and cheeks flushed. Elizabeth saw that Colonel Fitzwilliam eyed them with suspicion and moved to join them, but he was forestalled by Mr. Darcy's request that he remain.

Elizabeth had no time to consider the meaning of the gesture. Miss Darcy was before them, and she focused all her attentions on the poor young lady. Taking her hand, Elizabeth asked if Miss Darcy had left from London that morning. She answered with a slight nod, and Jane declared that she must come away upstairs to refresh herself. Miss Darcy suffered to be led away from the room and down the hall to the stairs, the remaining members of the household gawking silently at them — except for Mr. Collins.

"Miss Darcy!" he cried. "Niece of my esteemed patroness! I am honored to finally make your acquaintance! Here," he tried to put himself between Elizabeth and the heiress, "allow me to assist you!"

"Mr. Collins, please!" cried Elizabeth.

"My dear cousin," Mr. Collins sneered in haughty superiority, "as Lady Catherine de Bourgh's most trusted servant, it is only right that *I* attend Miss Darcy!"

Miss Darcy flinched. "Who... who are you?"

From the parlor, Mr. Darcy roared, "MR. COLLINS! Your attendance, if you please!" The man jumped as if struck, quickly made his excuses, and scampered into the room. Thus freed from the vicar's presence, Elizabeth and Jane maneuvered the skittish Miss Darcy up the stairs.

DARCY HAD SUFFERED A TOLERABLE night thanks to laudanum, but he was out of sorts when awaked at dawn by Mr. Macmillan and Mr. Jones. Their poking and prodding did nothing to improve his disposition, and the reapplication of the splint had been excruciating. Mr. Macmillan had mercy on his patient, and he had just administered a light draught of laudanum when Darcy was assaulted by his relations.

Confusion gave way to joy, which quickly turned to disquiet. Darcy doted on Georgiana and loved Fitzwilliam like a brother, but his delight in being in their agreeable presence was quickly overcome by alarm that his sister was in the same neighborhood that now housed Wickham. Concern for the former and disgust for the latter was augmented by wonder: How did Georgiana learn of his misfortune? Unless Miss Bennet sent his letter by express — and she gave no such indication — someone else had written to London. Who that could be, Darcy had no idea.

Darcy set that issue aside for the moment. His first thought was to protect Georgiana. Glancing over and beholding the kind faces of Miss Bennet and Miss Elizabeth gave him an excuse to speak to Fitzwilliam alone without Georgiana overhearing. The two ladies seemed agreeable to attending his sister, but Darcy was embarrassed by Georgiana's innocent question, "Are these the kind ladies you wrote of from Netherfield?"

He was sure his pale skin colored as he whispered, "Yes, they are. They have impressed me with their goodness. Go with them, and I shall see you soon."

He knew that Georgiana's innate reserve and shyness would give most people the wrong impression — that she was proud and above her company — but he trusted that the eldest Bennet ladies had better insight. He hid a smile as Miss Elizabeth took his sister in hand. The sight was much as he had dreamt lately — Miss Elizabeth ensconced as Mrs. Darcy at Pemberley and as a loving sister to sweet Georgiana.

However, his contentment was interrupted by Mr. Collins's presumptuous conduct. Darcy had shouted for the vicar, the laudanum having a liberating effect on his inhibitions. He did not want the man anywhere near him, but he had to get him away from Georgiana. Once the tall, heavy man entered the room, Darcy began directly.

"You overstep yourself, sir. I fancy myself owning tolerable forbearance, but I must warn you that I have an unforgiving temper. Take care that you never earn my displeasure, or you will suffer for it."

"I . . . I thank you, sir, for your generous warning!" came the groveling reply. "I shall endeavor to remember it if you would be so kind as to tell me how I have offended you."

Did the man have no wit at all? "It was my wish that Miss Bennet and Miss Elizabeth attend my sister. Had I any other intentions, rest assured I would have voiced them. Do not flatter yourself that you know *my* mind."

"Of course, of course!" Mr. Collins cried with a bow. "I would never dream of such a thing, noble nephew of my benefactor. But you could not have known I was without. No, you could not. Therefore, as a more suitable companion for your fair sister — "

"*Mr. Collins*, let me assure you that I am *never* unaware of your presence!" The youngest Bennet girls giggled, and even Mr. Bennet cracked a smile. "As for who is a suitable companion for my sister, I believe that *I* shall be the judge of that. You are dismissed. I wish to have a private conversation with my cousin." Darcy glanced at Mr. Bennet as Mr. Collins fled. "Mr. Bennet, if you would kindly excuse me."

With an insolent air, Mr. Bennet nodded his head and withdrew, followed by his wife and daughters, the men of medicine, and Bartholomew. Once the door closed, Darcy rounded on Colonel Fitzwilliam. "What the devil are you doing here, Fitz?"

Darcy's demand earned an amused chuckle from his cousin. "Good to see you, too, Cuz. How did you hurt your leg?"

"I fell off a horse. Do not change the subject. What are you doing here? Why did you bring Georgiana? You must take her back to London this instant!"

"Did that fall addle your brain, Darcy? We just got here. I am certainly not going directly back to Town, and neither is Georgie. The weather is beastly and the roads are treacherous. If Bingley's express had not been so dire, I think we would have waited a few days."

"Bingley!" Darcy groaned. "I should have known!"

"Perhaps I might have misunderstood Bingley's message, but the letter was so full of blots, I could only make out six words in ten. Georgiana was beside herself, and I was concerned, too."

"Well, now you see I am well attended, so you can take Georgiana back to London."

"Did you hear a word I said? The roads are too dangerous — "

"Wickham is here."

Fitzwilliam froze. "What? Wickham is here? In Hertfordshire?"

"Yes, he is in Meryton as we speak. He has joined the ——shire militia."

"Good God! Why did you not tell me? We cannot let him come anywhere near Georgiana!"

Darcy sighed. "Exactly my point. That is why you and Georgie must leave immediately."

Fitzwilliam began to pace about the room. "Blast! I was not exaggerating the state of the roads, Darce. They are bad and getting worse by the moment. Only a fool would be out there now."

"I know," Darcy said with a meaningful look at the colonel.

He did not miss Darcy's meaning. "Excuse us for caring, you ungrateful wretch!"

"Pardon my foul humor, Fitz, but you see my concerns."

"I do. But what are we to do?"

Darcy made to answer him, but there was a new commotion at the door.

"Good God!" the colonel cried. "What is *she* doing here?"

ELIZABETH AND JANE WATCHED AS Miss Darcy washed her face and repaired her appearance. She reluctantly agreed to come downstairs and take tea, and soon the heiress was seated in the Longbourn sitting room opposite the parlor serving as Mr. Darcy's sickroom. Mrs. Hill brought refreshments from the dining room for Miss Darcy's pleasure, but she refused anything but a cup of tea — cream, no sugar. The rest of the Bennet family attended her, even Mr. Bennet, but Mr. Collins stood preoccupied near the window and glanced out on occasion.

Elizabeth ignored the strange, tall man. She instead endeavored to engage Miss Darcy in conversation and found it to be challenging. She could tell it was not pride that stilled the young lady's tongue but an almost crippling case of shyness. She was not as Mr. Wickham described. Normally, Elizabeth would have wondered about that discrepancy, but she saw that the reserved and frightened girl needed immediate comforting and engaged all her considerable powers toward that end, setting other thoughts aside.

Lydia and Kitty quickly grew bored with the company and spent their time whispering and giggling while Mary simply stared — none of which seemed to make Miss Darcy any more at ease with her situation. Finally, Mrs. Bennet had her share of the conversation.

"Miss Darcy, what a lovely dress you are wearing! It cost a pretty penny, I should think. Do you not think so, Lydia? Yes, yes, very pretty. You must patronize the most expensive dress shops in London, I am sure of it! Pray, what did it cost?"

Miss Darcy was speechless. As for Elizabeth, she was happy one could not die of mortification, for if she could, her family would certainly be measuring her for her coffin at that moment.

"Miss Darcy," cried Jane, "I hope your trip here was not too taxing. The roads must have been in quite a state."

"They were poor," Miss Darcy allowed.

Elizabeth felt a need to take the girl's hand. "That you came at all shows a lovely devotion to your brother."

Miss Darcy looked wide-eyed. "He is all I have left in the world! If something should happen to him — "

"Nothing shall," Jane reassured her. "He is receiving the best of care."

"Oh, Miss Darcy, Jane is right," cried Mrs. Bennet. "Mr. Macmillan seems a very clever sort of man. He says he will save the leg, and even if he cannot, why a gentleman of Mr. Darcy's station would be able to get by very well with only one, with all the servants at his disposal."

"Mother!" Elizabeth begged to little avail.

"I only speak the truth," her mother claimed. "I am sure in any case that Mr. Darcy has well provided for his sister." She shot a glance at Mr. Collins's back. "*She* shall never have to worry about starving in the hedgerows!"

Elizabeth was afraid Miss Darcy was going to cry and tried mightily to think of something to say that would repair matters. It was at that moment that Mr. Collins began to do the most extraordinary thing: He started to hop about, clapping his hands.

"She is here! She is here! What joy!" With that, he fled the room. The other inhabitants were amazed at the exhibition they had just witnessed.

A dry-eyed Miss Darcy turned to Elizabeth. "Is your cousin always this…demonstrative?"

The front door was flung open. *Where is my nephew?* It was the voice of a woman of a certain age not used to being disappointed.

Miss Darcy paled. "Good God, what is *she* doing here?"

Chapter 5

Elizabeth saw that Miss Darcy was trembling anew, caused undoubtedly by the loud outcry of their intruder. She could do no less than offer comfort.

"Miss Darcy, I have no idea who that is. Should we investigate?" Elizabeth turned to Mr. Bennet. "Father, what is happening?" The voices in the hall grew in intensity as the mystery woman and Mr. Collins talked over one another.

Miss Darcy's grip on Elizabeth's hand was almost painful. "She must not know I am here! Please!"

The young lady was truly alarmed, and Elizabeth wondered whether there was danger to them all. Meanwhile, the others had left the room to see the source of the commotion, and after gaining Jane's assurance that she would remain with the distressed girl, Elizabeth joined her family.

In the hall was a tall, large, older woman with strongly marked features that might once have been considered beautiful. Her traveling cloak was soaked through, imparting a bedraggled appearance. Her air was not conciliatory, nor was her manner of receiving them such as to make her hosts forget their inferior rank.

"This is a very small park, and your portico is quite insufficient for inclement weather! It is beyond my understanding how my nephew found himself in such a place!" She glared at Mr. Bennet. "You are the owner of this hovel, I suppose."

Mr. Collins stood next to the woman, a sickly superior smile pasted on his ill features. "My lady, this is my cousin, Mr. Bennet, the *current* owner of Longbourn." He turned to the stately matron and bowed. "I have the great honor to present Lady Catherine de Bourgh of Rosings Park, Hunsford, Kent!"

So this was Lady Catherine! In her countenance and deportment, Elizabeth found some resemblance of Mr. Darcy. But the lady's speech was in tone so authoritative in comparison to her nephew as to make his proud discourse modest. Her marked self-importance brought Mr. Wickham immediately to Elizabeth's mind. From observation, she believed Lady Catherine to be exactly what he had represented. Mr. Wickham may have been wrong about Miss Darcy, but in this, he had been accurate.

"Enough of this prittle-prattle!" the good lady thundered. "You will take me to my nephew this instant!"

The clergyman scampered to do her bidding, and the door to the parlor was thrown open unceremoniously. Lady Catherine marched in without hesitation and cried out, "Darcy! What is the meaning of this? How came you to be housed in such degrading circumstances?"

The Bennet family stood without but could see into the room. Mr. Darcy was half-sitting up in bed. Colonel Fitzwilliam was beside him, the bed between him and Lady Catherine. Mr. Darcy was not sanguine; annoyance marked his features.

"Aunt Catherine," said Mr. Darcy with restrained emotion, "I am pleased to see you well. Tell me, how came you to journey to this place?"

Mr. Collins preened. "While humility is the first virtue of a clergyman, I am forced by honesty to report that I was the instrument by which my honored patroness was informed of your calamity."

Mr. Darcy whipped upon the man. "Are you saying you wrote to Rosings?"

"I did, by *express*," he admitted proudly. "No expense is too excessive in the service of my mistress!"

Mr. Darcy's eyes narrowed. "You take an eager interest in my concerns, sir."

Mr. Collins nodded his head. "I live to serve the Family de Bourgh."

"By thunder, you do not serve mine!" cried Mr. Darcy. "How dare you? How dare you interfere in matters that should be of no interest to you?"

Colonel Fitzwilliam laid a hand on Mr. Darcy's shoulder. "Easy, Darcy."

"By God, no!" Mr. Darcy railed onward. "Collins, I told you expressly that my business was not yours, yet you still chose to insinuate yourself into my concerns! You are treading a dangerous path, you sanctimonious fool, for I own an unforgiving temper, and your choice of profession shall not protect you from my wrath should you continue to anger me! As it is, if you do not get out of my sight in the next thirty seconds, I shall use whatever powers I have, either just or ill — including using my uncle, the bishop — to ruin you! GET OUT OF MY ROOM! NOW!"

Mr. Collins was deathly white, but whether it was from Mr. Darcy's threats or Lady Catherine's silence, Elizabeth could not tell. In a moment, the tall man was retreating up the stairs.

Lady Catherine huffed. "Darcy, if you are through berating my parson, get out of that bed. We are leaving for Rosings immediately."

"What?" cried Mr. Macmillan, who had by that time reentered the room. "Mr. Darcy cannot leave, madam."

"Who is this person?" Lady Catherine sneered.

"That gentleman is my physician, Aunt, and he is quite right," Mr. Darcy declared. "I am not well enough to leave. I am grateful for the hospitality from this fine, respectable family."

Lady Catherine was not swayed by this statement. "Nonsense! Hurry yourself along, or have your man gather assistance. Anne is waiting in the carriage."

"What?" cried Colonel Fitzwilliam. "You brought Anne here — to Hertfordshire in the rain *in November*?"

"Good God, madam, you have lost your mind," breathed Mr. Darcy. "Fitz — quickly!"

Colonel Fitzwilliam was already moving to the doorway, a quickness of action that surprised Elizabeth, even though she knew his profession. "Say no more, Darce! Bartholomew, attend me!" The two forced their way through the crowd and out the front door.

"There is no need for this, Darcy. We shall be on our way once you are in the carriage," Lady Catherine protested loudly.

"I am not leaving, and there is an end to it."

The front door opened again, and Elizabeth saw Colonel Fitzwilliam and Bartholomew half-carry a small, well-bundled person between them, rain droplets puddling on Mrs. Bennet's fine floors.

"Darcy, she is chilled to the bone!" cried the colonel. To Mrs. Bennet, he demanded, "Where is a fire?"

Elizabeth's mother jumped at the authority in the man's voice. "Here, in the sitting room. Quickly, sir. Oh, my poor nerves!"

She led the trio into the room they had lately vacated. The rest were undecided; curiosity over the new arrival battled with the attraction of the epic clash occurring in the parlor, for Mr. Darcy and Mr. Macmillan were as insistent in their demands for Miss de Bourgh's relief as Lady Catherine was outraged over their presumptuous interference. Finally, better manners won out, and the remainder of the Bennet family removed to the sitting room. Elizabeth had to drag a protesting Lydia by the arm.

The visitor was established in a chair close to the hearth. Miss de Bourgh, for it could be no other person, was dressed in heavy fabrics of high quality but poor fashion. The sleeves had not been seen in Hertfordshire society for many a year. The young lady herself was not at all the way Elizabeth imagined Mr. Darcy's intended. With his pride and hauteur, surely the master of Pemberley would seek out only the handsomest, most refined creature of the *ton*.

It was the work of a moment's attention to prove that Miss de Bourgh was nothing of the sort. Elizabeth was astonished at her being so thin and small. There was neither in figure nor face any likeness between her and her mother. Miss De Bourgh was pale and sickly. Her features, though not plain, were insignificant. She spoke very little, if at all, and when she did, it was in a light, almost incomprehensible whine.

This was the object of Mr. Darcy's esteem? This ill-looking, ill-acting wallflower? It was an astounding revelation that a man as exacting and penetrating an observer of his fellow man as Mr. Darcy undoubtedly was — a gentleman of great pride, presence, and intellect — would choose as the companion of his future life a woman as small, sickly, and insipid as his cousin.

But perhaps that was the answer to the mystery. Mr. Darcy was marrying for money and family like countless others of his station. It was a disappointment.

It was in Elizabeth's character to make such a pitiful creature comfortable. Already, Miss Darcy, who had *not* fled upstairs, and Jane had moved to talk to the heiress. Elizabeth saw she must have her share in the conversation, for the rest of her family gawked at the young lady as if she were a circus creature on display.

"Miss de Bourgh, may I pour you a cup of tea?" The lady responded to Elizabeth with only a shake of the head.

"Anne," said Miss Darcy, with some animation, "you must take something to warm you. Please have some tea" — the girl paused — "or perhaps something else?"

The girl's glassy eyes looked about the room. "Perhaps some sherry?" she rasped.

Elizabeth saw Colonel Fitzwilliam roll his eyes resignedly before turning to Mr. Bennet. "Might I trouble you for a glass of sherry, sir?" The glass was soon poured, and the girl sipped it greedily. The colonel sighed and requested that Miss de Bourgh show some moderation. Her response was to finish the drink and hold out the glass, a silent request for a refill. The second glass went down as quickly as the first. Miss de Bourgh decided to savor her third glass, but was no more talkative with her audience. Elizabeth spoke instead to her cousin.

"You seem very concerned over your cousin's comfort, Colonel. I hope she is not ill."

"Anne has been ill most of her life, Miss Elizabeth," he said. "She should not be out in such weather."

"I think it very romantic," cried Kitty.

"Romantic?" the colonel cried in response. "To chance her health for no reason? That is a strange description of romance, young lady."

Kitty was silenced, but Lydia was not. "She came to see her lover! What could be more romantic, even if he is only Mr. Darcy?"

Elizabeth did not think Lydia could be so crude, but her censure died on her lips as she beheld the reaction from the others.

Miss de Bourgh broke out in gales of laughter.

Miss Darcy was startled. "What are you talking about? Fitz, what is she talking about? Brother has not given in to Aunt Catherine's demands, has he?"

Colonel Fitzwilliam covered his eyes with a hand. "Oh, not that nonsense again!"

"Lydia! Be quiet!" Jane scolded.

"It is true!" Lydia stood firm. "Mr. Wickham said so!"

"Mr. Wickham?" Miss Darcy gasped.

Colonel Fitzwilliam was livid. "Deuce take him! What else has that scoundrel said?"

Miss Darcy was trembling again. "How do you know Mr. Wickham? What...what did he say?"

"Why, he is the most agreeable man in the militia, and he is our friend even if you are not!" Lydia crowed.

Miss Darcy gasped back a sob, rose to her feet, and dashed from the room with Jane in pursuit. Elizabeth berated Lydia for her words, but her sister only replied, "What did I say? It is only the truth!"

"Mr. Bennet!" cried Colonel Fitzwilliam. "Is it the custom of the Bennet family to insult their visitors?"

A red-faced Mr. Bennet stepped forward and broke his silence. "No, it is not. Lydia, to your room this instant!"

Lydia obeyed at once, crying her innocence as she fled. Kitty made to follow, but she was forestalled by a glare from her father. Mrs. Bennet, white-faced, sat back on the settee, fanning herself and mumbling something about her nerves. Meanwhile, neither Mary nor Miss de Bourgh said a word.

"I deeply apologize for this exhibition, Colonel Fitzwilliam," Mr. Bennet said with sincerity. The colonel was only slightly mollified.

"Miss Darcy is my ward as well as my cousin, and as such, her protection is my duty and pleasure. I will stand for no ill treatment of her from *anyone*. Do I make myself clear?"

"Perfectly, sir."

The colonel looked at the open doorway. "I should go to her."

"I am sure that my sister Jane is with her, and there is no kinder, gentler creature in the world. She will comfort her, if anyone can." Elizabeth paused. "If I may say so, you are in no state to see her — understandably, of course."

The gentleman was pacified. "Perhaps a few minutes' wait would be well."

"We are so sorry," cried Kitty, "but what did we do to upset her? Mr. Wickham said — "

Colonel Fitzwilliam's anger was reignited. "Wickham? You should have more wits than to believe anything Wickham says!"

"But... (cough)... but he is in the militia!"

The colonel moved closer to Kitty. "So, a red coat means honorable behavior? Miss Catherine, I have been a solider for fifteen years, and I have seen enough rogues and scoundrels in uniform to fill all of Meryton! Let me tell you what sort of man your Mr. Wickham is." To the entire room, he said, "He was the son of the late steward for my uncle, Mr. Darcy, may God rest his soul, and young Wickham was raised at that fine family's expense..."

DARCY, HALF-INTOXICATED BY THE LIGHT dose of laudanum, was far more expressive than usual with his difficult Aunt Catherine. She was known to her family as stubborn and willful at the best of times, and that she had dashed from Kent to Hertfordshire in such inclement weather and forced Anne to accompany her was pure madness. Darcy, contrary to his usual manner, was both disinclined and powerless to refrain from telling her so in forthright terms.

"It is past understanding," he said, his voice dripping with sarcasm, "how a woman who boasts of both motherly affection and superior intelligence could convince herself of the wisdom of bundling up her feeble daughter in a small coach and traveling over fifty miles in rain and mud with the sole object of forcing her nephew, suffering from a broken leg, to journey to Kent with her in opposition to both medical science and common sense. I had thought you foolish before, but this is beyond everything!"

Lady Catherine stared at Darcy in open-mouthed shock. "How dare you! I am not accustomed to such language as this. This is not to be borne! Immediately upon receiving Mr. Collins's express, I resolved to set off for this place and, out of the affection and goodness of my heart, to transport you to lodging more suitable to your station!"

Darcy would have none of it. "Even at the risk of my leg or life? How good of you, Aunt. And why bring Anne? Was it to 'accidentally' leave us alone somewhere along the road to Rosings for a sufficient length of time for Anne to be considered compromised? Out with it, woman!"

"Darcy! Honor, decorum, prudence — yea, even interest — commands that it is your family that cares for you and not some strangers in the wilderness. Yes, interest — for do not expect to be ignored by society if you willfully act against the inclinations of all. You will be censured, slighted, and despised by everyone connected with you."

"Madam," said Mr. Macmillan, "I believe you are overstating the case."

Darcy waved his hand in dismissal. "For the last time, Aunt, I am not leaving. Mr. Macmillan — "

"Is no one!" the grand dame declared. "My physician, Sir Anthony Carter, will attend you!"

"Carter!" cried Mr. Macmillan. "Tell me you have not employed that fraud! He is a menace!"

"*He* is the son of the Earl of — "

Mr. Macmillan was outraged. "The man is a butcher! I am not one to disparage my colleagues — but Carter! No amount of quackery is beneath him. There is not a respectable physician in all of London who will as much as speak to him!"

"They are jealous of his elevated station — "

"They are disgusted with his dangerous foolishness." To Darcy, Mr. Macmillan said, "If he is Miss de Bourgh's physician, I fear for her."

"Preposterous! There is nothing wrong with a little sherry in the evening! It improves Anne's stomach and calms her unsettled feelings of rejection by you, Darcy!"

Darcy laughed. "Aunt Catherine, Anne is half in her cups most evenings! Do you not see this?"

"Sir Anthony is aware of the ill effects — "

Mr. Macmillan proclaimed, "Sir Anthony Carter is a charlatan! Mr. Darcy, if I could have just five minutes with your cousin — "

Lady Catherine drew herself to full height. "You shall never touch my daughter, you cretin!" To her nephew she said, "Is there nothing I can say to change your mind?"

"No, there is not. By the way, allow me to be perfectly clear. I am not engaged to Anne, I never have been, and I have not the slightest intention of becoming so. I am my own master, and there is nothing in this world that can force me to become your son." He raised his hand and stopped her outraged protests. "I doubt any agreement was ever made with my mother, madam, but even if there was, it can have no standing with me. So please stop spreading your expectations as if they were settled facts. You embarrass me and demean yourself."

"Obstinate, headstrong boy! I am ashamed of you! Is this your gratitude for my attentions to you? Is nothing due to me, almost your closest relation, on that score? I am determined to carry my purpose. I will not be dissuaded from it. I am not used to submitting to any person's whims; I am not in the habit of brooking disappointment."

Darcy yawned. "*That* will make your ladyship's situation at present more pitiable, but it will have no effect on *me*."

Lady Catherine was astonished. "You refuse, then, to oblige me! You refuse to obey the claims of duty, honor, and gratitude. You are determined to ruin yourself — and Georgiana too — in the opinion of all your family and make your name the contempt of the world!"

"Neither duty, nor honor, nor gratitude," replied Darcy, "has any possible claim on me in the present instance. No principle of any of those obligations would be violated by my refusal to marry Anne. And with regard to the resentment of my family or the indignation of the world, I could not care less."

Lady Catherine's mouth flapped open. "And *this* is your true opinion of me and your family! This is your final resolve! Very well, I shall now know how to act. I hoped to find you reasonable, but depend upon it, I will carry my point. Your family will disown you!"

"*That* is a heavy misfortune," replied Darcy sarcastically, "but I find that Pemberley has such extraordinary sources of happiness necessarily attached to my ownership of it that I can, upon the whole, have no cause to repine."

Lady Catherine sniffed and moved to the door when, turning hastily round, she added, "I take no leave of you, Darcy. You deserve no such attention. *I am most seriously displeased!*" With that she quit the room.

Darcy sighed and turned to his shocked physician and valet. "Well, that was a long time coming. Might I get a bite to eat? I am famished."

COLONEL FITZWILLIAM FINISHED HIS STORY. "And Darcy sent him away after his outrageous request for the living, informing Wickham that he must be satisfied with the four thousand he had already wasted." He glanced at the door. "So, I hope you all understand that Wickham is not a man to be trusted with the truth."

Elizabeth's mind was in a whirl. Mr. Darcy exonerated? Mr. Wickham so wicked? Was it to be believed? She struggled with the concept and wondered whether she should voice her doubts when Kitty spoke for her.

"But…(cough)…but Mr. Wickham seemed so handsome — I mean, so reasonable!"

"A handsome face often hides a false tongue, for how else can the man be successful?" The colonel eyed Mr. Bennet. "My cousin and I have proofs of this, sir."

Mr. Bennet seemed half-amused and waved him off. "It will not be necessary, my good Colonel. I believe you. There is but such a quantity of merit between Mr. Darcy and Mr. Wickham to make only one good sort of man. For my part, I am now inclined to believe Mr. Darcy, but" — he turned to his daughter — "you shall do as you choose, Kitty."

Elizabeth noted that Miss de Bourgh seemed oddly untouched by the colonel's story. She attributed that to her already being aware of it. If that was so, then there could be no doubt Mr. Wickham had lied. Elizabeth was close enough to lean in and take the girl's free hand. "It must be a relief to you to see how well-cared for Mr. Darcy is."

Miss de Bourgh gave her a strange, unfocused look. "It is? I suppose it should be." She took a sip of her sherry, missing Elizabeth's incredulous expression. Elizabeth glanced at the colonel, but his shrug gave her no insight into the bizarre girl.

"I know it is not public yet," offered Mrs. Bennet, "but I hope Mr. Darcy's misfortune does not put off a rather important day."

Elizabeth knew her mother should not have mentioned the betrothal, but instead of any normal emotion, Miss de Bourgh looked confused.

"Important day? What are you talking about?"

"Mrs. Bennet — " Colonel Fitzwilliam began before Mrs. Bennet cut him off.

"You know, the big day!" She added a wink for good measure.

Confusion was still painted on the girl's face, so Mary spoke up. "Your wedding, Miss de Bourgh."

"What?" The girl almost dropped her glass. "Fitz, am I getting married? To whom? Has Mother done something? I do not want to get married!"

At that moment, Lady Catherine de Bourgh stormed into the sitting room. "Anne, we are leaving immediately! I shall not stay another moment in this place!"

The girl got unsteadily to her feet, and Colonel Fitzwilliam was forced to assist her. "Mother, am I getting married? They all say I am."

"Apparently not, for your cousin, whose name I shall not utter, has abandoned his duty to his family! Do not speak his name again, for he is dead to us! Fitzwilliam, attend us!"

"But, Mother," said Miss de Bourgh, "how can we call him Fitzwilliam if we cannot say the name Fitzwilliam? Should we not call him Richard?"

"Anne, enough! Let us leave." The grand lady took no leave of the Bennets, but instead turned on her heel and marched from the room, expecting the colonel and her daughter to follow. They did, with Miss de Bourgh giving the others a small wave. The Bennets remained seated, sharing glances of confusion and wonder until they heard the front door open and close.

"Well," said Mr. Bennet, "that was interesting!"

The next minute, Colonel Fitzwilliam reentered the room, but he was not alone.

"Good morning, everyone," said a cheerful Charles Bingley, still in his dripping overcoat. "I hope I find all of you well." He turned to the colonel. "Colonel Fitzwilliam and I are acquainted, but who was in the grand carriage that just left?"

"That was Lady Catherine de Bourgh," said Mr. Bennet as he eyed the pool of water growing at Mr. Bingley's feet. "Would you like to remove your coat, sir?"

"Oh! Forgive me!" He quickly removed the sodden garment and handed it to the footman who had followed in his wake. "My steward informed me of a carriage heading for Longbourn, and I rushed to see whether anything untoward had happened to my friend. I am happy you made good time, Colonel. Is Miss Darcy with you?"

"She is, Bingley, a…umm…bit indisposed. She is upstairs resting."

"Jane attends her," added Elizabeth.

Bingley smiled. "Oh, well, she is in the best of hands, then. Miss Bennet is an angel!"

"As for Darcy," said the colonel, "from what I have seen, he is as well as can be expected."

"BINGLEY!" called Mr. Darcy from the parlor. "IS THAT YOU?"

"There is certainly nothing wrong with his voice," said Mr. Bennet.

"Coming, Darcy!" Mr. Bingley called out before turning to the others. "If you would please excuse me, I must attend my friend."

"I had best come with you," said the colonel with a wink for the Bennets. As they made for the door, they were intercepted by Miss Darcy and Miss Bennet. Jane announced that Miss Darcy was recovered from her mortification, and once they saw that Lady Catherine had departed, decided to join the others. After sharing greetings, Miss Darcy kindly accepted apologies from the Bennets and went with the two gentlemen to see Mr. Darcy.

Mr. Bennet was already at the door of his book room. "I have had all the excitement I can stand for one morning. I do not wish to be disturbed until tea." With that, he closed his door firmly.

The others dispersed to attend to their usual activities, leaving Elizabeth in a state of confusion.

"You are leaving," Darcy commanded in a firm voice.

His sister's was soft but no less decided. "No, I will not."

"Georgiana, I am telling you to go back to London."

"And I am telling you I shall not. I will not abandon you while you are forced to remain here."

Darcy turned to his cousin. "Well, are you going to say anything?"

Colonel Fitzwilliam crossed his arms. "No, except that I agree with her. It makes no sense to send her away. Better to send for Mrs. Annesley when the weather clears."

"You *know* why I want her back in Town."

"She already knows about Wickham, Darcy."

Georgiana stood and crossed her arms as well. "Yes, I know he is here, but I am done hiding from him and my shame. I shall face the world like a Darcy—like *you*, Brother."

Darcy thought this was a bad time for Georgiana's spirits to recover from the near-disaster at Ramsgate, but he raised another objection. "I do not want my sister in an inn without my protection."

"Thank you for your faith in me, Darcy," cried the colonel with some heat.

"I am sorry. I did not mean any slight against you, but Georgiana is my responsibility. I will not rest quietly if she is in a public house outside of my eye."

"Never fear," chimed in Mr. Bingley. "She and the colonel may stay at Netherfield. We have room aplenty!"

"Stay out of this, Bingley," Darcy growled. "I am still angry with you for sending that express! Do not make things worse."

"Well, I think it a fine idea!" declared Georgiana. "Thank you, Mr. Bingley. I accept your offer."

Darcy was astonished at his sister's willfulness. "Georgiana, I forbid it!"

She looked at him with a twinkle in her eye. "It would be hard for you to do anything about it while you are abed." She blew him a kiss. "Richard and I shall go to Netherfield now, but we shall return tomorrow!"

Bingley offered the girl his arm while the colonel followed in their wake. "She is certainly becoming your sister, Cuz!" he said with a laugh in response to Darcy's renewed protests. In another moment, he was alone with the physician and his valet.

Mr. Macmillan cleared his throat, evidently embarrassed by the whole episode. "Umm...I should return to Netherfield, as well, Mr. Darcy. The weather prevents me from traveling to London, so I shall be by tomorrow. Is there anything I can do before I go?"

Darcy felt like a pouting child, but he did not care. "Is there any more of that brandy about? I could use a drink."

Chapter 6

THE THIRD DAY OF Darcy's forced exile in Hertfordshire began like the first two — with a splitting headache. However, Darcy resolved that he had enough of laudanum, and he absolutely refused Mr. Macmillan's offer of the potion. When challenged about his rejection, Darcy had a ready answer.

"Because I have been a damned fool on it, sir."

Earlier that morning after he awoke, Darcy had a long conversation with Bartholomew. He had vague memories of strange things, such as singing, shouting, and white soup, and he wanted to separate fact from fiction. What he learned did not please him.

"I *sang*, Bartholomew?"

"Yes, sir."

Bartholomew spoke in a dry, emotionless voice with undertones of condescension. It was an unfortunate affliction, and Darcy was never sure when the man was being impertinent. Bartholomew's tone and comportment were always the same, whether speaking of Darcy's cravat, the latest gossip below stairs, or the state of the weather. To his credit, Bartholomew was diligent and exceptionally loyal. Bartholomew could be truly frustrating to one's peace of mind, however, as the valet proved that morning.

"What did I sing?"

"I believe it was 'Spanish Ladies,' sir, but I could be mistaken.

Identification of drinking songs is not my forte."

"Please tell me no one heard me."

"That would be difficult, sir, as the entirety of the household was gathered outside. I suppose it possible no one paid attention."

"Was Lady Catherine here?"

"Yes, sir."

"Oh, good heavens! While I was singing?"

"No, sir. The singing occurred on the day of your injury. Lady Catherine came yesterday."

"What did I say to her?"

"I am sure I do not exactly recall."

"Bartholomew, tell me what you *inexactly* recall!"

"My best recollection is that you informed her ladyship you would not leave Longbourn, and you disagreed with her bringing Miss de Bourgh with her from Kent in this weather. Oh, and you would not be marrying Miss de Bourgh."

"Good God! Is that all?"

"I cannot say. There was a great deal of shouting."

Their conversation continued in the same vein, and by the end of it, Darcy gathered that he had insulted his aunt, told off a minister, yelled at his cousin, had his orders disregarded by his friends and family, and made a general spectacle of himself. As that sort of behavior was in every instance his abhorrence, he could only attribute this extraordinary breach of propriety to the influence of laudanum. He vowed never to use the vile stuff again, and Mr. Macmillan was forced to leave for London without dosing his patient.

Darcy suffered to take some white willow bark for his headache, but the concoction had no effect upon a new source of vexation: his cousin, Colonel Fitzwilliam, had come to call in the company of Mr. Bingley.

"So how are you feeling today," asked the colonel, "ready to bite someone's head off?"

"I apologize for my beastly behavior, Fitz. I can only excuse myself by pointing out I was under the influence of a very potent drug. Good morning, Bingley."

Bingley was annoyingly chipper. "I am happy to find you well, Darcy.

Do not worry about Georgiana. With the weather still wet, she remains at Netherfield. My sisters attend her."

Darcy did not find that news comforting in the least, knowing the Bingley sisters as he did. "Have you any word from Lady Catherine and Anne?"

The colonel shook his head. "I have heard nothing, but it is too soon for a message from either Town or Rosings. Surely, if anything untoward befell them, we should have heard. Do not fear. I am certain that Aunt Catherine has safely conveyed Anne back to Kent. You do not think a simple storm could stop her, do you? She would not permit it."

"True. I suppose I cannot convince you to do likewise and take Georgiana away from here?"

"Odd you should mention that." The colonel's easy smile belied a certain tension. He addressed the valet. "Bartholomew, we would like a little privacy — that's a good fellow."

Darcy waited until Bartholomew closed the door behind him. "He was not happy to be dismissed, you know. He fancies himself my nursemaid."

The colonel crossed his arms. "He must live with his disappointment. Darcy, we have to talk about Wickham."

"I agree. That is why Georgiana must be taken back to London. I do not know what will happen if Wickham learns she is here."

Bingley spoke up. "What is all this about Wickham? How does the presence of your late steward's son endanger your sister?"

Darcy had forgotten Bingley's attendance. "It is a private matter, Bingley."

"No, it is not," Colonel Fitzwilliam declared firmly. "I have thought this through all night and have come to the conclusion that we must deal with this matter once and for all."

"This problem concerns Georgiana, and I will not see her harmed," Darcy said darkly.

The colonel seemed amused. "You think you are more concerned about her welfare than I?"

"No, but I am her brother."

"And I am her guardian. I am older and wiser than you, not emotionally entangled, and still standing on my own two feet." He looked pointedly at Darcy's splint. "None of which you can presently claim. Therefore, mine is the voice that carries the most weight in the current circumstances."

"Are you enjoying yourself?" Darcy asked sourly.

"I am, actually." He grinned widely. "It is not often I have the upper hand over you."

Bingley spoke up. "Will someone tell me what this is all about?"

Darcy turned to his fair-haired friend. "My dear Bingley, I am sorry, but this is still family business — "

Fitzwilliam cut in, "He needs to know, I think. He can be of assistance."

"How?"

"I have a plan, and Bingley's disinterested involvement only helps." The colonel faced the other man. "Wickham has done more to Darcy than bedevil him for money that is not his and blacken his name with lies and half-truths. The reprobate tried to talk Georgiana into eloping with him last summer in an attempt to get his hands on her dowry."

Bingley was shocked. "The blackguard! Why, Miss Darcy is not yet sixteen!"

"You can see why we are disinclined towards the man."

"Indeed. Why has nothing been done to the scoundrel? He is dangerous!"

Fitzwilliam smiled. "Precisely."

"What can we do?" said Darcy. "I cannot take the chance that news of Georgiana's misstep becomes widely known. Her reputation would be in tatters."

"We must guard against that at all costs," Fitzwilliam agreed, "but there are other ways of ridding ourselves of Wickham. Think, Darcy! What does ole George do best besides charm young ladies?"

Darcy huffed. "He is no great card player — that is for certain."

Bingley chuckled. "Very true! I remember tales at Cambridge of how he was always short of funds from gambling."

"And that tells you — what?" Fitzwilliam prodded.

Darcy groaned. "You obviously have some idea. Stop imitating a Cambridge don and tell us, for heaven's sake. My head is splitting."

The colonel smiled. "The one thing Wickham excels at above all else is spending money. Who else could squander four thousand pounds and pile up debt besides in less than three years? How many times have you paid his bills in Lambton, Cambridge, and London? Debt is the key. I am certain that he already has run up accounts with the shopkeepers and tavern owners in Meryton during his short residence here. Let us buy them up — "

"I swore I would not do that again after the last time," Darcy declared.

"Yes, but this time we can have him thrown into debtor's prison." Fitzwilliam's wolfish smile gleamed.

"I say, that is brilliant!" cried Bingley.

The idea of his childhood playmate in debtor's prison was strangely painful to Darcy. "I…I do not know. Wickham has been foolish and greedy, but — "

Fitzwilliam rolled his eyes. "Oh, come now, Darcy! What can be your objection? If he threatens to expose Georgiana, I can have him 'persuaded' otherwise while in gaol. A few pounds to the right fellows and ole George will not be in a state to talk to anyone."

Bingley looked horrified, and Darcy narrowed his eyes. "I will not ask how you came to have such connections, but I insist that Wickham not be harmed if at all possible." Darcy looked out the rain-streaked window. "Not for his sake or mine but because it is not something of which my father would have approved. Many do not survive debtor's prison."

"Bah! If anyone deserves to be locked away in a dirty, disease-filled cell, it is George Wickham!" Fitzwilliam said with some heat. "But if your tender sensibilities are offended, we can always offer transportation to the colonies. Let Canada deal with him."

"With that stipulation, I will consider your plan," Darcy allowed.

Fitzwilliam rubbed his hands together. "It is very simple. Bingley and I will call on the local merchants and settle Wickham's accounts. Then I will approach Wickham's commander — "

"Colonel Forster," injected Bingley helpfully.

"Thank you, Bingley. I will inform Forster about Wickham's debts and ask him to investigate whether there are any outstanding debts of honor owed to his comrades. I am certain there are. Forster will see that

Wickham is a disgrace to the militia and will not interfere with having the magistrate order his arrest. Wickham will be sent to London to await trial, and we can give him a choice between prison and transportation. In any case, we will be done with him forever."

Darcy brooded. Wickham had long destroyed any affection Darcy once held for him, and there were times he could have throttled the reprobate, particularly after Ramsgate, but it was difficult to deal harshly with his father's godson. A little corner of Darcy's heart hoped Wickham would finally reform and become the man Old Mr. Wickham had been.

But Darcy could not afford to be merciful. Georgiana's reputation was at stake. Besides, Wickham's undoubted success with seduction meant that all the ladies in Meryton were at risk, even Miss Elizabeth. His sensibilities lurched at the thought of Miss Elizabeth at the mercy of Wickham. His heart hardened to the scheme.

"Very well," said Darcy. "It will be as you say. But for the plan to succeed, you need Mr. Bennet's aid." At the questioning looks he received, he explained. "You are a stranger here, Fitz, and Bingley, for all his affability, is as good as one. You need a resident of long standing to earn the complete support of the townspeople. The three of you will get far more cooperation."

Fitzwilliam was uncertain. "Will Mr. Bennet help? I must say I was not impressed with the man."

"He will once we explain the state of affairs. One last thing," Darcy added, "this is *my* problem, and *I* will provide the remedy. I cannot go with you" — he gestured at his leg — "but my purse can. *I* will buy up all the debts — no one else. I must insist on it."

Bingley protested, but Fitzwilliam was resigned. "I know very well I cannot talk you out of something when your mind is made up. Are you certain, Darcy?"

"I am. I will not be dissuaded. Bartholomew will go with you to make certain my will is carried out."

Fitzwilliam turned to Bingley. "Take no offence. His tone is often sharp when he is obstinate. He will apologize presently for his words" — he turned to Darcy — "but not his meaning."

One side of Darcy's mouth turned up. "Very true. I do beg your pardon most sincerely, but I *will* fund this enterprise."

"Then let Mr. Bennet be called," Fitzwilliam demanded. "It is time we finalized our plans."

THE LADIES OF LONGBOURN HAD retreated upstairs after breakfast so as not to disturb the gentlemen. To almost everyone's relief, Mr. Collins remained in his bedroom, pleading a stomach complaint.

Elizabeth tried to concentrate on her embroidery with limited success. The previous day's events had her mind in a whirl. Colonel Fitzwilliam's revelations about Mr. Wickham had been disturbing — to think that a man so handsome and charming could lie to perfect strangers with absolutely no hesitation! Elizabeth could scarcely believe it.

Neither Miss Darcy nor Miss de Bourgh resembled Mr. Wickham's description in the least. It was plain to see that Miss Darcy was not proud but painfully shy. The affection she had for her brother, and he for her, could not be doubted. And Miss de Bourgh was no belle of society. Rather, she was a sickly and somewhat strange individual with a partiality for sherry — not a lady one would expect to be the intended of one of the most eligible men in the kingdom.

The hullaballoo at the end of the de Bourghs' visit seemed to put the final nail in the coffin of any union between Rosings Park and Pemberley. Mr. Darcy was not to marry Miss de Bourgh. Elizabeth could only wonder whether the gentleman had changed his mind, shamefully abandoning his betrothed, or whether the engagement had, in fact, not existed at all. The testimony of Mr. Collins was suspect, and as much as Elizabeth wanted to know the truth, she could not in good conscience question the colonel or Mr. Darcy about it.

What Elizabeth could *not* put out of her mind, however, was why she even cared.

Besides her musings, there was another cause for Elizabeth's inattention to her work. Her mother and Jane were still scolding Lydia for her earlier behavior, and her youngest sister was taking it poorly.

"But I do not see where I was wrong," she insisted. "I only said Mr. Wickham was our friend and that Miss Darcy was not. How can she be our friend when we just met her?"

Jane continued to explain. "Lydia, can you not see how rude it was? You implied that we do not want to be friends with her."

"I said nothing of the sort! I am willing to associate with her, but I hate her brother! I am sure that Mr. Bingley would have held a ball for us if not for Mr. Darcy's stupid fall!"

"Oh, you foolish girl!" cried Mrs. Bennet. This was a wondrous occasion as it was exceedingly rare for her to berate her favorite. "By insulting Miss Darcy, you anger Mr. Darcy! My Brother Philips says that Mr. Darcy can sue us out of house and home should he choose to do so! We must not do anything to displease him!"

"But what of Wickham?"

Elizabeth had enough. "Lydia! We told you what Colonel Fitzwilliam said. Mr. Wickham has not been truthful with us."

"Yes," said Kitty, disagreeing with Lydia for the first time. "The colonel said not to believe anything Mr. Wickham says."

"But Wickham is so handsome and pleasant, and the colonel is so old, severe, and plain!"

"Lydia, enough!" Mrs. Bennet wagged her finger at her. "Colonel Fitzwilliam has the right of it! After all, he is in the regulars and the son of an earl! He is far better than a poor lieutenant of militia, no matter how charming! Your father has decreed that none of us acknowledge Mr. Wickham's existence ever again! You will do as you are told, or you will be kept in the house until that scoundrel leaves the neighborhood!"

"But, Mama —"

"Oh, what you do to my nerves! Cease this caterwauling! You would do better to save your breath and try to catch Colonel Fitzwilliam's eye. He has far more to give, I will wager!"

Lydia's eyes popped open. "Mama!"

"And Mr. Darcy is not so bad," her mother continued in a calmer voice. "He has been very complimentary to Cook, and I have no doubt he has a kitchen full of French cooks at his Pemberley. Look how he defended us before that horrid Lady Catherine." She turned to Elizabeth. "I am sorry, my love. I shall try to bear her as best I can for your sake, but she is a most disagreeable person!"

Elizabeth blanched. Her mother still planned on her marrying Mr.

Collins! "Mother — "

"Unlike Mr. Darcy," her mother gushed. "He improves upon acquaintance. So handsome and so rich!" She looked at her daughters. "How fine it would be to have four daughters married! I would go distracted! Yes, Mr. Bingley for Jane, Mr. Collins for Lizzy — "

"Mother!" cried Elizabeth and Jane together.

"And if Lydia can secure Colonel Fitzwilliam — "

"*Mama!*" cried Lydia.

"Why, that would leave my last two darling girls for Mr. Darcy!" She eyed a perplexed Mary and a hopeful Kitty. Mrs. Bennet's face fell. "Oh, well, I suppose a man as grand as Mr. Darcy would have his choice of the cream of society, but it is a delightful conjecture!"

MR. BENNET SAT BACK IN a chair in the sickroom, hands clasped over his midsection. All the gentlemen awaited his response to Darcy's full rendition of his family's dealings with George Wickham.

"I thank you for this intelligence, sir. Your Mr. Wickham is a nasty piece of business, it seems. The information regarding your sister will go no further, I assure you, Mr. Darcy. As for my house, I had already announced that Longbourn is closed to him. I shall now reinforce my decree by forbidding any future contact with the rascal in Meryton, as well."

The four others shared a look. "That is advisable, sir," allowed Fitzwilliam, "but we had in mind a more permanent solution to our problem." He then outlined their plans.

At the end of the colonel's recitation, Mr. Bennet nodded. "Your plans sound effective — and expensive. I wish you good fortune."

"Mr. Bennet," Colonel Fitzwilliam patiently said, "there is a reason we have brought you into our confidence. We need your assistance."

"Me? Whatever for? How can I help you?" Mr. Bennet frowned. "You do not need money, do you? For if you do, I must sadly decline."

"It is not a matter of funds but of legitimacy," said Darcy. "We must go and speak to your neighbors. Your presence in our group as head of one of Meryton's most prominent families will help loosen tongues and encourage trust."

"I thank you for the compliment, but I would rather not."

"But, sir," cried Bingley, "we need your assistance most urgently!"

"Oh, I do not think so," Mr. Bennet gently rebuffed him. "You are popular enough about the village, Mr. Bingley, and I am sure the merchants will be more tempted by the money in your purse than by the attendance of an old man like me. Besides, this sort of business is not my cup of tea."

"I must insist upon you participation, no matter your personal aversion to it," Darcy said. "This enterprise cannot have any possibility of failure, for there is more to this state of affairs than a few debts." He had anticipated Mr. Bennet's reluctance and launched into his prepared argument. "Forgive me, sir, but your daughters may be in danger."

"Oh, come now. I may be a gentleman, but compared to you, I am a pauper. My girls are too poor to be the target of a fortune hunter."

"Lack of funds will not stop Wickham in matters of this sort." Darcy paused. "Nor status of birth."

Mr. Bennet blinked. He had obviously thought Wickham not as bad as this. "You are saying he is capable of dallying with a lady of gentle birth? To affect the ruin of a girl that is by no means defenseless?" He sat up. "By Jove, it is so great a violation of decency, honor, and interest as to make it difficult to believe even Mr. Wickham capable of it."

Darcy was grim. "I believe him capable. Indeed, I *know* him capable. I possess proofs that cannot be denied showing that he has been profligate in *every* sense of the word, that he has neither integrity nor honor, and that he is as false and deceitful as he is insinuating. Even now, I support two consequences of Wickham's debauchery at Pemberley — one a farmer's daughter, the other the only child of a local attorney. Both were promised marriage, but after the ladies found themselves in distress, Wickham was nowhere to be found."

Mr. Bennet turned white. "I see." He seemed to consider his guest's claims. "The assistance provided to those poor unfortunates — you are very generous, sir. Many would do differently."

Darcy shrugged. "They are my people. What say you, sir? Will you join us?"

Mr. Bennet sighed resignedly. "It seems I must."

"Excellent." Colonel Fitzwilliam shook his hand. "We shall begin first thing tomorrow morning."

"I was afraid you would say that."

Darcy raised an eyebrow. The others took Mr. Bennet's words as a joke.

Fitzwilliam continued. "We require one thing of you, sir: a list of the merchants in Meryton that a solider would most likely frequent and who are not opposed to extending credit. That way we may be able to plan our calls with greater efficiency."

Mr. Bennet looked pained. "You need this today?"

"Within the hour would be best," the colonel said.

"Shall I get you pen and paper, sir?" offered Bartholomew.

Mr. Bennet groaned and got to his feet. "No, I have sufficient store of both in my book room." He made for the door but turned back just as he reached it. "Today?"

"Yes, if you please." Fitzwilliam smiled.

Mr. Bennet sighed again, turned, and left, saying as he closed the door behind him, "The things I do for my family."

Chapter 7

THE NEXT DAY DAWNED as cloudy and rainy as the days before, thwarting Elizabeth's plans for a long walk. The weather prevented any visit from the ladies in residence at Netherfield but not from the gentlemen. To the surprise of all and the consternation of some, the object of Mr. Bingley and Colonel Fitzwilliam's visit was not to call on Mrs. Bennet and her daughters but to collect her husband to accompany the gentlemen on what was described cryptically as "business in the village." Mr. Bennet had given no indication that he was to undertake such an errand and, as he left, gave no clue as to what the business might be. This, of course, gave rise to much speculation by the Bennet ladies, so much so that hardly anyone noticed that Bartholomew had joined their company.

The ladies were in the sitting room, and many were the theories bandied about. Mrs. Bennet was sure that Mr. Bingley had run into difficulties at Netherfield and needed Mr. Bennet's assistance. Lydia was having none of that. She was convinced, despite the total absence of corroborating evidence, that the gentlemen were instead planning a surprise ball for the coming week, a conjecture eagerly endorsed by Kitty. Mary was certain that such sensible men would not waste their time on trivial matters, but she could give no opinion as to their real business. Jane was undecided, as was Elizabeth, but unlike her sister, Jane voiced that it was indeed possible that either Mrs. Bennet or Lydia was correct.

Kitty, true to her inconstant personality, wondered aloud if they both could be correct, a suggestion roundly rejected by the others assembled.

Jane had just turned to ask Elizabeth's opinion when Mr. Collins made his first appearance downstairs in two days.

"Madam," said he to Mrs. Bennet, "as you know, my leave of absence from Hunsford extends only for another week. Therefore, may I solicit the honor of a private audience with your fair daughter Elizabeth during the course of this morning?"

One could hear a pin drop in the aftermath of this request. Before Elizabeth had time for anything but a blush of surprise, Mrs. Bennet answered, "Oh dear! Yes, certainly. I am sure Lizzy will be very happy — I am sure she can have no objection. Come, girls, come away. I need you all upstairs."

The matron gathered her work together, and the other girls rose to their feet in differing manners of expression — Jane concerned, Mary shocked, and Kitty and Lydia amused.

"Mama, do not go, please," Elizabeth called out. "Mr. Collins must excuse me. He can have nothing to say to me that we all cannot hear."

Mrs. Bennet paused for a moment, hesitated, and then said, "No, Lizzy. I desire that you stay where you are." Upon seeing Elizabeth's vexed and embarrassed look, she added firmly, "I *insist* that you stay and hear Mr. Collins." She concluded in a more hopeful voice, "All will be well, my dear."

Elizabeth could not oppose such an injunction, and after a moment's consideration, she deemed it wise to get it over as soon and as quietly as possible. She sat down again. Mrs. Bennet and the others walked off, and as soon as they were gone, Mr. Collins began.

"Believe me, my dear Miss Elizabeth, your modesty, so far from doing you any disservice, rather adds to your other perfections. You can hardly doubt the purport of my discourse; my attentions have been too marked to be mistaken. Almost as soon as I entered the house, I singled you out as the companion of my future life.

"But before I am run away by my feelings on this subject, perhaps it will be advisable for me to state my reasons for marrying — and, moreover, for coming into Hertfordshire with the design of selecting a wife, as I certainly did."

The idea of Mr. Collins, with all his solemn composure, being run away with *any* emotion made Elizabeth so near laughing that she could not use the short pause he made to gather his thoughts to stop him from continuing further.

Mr. Collins then launched into a rambling monologue on the subject of his motives for matrimony. Every girl dreams of a declaration of love and devotion from her lover, and Elizabeth was no different. Mr. Collins's speech, for all his talk of emotions, was as far from this lady's ideal of a proposal as any man could make. Rather than beauty, character, kindness, and love, Mr. Collins spoke of duty, economy, and deference. The most outrageous statement he made indicated he was led to seek an alliance with the family at Longbourn not out of a personal desire to bridge the breech between the Bennet and Collins families, but solely on the advice of Lady Catherine de Bourgh! He claimed that, should his choice of wife satisfy the exacting standards of that august personage, the grand dame would condescend to visit her.

"Allow me to observe, my fair cousin," he said, "that I do not calculate that Lady Catherine de Bourgh will hold her most justifiable resentment over her nephew's un-gentlemanly abandonment of the lovely Miss de Bough against you or your family as long as proper deference is paid. No one of your station could influence someone of Mr. Darcy's rank. Therefore, there must have been some great negligence in *his* upbringing for him to so throw off all notions of duty and what is owed to my most exalted patroness, his aunt."

The reader may be assured that this statement did away with any amusement Elizabeth may have felt in listening to his ridiculous proposal, but Mr. Collins continued too quickly to be interrupted.

"The fact is, as I am to inherit this estate after the death of your honored father, I could not satisfy myself without resolving to choose a wife from among his daughters, that the loss to them might be as little as possible when the melancholy event takes place. This has been my motive for securing my life's companion from Longbourn instead of my own neighborhood, and I flatter myself it will not sink me in your esteem."

Mr. Collins was wrong — very wrong. Any respect Elizabeth might have had for the gentleman due to his profession dissipated as her anger rose at the clergyman's crass reference to the entail. She had decided within five minutes of meeting him that Mr. Collins was the last man on Earth she could be persuaded to marry, and every word now uttered by the vicar reinforced that resolve.

Mr. Collins was, of course, ignorant of his object's revulsion of his person. "And now nothing remains for me but to assure you in the most animated language of the violence of my affection," he pompously proclaimed. "To fortune I am perfectly indifferent, and shall make no demand of that nature on your father since I am well aware that one thousand pounds, which will not be yours till after your mother's demise, is all that you may ever be entitled to. On that head, therefore, I shall be uniformly silent, and you may assure yourself that no ungenerous reproach shall ever pass my lips after we are married."

Elizabeth felt it was absolutely necessary to interrupt him now. "You are too hasty, sir. You forget that I have made no answer. Let me do it without further loss of time. Accept my thanks for the compliment you are paying me. I am very sensible of the honor of your proposals, but it is impossible for me to do otherwise than decline them."

To Elizabeth's surprise, the man only smiled. "I know it is usual with young ladies to reject the addresses of the man whom they secretly mean to accept when he first applies for their favors and that sometimes the refusal is repeated a second or even a third time. I am, therefore, by no means discouraged by what you have just said and expect to lead you to the altar ere long." He took a step towards her. "Let us seal our inevitable agreement with a kiss."

"No!" Elizabeth cried, to no avail. Mr. Collins continued towards her, for he was not to be denied. She spun about, took to her heels, and dashed out of the room.

Mr. Collins followed closely. "Such behavior is uniformly charming!"

Rather than flying up the stairs, the impulse of a moment found Elizabeth in the parlor occupied by Mr. Darcy and the maid Sally. She did not falter at their astonished looks but continued into the room until Mr. Darcy's sickbed was firmly between her and the door — and her most determined suitor.

"Mr. Collins," she panted, "I do assure you that I am not one of those young ladies who is so daring as to risk their happiness on the chance of being asked a second time! I am perfectly serious in my refusal. You could not make *me* happy, and I am convinced that I am the last woman in the world who would make *you* so."

"What the devil is going on?" asked Mr. Darcy.

"Mr. Darcy, this is a private matter," said Mr. Collins. "Elizabeth, come away. It is not proper for my betrothed to be in the room of a gentleman."

"Excuse me?" sputtered Mr. Darcy before turning to Elizabeth. *"Betrothed?"*

"Mr. Collins is mistaken," Elizabeth insisted. "I have refused his proposals. He must withdraw."

"You must give me leave to flatter myself, my dear cousin," returned the clergyman with a smile, "that your refusal of my addresses is merely words of course. It does not appear to me that my hand is unworthy of your acceptance or that the establishment I can offer would be any other than highly desirable. My situation in life, my connections with the family of de Bourgh, and my relationship to your own are circumstances highly in my favor."

"Mr. Collins," said Mr. Darcy, "the lady has refused you."

"Inconceivable! She knows better than that." Mr. Collins turned to Elizabeth, and his smile dissolved into a sneer. "My *dear* cousin, you should take it into further consideration that, in spite of your manifold attractions, it is by no means certain that another offer of marriage may ever be made you. Besides, *I* will one day be the master of Longbourn, and I shall extend my charity to my *family*," he emphasized the word, "as Our Lord commands."

Elizabeth gasped at the flagrant threat. Mr. Collins had virtually avowed that should Elizabeth not marry him, Mrs. Bennet would indeed starve in the hedgerows! She could say nothing at present, but Mr. Darcy felt no such restraint.

"How *dare* you, sir." Mr. Darcy did not bellow as he had when under laudanum. He did not even raise his voice. Instead, he enunciated in a cold, clipped, unemotional manner. The effect was that each word slammed into Mr. Collins like a blow. "How *dare* you speak so to the daughter of a gentleman? You would use your power over a young lady's family to satisfy your base desires? By God, sir."

Mr. Darcy, red-faced and furious, threw off the bed sheet and struggled to rise, causing Mr. Collins to cringe in fear. Fortunately for Elizabeth's sensibilities, he wore breeches. Sally dashed to Mr. Darcy's side, but he would not heed her requests to lie back and instead used the young maid's shoulder as support. His look was deadly, his appearance frightening. His eyes were blazing, and had they been swords, Mr. Collins would be pinned against the opposite wall.

Mr. Collins tried to placate him. "Sir…sir, you misunderstand! I meant no such thing!"

Mr. Darcy was relentless. "I warned you, man. I warned you against angering me. You should be happy I am immobile, for if I could stand on my feet unaided, you and I would meet on a field of honor, you *scoundrel*. I would take great pleasure in puncturing your pompous exterior and feeding your carcass to the pigs. You are no gentleman and deserve no courtesy whatsoever." Mr. Darcy lowered his voice further. "Heed what I say, for my mind is no longer clouded by laudanum, and I will fulfill this vow: You *will* withdraw, man, and you will no longer impugn yourself upon the ladies of this house, or heaven help me, I will see you *destroyed*."

Elizabeth was transfixed by the scene. Judging by Mr. Darcy's frigid voice, his trembling fists, and Mr. Collins's blanched response, she had not a shred of doubt that Mr. Darcy meant every word he said and that Mr. Collins knew it, too. Sweat broke out on the parson's face even though the air was rather cool. He took first one and then a second step backwards before fleeing the man who had just declared himself the Bennet family champion.

Once the echo of Mr. Collins's flight up the stairs died away, Mr. Darcy sagged against the bed, a groan escaping his lips.

"Oh, sir!" cried Sally. "Now see what you've done! You've done that rascal proper, but you've taxed yourself overmuch! You must lie down, sir!"

Mr. Darcy's distress spurred Elizabeth into action. "You must return to bed," she demanded as she moved to help the maid.

"Miss Elizabeth, do not," he weakly protested. "It is not suitable that you assist me."

Elizabeth would hear none of it. "For what you did for me, it is the least I can do. Come, Sally, gently now." Between the two of them, Mr. Darcy was reestablished in the bed, Elizabeth trying valiantly not to take notice of his state of undress or the solid muscle beneath his nightshirt. Trying — and failing.

Mr. Darcy's face was white with pain. "Are you well, Miss Elizabeth? I hope you did not take fright."

Elizabeth shook her head. "Goodness, no! I am only thankful for your actions. But you are the one in pain, not I. Is there anything you can take for your present relief? A glass of wine — shall I have one fetched for you?" Sally began moving towards the sideboard, but Mr. Darcy forestalled her.

"No, I am well." He smiled. "I only want…" His voice trailed off, and his eyes darkened as he stared at her. Elizabeth could not move for the world. Mr. Darcy's lips moved as if he meant to say something but made no sound. Finally, he broke his gaze on her and said, "A bit of rest is all I need. It was an honor to be of service to you."

"Please do not do it again!" Elizabeth begged. "You might have re-injured yourself! You must take care and get well." As an afterthought, she added, "Think of your poor sister!"

Mr. Darcy closed his eyes and chuckled. "I am well rebuked. It shall be as you say."

Elizabeth smiled. "Good. I will leave you in Sally's capable hands. Rest now, good sir knight, for one never knows when another damsel in distress might be in need of a hero."

She excused herself and made her way to her bedroom upstairs, taking care that the hallway was empty of any sign of Mr. Collins.

ELIZABETH DID NOT EMERGE FROM her chamber for some time, but that did not mean she was alone. First, her mother and then all her sisters invaded the sanctuary she shared with Jane. Elizabeth suffered interrogation, laughter, consolation, and condemnation from her relations.

As expected, Mrs. Bennet was particularly distressed. If Elizabeth heard *"How could you do this to your poor Mama? We shall be thrown to the wolves after your father is dead!"* once, she heard it a hundred times. Mary and Jane expressed doubts over her account of Mr. Collins's actions. They were sure there had been some mistake — Mary, because a man of the cloth could do no wrong, and Jane, because of her innate belief in the goodness of everybody. Strangely enough, Mrs. Bennet did not join their chorus. *Her* concerns were more over what Mr. Collins's future actions could be. Kitty and Lydia thought it all great fun, and the youngest had to be restrained from going to Mr. Collins's room to ask him about the incident.

Elizabeth did report Mr. Darcy's participation in the event, but she minimized his actions. She simply testified that the gentleman had recommended to the clergyman that he should take the lady's refusal at face value and bother her no more. She certainly did not relay the fact that Mr. Darcy had as good as threatened the vile vicar's life because of the man's insults to her and her family. Their reaction to the information she did provide was surprise, except for Jane, and all commended the gentleman for his consideration. The response was nothing to what it would have been had the others known the full extent of Mr. Darcy's declarations, Elizabeth knew.

Elizabeth was one to mull thoughts over obsessively, and *this* was a subject ripe for intensive retrospection. Until Elizabeth could decide what it all meant, she would share it with no one — not her mother, her sisters, or even her beloved Jane.

Almost two hours passed before she heard that her father had returned. Elizabeth hurried to the book room, knowing she had to tell her father *something* of what had happened during his mysterious absence. The extent of that information she had not yet determined. By the time she gained entrance to her father's inner sanctum, she discovered her mother was of like mind and was already protesting to her husband, even before he took his ease behind his desk.

Mrs. Bennet wailed in fine form. "Oh, Mr. Bennet, we are ruined! Lizzy has refused Mr. Collins, and we shall starve in the hedgerows! Whatever shall we do?"

Mr. Bennet, obviously exhausted and irritated as well as damp, did not seem to be as diverted with this information as Elizabeth had anticipated. "What is it you are going on about, Wife? What is this about Mr. Collins?" He noticed the attendance of his favorite. "Lizzy! Will someone tell me what has happened?"

Between the two ladies, Mr. Bennet was informed of the morning's activities.

"So, am I to understand," Mr. Bennet said slowly in his usual place seated at his desk, "that Mr. Collins made Lizzy an offer of marriage, which was refused, but Mr. Collins would not accept this rejection until Mr. Darcy intervened?" At Elizabeth's nod, he asked, "How on earth did Mr. Darcy come to be involved in this business? Was he in the room?"

Elizabeth blushed. "No, Father — rather, we were in his room."

"How did that happen?"

Mortified at seeing how this chain of events must look, Elizabeth was forthright. "Mr. Collins was rather animated in his expectation of an acceptance of his proposal, and I thought distance would be advantageous. Before I knew it, I had taken refuge in the parlor, but Mr. Collins followed. That Mr. Darcy was a witness to this was unintentional, I assure you."

Mr. Bennet eyed her. "Was it now? Was it indeed? I suppose it matters not as his services were required." He rubbed his face. "Blast, the last thing I want is to be further indebted to that man!" He started and dropped his hands. "Did Mr. Collins harm you, Lizzy?" His voice was sharp.

"No, Father! But his presence was an imposition."

Mr. Bennet relaxed. "Do you stand by your refusal?" She nodded, and Mr. Bennet grimaced. "Excellent, for I tell you now, I should have refused to give that man my permission in any case."

"But, Mr. Bennet!" cried his wife anew. "What will happen to us should the Lord take you away? Mr. Collins will not be predisposed to be kind to us! He will throw us out of the house!"

Mr. Bennet turned to his wife. "You would have one of your daughters married to that dolt?"

Mrs. Bennet glanced at Elizabeth, biting her lip. "I... I must think of all the girls should evil befall you, my dear."

In a flash, Elizabeth understood. Her mother did not hold Mr. Collins in any particular regard. Rather, she thought marriage by one of her girls to the odious Mr. Collins was the lesser of two evils. Elizabeth, being the second in line was the obvious choice. Jane, almost engaged to Mr. Bingley, was not available. Mary, at barely eighteen, was almost too young for marriage, and Kitty and Lydia were practically children.

Mr. Bennet groaned. "This is my fault." He held his face in his hands. "My dear, forgive me. I should not have teased you so all these years."

"Teased me? What do you mean?"

Mr. Bennet sighed. "It is all in my will. There will be enough money set aside to provide you a cottage in the case of my demise and a little more besides. Though not in the style to which you have become accustomed, Mrs. Bennet, you certainly shall *not* starve in the hedgerows."

"A…a cottage?" Mrs. Bennet could hardly believe it. "I am to have a cottage?"

"Yes. I am sorry it is not more."

"Oh, Mr. Bennet!" The lady dashed to her husband and, to Elizabeth's amazement, embraced and kissed him. "A lovely little cottage! All that is delightful! Oh, you take such good care of us, my dear! A garden — shall it have a garden?"

Mr. Bennet freed himself from his wife's assault. "It has not been purchased yet, but I see no reason why it should not. I leave those details to my Brother Philips — "

Mrs. Bennet was beside herself. "Of course, it shall have a garden! Two gardens — one for flowers and another for vegetables! Clever Mr. Philips! Thoughtful Mr. Bennet! We are saved forever! Oh, my dear, I knew you should not be so clever for nothing!" She turned to Elizabeth. "Lizzy, my love, I hope you will forgive me foisting that horrid parson on you, but I saw no other way!" She frowned. "But now I can finally give that revolting man a piece of my mind!" With that, she stormed out of the book room.

Elizabeth, stunned by the series of events she had witnessed, stood in a corner. For his part, Mr. Bennet stared out of the window, watching the drizzle.

"Leave me, Lizzy. I have work to do."

Elizabeth made to go but could not. "What troubles you, Father?"

"For the second time today, I have been reminded how inadequate a master and provider I have been. I have done more this morning for the village than I have done in all the years I have lived here." He sighed. "I will certainly get credit for it, but all I did was stand about and look important. Other men paid the price. I am thoroughly ashamed of myself."

Elizabeth was concerned. "What happened this morning with Mr. Bingley and Colonel Fitzwilliam?"

He seemed distracted at first and then said, "Nothing dire, I assure you. It is just that I have been forced to admit to myself I am not the man I pretend to be."

"You are the best of men!" Elizabeth did not quite believe that, but she loved her father.

Mr. Bennet would have none of it, however. "Say nothing of that. Who should suffer but myself? It has been my own doing, and I ought to feel it."

"You must not be too severe upon yourself," replied Elizabeth.

"You may well warn me against such an evil; human nature is so prone to fall into it. No, let me once in my life feel how much I have been to blame." He chuckled without mirth. "I am not afraid of being overpowered by the impression. It will pass away soon enough." He pulled out a sheet of paper. "I am writing to your Uncle Philips and later to your Uncle Gardiner," he said as her wrote. "I am determined to devise ways of economy, thereby leaving more for your mother when my time comes." He glanced at Elizabeth. "It will mean fewer fine dresses for you, my dear. I hope you understand."

Elizabeth could feel panic creep up her throat. "I care not about that! Are you well? You have not received bad news?"

Mr. Bennet blinked. "No, I am perfectly well." He smiled for the first time. "Fear not, child, I am not going to die. My plan is to be responsible and set more aside, that is all. Come, give me a kiss and leave me to this task. I shall see you all at tea."

A relieved yet puzzled Elizabeth dutifully kissed her father's cheek and left the place. As she closed the door behind her, she beheld her mother coming down the stairs in triumph.

"So much for him!" Mrs. Bennet cried with a snap of her fingers. "He is leaving directly," she said of Mr. Collins, "but not without hearing just what I think of him and his patroness!"

"Mr. Collins is leaving Longbourn?"

"And good riddance, say I! Who needs the big oaf with all his prattling about his esteemed Lady Catherine de Bourgh? A pox on both of them!" She took Elizabeth's hands in hers. "Do not worry, my love. When Jane secures Mr. Bingley, he will certainly throw you and your sisters in the path of other rich men!" An idea seemed to occur to her. "Perhaps…" She glanced at the parlor door.

"Mama?" asked Elizabeth, dreading the answer.

"Of course! He is so clever, but so are you!" She looked hard at her second daughter. "But you must do away with your high ways and outspoken opinions, Miss Lizzy! Mr. Darcy expects deference!"

"Mother!"

Mrs. Bennet took Elizabeth's face between her hands. "True, you have not Jane's beauty, but you are pretty enough. If we do something with your hair," she glanced at Elizabeth's dress, "and your *décolletage*."

"MOTHER!"

Her mother smiled, a familiar glint in her eye. "Just go upstairs and make yourself presentable for tea, Lizzy, and leave everything to me. Mr. Darcy will be here another month, at least. Plenty of time — oh, yes, plenty of time!"

To Elizabeth's horror, Mrs. Bennet kissed her cheek and left for the kitchen, humming a song — *a love song*.

Elizabeth knew the Matchmaking Monster of Longbourn had a new target.

MEANWHILE, SAFELY INSIDE DARCY'S MAKESHIFT sick room, Colonel Fitzwilliam and Bartholomew were giving their report to Darcy, Mr. Bingley having returned to Netherfield directly from Meryton. Darcy was minding none of it. His head instead was filled by the events of that morning.

What in the world had induced him to speak in that manner? Never, even with Wickham, had he been as angry. True, he could not stand by while Collins made his vile insinuations; no true gentleman could. But there were other, more proper ways of extracting Miss Elizabeth from her mortifying situation — ways that would not have him break the rules of propriety in defending the lady. Why, he had all but declared an interest in Miss Elizabeth Bennet!

I must stop deceiving myself, he thought. *I cannot blame this on a mind clouded by concoctions. I AM interested in Miss Elizabeth. She is the most captivating creature I have ever beheld. She bewitched me at Netherfield, and nothing at Longbourn has dimmed that certain glow that surrounds her as she walks into a room. And her eyes! There is not a lady in the country that is her equal in wit, beauty, and kindness. But marry her? Make her my wife and mistress of Pemberley? Is it feasible?*

Darcy's initial objection to Miss Elizabeth, other than that stupid comment at the assembly, was her family. They were undoubtedly ridiculous, something that surely would be a degradation to his name, his standing, and Georgiana's chances of a suitable alliance. But Lady Catherine's visit — what he could remember of it — had been a revelation. She and Anne were worse than ever. Lady Catherine's choice of vicar proved her judgment was as deficient as her parenting skills. How could Darcy condemn Miss Elizabeth's family for behavior that paled in comparison to his?

To be honest, he had been treated with the utmost care and compassion by all the occupants of Longbourn, save Mr. Bennet. *That* gentleman was insolent and indolent; his saving grace was his obvious affection for his children. Could Lady Catherine say the same?

Darcy, for himself, cared not a whit for society. Dare he make an offer for the fair Elizabeth? If he could be assured that Georgiana would not be harmed by an alliance with Longbourn —

"Darcy!" cried Colonel Fitzwilliam. "Have you heard a word I have said?"

His musings broken for now, Darcy returned to his guest. "Of course, Fitz. Pray continue."

The colonel held up a sheaf of papers. "Twenty-two pounds, eight shillings, eleven pence. It is unbelievable how much debt Wickham can accumulate in less than a week! Twenty-two, eight, and eleven — a quarter of his annual pay! At that rate, he would bankrupt all of Hertfordshire in six months!"

"Wickham is not good at much, but he is good at that." Darcy turned to Bartholomew. "Did you have enough money?"

The valet held up Darcy's wallet. "Fortunately, sir, most of the merchants were willing to accept a bank draft. There will be no need of additional funds."

"You were right about Mr. Bennet's attendance," the colonel admitted, "otherwise, I think it would have been cash only."

"Will it be enough?"

The colonel nodded. "Once I have a word with Colonel Forster, we can add Wickham's gambling debts to the total. Knowing ole George, they should be substantial. We will have enough to have him taken up. Once he gets to London and the report of his arrest is in the papers, I am sure all his creditors in Town will make themselves known. We will have all the leverage we need."

"And if he is not a fool, he will be on a ship bound for Halifax," Darcy mused.

"You know my opinion of that," said Fitzwilliam darkly, "but I agreed the worthless scum should have a last chance. As long as I never set eyes upon him again, I am satisfied."

"So am I," Darcy admitted.

A loud banging from the hallway caught their attention, and Bartholomew opened the door to investigate. The three beheld a red-faced Mr. Collins struggling with a trunk near the front door, complaining the whole time.

"Is there no one in this cursed place who will assist me? I shall remember this when I come into my inheritance!"

Darcy sat up. "Is that so, Collins? Have you forgotten already what I told you?"

The tall man jumped and yelped. He did not know he was being observed, his back being to the door. "Ah, Mr. Darcy! No, sir, I have not forgotten! It is forever implanted in my mind!"

"I doubt that," Darcy replied. "You are leaving? Excellent choice. Bartholomew, find Mrs. Hill and have her fetch a few stout fellows to remove this man from the premises."

"At once, sir." Bartholomew left through the other door. Fitzwilliam made to close the door to the hallway, but Darcy stopped him.

"Collins," he said in the same, low dangerous voice he had used before, "it is my practice to treat servants with respect. As a man who claims to have taken orders, I will expect no less from you. For your sake, I would not like to hear differently about your behavior. Do I make myself clear?"

"Per...perfectly, sir! I shall endeavor to remember your generous words of instruction, so similar to those my esteemed patroness has imparted to me regarding the lower classes — "

Darcy had had enough. "Fitzwilliam, please close the door."

Chapter 8

I T WAS SUNDAY, A grey and threatening Sunday, but remaining at home was out of the question for the Bennets. Church must be attended, and most of the inhabitants of Longbourn busied themselves donning their Sunday best — most, but not all.

Fitzwilliam Darcy was a faithful churchgoer, but his leg forced him to forgo services that day. However, he was determined to appear his best, anticipating that his sister would want to spend the Lord's Day with him. A sponge bath refreshed his body, and his clean shirt awaited only a shave before Bartholomew did his magic with the cravat. Unfortunately, Darcy's traveling razor had become dull.

"Forgive me, sir," said an irritated Bartholomew. "I cannot get the blade to hold an edge. Oh! I have cut you!"

Darcy assured his valet that he hardly felt the mistake, a claim that did little to pacify his manservant.

"There must be a half-way decent bladesmith in this wilderness," Bartholomew grumbled as he applied a cloth to Darcy's face. "I must find one tomorrow."

Just then the door flew open. "Mr. Darcy," cried Miss Bingley, still wearing her bonnet and pelisse, "we came with your sister and cousin to attend church with the Bennets, but I just *had* to look in on you... you..."

Darcy watched as Miss Bingley's face paled. He then remembered that Bartholomew was still sopping up blood from his chin. "Bingley, come quickly!"

It was too late. Miss Bingley's eyes rolled up, and the lady fainted dead away. Instantly, Bingley, Hurst, and Colonel Fitzwilliam tried to assist the unconscious woman without success. It was left to Mr. Bennet to provide relief.

"Oh, not again! Mrs. Bennet — your smelling salts if you please!"

THE PARTIES FROM LONGBOURN AND Netherfield walked into the Meryton church together, the somewhat recovered and plainly embarrassed Miss Bingley much more quiet than usual. As her male relations were otherwise occupied — Mr. Hurst with his wife, and Mr. Bingley attending Jane — she used Colonel Fitzwilliam's supporting arm to help her down the aisle.

Elizabeth smiled. Surely when Miss Bingley dreamed of being on the arm of a gentleman from Derbyshire, a colonel of infantry was not what she had in mind!

Elizabeth's amusement vanished as she became aware of the whispers and furtive glances from the congregation. She had a sinking feeling she knew the cause, and another moment proved her right. There, in a corner of the church, Mr. Collins was speaking to Sir William Lucas. Elizabeth grew mortified. All of Meryton was aware of Mr. Collins's removal from Longbourn. Goodness knew what stories were being bandied about!

Elizabeth glanced at her relations. Jane was preoccupied with Mr. Bingley's close attentions, Lydia and Kitty were engaged in their usual gossiping and giggling, and Mary was deep into her Bible. Only her parents seemed aware of the murmurings, and they reacted in very different ways. Her father was obviously bored by the whole exercise, while her mother, cheeks red with embarrassment, raised her chin and sat straight in the pew next to Elizabeth, looking neither left nor right. She reached over and squeezed Elizabeth's hand.

"Never mind them," Mrs. Bennet whispered, indicating the townspeople. "Gossip is all they have. We have better waiting for us at home." She accented her declaration with a wink.

Elizabeth's mortification was complete.

The service passed without further incident, but the rain had returned. While waiting for the carriage, Elizabeth had time to speak with her good friend, Charlotte Lucas.

"It is the talk of Meryton," Charlotte disclosed in a low voice. "Everyone knows that Mr. Collins has quit Longbourn, but there is no accord as to why. Some say he was driven out because of some unrevealed misbehavior by him. Others say that he had grown tired of Mrs. Bennet's insistent matchmaking." She looked at her friend expectantly for an answer.

Elizabeth blushed. She longed to be frank with Charlotte, but a crowded church was not the proper place for such a discussion. "There is a reason he has left our house, and the blame must be all his. More than that I cannot say, but if you come to Longbourn tomorrow, you shall know all."

Charlotte's eyes grew wide, and she stole a glance at her mother across the church. "I am happy you told me this much. Mother was quite put out when she heard the news of Mr. Collins's removal, and she is determined to show the man the civility she says he deserves. She means to invite him to Sunday dinner." She continued in a whisper, "I think she wants me to take your place."

Elizabeth looked over. Sure enough, Lady Lucas was deep in conversation with Mr. Collins.

"Charlotte, take care! I must leave now, but promise me you shall do nothing, agree to nothing, until we talk tomorrow!"

Charlotte readily agreed, and the two parted, Elizabeth still unsettled. She was glad for her own escape from the foolish clergyman, but she wondered whether Charlotte could withstand both Mr. Collins and her parents. She knew her friend was all but acknowledged a spinster and that she was painfully aware she was a burden on her family. Elizabeth prayed that Charlotte would resist any entreaties until they spoke again.

Once in the family carriage, Elizabeth learned that the Bingley party was to return to Netherfield, but Mr. Darcy's relations were firm in their intention to dine with him, regardless of the rain. The two carriages made good time in the inclement weather, and all were soon safe and dry at Longbourn. As Mr. Darcy could not join the others in the dining room, Mrs. Bennet had Mrs. Hill set up a small table for Miss Darcy and Colonel Fitzwilliam in the parlor. The young lady and the officer could hardly find the words to express the appreciation they felt, and a very flattered Mrs. Bennet took her usual place at table with a self-satisfied smirk.

Sunday dinner at the Bennets was a matter of routine, for Mr. Bennet, contrary to his usual behavior, was very particular about it. It was Elizabeth's favorite meal because her father, basking in the pleasure of enjoying his preferred dishes, was gregarious and forgiving of the foibles of the more foolish members of the family.

Alas, today was not a usual day. It began with the presentation of the main course.

"Madam," cried Mr. Bennet, "what is this?"

"I beg your pardon, Mr. Bennet?"

"This!" He gestured to the platter of meat set before him in preparation for the ritual carving. "This is not roast beef. This is a leg of lamb!"

"House-lamb is all we can get in November. We cannot get good grass-lamb until spring, you know."

Mr. Bennet rolled his eyes. "You misunderstand me. What I want to know is why we are having lamb at all. And — good heavens, is that potatoes? Where is the Yorkshire pudding?"

"Potatoes are much better with lamb."

"Mrs. Bennet, this is Sunday. We *always* have roast beef and Yorkshire pudding on Sundays!"

"Yes, but we have guests." Mrs. Bennet smiled and looked at Elizabeth. "I understand *Mr. Darcy* is partial to lamb."

Elizabeth's face turned bright red while her two youngest sisters giggled uncontrollably.

Mr. Bennet glowered. "Mrs. Bennet, this is *my* house, not Mr. Darcy's, and I expect roast beef on Sundays!"

His wife waved her napkin in an unperturbed manner. "Oh, you may have your old roast beef next week! Indeed, you like Cook's lamb."

"That, madam, is beside the point. You are spending *my* money on Mr. Darcy's lamb!"

Mrs. Bennet was unmoved. "I insist you carve. The rest of us are waiting."

Mr. Bennet was all irritation as he attacked the mass of meat before him. Usually very careful, he made a hash of it, but Elizabeth could forgive him his mood. All her life she could depend upon roast beef and Yorkshire pudding for Sundays. It was her father's favorite dish, and for his preferences to be set aside as a result of Mrs. Bennet's scheming was not only unfair in Elizabeth's eyes, but unnecessary.

True, Mr. Darcy had been a bit more accommodating of late. He had apparently forsaken the snobbish air he so effortlessly displayed at Netherfield during Jane's illness, and he had been very forceful in his dealings with the obnoxious Mr. Collins and his equally unpleasant aunt. But that signified little to *her*. Elizabeth was still the lady judged not tolerable enough to make an adequate dance partner. It was not easy to recover from such a blow to one's pride.

Mr. Darcy's recent good behavior was the result of the gentleman finally remembering his manners — that was all, Elizabeth decided. For her part, she would respond in kind. The two might no longer be enemies, but acquaintance is not admiration. Mrs. Bennet's ambitions for her second daughter were doomed to failure.

Mr. Bennet's mood did not improve upon the presentation of dessert.

"Baked apples? But where is the trifle?"

"Oh, Mr. Bennet," laughed his wife, "we have trifle all the time! The apples were so nice this week. I knew we must have some. Nice and warm on a cool and wet November day. Look, Cook added currants. It smells heavenly, does it not, Jane?"

"I do not like currants," whined Mr. Bennet. "I like my trifle! Is it too much to ask that I be satisfied *one* day a week?"

This last statement from Mr. Bennet was one too many, and all the girls looked on with wide eyes as their mother threw down her napkin. "I will have you know that I have set a good table for you these four and twenty years! Such a thing to say to me!"

Mr. Bennet remembered himself and apologized, not very graciously, but it was accepted by his wife, and all attended to the apples. They were delightful, an opinion echoed from outside the family.

Colonel Fitzwilliam appeared with a plate, the smile on his face making his plain features very pleasant. "Mrs. Bennet," he cried. "Allow me to convey the gratitude of my cousins and myself for a wonderful dinner!"

"You are very welcomed, Colonel," Mrs. Bennet simpered, giving her husband a look of triumph. "It has been said I serve the best dinner in Hertfordshire, and I believe I can give a good account of myself, even in Town! I am happy you enjoyed it. Mr. and Miss Darcy did so as well?"

The colonel laughed. "Indeed, they did! In fact, my cousin sent me to see if any of those delicious apples were left. He is not one for second helpings, but he cannot resist a baked apple, particularly with currants!"

"Is that so?" Mrs. Bennet looked as if butter would not melt in her mouth. "Well, here is more. Hill will fill your plate."

Colonel Fitzwilliam turned his back and did not see how dark Mr. Bennet's look became, but the change in her father's countenance did not escape Elizabeth's notice. He waited to explode until the cheerful colonel left the room.

"*Mr. Darcy* likes baked apples, does he?!" Mr. Bennet stood up in a huff. "Mrs. Bennet, you may name me exceedingly displeased!" He stalked off, declaring that he was going to his book room and was not to be disturbed. Elizabeth was thankful that he did not slam the door.

Mrs. Bennet did not seem affected in the least. "Oh, he will sit and storm for a while. Let him stew." She smiled at Elizabeth. "The important part is that Mr. Darcy is well pleased!" With that, she rose to go to the kitchen to thank the cook.

Elizabeth's sisters stared at her, and the object of their examination dearly wanted to escape to the woods if only the weather would permit it. It did not, however, and the others began directly to question her.

"Lord, Lizzy, is Mama trying to match you with Mr. Darcy?"

"Lydia, I am sure that is not what Mama is doing."

"It appears so, Jane. How funny! Mr. Darcy is so dull!"

"Mr. Darcy is a respectable gentleman, Kitty. He is serious, not dull, although I must wonder at his disrespect for a member of the clergy."

"Oh, hush, Mary! (cough) Mr. Darcy is worth a hundred of your stupid Mr. Collins!"

"Kitty, he is not *my* Mr. Collins!"

"Perhaps not, but Mama would have Mr. Darcy be Lizzy's! Haha! If only he had a red coat, he would be as handsome as Wickham!"

"Lydia, for shame! Mr. Wickham is a scoundrel."

"I know that, Jane, but he is a *handsome* scoundrel."

"If Mr. Darcy marries you, Lizzy, how many carriages would you have?"

"Money is the root of all evil."

"Oh, hush, Mary!"

There was nothing for it but for Elizabeth to flee above stairs.

"I SAY, DARCE," SAID COLONEL Fitzwilliam, "these baked apples are almost as good as the ones served at Pemberley!"

"I agree," said Darcy. "Apparently, Mr. Bennet has a source of cinnamon — it must be his relations in trade."

"I have no idea what cinnamon is, but if it makes apples taste like this, then I must have Father procure some for Matlock."

Darcy, knowing how frugal and English his uncle was when it came to his table, did not expect that Fitzwilliam was serious. It was a long-standing difference between Pemberley and Matlock, for the earl considered all things French to be foreign and unnecessary — except for wine and Cognac, of course. At Pemberley, it was another matter entirely. Darcy's cooks were well versed in the French style, and lately there had been attempts at Italian *pasta* and even the exotic *curry* of India.

Georgiana ate her dessert with a thoughtful expression. "Has Mr. Collins left Longbourn?" Assured that he had, she became concerned. "I do hope that the Bennets are not blamed for that. There were strange looks directed at them during the church service."

The colonel was nonchalant. "Small society as found in the country must have their gossip, Georgie. What other entertainments are available here in the wilderness?"

"If memory serves," responded Darcy drily, "the *ton* indulges in its share of gossip and scandal and more besides, even with all the diversions that may be enjoyed in Town."

The colonel laughed. "Well said! Although you must admit that gossip is paramount among the pastimes in London! Things would be so dull without it."

For some of us, thought Darcy. Aloud, he asked his cousin how long he was to stay in Hertfordshire.

"My plans are not fixed," the colonel admitted. "I have received indefinite leave from Whitehall." He grinned. "It helps having a father in the House of Lords, what? The length of my stay depends on you, Darcy, and how fast your leg heals. I shall stay until you are well enough for removal to London and civilization."

"Well, I like it here," said Georgiana. "I only hope that Mrs. Annesley is not too lonely."

"I am sure your companion is well and has enjoyed her short respite from her duties," said the colonel. "She will join us once the weather clears. That reminds me." He moved to the window and looked outside. "Yes, I *thought* the weather was letting up. We should return to Netherfield before the rains return in earnest."

Georgiana was not happy. "I want to spend more time with Brother!"

Darcy's heart was touched by his sister's devotion. "As much as I enjoy your company, my dear, our cousin is right. You must not endanger your health."

"I am not like Anne; a little rain will not bother me!"

Darcy could hardly believe how quickly Georgiana's sprits had revived in Hertfordshire. It made him almost happy that he had broken his leg — almost. "If my sister should fall ill, it would bother me a great deal. Please do as I ask."

"Oh, very well." The girl pouted for a minute before an idea seemed to occur to her. "If we must go, I should take my leave of the Bennets, especially Mrs. Bennet." She stood and, with an insincere smile, said, "It would not do for me to fail to thank her for her hospitality. I should not be a moment!" The two gentlemen watched her depart.

"She is going to grow to be a handful, I think," observed the colonel. "I do not envy you."

Darcy was too happy to see his sister smiling again to be concerned about such things. "She has been through much. I can indulge her a little."

Mrs. Hill came in. "Begging your pardon, sirs, but I just spoke to Miss Darcy, and she said that you were preparing to leave. Shall I have

Mr. Hill fetch the carriage?"

Darcy was pleased at the efficiency of the housekeeper. "Very good, Mrs. Hill. Directly, if you please." A quick curtsy and the servant was gone.

Darcy and Colonel Fitzwilliam spent a little time talking over politics until Georgiana's return with Mrs. Bennet and Jane. The Bennet ladies bade their visitors goodbye at the door while Darcy wondered why Miss Elizabeth had not joined them.

Darcy's thoughts had become increasingly occupied by fine eyes, curly hair, and impertinent remarks. He thought he had been winning his struggle against Miss Elizabeth's now undeniable attractions, but the incident with Mr. Collins overthrew such fantasies. He was lost — he had as much as declared himself during his defense of the lady. There was nothing for it but to make clear his intentions in form.

And why should I not? he asked himself. She was a gentleman's daughter and, therefore, his equal. True, she had not the benefit of a season in Town, but what of it? In Darcy's opinion, society had ruined more ladies than it helped. Elizabeth was kind and intelligent, not the least bit mercenary, and she possessed a quality missing from many: courage. Her strength of character stirred his blood as thoroughly as did her light and pleasing figure. She was just the sort of companion his dear sister Georgiana needed — and himself.

The lady was not indifferent to him, he knew. The spark in her eyes just yesterday as she helped him back to bed sent a jolt through him that left him speechless. He was bewitched by her plump, moist lips; he ached to taste them — to lose himself in her arms.

Just then, Mrs. Bennet returned, and Darcy was glad for the blanket across his lap. Otherwise, he was sure to be ashamed of himself.

"Are you feeling any better today, Mr. Darcy?" asked the matron. "I must say, you are looking well, as is your sister — a lovely young lady. You should be very proud of her. She is welcome anytime to Longbourn — and your cousin, the colonel.

"I understand you enjoyed the dinner. I shall tell Cook that you were pleased. It is important to set a good table and impress one's guests, as I have constantly instructed my girls. Oh, they all know their duties, I can assure you! Lizzy is particularly attentive to such things, but then, so are all the girls. Yes, running an estate like Longbourn is not very different from Netherfield or even Pemberley, I daresay. Why, they are all houses, some larger than others. The only difference is the size of the staff. You are satisfied with the attention we have shown, are you not?"

The lady's transparent fawning and boasting almost undid Darcy, but he was able to marshal his expression into a properly appreciative visage though he did have to bite his tongue to stop from snickering.

"I have no complaints at all, madam. Mrs. Hill and Sally have been most attentive. And I shall say that the food is as good as I have had in any house I have visited."

"Bless you, sir, but it is nothing!" Mrs. Bennet simpered. "It is just a matter of proper household management. As I told Mr. Bennet, 'We do not have to worry over our girls, for wherever they go, they shall run the finest house in their neighborhood!' Well, I should leave you to rest. I shall let your man Bartholomew know your relations have departed."

Mrs. Bennet closed the door behind her, leaving a very pleased Darcy. He expected that Mrs. Bennet would not be averse to having Miss Elizabeth become Mrs. Darcy, but to have her so blatant about it was actually comforting. All that remained was to get well enough to propose to the charming Elizabeth.

Darcy smiled, anticipating her response.

Chapter 9

THE RAINS FINALLY ENDED; the sun shone merrily the next morning. Elizabeth could hardly restrain herself long enough to make a proper toilet and choke down a bit of breakfast before seeking the solitude and serenity that only a walk in the countryside could provide.

The air was cool and still, and the woods were ablaze with color. Elizabeth's shoes made an agreeable crunch on the new-fallen leaves as she progressed on her ramble. Finally, assured she was indeed by herself, she turned her thoughts from a simple appreciation of nature to the issues that had plagued her sensibilities during the past week.

She disliked Mr. Darcy, and he disliked her. Until his accident, nothing could have been more firmly decided in her mind. He was snobbish, proud, disagreeable, and worst of all, he had insulted her appearance. The man was above his neighbors. He paid no attention to anyone who was not part of his immediate party, and when he did, it was only to observe their faults with a satirical eye. It was the reason Lizzy accepted Mr. Wickham's tale of woe so readily.

Now, almost every expectation was exploded. Since his injury, Mr. Darcy had been undeniably correct and polite to almost everyone and treated the staff of Longbourn with kindness and consideration seldom seen from one of his station. He took the blame for his accident upon himself, at least publicly. Even when addled by laudanum, his outbursts were not directed at the Bennet family and their staff, but in their defense. Mr. Wickham's story was proven to be a lie. Mr. Darcy had practically thrown his unpleasant and overbearing aunt out of the house. Miss Darcy proved to be sweet, devoted, and painfully shy — not proud at all. The gentleman's cousin, Colonel Fitzwilliam, was steadfast in his praise of the man. And most unsettling of all, Mr. Darcy had gallantly risked his health to defend Elizabeth against the unwanted advances and outlandish insinuations of Mr. Collins — for all intents and purposes naming himself the protector of the Bennet family.

Elizabeth was coming to the uncomfortable conclusion that she may have been wrong about Mr. Darcy. For a person who prided herself a careful observer of others, it was a painful supposition. Lizzy knew few who were her superior in understanding though her father and the Gardiners quickly came to mind. She valued Jane's saintly sweetness and consideration for others, but there were times when Lizzy considered her sister naïve in the ways of the world. Owning much affection but little respect for the rest of her family, she depended upon her own wit and intelligence to guide her through life.

To be so wrong in her opinions when she had been so certain was a hard business with which to wrestle. Every time a small voice in her head said that Mr. Darcy was a good man, her darker feelings reasserted themselves.

No matter his present manners, Mr. Darcy had been silent, grave, and indifferent almost every time they had met publicly. In more private settings such as Netherfield, he impressed her with his arrogance and condescension. Boasting of knowing only a half-dozen truly accomplished woman, indeed! Who were these paragons of womanhood? Certainly nobody Elizabeth had ever met!

Perhaps he meant his sister, her better angels whispered.

Well, yes, maybe — but what of the others? Viscountesses and ladies of fortune, no doubt — the cream of the First Circles of society in London. No wonder Mr. Darcy so despised the people of Hertfordshire. How else was one to explain that he could sit next to poor Mrs. Long for a half-hour without once speaking to her?

That annoying inner voice spoke again. *Are you not protesting too much?*

No, of course not! In fact, she cared not a whit about the tall, proud man! He had been exceedingly rude to her father. Mr. Darcy acted as if he was the master of Longbourn rather than a guest. What sort of gentleman diminishes his host?

What sort of husband diminishes his wife as my father does?

Elizabeth groaned aloud. This sort of musing only served to increase rather than alleviate her confusion. She vowed to think upon the man no more and instead enjoy what was left of the autumn foliage. She expected that Charlotte would soon be at Longbourn, and they had much to discuss.

DARCY HAD JUST FINISHED HIS breakfast when an excited Mrs. Hill opened the door. "Oh, sir! Begging your pardon, but there is a wagon outside just come from Town with something for you!"

Darcy had no idea what it could be, but with his injury, he could only wait until Mr. Hill brought in a large wooden object. It was a plain wood chair, straight-backed with arms, not very different from what he had seen in a poor farmer's house. What made it different was attached to the bottom of the four legs.

"Here it is, sir, although I've never seen th' like before, or the other one too," the servant said. "There be wheels on the legs." Indeed, there were four small wheels affixed to each leg.

"It is a wheel-chair," explained Darcy as Hill placed the chair before him. "Bartholomew, see to the driver."

"There's a note too, sir," said Hill. He handed it over as Mrs. Bennet came into the room.

"Oh, Mr. Darcy! What an ingenious thing — a wheel-chair! Mrs. Golding's father used one years ago before he died. Consumption — a sad business. I remember the family burning the bedding afterwards."

Darcy looked up from the note. "It is from Mr. Macmillan, and he mentions two chairs. Where is the other one, Hill?"

He jerked a thumb over his shoulder. "That one's outside, as it's too big fur th' house, I'm thinkin'."

The mystery was solved by Bartholomew. "There is a Bath chair outside, sir. I have paid the driver."

"A bath chair?" cried Mrs. Bennet. "Why would anyone need a chair to take a bath?"

"Seems a bit too big ta take a bath with, ma'am," observed Hill.

Darcy somehow prevented the rolling of his eyes. "It is a Bath chair — a rolling chair used in Bath to transport invalids or people affected by gout to take the waters. Help me, Bartholomew."

At once, the valet grasped Darcy under one arm, and he was joined the next instant by Hill. Together, they maneuvered Darcy into the wheel-chair with only a small gasp from the patient. Once a blanket was draped about Darcy's shoulders, Bartholomew pushed the chair on its small, rickety wheels towards the still open front door. Outside was a large wheeled contraption made of wicker, shaped like an overgrown slipper. Two large carriage wheels adorned either side of the vehicle, while a smaller third wheel extended from the front, a long rod rising up and back from it.

"Goodness me!" cried Mrs. Bennet. "How does it work?"

"One sits in the chair," Darcy explained, "and a man pushes it, while the occupant steers it by way of that rod, like a rudder on a boat, only in reverse."

"How very clever indeed! I should have seen one before, for I always wanted to go to Bath, but Mr. Bennet is not fond of crowds and would not make the trip."

Darcy had a sudden urge to escape the house and enjoy the outside air. He disregarded the pleas from Mrs. Bennet that it was too cold and had Bartholomew and Hill help him into the Bath chair. He suffered to have Mrs. Bennet stuff additional blankets about his person before ordering Hill to push him towards the rose garden on the side of the house.

Hill parked the chair beside a very thick rosebush, one not yet pruned back for winter. He was in the warm sunshine and still in view of the house. Hill then excused himself to return to his usual chores, alerting the nearby gardener to save an ear for Mr. Darcy.

Darcy looked about and could just make out a set of benches on the other side of the bush. He thought this would be a pleasant spot, especially when the bush was in full bloom, and the blossoms gave up their scent. He wondered whether it was the same fragrance Elizabeth wore.

He chuckled. Would she be surprised to learn that he had paid her such attention as to attempt to guess her choice of rose water? No, not surprised, not her! Flattered yes, but not surprised. She was as sharp as she was beautiful, and his attentions had been too marked.

Darcy settled back into the chair, allowing himself to daydream about roses and Elizabeth.

CHARLOTTE WAS GOOD UPON HER time, and after sharing an affectionate greeting, the two walked about the fading gardens of Longbourn.

"I have news of Meryton," Charlotte said almost at once. "It is the talk of the village that Mr. Wickham has been arrested. It is said there are debts and claims of honor against his name and that Colonel Forster has turned him over to the magistrate."

Elizabeth was shocked indeed at such news although less than she would have been prior to Colonel Fitzwilliam's visit. Still, she could not help but be concerned. "Taken up for debt! This is a serious business indeed! Is there no way Mr. Wickham can settle his accounts?"

"There is no firm estimate as to the amount," said Charlotte, "but the gossip has it that it is more than his pay could possibly support. I am afraid it is debtor's prison for him."

"I will admit that my opinion of the gentleman is not as high as it once was," Lizzy allowed, "but it pains me that one of my acquaintances should have to suffer gaol. It is a terrible place. And what of the merchants! Mr. Wickham shall be punished, but how will they recover their losses?"

Charlotte looked at her friend with a strange expression. "Do you not know?"

"What do you mean?"

"Why Eliza, all of Mr. Wickham's debts with the merchants of Meryton were bought up by Mr. Bingley, Colonel Fitzwilliam — and your father."

"My father!" Lizzy cried.

"Indeed. He was seen in the company of the other two gentlemen going into all the establishments in the village on Saturday. My brother says that Colonel Fitzwilliam was the one who spoke with Colonel Forster."

"I knew nothing of the sort," Elizabeth said most urgently. "But this means my father holds Mr. Wickham's debts. He must be the one to bring charges against him!"

"Along with the colonel and Mr. Bingley, yes. I must say that the three of them are very popular with the shopkeepers."

Elizabeth said nothing as she considered this surprising intelligence. The Bennets, while comfortable, were certainly not rich. Even if the debt was split three ways, her father's portion would be felt by them all. Was that why he said he planned to practice economy? Why would he involve himself in such matters? Mr. Bennet cared little for what happened in Meryton. Why this sudden interest? Why would he turn his attention to a man who had lied about and cheated Mr. Darcy?

Remembering Miss Darcy and Colonel Fitzwilliam's unease upon learning that Mr. Wickham was residing close to Longbourn and Netherfield, Lizzy began to think that somehow Mr. Darcy colluded in this. Did he demand that Mr. Bennet act to remove a perceived threat against his sister? Mrs. Bennet had said that Mr. Darcy could bring suit against Longbourn for his injuries. Did the man use that to intimidate her father into spending his money so that Wickham would be arrested?

Her silence during this contemplation caught Charlotte's notice. "Eliza, are you well?"

"I am very well," was her instant reply, silently promising herself that she needed to speak to her father. "I am all attention."

"Then, I must thank you for your warnings about Mr. Collins. He came to Sunday dinner yesterday, and I am afraid he had no very kind compliments for your family."

"I am sorry to hear that, but I understand his anger."

"Lizzy, you said yesterday that you had news of Mr. Collins. Can you not share it with me now? I must say that his attentions towards me became marked during his visit, and my mother now has the idea that she would like very much to see me as the future mistress of Longbourn."

Elizabeth grasped her friend's hands. "You must resist him! He is not the man he seems!"

"Elizabeth, you are frightening me!" Charlotte cried.

The two continued their stroll through the gardens, Elizabeth sharing the events of the last week in a low voice. Charlotte was, of course, surprised and concerned, particularly over Mr. Collins's very improper threat against the Bennet ladies.

"Goodness! Your warnings are timely indeed! It sounds as though Mr. Collins has not taken his vocation seriously to say such things to you!" The two walked on in meditation on how the character of men often did not match their profession.

Charlotte came to a sudden stop. "Mr. Darcy was very gallant!" she blurted. "He must admire you!"

Elizabeth almost stumbled over a tree root. "What? What did you say?"

"Eliza, did you injure yourself?" Charlotte saw that Elizabeth was very red, even in the November cool. "You should sit down."

Elizabeth's flush had nothing to do with her misstep, but she kept that to herself. "There is a bench just down the path near the rose garden."

Charlotte insisted they go there without delay, and soon the ladies reached their destination. They sat with their backs to the rose bush, looking out towards the field beyond. By now, Elizabeth had recovered enough to answer her friend.

"I must tell you that you are as wrong about Mr. Darcy as you could be. I am but the daughter of the man in whose house he is forced to take up residence. I can mean nothing to him."

"I think you are wrong," said the other. "Consider his defense of you. Can there be any reason for his interference but that of the deepest love?"

"No, no, no! That cannot be! Mr. Darcy loves no one but himself!"

"Eliza!" Charlotte cried in disapproval.

But Elizabeth heard nothing. Charlotte's conjectures were too close by half to Elizabeth's own internal struggle with the mystery of Fitzwilliam Darcy. She had not the time to work out the meaning of the gentleman's seemingly conflicting actions, and she wished with all her heart that, until she could come to some resolution about Mr. Darcy, Charlotte would keep her romantic musings to herself. As was her wont when agitated, Elizabeth expressed opinions that were not necessarily her own.

"It is true! Since coming to the neighborhood, Mr. Darcy has been aloof and standoffish. He has spoken to no one outside his own party. And he has been worse since his injury. He has all but taken over Longbourn. The servants are at his beck and call, and he treats them as if they were his own."

"Elizabeth, surely you exaggerate. Mr. Darcy is a gentleman. Besides, he is in his sick bed. Should not the servants attend him?"

"Of course, they should, and they do," Elizabeth conceded, "but Mr. Darcy asks no one's pardon when he gives his orders. He has diminished my father at every turn. My father is master of Longbourn, but Mr. Darcy treats him no better than a servant!

"And the rest of my family! Mr. Darcy has that manservant of his tell my mother and sisters to comport themselves in silence, else they will disturb Mr. Darcy's precious rest! He has made changes to our dinner menu without so much as a by-your-leave. A servant ordering my family about — it is unsupportable!"

Charlotte attempted to calm her friend. "You know your younger sisters and mother are very boisterous; you have said so yourself many a time. Is it not right to ask for peace and quiet for a bedridden man? And certainly your mother cannot object to providing meals her guests would enjoy?"

"You take an eager interest in Mr. Darcy's welfare! I wonder whether you do not admire him yourself."

"Eliza! I will not berate you when you are so impassioned. I will say that, of course, I admire Mr. Darcy as I would any worthy gentleman. His place in the world has earned him some deference."

Unknowingly, Charlotte had touched upon the very subject that had troubled Elizabeth the past week — the gulf between her family and his.

"This is insensible," Charlotte continued. "You know it to be insensible." She smiled. "What was it the Bard said? *The lady doth protest too much?*' I believe there is some admiration in your denials."

Elizabeth was not best pleased that her own conscience and Charlotte voiced the same conjecture about Lizzy's antipathy for Mr. Darcy. She shot back in defense, "How unfortunate for me that you quote Shakespeare! In my turn, I will say, *Love looks not with the eyes but with the mind.'* Remember I was the lady he said was not tempting enough to dance with at the assembly. No, you and I must disagree on this. He thinks as little of me as I do of him. Mr. Darcy has done nothing but impress me with his conceit and selfish disdain for the feelings of others. I assure you that I think very meanly of any gentleman who comes from Derbyshire, whether he wears a blue coat or red!"

"Yes, Mr. Darcy is very handsome in his blue coat," Charlotte teased.

"Charlotte!"

"Very well, I know there is no turning you when you are so fixed." Charlotte sighed. "I would only advise you to keep your opinions of the gentleman to yourself. It would not do to insult that man."

Charlotte's calm warning did much to soothe Elizabeth's ruffled feelings. "And I will not refuse such good counsel even though I had already come to the same conclusion. As far as Mr. Darcy is concerned, he shall receive every courtesy no matter how little he shows in return."

"Very wise," returned her friend, but Charlotte's knowing glance told Elizabeth that her companion had not changed her opinion. "I understand from Maria that there is a new calf?"

Thankful for the change of subject, Elizabeth smiled. "Yes, and if you would like to see it, we can go to the barn directly by the path here."

"Then, by all means, lead on."

THE GARDENER WAS HARD AT his labors when he was interrupted by a nasally superior voice.

"Here, now!" cried Bartholomew. "I was told you were to attend to Mr. Darcy! Where is he?"

The man remained kneeling, only turning halfway to eye the intruder. "An' ain't th' man himself not twenty yards away by them rose bushes there?" He gestured with a trowel. "Look there — there's that contraption, an' him sittin' in it. I might be gettin' on in years, but there's ain't nothin' wrong with my ears!"

Bartholomew glared at the gardener, but he was unsuccessful in intimidating the man, who by then had returned to his weeding. With a theatrical humph, the valet walked quickly over to his employer.

"I am sorry the servants here have been so lackadaisical in carrying out their — Oh sir, how pale you are! You must be chilled! You must come inside at once!" Bartholomew pulled the blanket on Mr. Darcy's lap up around his shoulders. "I will have you warm in no time, Mr. Darcy!" The agitated valet swiftly moved to push the Bath chair to the front of the estate.

A few fallen leaves were on the grass, and the wheels of the chair made a crunching sound as they rolled, which accounted for Bartholomew's failure to hear a painful sigh from within the vehicle.

Chapter 10

Darcy made not a sound as Bartholomew and Hill assisted him from the Bath chair and into the house. No grunt of discomfort escaped his lips as he was maneuvered into the wheel-chair. The servants might have thought to congratulate themselves on their care, but they would be wrong. Darcy was uncomfortable; the manhandling caused him pain, and a headache was descending upon him. Another man at least would have whimpered.

Fitzwilliam Darcy was not like other men. For a Darcy to complain was ungentlemanly; such had been his lesson from a young age. Besides, his mind was exceedingly — and distressingly — preoccupied.

"Sir," asked Bartholomew, "shall we return to your bedroom?"

"No," said Darcy at once. "I need a change of scenery. Pray take me somewhere else."

Bartholomew pushed Darcy into the sitting room, and the manservant was happy to see a fire in the grate. Positioning his master in an armchair and footstool close to the fireplace and told by the same that he wanted nothing but peace, the valet returned to the parlor sickroom and his duties there.

Darcy stared at the coals, continuing his contemplation of the conversation he inadvertently had heard in the garden. The two ladies may have spoken in low tones, but the slight breeze carried every word to Darcy's increasingly distraught ears.

Miss Elizabeth hated him! It was inconceivable, but it was true. He had heard the lady's denouncement of him from her own lips! She found him proud, aloof, and overbearing — his manners bad, his actions painful, and his attentions to *her* ignored. How could this have come to pass?

Darcy saw at once the seeds of his disappointment — his own unthinking words to Bingley at that blasted assembly! Darcy disliked public gatherings generally and crowded dances particularly, both in Town and in the country. He was always uncomfortable with strangers and distant acquaintances. He never knew what to say; he had no ear for conversation like Bingley or Fitz. He had borne this cross all his life.

The Meryton event was untimely as well. It had been mere weeks since Ramsgate, certainly less than two months. He only said what he did to Bingley to have his friend leave off. He would have said the same about a princess of the realm. Darcy did not intend that the lady would hear his words, but he had no idea that she would have taken them so seriously. Why had he spoken so loudly?

Was it any wonder Miss Elizabeth gave no credence to his attentions? She had taken his words to heart. She had disliked him from the very beginning. His joke about his "tolerable leg" had fallen as flat as he had from his horse.

But what of their conversations at Netherfield? He treated her as he treated no other woman in his life. He tried to be careful, tried not to raise expectations, but he could not help himself. He listened to her, debated her, and laughed with her.

Darcy reconsidered Miss Elizabeth's actions. Perhaps she was laughing *at* him.

"Mr. Darcy has done nothing but impress me with his conceit and selfish disdain for the feelings of others," she had said. How could he have done that?

Snippets of conversations with Miss Elizabeth returned to him — of dances refused, of accomplishments of women, of implacability of temper, of whether pride could be held under good regulation.

"Your defect is a propensity to hate everybody," she had said. Had she really believed that about him?

Apparently she did.

Oh, good God!

Darcy fell into a temper, a debate raging in his mind. Justifications for his actions and conduct warred with the reality that the *perception* of his character by the one woman in the world he wanted to impress was unfavorable. His headache only added to his misery.

It was during this silent struggle that Darcy's solitude was broken by Miss Mary Bennet. She entered the room with a sheaf of music under one arm, obviously intending to practice upon the pianoforte in the corner. She started at Mr. Darcy's presence.

"Oh, you are out of your room! I did not know you could — pray, excuse me. I shall practice another time." While her words were all that was correct and polite, her tone was not. She was disappointed and peeved at the hindering of her intended activity.

Darcy heard the unpleasantness in her voice, and his initial inclination was to thank her for leaving, but just then Miss Elizabeth's words returned to haunt him. *"Conceit and selfish disdain for the feelings of others."*

Is that what you believe, Elizabeth, my fine country beauty? Well, we shall see about that!

"No, Miss Mary, do not leave, please," he said kindly. "This is your house, and you obviously look forward to your time with the instrument. I am the guest here. Pray, come and practice. I hope my presence does not disturb you."

Mary looked askew at Darcy, her expression clearly saying that she was surprised at his statement. She paused for a moment and then slowly made her way across the room to the pianoforte. She sat down, ruffled through her music for a selection, and proceeded to play.

Almost at once, Darcy regretted his gallantry. Mary had selected a ponderous religious canticle, and unfortunately for Darcy's ears, the chord changes were beyond the lady's talents. What was worse, Miss Mary thought she could improve her performance by attacking the keyboard. Gritting his teeth, he tried to suffer through her recital, but the loud poundings from both the pianoforte and his head were too much for him.

Mary must have noticed his discomfort, for the music ended abruptly, her face flushed in mortification.

"It is apparent you are not enjoying yourself, sir. I think it best that I leave."

Darcy was determined to prove Miss Elizabeth wrong. He would be a pleasant gentleman, no matter how it hurt. "I am afraid I must admit to a headache. I regret that such a...passionate...performance is more than I can bear at present."

"I am very sorry," she mumbled, her eyes watering.

"But stay, I beg you," continued he. "I am sure that music is just the thing I need to soothe my head. Perhaps something lighter and softer?" *Please!*

"Are you certain?"

"Yes. My sister's playing has had just that effect, and I suspect yours will, too."

Mary frowned, doubt written on her face, but she dutifully searched through the music before her. "Here is a lullaby that might serve."

The room was soon filled with a light and cheery air, played at a soft volume, and to Darcy's surprise, the pain in his head did lessen somewhat. He sat back in the armchair, the sounds washing over him, and felt rather pleased with himself.

The music done, Mary asked with trepidation, "Is your head any better, sir?"

"Indeed it is," Darcy answered truthfully. "You played that piece beautifully."

"You...you *liked* it?" It was apparent that Mary did not hear much praise for her playing.

"Yes. Would it be too much to ask for another?"

Mary's eyes opened in astonishment before a bright smile broke out. It made her look rather pretty, Darcy considered. The girl immediately searched the pages for another lullaby, eager to fulfill her audience's request.

As she bent to her music, Darcy surreptitiously observed the young lady. Her eager desire for approval was much like Georgiana, he saw, although her talents were not of the same caliber. But, did not Georgiana practice constantly, and had she not the benefit of music masters? Mrs. Annesley aided his sister in her studies of languages, art, and music, as well as serving as her companion. This poor girl lacked his sister's advantages. How much might Miss Mary improve with help? Darcy lightly applauded at the conclusion of the song.

"You liked it, too?" Mary clasped her hands together in elation. "Oh, I am so glad!"

"I did. You enjoy playing very much, I see."

"I do, but I do not receive many requests to continue." Mary looked at him with big, watery eyes. "You are the first." Her lip trembled.

His heart breaking, Darcy replied, "I am honored to be the first of many, I expect."

Mary made a sound half-way between a sob and a giggle. "Would you like another song? I am not tiring you?"

Darcy smiled. "I am at your disposal."

Mary took a breath to collect herself and had just begun playing when they were interrupted by Mrs. Bennet and, to Darcy's surprise, Georgiana.

"There you are, Mr. Darcy!" Mrs. Bennet cried. "Who is that playing? Mary? My goodness child, why are you bothering Mr. Darcy?"

Darcy interjected before Mary could take offence. "I have enjoyed the concert very much. Georgiana, welcome!"

"Brother, I am so happy to see you up and about." Georgiana had a mysterious twinkle in her eye as she gave Darcy a kiss on the cheek. "Miss Mary, please do not stop. That song was very pretty."

"I thank you, but surely you wish to spend some time with your brother."

"I shall — after my trunk has been unpacked."

Darcy's ears pricked up. "I beg your pardon?"

"Your room is all ready," Mrs. Bennet gushed. "Mrs. Hill had the staff clean the guest room from top to bottom after that unpleasant Mr. Collins quit it. You and your companion shall be as comfortable in there as any room in all of Hertfordshire, I declare!"

Georgiana smiled. "I am sure of it. Thank you for all you have done."

"I beg your pardon?" Darcy repeated sharply.

Mary brightened. "Are you staying at Longbourn, Miss Darcy?"

"Yes!" said the heiress. "Perhaps we may play the pianoforte together.

My companion, Mrs. Annesley, will be coming soon. Would you care to join me for my music lessons?"

Mary was beside herself. "What a wonderful idea!"

Darcy lost his composure. "Will someone please tell me what is going on?"

"You do not need to raise your voice," Georgiana scolded him. "Now that Mr. Collins has left Longbourn, there is a room available for me. Mrs. Bennet was kind enough to agree to house both Mrs. Annesley and me while you are convalescing."

"But…but Netherfield — "

His sister cut him off firmly. "Netherfield is too far away for me to take proper care of you. And I *shall* take care of you."

"Is your companion without, Miss Darcy?" asked Mrs. Bennet.

"No, madam, but her letter said she should arrive in Hertfordshire this afternoon. Colonel Fitzwilliam will direct her to Longbourn when she reaches Netherfield."

"Well, we will make her very welcome when she arrives!"

"Georgiana, I really must protest — "

Georgiana would not hear his objections. "It is quite useless, Fitzwilliam; I am decided." She turned to Mrs. Bennet. "May I see the room now?"

"Of course, of course! Right this way. Mary, attend us. Good day, Mr. Darcy. Hill! Oh, Hill! Miss Darcy is here! See that her things are brought upstairs. Hill, where are you?"

A moment later, a bewildered Darcy found himself all alone in the sitting room. He did not like his will overruled, but he had to be thankful that his injury had reignited Georgiana's confidence. It had reignited his headache as well.

It seems you were wrong, Elizabeth, he mused. *If I am such an overbearing ogre, how is it that I have lost control?*

CHARLOTTE ENJOYED MEETING THE CALF, and the distraction gave Elizabeth time to reconsider her conversation with her friend. To her shame, she knew she had been unfair to Mr. Darcy. Yes, he had been overbearing at times, but he was in pain — because of *her* carelessness, she reminded herself. She also recalled that she was a less than compliant patient when she was ill.

To give Mr. Darcy his due, he had been kind to her mother and sisters, and he had been very good to the servants. She wished Mr. Darcy would treat her father better, but Mr. Bennet had been very difficult of late. Elizabeth was still concerned over the issue of buying Mr. Wickham's debts, but after further contemplation, she realized that no one could force her father to spend funds if he was unwilling. If Mr. Bennet had participated in helping the merchants of Meryton, she expected her father thought he could afford it.

Surpassing all else, the service he had rendered in protecting her from Mr. Collins was so great as to make her now feel ashamed of her slights against Mr. Darcy's character.

She confessed all to Charlotte, and even though they still disagreed as to Mr. Darcy's opinion in regard to herself, Elizabeth parted from her friend with a relieved conscience and a resolve to treat Mr. Darcy better.

Elizabeth re-entered Longbourn in the middle of the hustle and bustle of Miss Darcy's surprising arrival. She was thankful to have the opportunity to spend more time with Miss Darcy; she felt that many of the answers to the mystery of her brother lay with the young lady.

But Mr. Bennet watched the proceedings grimly. "Well, Lizzy, what say you to this turn of events?"

"I am sure Mr. Darcy will be pleased to enjoy more of his sister's company."

"Of course. But it falls to me to have two more mouths to feed. Yes — *two* more. Miss Darcy's companion is to join us before the day is done. Mr. Darcy's misadventure is becoming more expensive by the day." With that, Mr. Bennet retired to his book room.

Elizabeth blanched. While the Bennets were far from destitute, surely her father would feel the additional expense. Her inattention had cost her father a great deal of money, she reflected with remorse. She decided not to bring up the subject of Mr. Wickham's debts.

All of Elizabeth's sisters greeted their new guest warmly, save Lydia. With the news of Wickham's fall from grace, which she alone bemoaned, and wary of offending the heiress again, Lydia gave the girl a wide berth and remained uncharacteristically silent when in the same room. Lydia's pouting face was an embarrassment to Elizabeth, but Miss Darcy showed her good breeding and pretended not to notice.

Every moment Elizabeth spent in the young lady's company raised her opinion of Mr. Darcy's sister. She was good natured and unpretentious, and the initial shyness displayed upon her introduction to the Longbourn family was much reduced. Miss Darcy was a wonderfully charming girl of sixteen and, unlike Lydia, had no intention of acting as if she were older. By the time tea was called, Elizabeth was well on her way to loving the girl as much as if she were a sister.

Tea brought several guests. Mr. Bingley came, to Jane's understated delight, as did Colonel Fitzwilliam, which sent Kitty and Lydia into raptures. Miss Bingley and the Hursts were also in attendance, which pleased no one. They did not hide their surprise and disapprobation of Miss Darcy's removal to Longbourn, and only the colonel's enthusiastic endorsement of his ward's actions stopped their subtle disparagement of the scheme.

There was also a new addition to the party: Mrs. Annesley, Miss Darcy's companion, had arrived from Town. She was a stately woman of a certain age, well versed in manners and conversation. Both Darcys were pleased to see her, but Elizabeth was surprised at Mary's reaction. Seldom had her pious and withdrawn sister seemed so happy to make a new acquaintance. Elizabeth could only wonder at it.

Still feeling guilty for her unfortunate conversation with Charlotte about Mr. Darcy, Elizabeth endeavored to atone for her lapse in good manners. She made every attempt to pay the gentleman particular attention. She tried to engage him in conversation, kept her witty observations to herself, and smiled more than usual.

However, she was less successful than she hoped. While Mr. Darcy accepted her attentions with civility, Elizabeth could do nothing to arouse his interest. He seemed essentially as he was when he first came to Hertfordshire — coldly polite and saying only the bare minimum before falling silent. Having enjoyed his more pleasant behavior over the last few days, the lady was vexed to see him go back to his taciturn ways.

Vexation soon turned into mortification when it quickly became apparent to Elizabeth that Mr. Darcy was only reserved with *her*. With everyone else, he was open and friendly. He complimented Jane on her dress, spent several minutes in conversation with Mary, and even laughed at one of Mrs. Bennet's silly jokes! His contradictory behavior to *her* was so obvious that her mother sent Elizabeth a nervous, quizzical look, as if to ask what she had done to displease the gentleman.

Mr. Darcy was an enigma, Elizabeth concluded.

With so many talented ladies in the room, it followed that the instrument was opened and put to good use. Miss Darcy refused the opening honors, a post Miss Bingley filled with alacrity. Her performance was of a kind like those in the past — technically correct, but rather mechanical and cold. It was then Elizabeth's turn, and her playing won approval from all — it was the only spark she could generate in Mr. Darcy's eyes that evening.

Mary was delightfully surprising. Rather than some over-long dirge, her simple county tune was so well received that she was encouraged to play an encore. Never had Elizabeth seen Mary so happy. The strange thing was the affectionate look she sent to Mr. Darcy and the gentleman's small smile in return. The exchange made Elizabeth wonder whether her plain sister was falling in love with their guest.

Finally, Miss Darcy was compelled to take to the pianoforte; Colonel Fitzwilliam attended to the turning of the music. The young girl played a beautiful song from Mozart's *Don Giovanni*, singing in flawless Italian. Elizabeth listened with increasing delight to the song, her mind returning to a memory. Years ago, her uncle, Mr. Gardiner, had taken her to the opera to hear *Don Giovanni*, and Miss Darcy's performance was the equal of the lead soprano.

Suddenly, Elizabeth realized something. Miss Darcy was not singing the lyrics phonically, as if they were musical notes as most ladies did when singing in something other than English. No, Miss Darcy was obviously fluent in Italian, and she performed the song as if she were a professional on the stage.

Miss Darcy is fluent in Italian, she concluded, *and I dare say French and Spanish, too. I would not be surprised that her command of the Germanic languages is just as notable. If the library at Pemberley is half as grand as*

Miss Bingley alluded —

Oh, my goodness! Miss Darcy IS one of those half-dozen truly accomplished women of whom Mr. Darcy spoke! I mocked him, thinking he was exaggerating, but he was not. He was speaking of his sister!

Abashed at her foolishness, her eyes flew to Mr. Darcy. He was sitting happily, watching his sister with unmistakable pride and affection. She did not know whether he felt her eyes on him or it was just a coincidence, but in the next moment she was locked in his gaze. His look was searching, unreadable — and then it clouded over. He frowned, broke contact, and returned his attention to the performance.

Elizabeth's heart sank. She was now certain that Mr. Darcy was displeased with her, and she knew not why.

Chapter 11

ELIZABETH STOLE OUT OF the house even earlier than was her custom. She had not slept well the night before and longed for the clarity of mind a long morning walk often afforded her.

Unfortunately, that lucidity eluded her. She could not understand Mr. Darcy's sudden coldness towards her. Since his accident, the gentleman seemed...*gentle* in his dealings with her and her family. He treated the servants well, he won over her mother, and even serous Mary was taken with their guest. Only Mr. Bennet and Lydia proved impervious to his newly-displayed charm.

Mr. Darcy's impassioned defense of her before Mr. Collins, now that she had time to think upon it, had given birth to new and strange thoughts. Mr. Darcy had declared himself champion of the Bennets, but only a lover would take a family with no advantageous connections under his protection. Did that mean...could that mean...? Was Mr. Darcy in love with her?

Impossible! Mr. Darcy did not like her — she was sure of it! He was just being kind, was he not?

A realization came to Elizabeth. Perhaps Mr. Darcy made his assertion to Mr. Collins in stronger terms than he intended. Of course! Mr. Darcy had no intention of making her an offer of marriage, and his new reserve in regards to her was to make that clear to all. He knew that he had raised expectations and was trying to undo the damage by tamping down any false hopes he may had inadvertently created. Mr. Darcy was attempting to protect both their reputations, as a true gentleman should.

This new thought now settled in her mind, Elizabeth wondered why she was not content. She was still uneasy. Surely she was not…*disappointed*?

Of course not!

A rabbit skipped across the path, and Elizabeth surrendered to a sudden urge to follow. She made her way into some bushes that had not yet lost their leaves and crouched down to find the burrow, but she could find no sign of the hare. Giving up the search, she was about to stand and return to the lane, when she heard horses approaching. Elizabeth was embarrassed at her childish pursuit of the animal and decided to remain concealed.

The sound of Miss Bingley's voice convinced Elizabeth that she had made the correct choice. She did not want to give the unpleasant snob any more reasons to disparage herself or her family. If Miss Bingley saw her climb out of the brush, Elizabeth was sure that she would never hear the end of the mocking. She sat down and waited for the riders to pass, for Miss Bingley had a companion.

This outcome was not what Elizabeth had hoped. Instead of continuing down the path, the riders turned just before her location and made their way through the underbrush into a pasture. They stopped, not ten feet away from Elizabeth's position.

Now here was an unfortunate spot! Elizabeth was trapped; she could not move without giving away her location, and that would result in an awkward explanation. But she could clearly overhear the pair's conversation from where she was hidden, and that was very rude.

There was nothing for it. Elizabeth accepted the lesser of two evils and sat as quietly as she could. She could only see parts of horses and not the riders, but the voices were clearly that of Miss Bingley and Colonel Fitzwilliam. The two were taking in the vista of the pastureland before them, the pale November morning sun painting the vast field of brown and gold.

"Are you enjoying your ride?" Elizabeth heard the colonel ask his companion.

"Yes!" Miss Bingley answered with more cheerful enthusiasm than

Elizabeth had ever heard before from the lady. "The countryside can be *so* devoid of diversion, except for riding. This is a pretty prospect! There is something to be said for Netherfield, but little else. It is nothing to your home in Derbyshire, I am sure." Her conversation was easy and pleasing.

"Yes, Matlock is more rugged, unforgiving — ha, and cold! The ground here is gentle and rolling. Not as pleasing to the eye, but kinder to the horses. Now, if you wish to ride in lush green fields, Kent is your place in springtime."

"Your aunt lives in Kent, I recall. You must enjoy Rosings."

"It is very easy to enjoy the place." There was a pause. "To withstand the company there, however, requires fortitude."

Miss Bingley giggled softly and then grew quiet. Elizabeth was puzzled and intrigued by this pleasant Caroline Bingley. She strained to put herself into a better position to see the pair without giving herself away. The lady spoke again.

"I believe it is time to return." Her voice held a bit of an edge.

"If you wish," returned the colonel carefully. "Have you appointments for the afternoon?"

"Of course — to visit with Miss Darcy! Surely, she must be rescued from the excruciating company she is suffering." Miss Bingley's voice had returned to her usual superior manner. Elizabeth relaxed; for a moment, she was apprehensive she had been wrong about Caroline, too.

"I do not think Georgiana finds caring for her brother excruciating," Colonel Fitzwilliam said.

"That is not the company of which I speak. Oh, it is all well and good for dear Miss Darcy to so sacrifice her sensibilities in service to her brother, but really! It is such an uncultured, backward family with whom she is now forced to contend!"

Elizabeth seethed at Miss Bingley's gross insult.

Miss Bingley continued on. "To be blunt, Colonel, I cannot see how you permitted your cousin to leave the refinement found at Netherfield and go to Longbourn and those country nobodies."

Elizabeth did not know whether she had the strength to remain silent given the inducements to defend her family against such an ill-bred attack.

"Miss Bingley," said Colonel Fitzwilliam evenly, "you should not speak so of your betters."

Miss Bingley gasped. Elizabeth was shocked senseless. The colonel continued.

"Mr. Bennet is a landed gentleman of respectable reputation. He is not affluent and does not socialize in Town. That is unfortunate, true, but his daughters are gentle-born. The family is known to and approved by Mr. Darcy, Georgiana's brother and head of their house. The Bennets are acceptable acquaintances for my ward."

"But, but…" Miss Bingley tried to defend herself. "Their manners, their lack of connections —"

"Their connections are poor and their manners could be better, but the Bennets do not have to prove themselves. These deficits hurt their standing but do not eliminate it. It is a family of property."

"Nevertheless —"

"Miss Bingley, must I be blunt? Mr. Bennet did not come from trade."

It was fortunate that Elizabeth was sitting down else her legs would have given way. She did not have to see Miss Bingley's face to know it was awash in mortification.

"My dear Miss Bingley, the time has come for us to have a hard conversation. I speak to you as a friend. You must stop — you must withdraw — or you will ruin your reputation."

"How dare you!"

"Do you think me blind? You only pay attention to Georgiana to please Darcy! You are wasting your time. I tell you now that the daughter of a tradesman shall never be mistress of Pemberley."

Miss Bingley tried to speak, but instead she burst into sobs.

"Blast it!" cried Colonel Fitzwilliam. "Forgive my rough speech; I am too used to life in my tent."

"You cruel, cruel man! Such hateful lies! I shall prove you wrong!"

The colonel spoke with more kindness. "Miss Bingley, you must be honest with yourself. It is not my cousin you desire but Pemberley and the connections in Town that come with it. Can you not see how ill-suited such a match would be for you? Darcy is quiet and reserved. He despises London society and balls and parties — everything you enjoy.

He loves Pemberley and country living as much as he hates London. Even if you were gentle-born and acceptable to my cousin, you would be miserable. You would be locked up in Derbyshire, longing to be free. You would loathe such a life — and him, eventually."

"Stop it! Stop it! I will hear no more!"

Fitzwilliam's voice rose. "You will hear it all. You will hear the truth. I shall be a friend to you against your will. I tell you Darcy only sees you as the sister of his friend. But if he did admire you, he would do nothing, for you can never be acceptable. He is a gentleman, head of a distinguished family, with money in the funds. He has no need to marry a generous dowry, and all of London knows it. A gentleman's daughter would be barely acceptable to the *ton*, and the expectations of his family are much higher. In such circumstances, a tradesman's daughter would be despised and ignored by all, and Georgiana's prospects would be damaged.

"These facts are obvious to everyone in London. Should you ignore my counsel, your character will be fixed by the *ton* as the most determined flirt that ever made herself and her family ridiculous. My dear girl, you *must* give up this quest, for his sake and yours."

Miss Bingley's sobs were redoubled, and she immediately urged her horse back to Netherfield. Elizabeth heard Colonel Fitzwilliam utter a rather colorful oath, which should have shocked her had she not already been astonished by the conversation she had overheard. The officer then urged his mount to follow, and Elizabeth now had her opportunity to escape. She had much to think of as she made her way back to Longbourn.

It was Georgiana's idea to go out of doors after breakfast, and she would not be denied. So it was, after Hill and Bartholomew helped him into the Bath chair, that Darcy found himself again near the rose gardens of Longbourn, this time in the company of his sister and Mrs. Annesley. Darcy was unhappy with his sister, for in her intention to be kind — she well knew her brother enjoyed fresh air immensely — Georgiana had inadvertently reminded Darcy of his wretched experience of the day before.

Darcy had not slept well, brooding over Elizabeth's behavior at tea and dinner. Had he not known better, he might have been deceived into thinking that he had improved Elizabeth's opinion of him. She seemed to go out of her way to engage him in conversation. Her smiles, brighter than ever, were more than once directed his way. Her playing always stirred him, her sweet voice and lack of artifice filled his mind and soul, and yesterday's performance at the pianoforte was more enchanting and enticing than ever. He wished that it was for him.

But he *did* know better. He had heard from the lady's own lips what she thought of his character. *"As far as Mr. Darcy is concerned, he shall receive every courtesy, no matter how little he shows in return,"* she had said. Yesterday evening had been an act. Miss Elizabeth had been mocking him, just as at Netherfield.

The realization was bitter last night and remained so in the morning. He knew he was poor company for Georgiana, but he could not summon the energy to attend her as he should. He was, in a word, sulking.

Georgiana pointed out a pleasant aspect in the garden in a vain attempt to engage her brother before exclaiming, "Well, here is Miss Kitty! What brings you outside so early?"

Darcy saw the startled girl sitting on a bench, trying to hide something. "Good — (cough) — good morning." She rose to her feet, her hands behind her.

"Did we disturb you?" Georgiana tried to see what the girl was concealing. "Was that not a sketch pad?"

"Georgiana," scolded Mrs. Annesley gently. "We should not pry."

"Oh, no, you are not disturbing — (cough) — I was not doing anything." The girl was very flustered, her face beet red. Without much consideration for what he was doing, Darcy took pity on her.

"Miss Catherine, we would by no means interrupt you. My sister was only showing interest in your activity. We will leave you in peace."

"I am so sorry," cried Georgiana. "I did not mean to embarrass you. It is just that I enjoy drawing, and if you do, too, I would be happy to see your work."

"Oh!" Kitty hung her head. "I am not offended — (cough). I draw a little, but it is nothing. Surely nothing compared to what you can do."

Apparently, Miss Kitty coughed when agitated. Darcy said gently, "We would not think of distressing you, and if you would rather not show us your drawings, we will not be offended. But we are sincere in our interest. I would very much like to see your work."

Kitty looked them all in the eye, biting her lip in indecision and anxiety. A moment passed, and then the girl brought out the pad from behind her back and thrust it at the others. "Here! Look at it if you like."

A smiling Mrs. Annesley approached the girl as if she were a frightened fawn and took the pad from her trembling fingers. She returned to the chair and opened the pad in such a way that all three could see Kitty's etchings.

After viewing the first few, Georgiana exclaimed, "Why, these are very good!"

Indeed they were, Darcy saw. Kitty was obviously untrained, and her charcoal sketches of landscapes were only tolerable, but she had a remarkable talent for portraiture. Page after page was filled with portraits of the Bennet family, posed in profile, full face, and three-quarter. Most extraordinary were the ones done surreptitiously, catching the Bennets reading, sewing, or playing the pianoforte.

"Oh, do you think so?" Kitty asked doubtfully.

"Yes, miss," said Mrs. Annesley. "You have a fine eye."

Darcy could not help but agree. Kitty was talented. She was able to capture one or two features that made each portrait unique to the subject. Jane's half-smile, Mr. Bennet's smirk, and Elizabeth's eyes. Oh, yes, Elizabeth's mesmerizing eyes!

"Have you ever tried watercolors?" Mrs. Annesley asked.

"No," the girl blushed in return. "I…I have never asked Papa to buy watercolors for me." Then in a rush, she exclaimed, "I do not talk about drawing very much. It is a waste of time, after all. I mean, Jane and Lizzy are kind, and so is Maria Lucas, but I am not as good as Jane with her needlework or Lizzy and Mary on the instrument. Mama wants me to improve myself and…and Lydia teases me — (cough)." She choked back a sob.

Georgiana frowned, took the sketchbook from Mrs. Annesley, and marched over to Kitty. "I think you are very talented," she stated firmly, handing the pad to its owner, "and I would like very much to draw with you. Would you permit me?"

"With me? Truly?"

"Yes. I shall return to the house for my pad, and then we will draw together. Perhaps," she turned with a cheeky grin, "we will draw my unfortunate brother. It will be a contest! Will that not be great fun?"

Kitty agreed it would be so, and Georgiana made her way quickly to the house. While she was gone, Darcy spoke to Kitty.

"Miss Catherine," he said with mock seriousness, "I will agree to this scheme of yours, but I tell you now that I do not pose for free. Indeed, there will be a price to pay."

Kitty took him at his word and nodded nervously. "I only hope it is not too much. Lydia has borrowed all my money for a new bonnet."

Darcy smiled. "I do not want money, but I have a condition for my cooperation. A drawing."

"A drawing? You want one of my drawings? Which one?"

Darcy almost asked for her portrait of Elizabeth, but he resisted the impulse. "I have a commission for you. I will agree to sit for you, but in turn you must eventually produce a portrait of Georgiana."

"Truly? Very well, I will. Thank you, Mr. Darcy! You are so very nice, no matter what everyone else says!" Kitty caught herself and blanched, one of her hands flying to her mouth. "Oh, I should not have said that! — (cough, cough) — I am so sorry!"

Mrs. Annesley gasped a little, and Darcy's smile faded a bit.

"Mr. Darcy has done nothing but impress me with his conceit and selfish disdain for the feelings of others." Elizabeth was not the only one who felt that way, apparently. Darcy knew he had damaged his reputation, and there was work to do if he meant to repair it. He spoke as kindly as he could.

"That is quite all right. We are friends now, and I trust you will let me know if I misbehave again."

Kitty clearly could not make out what Darcy was talking about. "All…all right." She then smiled. "And will you do the same for me?"

Darcy's smile returned. "It is a bargain," he said as he extended his hand from the chair.

Kitty giggled as she shook his hand to seal the agreement. Moments later, Georgiana returned with her pad and one for Mrs. Annesley. The three ladies took their places and withdrew their charcoals, and Darcy suffered having his likeness captured for the next hour.

Returning to Longbourn, Elizabeth felt like a leaf buffeted by the wind. One by one, her firmly entrenched opinions were being overturned.

Elizabeth could not like Miss Bingley, but she would have to have a heart of stone not to feel distress on that lady's part after overhearing what she had. Colonel Fitzwilliam's harsh set-down was very difficult for Elizabeth to hear, and it was not even directed at *her*. Miss Bingley's sufferings could not be imagined.

The colonel's tacit approval of the Bennet family was confusing. Elizabeth knew they were but simple country folk. The Bennets never went to Town and never endeavored to involve themselves in the social activities of the *ton*. Elizabeth was sure that, in the unlikely event her father attempted such a thing, the *Quality* would reject their overtures with derision and disdain. She never considered her family as even a minor part of the aristocracy, but apparently the colonel did. Were the Bennets the superiors of the Bingleys in spite of Mr. Bingley's five thousand a year? It was an astonishing concept and, Elizabeth blushingly admitted to herself, very flattering.

Colonel Fitzwilliam also reinforced Elizabeth's expectations of Mr. Darcy. More than ever, she was convinced that he was destined for a great lady of London as was expected of a man of his stature. It was silly to think his current behavior was anything but that of an honorable gentleman attempting to preserve his good name and not become the subject of gossip by paying too much attention to a lady for which he could have no true interest.

Mr. Darcy was a good, if proud, man — a very good man. Elizabeth wished him well. Perhaps he would marry one of those half-dozen accomplished women he knew. Perhaps he already knew the choice of his heart and only waited to recover to claim her as his own. Elizabeth hoped this mystery woman would be kind to Mr. Darcy.

Walking past the sitting room, she heard the pianoforte in use. Curiosity won out, and upon entering, she observed Mrs. Annesley demonstrate fingering for the benefit of Mary and Miss Darcy.

"Miss Elizabeth! We were just sitting down for lessons. Would you like to join us?" Miss Darcy was all smiles.

Elizabeth saw Mary's look of disappointment and demurred. "Oh, no. I should not disturb you."

Mrs. Annesley now spoke. "Let me assure you that your presence, rather than diminishing our enjoyment, would only increase it. We would be happy to have you."

Mary bit her lip and said, "Yes, Lizzy. Please stay."

Elizabeth capitulated to the entreaties, silently vowing to allow Mary the majority of the attention. The four ladies passed the next hour contentedly, and in Mary's case, joyfully. As they quitted the room — Miss Darcy remaining for her German lesson from Mrs. Annesley — Mary uncharacteristically seized Elizabeth's hand.

"Oh, that was so delightful!" she cried. "We shall practice every day with Miss Darcy and Mrs. Annesley while they are here, shall we not, Lizzy?"

Elizabeth assured Mary that they should, touched by this affectionate display from her normally serious sister.

Tea brought Mr. Bingley and Colonel Fitzwilliam, but not Miss Bingley or the Hursts. Mr. Bingley apologized for his sister's sake; a sudden headache must be her excuse, and Mrs. Hurst stayed to attend her. A glance at Colonel Fitzwilliam showed that gentleman was uncomfortable, and Elizabeth lowered her head, hoping her countenance did not give the lie to Mr. Bingley's statement.

The rest of tea passed uneventfully. Colonel Fitzwilliam rallied and was his usual charming character, Mr. Bingley had eyes only for Jane, and Mr. Darcy was less severe with her. Now aware of Mr. Darcy's design, Elizabeth found herself relaxed in his company and spoke as she always did, her wit now undiminished by worry. More than once she was in conversation with their invalid guest, happily debating some point of contention. When she turned her attention to Mrs. Bennet, she saw that, while her mother was confused and sometimes alarmed at the pair's banter, she was also pleased with the apparent peace between her second daughter and their most honored guest. Elizabeth sighed.

There was no way of convincing her mother that her matchmaking schemes were in vain.

There was only one small mystery. Today it was Kitty's turn to gaze reverently at Mr. Darcy. Elizabeth shook her head — first was Jane's admiration, then Mary's adulation, and now Kitty. Was it every Bennet girl's fate to fall in love with Mr. Darcy, save Lydia and herself?

Mr. Bingley and the colonel could not remain for dinner, citing Miss Bingley's indisposition. The meal passed without incident — roast beef and Yorkshire pudding had returned to the table, even though it was a Tuesday — but the same could not be said for afterwards. While Miss Darcy entertained the group at the pianoforte, Lydia sat and grumbled.

"Lydia, please," Mary scolded softly, "Miss Darcy is playing."

"Oh, who cares about that?" Lydia shot back, not lowering her voice at all. "Today is the twenty-sixth! We should be at Netherfield, dancing the night away with all the handsome officers! Instead, Mr. Bingley's ball is canceled, and we must sit bored at home. It is unfair!"

"Lydia, please, lower your voice," Jane advised. "It is no one's fault that the ball had to be postponed."

"Yes, it is," Lydia cried. She pointed at Mr. Darcy. "It is all *his* fault!"

Up to now, Miss Darcy dutifully continued her piece. But at Lydia's outcry, she stopped. Heedless of the spectacle she was making, indeed, reveling in the attention, Lydia continued.

"If Mr. Darcy had not broken his leg in that stupid manner, Mr. Bingley would not have cancelled the ball, and we would be dancing now! I believe he did it a-purpose! You saw how he insulted you at the assembly, Lizzy. He hates dancing!"

The entire room was aghast at Lydia's outlandish pronouncement. Both Mr. and Miss Darcy turned pale, but before Elizabeth or Jane could take Lydia to task, correction came from a most unexpected corner.

"You naughty, naughty girl!" cried Mrs. Bennet. "How can you say such a thing about Mr. Darcy? He has suffered a serious accident, and it is only by God's grace that he did not lose a limb! He is very welcomed here, and he deserves our pity and care. Oh," she fanned herself, "you will give me a case of the nerves, you ungrateful child! Dancing — who cares about dancing! You can dance any old time at the assemblies! You will apologize to Mr. Darcy right away — and Miss Darcy, too — or you will be sent to your room!"

"Yes," cried Kitty, "Mr. Darcy has been very nice, and you are being mean to him! For shame!"

Lydia, who well knew she was her mother's and sister's favorite, was shocked into tears.

"Lydia," said Mr. Bennet finally, "we are waiting."

"Oh, everyone hates me!" Sobbing, Lydia dashed from the sitting room and up the stairs. After a moment, Jane and Mary rushed to Miss Darcy's side to reassure the shaken girl. Meanwhile, an anxious Mrs. Bennet turned to Mr. Darcy.

"Sir, I hope you will forgive my youngest. She enjoys dancing very much, and her disappointment must be her excuse. She is young and spirited, not mature like my other girls! Oh, yes, my girls are very kind and level-headed, especially Lizzy! You will find no more sensible girl than my Lizzy!"

Elizabeth, already blushing in mortification over Lydia's antics, flushed deeper hearing her mother's uncalled-for praise.

Mr. Bennet, clearly askew at his wife's proclamations, nevertheless echoed her sentiments. "Yes, my girls are usually more sensible than that and know better than to insult a guest, particularly one forced to use a wheel-chair. My apologies, sir."

"Accepted," Mr. Darcy said shortly. He glanced at his sister, deep in conversation with Jane. "Miss Lydia's youth must be her excuse." He turned back to Mr. Bennet. "I know we are a burden to you all."

"Of course not!" Mrs. Bennet exclaimed.

"Once again, I must agree with my wife, as unusual as that may be," said Mr. Bennet. Elizabeth winced slightly. She hoped Mr. Darcy did not detect the derision in her father's voice. "You are welcomed here for as long as you can bear it."

Her parents then moved to speak to Miss Darcy, which gave Elizabeth a chance to add her own regrets. "I am so sorry for what you have endured, Mr. Darcy! We do not deserve your forgiveness."

For a disconcerting moment, he stared hard at her, searching her face. He then sighed. "It is quite all right, Miss Elizabeth. It is *all* forgotten."

He gave her a small smile. "I suppose none of us are immune from saying things we do not mean — for giving offence when none is intended."

Elizabeth blinked. Was Mr. Darcy apologizing to *her*? *Why*? "We are all poor sinners. None of us is perfect."

There was that penetrating stare again. She could almost feel his gaze caressing her skin. "Some of us, perhaps," he said huskily. His closed his eyes for a moment, and then looked at Jane and continued in a lighter vein. "Your sister, for example — would you not say she is a perfect angel, as some have said?"

Elizabeth laughed. "Yes, Jane is as perfect as can be and shames us mere mortals!" The moment was past, and Mr. Darcy appeared weary. "I believe you are tired, sir."

"Yes, it has been a long, trying day." He glanced at her. "I believe I shall surrender — to rest," he said cryptically.

"I shall summon Mrs. Hill, then. Good night, sir."

"Good night, Miss Elizabeth."

Elizabeth went in search of the housekeeper, convinced that it was a sign of Mr. Darcy's fatigue that he lingered slightly over the syllables of her name.

Darcy *was* tired, and he longed to surrender. He was tired of fighting his attraction to Elizabeth, and he longed to surrender to her charms. Her liveliness during tea, her intelligent conversation during dinner, and her genuine regret for Lydia's actions had completely overset Darcy's intention of putting distance between himself and the girl in less than a day. No one outside of the Drury Lane stage could be that good an actress. Her sincerity could not be denied. Elizabeth may have been angry with him yesterday, but she seemed to think better of him today.

Not that it mattered. Darcy knew he had found the woman he wanted. Now he must prove worthy of her.

Perhaps Elizabeth's opinion of Darcy was not as high as he wished, but he was now persuaded that the lion's share of the fault lay with him. Since Darcy tried and failed to give her up, it remained for him to undo the damage he had done. He was decided: He would win Elizabeth's heart no matter how long it took.

While Mrs. Hill moved him back into the parlor bedroom, Darcy leaned back in his wheel-chair, contemplating a lovely set of eyes gazing at him in concern and friendliness. Great was his surprise with what awaited him.

Sally, the maid, was in Bartholomew's arms, weeping.

"What is the meaning of this?" Darcy demanded.

"Sir! It is not what it seems!" cried an unsettled Bartholomew. To Sally, he pleaded, "Please, girl, you must stop this now!" For her part, Sally buried her head deeper into the valet's chest and cried harder.

Mrs. Hill quickly closed the door behind them and moved to the pair. "I'll see to this, Mr. Darcy. I know what ails her." She gently placed her hands on the maid's shoulders. "Come, child, enough of this. You'll give Mr. Darcy a poor impression of you. Rest is what you need. Come with me." To Bartholomew she said, "I hope she wasn't too much of a bother."

Bartholomew's expression said that he thought she indeed had been a very great bother, but he only nodded and quickly backed away from the pair. Darcy waited until the two women left through the servants' entrance before he began his interrogation.

His valet was rattled by his experience. "I had just returned from my meal in the kitchen when I found Sally standing by the window, crying uncontrollably," he explained. "I, of course, enquired as to what the matter could be. The girl would not talk at first, and then she threw herself at me, clinging as if she were drowning. It was *most* disconcerting, sir."

Knowing Bartholomew to be a confirmed bachelor, Darcy could only agree. "Do you know why she is distressed?"

"Yes, sir. She spoke at length."

Darcy pursed his lips. Sometimes he wondered whether his closed-mouth servant enjoyed this game of compelling his employer to wheedle information out of him. "Then I require that you tell me what she said."

"As you wish, sir. It seems Sally lives at home with her widowed mother, who until recently was employed as a cook in a house in Meryton. The family has this week quit Hertfordshire for Cornwall, never to return, leaving Sally's mother with only a recommendation."

"That is unfortunate," said Darcy. "Surely, if the woman is of good character, she will secure employment soon."

"Unlikely anytime soon, I am afraid to report, as there is no work to be had."

Darcy frowned. "It is all very sad, but even with the small amount Sally makes working for the Bennets, they should get by with charity from the local parish until a position is secured if Meryton is anything like Lambton."

"I am sorry to say that Meryton does not enjoy the patronage of a generous family as Lambton does," he nodded to his employer, "but there is more."

"Go on, Bartholomew."

"Yes, sir. There is a brother. He left home to seek his fortune in the factories in Birmingham, but he fell afoul of one of the machines. The surgeon did what he could and saved his life, but he lost an arm. He has come home to recuperate."

Darcy was uneasy. Perhaps two people could live on the merger earnings of a housemaid with assistance, but not three. "This is troubling, indeed. Is the brother out of danger?"

"It seems so, but of course there is no employment for him, either. He cannot work the fields or go back to the factories, not with one arm. It is a bad situation."

Darcy said nothing. Bartholomew seemed to recognize the look on his employer's face. "I regret bringing this to your attention, sir. It is bothering you. I am very sorry for Sally, but there is nothing to be done."

Darcy did not agree, but he kept his thoughts to himself. Instead, he requested that his valet undress him for bed. Once Darcy was abed, Bartholomew was glad to see a contented expression on his employer's face. He may have thought it was the comfort of fresh sheets, but he would have been wrong.

Darcy was working over the problem of Sally and was having a marvelous time. Nothing suited him as did being useful to others, and here was the perfect opportunity for him to engage in his favorite activity — solving someone else's dilemma.

Chapter 12

AT BREAKFAST, ELIZABETH LEARNED Mr. Bingley had arranged a shopping expedition to Meryton that morning. Jane, Mary, and Kitty were to go with Miss Darcy and Colonel Fitzwilliam. Georgiana invited Elizabeth, but she declined as Charlotte was expected to visit. Lydia's name was not mentioned. Due to her behavior the evening before, she was forbidden to leave Longbourn or entertain visitors for the next two days.

At the appointed time, a carriage appeared containing only Mr. Bingley. Colonel Fitzwilliam chose to ride alongside on his tall charger. Neither Miss Bingley nor Mrs. Hurst accompanied their brother, and Elizabeth began to worry about Miss Bingley's state of mind. Obviously, Caroline had taken the colonel's words very hard, and in her mortification, she could not face the outside world, even to visit Miss Darcy.

The party was assembled, and Elizabeth noticed the presence of Mr. Darcy's manservant. As Bartholomew helped the ladies into the coach, Elizabeth assumed the man was running errands for his master in the village. Mr. Bingley stood by his horse, heretofore secured to the back of the carriage, having a private word with Jane, when there was a squeal from the house.

"What is going on?" cried Lydia. "Where is everyone going?"

Jane answered her wayward sister. "We are all to Meryton. Mr. Bingley was kind enough to take us shopping —"

"I want to go, too! Wait there and I will get my pelisse and bonnet."

Mrs. Bennet stopped her. "You are indeed *not* going, young lady! You know very well you are to stay in the house until Friday. Now, be a good girl and return inside."

"But, Mama, *pleassse*! I will be good! Mr. Bingley, please tell Mama you want me to come!"

Mr. Bingley was clearly uncomfortable. "It is not my decision to make."

Elizabeth stepped over to her sister and tried to calm her down. "You must listen to Mama and go inside. Pray stop making a scene."

Lydia would have none of it. "But I want to go! Mary and Kitty are going!"

"Because we were invited," Kitty shot back from the carriage. "Mary and Georgiana are to select music while I will shop for a set of watercolors."

Elizabeth did not know what surprised her more: Kitty's familiar use of Miss Darcy's name or that her submissive sister had stood up to Lydia.

"You should not expect nice things when you are so mean to people," Kitty continued. "Please stop. You are embarrassing our guests."

Kitty's rebelliousness shocked Lydia silent, and Mrs. Bennet took her youngest by the arm. "Yes, Kitty has the right of it! Go inside the house this instant! Oh, what you do to my nerves!"

Lydia looked about but only beheld stern expressions or averted glances. With a sob, she turned and ran back indoors. The shopping expedition left under a small cloud of unpleasantness, and Elizabeth could only marvel at the changes at Longbourn.

Mama punishing her favorite? Kitty challenging her idol? Mary willingly going shopping? What was happening to her world?

Darcy was in the sitting room across from the parlor, attending to his correspondence. It was not too daunting a task as there was little to command his attention at Pemberley during that time of year. The harvest in and repairs completed on the tenants' houses, the steward's concerns were now relegated to plans for the spring planting months hence.

The letters from Town were a different matter. His banker was concerned over uncertainties for trade due to the political tensions between the government and the former American colonies. And his solicitor had sent him yet another counter-offer for that property in Ireland. Darcy was working through the complicated terms — frowning, for he suspected that his solicitor was correct in alleging chicanery by the seller — when the door was flung open.

"Oh, it is you," said a surprised Miss Lydia.

Darcy was busy and did not want to be disturbed, particularly by Elizabeth's spoiled young sister, but he had been too well trained not to offer civilities. "May I help you, Miss Lydia?"

"No," said the girl as she turned to leave. But she halted her progress and turned back to him. "Yes. Mama says I should apologize for yesterday." She spoke as if every word were wrenched from her mouth.

Darcy put the contract down. "Yes?" he said expectantly.

Lydia's toe made circles in the carpet. "I am sorry. What I said yesterday was silly. I mean, you would not break your leg on purpose to stop a ball, even if you do hate dancing. You would just stand in a corner and say mean things about Lizzy like you did at the assembly."

It was the strangest apology Darcy had ever received, and her comment about his behavior at that blasted assembly drove all thought of work from his mind. Did all of Hertfordshire know of his unfortunate remark? No wonder Elizabeth had a low opinion of him!

"I suppose I should apologize to Miss Darcy, too. Did I hurt her feelings?"

Darcy considered his words. "I think an apology would be welcomed. However, do not bother if you are not sincere."

"Oh, but I am!" the girl assured him. "I mean, Miss Darcy is kind and spends time with my sisters, and she dresses so well. I would not like it at all if *she* disliked me."

Darcy tried to make sense of Lydia's bizarre statement when Mrs. Annesley came into the room. "Do not let me disturb you, sir, but I wanted to tell you that Miss Georgiana and her party have left for Meryton." She gave Lydia hardly a glance.

"Excellent — and Bartholomew accompanied them?"

"Yes, sir. He has your instructions."

"Very good. Miss Mary and Miss Kitty will get the items they need.

It seems you have a free morning today."

"I have some letter-writing that needs my attention. I look forward to hearing the music Miss Mary chooses this afternoon. I know Miss Kitty is excited about trying watercolors, so we shall use them first thing tomorrow. Is there anything you need, sir?" Assured he was fine, Mrs. Annesley left the pair.

Lydia pouted. "You see? She did not so much as acknowledge me! Everyone hates me!"

"And when was the last time you greeted Mrs. Annesley?" Darcy gently pointed out. "She is my sister's companion. You are a lady of this house. It is your duty to speak to her first. Civility goes both ways."

Lydia plopped into a chair. "I do everything wrong!"

"Your sisters show more proper behavior. You should follow their example."

Lydia wagged her feet. "I suppose," she admitted, showing no inclination to leave.

Darcy, too polite to have the girl removed from the room, bent back to his work. A few minutes passed, and after he made a few more notes for his planned letter to his solicitor, he was interrupted anew.

"What are you doing?" asked Lydia.

Darcy sighed. The girl was bored and thought nothing of breaking his concentration. "I am working. If you would excuse me —"

"Are all those letters?" Lydia obviously could not take a hint.

"Yes. This stack is from my banker in Town," he indicated a pile, "this stack is from my solicitor, and these letters are from Pemberley."

"No invitations to parties? Just business matters?"

"Yes, just business matters." Darcy did not say that he instructed his people not to forward invitations unless they were from a small, select group of people — his family or close friends.

"How boring! I thought you were rich. Do not rich people have people to take care of all that?"

"Miss Lydia, if I did not attend to matters such as these, I would not be rich for long."

The girl seemed to think about that. "Papa gets letters of business, but he leaves most of those matters to the steward. Do you not have a steward?"

"I do, and he is a fine, intelligent, and hardworking man. But as I am ultimately responsible for Pemberley, we remain in close consultation."

"I am glad we have Papa and our steward. I would hate to do all that work."

"Well, there is only me."

"Really? What about your father?"

"My father has been dead these five years, Miss Lydia."

"Oh." She seemed to think about that too. "I should hate it if anything happened to Papa. I mean, he teases me, and he can be strict, but ... but he is my papa. You understand? Besides, Mama says if Papa died, Mr. Collins would have us starve in the hedgerows."

Darcy recalled the tall, heavy, detestable man, and with sudden, furious resolve, silently promised himself, *Not if I have anything to say about it!*

Lydia continued. "Is your mother gone, too?"

Darcy nodded. "It is just Georgiana and myself."

"Oh. You are a good brother to Miss Darcy."

"I try to be. She is all I have." Darcy had no idea why he was opening his heart to this strange girl.

"She has beautiful dresses and pianofortes and jewels — she *does* have jewels, does she not? Big emeralds and rubies and pearls?" Lydia's eyes gleamed. "Oh, I wish I had a rich brother!"

"There is more to being a good brother than dresses and trinkets. Georgiana has had the opportunity to study under masters of art, music, and literature. These are gifts that will last a lifetime, long after the dresses are rags and the trinkets are forgotten."

Lydia deflated a bit. "I still wish I had them. Miss Darcy is very accomplished, though."

"She has worked very hard to become so."

"Miss Bingley thinks she is accomplished, but she is nothing to Miss Darcy," Lydia said with no little spite. "Neither are we."

"I disagree," Darcy said. "True, you ladies have not had Georgiana's advantages, but you and your sisters have made the most of what you have."

"Perhaps. Lizzy is good on the pianoforte, and Jane does beautiful embroidery." She gazed at the fireplace. "But the rest of us have no talent at all."

"Miss Lydia, you do a disservice to your sisters. Miss Mary is working very hard to improve herself on the pianoforte, and Miss Kitty's drawing is very fine." He lowered his voice. "You should not tease your sister. She has done a lovely portrait of you."

Lydia looked up, puzzled. "Is that so? She never showed that to me."

"Can you blame her? She says you mock her work."

Lydia shrunk back into the chair. "I . . . I do not mean to hurt her feelings! I just — oh!" She hung her head, as a tear ran down her cheek. "It is just that they can do all that and I cannot."

"Have you tried?"

"Yes, but the pianoforte is so hard, and all my drawings look as if Cassandra had an accident on the paper."

Darcy sat back, observing the wretched girl. "You remind me of someone I know."

"Who? The village idiot?" she mumbled into her chest.

Darcy bit his lip so as not to laugh. "Let me tell you a story. Once upon a time, there were two sisters — two princesses. Both were very beautiful, but that was all they had in common. The elder princess was kind and good and paid attention to her lessons. She became very accomplished and attracted many admirers. She had her pick of any man in her father's kingdom, and many knights and earls and dukes vied for her hand. But instead, she fell in love with an untitled gentleman, renowned for his wisdom, wealth, and good humor."

The story caught Lydia's attention as he continued. "Her father, the king, was surprised at his daughter's choice and questioned her closely about it. She was steadfast and would not give up her lover, and in his turn, the gentleman made an excellent impression upon the king. The king granted his permission, and the pair made a very happy marriage. They raised their children to work hard, respect all people, and marry with affection."

"Was the gentleman handsome?" asked Lydia.

"I suppose he was. Allow me to finish my story. The younger princess was not kind to those beneath her and did not attend to her lessons.

She found them difficult. She was also very proud. She wanted to be the best at anything she did and cried very much when she was not. But she could never be as accomplished as her sister because she would not put forth the effort.

"She finally decided that if she could not be a true proficient, she would not try at all. Why should she play music or draw or write? She was a princess, after all. She would have people do that for her. She also decided that as she was a princess, she should marry only for rank and prestige.

"Unfortunately for her, tales of her pride and haughtiness were told throughout the kingdom. Few nobles wanted to spend their lives shackled to such an unpleasant woman, even if she were a princess. After many years, the king finally found a knight willing to marry her. The princess agreed, for she had no other suitors. However, the two did not get along, and their marriage was filled with acrimony. Their arguments would only end with his untimely death a few years later.

"The princess lived on as his widow, holding court in the knight's ancestral home. Few came to visit, for those who did quickly tired of her boasting and conceit. To the end of her days, the princess would belittle her betters by proclaiming that her unimpeachable taste was superior to all, and that she would have been an extraordinarily accomplished woman if she had so desired it."

"What a silly woman!" said Lydia, who had hung on every word. She paused a minute. "You think I am like the younger princess?"

Darcy smiled kindly. "You do not have to be. Look to your sisters' example. Miss Mary and Miss Kitty went to Meryton not to buy bonnets or finery but to acquire items that will help them become accomplished in their chosen art."

"I was wondering about that. Mary only spends her money on religious books, and Kitty has no money as I borrowed it all for a..." Her voice trailed off. "Wait! How do you know what they are buying in Meryton? From what you said to Mrs. Annesley, you already knew!" She pointed accusingly at Darcy. "You do know! *You* are buying their music and paints!"

Caught, Darcy said nothing.

Lydia frowned. "Why are you doing that?"

"They truly wish to become proficient in their avocation." He gave Lydia a hard look. "*And* they have been kind to my sister."

"I am sorry about that!"

"So you have said."

Bold as brass, the girl asked, "If I apologize to Miss Darcy, will you buy me something?"

"Do you believe I buy my friends or my sister's friends, Miss Lydia?"

Lydia cringed. "I am sorry! I say stupid things sometimes!"

You seem to make a habit of it, Darcy thought wryly. "Besides, do you have an avocation?"

"I do not know. What is an avocation?"

"Something you enjoy doing — something in which you want to become accomplished."

"Oh." Lydia looked out the window. "I do enjoy something, something above all else, but Papa will not let it become my *avocation*."

Darcy shuddered to know what it could possibly be, but he had to ask for form's sake. "What is it?"

"Riding." She turned to him, visibly unhappy. "I love riding and jumping and all those good things, but Papa never lets us ride the horse! It is always being used on the farm. What is the use of *learning* how to ride if one never *gets* to ride?"

Of all the things Lydia could have mentioned, Darcy had to admit riding was one of the last things he expected. "Do any of your other sisters ride?"

"We all learned, but only Jane and I enjoy it. Lizzy is positively frightened of horses! I do not think she has been on one since her lessons. Mary and Kitty do not care one way or the other. I would say that Jane and I are the only ones who would like to be considered horsewomen."

Lydia reinforced Jane's revelation of Elizabeth's aversion to horses, and it explained much about his accident. He set aside contemplation of the reasons for Elizabeth's aversion until later, sat back in his chair, and studied the unhappy girl before him. "If you had a horse for your own use, what would you do?"

"Will you get me a horse?" cried Lydia hopefully.

Darcy held up his hands. "I did not say that! This is a speculative exercise. Imagine you owned a horse. How would you treat it? It is a great responsibility, owning a horse."

"Oh," she said disappointedly. "Well, I would ride him every day, of course. I would make sure the groom fed him well and that he had clean hay in his stall at all times. I would brush him and put ribbons in his mane and tail and feed him carrots. And…and" — she blushed — "I would bury my face in his neck and kiss him and smell him. I just love the smell of a horse!"

Darcy had to admit that he did as well.

"Nobody knows," Lydia said, "but when I can, I go the barn and just sit with our horse and talk to him and give him sweets. The groom keeps my secret."

Darcy smiled. "Being a good horsewoman is a worthy avocation."

"Much good it will do me as I have no horse." She smiled sadly. "Thank you for listing to me and not teasing me. I suppose I should go do my chores."

"That would be best. And I must go back to my work."

She rose from the chair and eyed the stack of papers. "Perhaps being rich is not good fun after all. Good day, Mr. Darcy."

"Good day, Miss Lydia."

Darcy had just returned to his stack of correspondence when Lydia had one last word from the door.

"Mr. Darcy? I am sorry about your father and mother. You must miss them."

"Thank you, Miss Lydia." *Yes, I do — every day of my life.*

AS MUCH AS ELIZABETH WANTED to go shopping with Miss Darcy, she was glad she met with Charlotte. Apparently, Mr. Collins had not ended his attentions. Rather, he seemed more determined than ever to secure a bride in Meryton, and he had selected Charlotte as the most agreeable candidate.

"Oh, Eliza," cried her friend, "Mr. Collins is relentless! He has worked upon my mother's desires that I secure a husband so diligently that she is acting in a manner more like your Aunt Philips!"

Elizabeth was not deceived by Charlotte's choice of relation. She knew she meant to say *Mrs. Bennet*. Still, it was distressing that Charlotte should find herself in such a predicament! Her friend had begged her father to refuse any application from the pernicious parson, but she feared that he might give way if Lady Lucas demanded the marriage.

Once Charlotte returned home, Elizabeth directly petitioned her father to come to her friend's aid. It took a quarter-hour to secure Mr. Bennet's promise to talk to Sir William and tell the knight what he knew of Mr. Collins's character.

Even though she was successful in her mission, Elizabeth was unhappy with her father's reluctance to do the right and proper thing without being first hounded into action. He had shown himself repeatedly to be selfish and indolent, complaining about the imposition of Mr. Darcy. In comparison, Mr. Darcy was a paragon, for all his faults.

She could not have known it, but her opinion of Mr. Darcy would be even higher before the day was done. During music practice, she learned that Mr. Darcy had provided the funds to purchase the sheets of music that were now Mary's most prized possession. At dinner, Kitty was ecstatic over her watercolors, and a full five minutes were insufficient to express her deep gratitude for Mr. Darcy's generosity. For his part, Mr. Darcy seemed genuinely embarrassed by the attention, something that appeared not to be unusual given Miss Darcy's amused reaction to her brother's discomfort.

A subdued Lydia had given a contrite apology to Miss Darcy upon her return to Longbourn. Georgiana, being well bred, accepted the girl's words with modesty and sincerity. At dinner Lydia was much quieter than customary. Elizabeth dismissed it; her sister was probably worried about her punishment being extended if she did not behave.

Mr. Bingley and Colonel Fitzwilliam returned for dinner, once again without the company of Miss Bingley or the Hursts. Elizabeth did not know the depth of Mr. Bingley's concern for his sister, for he was too busy talking and gazing at Elizabeth's sister. Jane was much affected by the attention — affected, that is, by Jane's standards. Her blushing and the averting of her eyes spoke volumes to Elizabeth. She knew that Jane had come to know what it was to love and be loved in return.

In her joy, Elizabeth flashed a brilliant smile at Mr. Darcy. He seemed both befuddled and pleased at the gesture, and Elizabeth realized her blunder. It would not do to send their guest the wrong message — not while he was trying to be a gentleman!

Speaking of gentlemen, Colonel Fitzwilliam was his usual charming self, but to Elizabeth, it seemed a façade, an act. She wondered at it. Did he regret his harsh words to Miss Bingley, or was he worried about something else? Mr. Wickham was still under lock and key in Meryton and had not yet been transported to London to face gaol. Might he be concerned that the man might talk his way free? If so, the colonel did not know the magistrate. That gentleman hated debtors with a passion. There would be no escape for Mr. Wickham.

The separation of the sexes was long that night, and it gave Elizabeth the chance to spend time in conversation with Miss Darcy. By the time the gentlemen rejoined them, the two had agreed to use their Christian names.

Mrs. Bennet insisted on cards, and Elizabeth found herself, by her mother's design, partnered with Mr. Darcy. It was almost too easy — their competitors were Jane and Mr. Bingley — and though Jane was attentive enough, Mr. Bingley made so many errors that one might think him a simpleton if one did not know the cause of his distraction. To Elizabeth's amusement, she caught Mr. Darcy rolling his eyes more than once during the game, a gesture that made the gentleman more approachable than ever before.

Late that night as she readied for bed, Elizabeth was happy she had finally come to understand Mr. Darcy's nature and character. And just in time, too, for if she was not careful it would be all too easy to fall in love with the gentleman.

When Darcy and Colonel Fitzwilliam were alone in his room, the colonel poured them both a brandy. "To your health, Cuz, and to our removal to Town," he offered as a toast.

"What?" asked Darcy. "You wish to leave Hertfordshire?"

"Do you not?" the officer shot back. "Would you not be more comfortable in your own house? When can you leave?"

"Fitz, my injury occurred but a week ago. Mr. Macmillan advised that I not be moved for another month at least."

"Christmas, then? I hope the roads hold up." The colonel walked restlessly about the room. "Bingley was in rare form tonight. I suppose he will offer for Miss Bennet soon."

"Do you think so? Bingley has been in love before yet has managed to escape matrimony."

"Not this time. Did you not see the fool he has been making of himself over that girl? It is embarrassing."

Darcy thought about that and his better understanding of Jane Bennet. "Yes, he has been more taken by Miss Bennet than by any other young lady. If he is serious about it, he should act."

"It will not be a brilliant match for him; it will not help his standing in society."

"True, but I do not think that has ever been Bingley's ambition. He wants a pretty and quietly charming lady who truly cares for him. If Miss Bennet loves him — and she very well may — she would meet his every expectation." Darcy chuckled. "It is *Miss* Bingley that would suffer the disappointment."

"Quite," said the colonel sharply before turning to the window, staring out into the darkness. "Oh, I long to leave this miserable wilderness and return to civilization! How can you bear it?"

Darcy was surprised at the earnestness in his cousin's tone. "This is a dark mood! I thought you enjoyed the countryside."

His back still to Darcy, the colonel replied, "I spent too much of my time 'enjoying the countryside' from a tent in Spain. I think I shall go to Town for a few days." He swallowed the rest of his drink, turned, and smiled. "Forgive me for distressing you. I shall be all smiles from now on."

Darcy thought the colonel's explanation was too glib by half but kept his observation to himself as his cousin moved to the sideboard and refilled his glass. "Have you heard recently from your brother?"

Colonel Fitzwilliam was surprised by the question. "Horace? I saw him before I left London. He and the viscountess are well."

"And how are things at Argyle Manor?"

"Short-handed as usual. He never can make up his mind about staff. It drives Lady Eugenie to distraction." He laughed. "I am not saying that is a bad thing."

Darcy knew well the mutual loathing between the viscountess and the colonel. "Do you think he would take on a new cook?"

"If it would make dinners at Argyle more palatable, he should jump at the chance. Do you have someone in mind? You know he can deny you nothing."

"As a matter of fact, I do — a local woman with excellent references. She has a daughter trained as a maid and a grown son — hard-working, but he has lost an arm in the factories. I would hope he could take the lot."

"There is room for extra staff at Argyle, I am sure. The son lost an arm, you say? Horace would probably make him a footman and tell everyone the man was a veteran of the wars just to irritate me."

"Good. I will write him tomorrow."

The colonel frowned. "Why are you concerned with Horace's domestic deficiencies? What is this unnamed family of servants to you?"

"You recall the maid attending me — Sally? I speak of her mother and brother. They are facing hard times as the mother lost her position when her employers left Hertfordshire."

"Anyone with common sense should leave this wretched place. Ah, here you go again, saving the world! I wonder at you, Cuz. One of these days, your intrusion into other people's business will get you in trouble."

"It has done me no ill yet. Will you take my letter to the viscount?"

"I suppose I can suffer a half-hour's visit with my dear brother and sister. I will be your courier."

"Will you return?"

"Yes, in a few days. I shall not abandon you or Georgiana."

"Thank you. One last request: Bring two or three of my horses back with you."

The colonel nodded. "I planned to bring Georgiana her horse — hold, you said two or three? Why? You cannot ride."

Darcy smiled. "Just do as I ask, please."

Chapter 13

THE NEXT FEW DAYS were little changed from the ones before
them. The weather remained mild for November. Elizabeth
never missed a morning ramble while Darcy spent his time
after breakfast outdoors in the Bath chair, posing for Georgiana and
Kitty's amusement, often with Cassandra in his lap. In the afternoons,
Mary, Elizabeth, and Georgiana practiced with Mrs. Annesley. Jane
would sit and listen, working on her embroidery. Lydia would disap-
pear for hours at a time, and only the groom and Darcy knew where
she was to be found.

Like clockwork, Mr. Bingley would arrive for tea, the only event save
meals that could coax Mr. Bennet to abandon his book room. Colonel
Fitzwilliam had left for London, but he was expected to return, to the
relief of the younger members of the Bennet household. Of Miss Bingley
or the Hursts, nothing was seen, but only Elizabeth and Jane showed
any concern over their absence. Mrs. Bennet, good hostess that she was,
would normally be curious about Mr. Bingley's missing relations, but she
was too occupied entertaining the gentleman himself, thereby helping
her eldest daughter secure the lessee of Netherfield.

Mrs. Bennet was also pleased at the affability between her second
daughter and their august guest. True, Mrs. Bennet often found herself
confused and sometimes shocked listening to their strange exchanges,
which to her mind sounded like arguing. They were certainly nothing

like the gentle conversation shared between Jane and Mr. Bingley. *That* was proper courting. Elizabeth and Mr. Darcy seemed to be debating most of the time. What sort of courtship was that? However, the two seemed to enjoy their discussions — Elizabeth was all smiles, and Mr. Darcy was very pleasant as he spoke to Elizabeth — so Mrs. Bennet was only somewhat alarmed.

Fanny Bennet understood she was not an astute woman. Her husband was considered by all of Meryton exceedingly intelligent for all the good it had ever done him, and she knew Elizabeth was Mr. Bennet's equal. Mr. Darcy's intellect was undisputed. Mrs. Bennet expected that Elizabeth would never be happy if she did not esteem her husband. She considered Mr. Darcy her daughter's superior in wealth and learning, and if debating was how clever people made love in a crowded sitting room, who was she to gainsay it?

As long as there was a marriage at the end of it.

Now you, gentle reader, might think that Elizabeth and Darcy were well on their way to an understanding. Alas, you would be wrong. For, you see, as intelligent and perceptive as these two persons were, preconceptions continued to cloud the pair's thinking.

Elizabeth's esteem for Darcy grew by the day. Truly, she thought, he was among the best men she had ever met. In fact, he was fast becoming her secret ideal of perfection, and he was in danger of being placed on a pedestal to be worshiped from afar — afar because Elizabeth presumed there was no future for the two of them. This good, decent, generous, and handsome man was one of the richest landowners in Britain. According to something Colonel Fitzwilliam once mentioned, Mr. Darcy's family came over with the Normans in 1066. The history of the family spanned that of the kingdom. He was a consort fit for the daughter of a duke.

Elizabeth took care not to fall in love with the gentleman; for the child of an obscure country squire to even dream of something more than friendship was simply absurd.

Darcy's thoughts were less conflicted. He had surrendered to his desire for Elizabeth Bennet. He had fixed the idea in his mind that he would have her as his wife. He was humbled by learning of her previous opinion of him and his manners. He labored to prove himself to her, and as the days passed, he thought he was making extraordinary progress in changing the lady's mind.

His attraction to Elizabeth was fueled by more than her undeniable beauty; he had put his stupid statement at the assembly completely out of his mind. She was witty, learned, charming, and kind. She loved the countryside as much as he did. He also perceived that she possessed the proper strength of character he desired in the future mistress of Pemberley. Darcy wanted no shrinking violet as his bride, forever hiding in his shadow. No, he wanted and needed a woman who would be his partner and confidant, as well as his lover and the mother of his children — someone who could manage his house, stand up to the slings and arrows of society, and provide the love and serenity he craved.

And why should he not marry Elizabeth? He was only a gentleman, and she, a gentleman's daughter. She was certainly his equal, no matter what others, particularly his Aunt Catherine, might say.

Darcy was pleased that Elizabeth seemed to enjoy his company. There were times he was tempted to express more of his admiration — indeed, even to flirt — but he checked himself every time. Darcy was a proud man, and he would not make love to his choice while he was a helpless invalid. To rouse her pity was his abhorrence.

And though he would not admit it to himself, he was also reluctant to risk a considerable improvement in their dealings with one another by being more open. He was, in a word, scared.

Darcy should have remembered his family motto, *Fortune Favors the Bold*. It would have saved much heartache later.

THE BENNETS DUTIFULLY PROMENADED TO church on Sunday, the matriarch of the family proud that their number included the illustrious Miss Darcy of Derbyshire. The young lady even sat in their family pew, and the group enjoyed the adjacent attentions of the Bingley party. The service passed either quickly or slowly, depending on the participant's point of view, and at the appointed time, the congregation gathered outside the church for fellowship and gossip. The air was abuzz with talk about the absence of a certain clergyman from Hunsford.

The seemingly recovered Miss Bingley thanked Mrs. Bennet for the invitation to Sunday dinner at Longbourn, and were it not for some undisclosed matter at Netherfield, the Bingleys and Hursts would have been more than happy to accept. But decline they must. Elizabeth did not need a gypsy's crystal ball to tell her that Mr. Bingley was not happy about his absence from the Bennet table.

This turn of events gave Elizabeth leave to accept an invitation from Lady Lucas for dinner. Permission was quickly secured from Mrs. Bennet, and soon Elizabeth was in Charlotte's bedroom in deep conversation, the subject being the abandonment of Meryton by Mr. Collins.

"Eliza, I must thank Mr. Bennet for his counsel to my father. He would not tell me what he was told, but whatever it was, it was enough for Father to be distressed by Mr. Collins's attentions towards me. On Friday when Mr. Collins came for tea, Father had him come into his study for a private talk. We in the parlor could not make out the words, but we soon heard raised voices. We grew alarmed, and my brother was about to see what the argument was about when the door flew open and Mr. Collins emerged, his face very red. He did not take his leave of us but quit the house directly, mumbling to himself. We learned later that he left the inn at Meryton in an angry mood that very evening, taking the mail coach to London. It is believed he has returned to Kent."

"My goodness!" cried Elizabeth. "How very singular! Did Sir William say anything about his conversation with Mr. Collins?"

"No, he did not, except to say that Mr. Collins was *persona non grata,* and he was not permitted to enter Lucas Lodge again. Father so much as commanded that should Mother, Maria, or I encounter him in the village, we were not to speak to him but rather cross the street directly and either seek shelter in a shop or return home."

Elizabeth allowed this was an extraordinary demand from the habitually affable knight.

"It was," Charlotte agreed. "Father only uses Latin when he is most upset."

Elizabeth was pleased that her father had kept his promise to warn Sir William about Mr. Collins, but she was concerned. For Sir William to grow so incensed about the clergyman, Mr. Bennet must have told him about his attempted assault on her. Sir William Lucas was a good and kind man, but he was not known to keep a confidence. Could Elizabeth depend upon the knight not to spread tales about Mr. Collins's perfidy all about Hertfordshire, using her own unfortunate interactions with the man as an example?

Charlotte continued. "Mother was, of course, taken aback by this turn of events. I am afraid that she had set her cap on my catching Mr. Collins. But after a long, private talk in my father's study, she seemed more sanguine over the incident and has not spoken of it since. Maria is full curious but can get no details from our parents. Eliza," she took Elizabeth's hands into her own, "I believe your father must have shared some of your adventures with Father, but do not fear. Not a word of them shall leave this house, I am persuaded."

Elizabeth was relieved to heard Charlotte's words.

"But I have a question." Charlotte's brow wrinkled. "I said that Mr. Collins was mumbling to himself in an angry manner when he left the house. I could not make out anything he said, save two words: *Mr. Darcy.*" She turned to her friend. "Whatever could he mean?"

Elizabeth was astonished that Mr. Darcy's name was mentioned in this matter, but she was able to maintain a reserved countenance as she replied that she had no idea to what Mr. Collins was alluding. It was a lie, of course. Elizabeth knew full well why Mr. Collins spoke his name.

Her father must have given a full accounting of Mr. Collins's actions at Longbourn, including Mr. Darcy's spirited defense of her. This was distressing news indeed! Elizabeth had not yet come to a satisfactory conclusion over the meaning of Mr. Darcy's words and behavior then or of his actions since. Until she did, she would be mortified if all of Meryton became acquainted with the incident.

Elizabeth was unhappy about deceiving her friend, but there was nothing for it. She was not prepared to speak about Mr. Darcy to any-one, and this was intelligence that must be contemplated in detail at a more appropriate time.

As it was Sunday and he could not attend services, Darcy thought he might as well read some Scripture in observance of the day. He looked up from his Bible just as a giggling gaggle of pretty young ladies burst into his room, still in their bonnets and coats. Cassandra, who had taken her usual place in his lap, was not disturbed by the interruption of her mid-morning nap.

"Oh, Mr. Darcy, wait until you hear what we heard!" cried Kitty.

"You will never guess," proclaimed Lydia. "It is all too funny!"

"No, you will all get it wrong," Mary declared. "I should tell Mr. Darcy."

"Oh, Brother," said Georgiana, who knelt by his chair and took his hand, "it is all over Meryton that Mr. Collins has been chased away from the neighborhood!"

"Georgie! I wanted to tell him!" Kitty took Darcy's other hand. "We heard that Sir William Lucas turned him out of his house."

"Denny said Mr. Collins was running through the streets like a dog with his tail between his legs!"

"Lydia, how rude! I am sure that Mr. Denny knows nothing about it. But it is true, Mr. Darcy, that Mr. Collins has quit Meryton. He did not even stay for Sunday services! Is that not strange for a man of the cloth?"

The girls were all talking over one another, and Darcy found he could not get a word in. It was left to Jane to restore sanity to the scene.

"We should not judge other people's actions, Mary," she said as she entered the room, her coat and bonnet already handed to a servant. "All could be perfectly reasonable. What is not reasonable is that you have assailed poor Mr. Darcy while still in your out-of-doors clothes. Pray give the man some air."

"Yes, yes, Jane has the right of it!" cried Mrs. Bennet. "Where are your manners? You act like wild savages in your bonnets and coats — except you, Miss Darcy, of course! Why, no one could accuse you of uncivilized behavior, I am sure."

"Actually, I believe you were correct in your first observation, Mrs. Bennet," said Mrs. Annesley. "Come, Georgiana, please restrain from assaulting Mr. Darcy until you are more presentable."

Mrs. Bennet gathered her brood in, chattering all the time about preparations for Sunday dinner and how sad it was that Mr. Bingley could not attend and good riddance to Mr. Collins. Georgiana obediently followed her companion from the room, leaving only Jane and Mr. Bennet with Darcy and the maid Sally, who was puttering about.

Darcy spoke to the gentleman. "Is it true, sir, that Mr. Collins has quit Hertfordshire?"

"Yes," Mr. Bennet quipped. "It seems my talk with Sir William Lucas had a most stimulating influence." The grin slipped from his features. "I am more determined than ever to postpone the event that places *that* man in charge of Longbourn, as I am certain he has no kind feelings towards his family or neighbors."

"Amen to that. If there is anything I can do — "

"You have done quite enough already!" Mr. Bennet said gruffly. He seemed to catch himself. "I thank you for everything you have done, but this matter should fall to its proper place. Well, I will be in my book room. I shall see you at dinner." With that he left the room.

"I am sorry, Mr. Darcy," said Jane. "My father is — "

"Say no more, Miss Bennet, I quite understand. We all have our pride. Indeed, I should act in exactly the same manner, should the tables be turned."

"Somehow, I doubt that." She gave him a small, sisterly smile, and then glanced at the creature in his lap. "You have made a conquest of Cassandra. Lizzy will be jealous. Is your leg giving you much pain today?"

Darcy reported he was well, and the two fell into an easy conversation, Jane making herself comfortable in a nearby chair. It was not long before Darcy asked about Bingley, and he was able to comprehend the disappointment hidden in Jane's expression as she relayed Miss Bingley's excuse for her family's absence from Longbourn that day. Darcy was more convinced than ever that Jane had feelings for his friend and hoped, rather than expected, that they were of the most fervent kind. He practiced patience — it would not do to openly question the young lady about Bingley — and was soon rewarded.

Jane absentmindedly picked up a book and fiddled with it before remarking, "I believe you are very fortunate in your friends, Mr. Darcy. Colonel Fitzwilliam has been most obliging, going to Town on your behalf. And Mr. Bingley — he speaks about you constantly, singing your praises."

Darcy smiled. "Bingley is very kind. I am sure I deserve no special commendation."

Jane glanced at him. "He says you are his dearest friend and ablest counselor. He looks to you as an elder brother. I do not believe he is given to hyperbole. How long have you been friends?"

Darcy explained that they had met at Cambridge, when Bingley was just starting his terms, and Darcy was an upperclassman. Something drew Darcy to the younger man. He took young Bingley under his wing, and they had been fast friends ever since. "Bingley was new to society, and there were many pitfalls. I was able to advise him.

"You must understand," Darcy was quick to add, "Bingley is an excellent fellow. He has great natural modesty with a stronger dependence on my judgment than on his own. He wishes to be a gentleman, and he is afraid of making a mistake. But his principles are of the highest quality. I am proud that he is my friend." Jane smiled a little, and without knowing why, Darcy blurted, "He is a deliberate man, but once he makes up his mind, he is unshakable. He would never mislead someone."

Jane blushed and turned away, and Darcy knew that he had hit upon the crux of the matter. Jane was attached to Bingley but was becoming unsure of his friend's intentions. This would never do. Darcy knew he must have a talk with Charles.

Jane recovered and immediately changed the subject to the weather. Darcy followed her lead, becoming more convinced than ever that Jane was very much like himself in temperament when it came to private matters, hiding her feelings from the world at large and showing a façade of contentment and composure. Did she conceal the same passionate impulses with which Darcy was forever struggling? He expected it was so.

Darcy knew he was attracted to open, pleasant, intelligent people, like Fitzwilliam, Bingley — and Elizabeth. If Jane's temperament was very much like his, he thought that Bingley would be just the man to suit her while her steadiness would be a rock his friend could depend on.

Just then, the sister of the subject of their conversation burst into the room, followed by the man himself.

"Oh!" cried Jane as she rose. "Miss Bingley, Mr. Bingley! You are most welcome to Longbourn — but I thought you could not come today."

Caroline, white as a sheet, stuttered, "Yes, well, I am afraid we cannot stay for dinner, but I — Charles and I wanted to visit with Mr.

Darcy — and your family, of course."

Caroline's disjointed claims were patently false, but Darcy knew not what the woman was about. For Bingley's part, he seemed as confused by his sister's behavior as the rest, but he focused his attentions towards Jane.

"Where is the rest of your family, Miss Bennet?" asked he.

Jane explained that her sisters and Georgiana were occupied, but should be joining them soon in the sitting room. Bingley suggested that they repair there to await them, and the others agreed, Caroline declaring that she would accompany Mr. Darcy. Darcy selflessly gave Jane and Bingley an occasion for privacy and encouraged his friends to precede them. Caroline's countenance bespoke of a desire to have a private conversation with him. Sally followed the young people out to fetch both Bartholomew and the wheel-chair.

Darcy waited as Caroline paced about the room in a distressed manner. "What is *that* in your lap?" she finally said.

"It is a cat, Miss Bingley."

"Certainly it is bothering you. Shall I have a servant remove it?"

Darcy glanced down at the purring animal. "Cassandra is content, and so am I. We shall leave things as they are for now."

Caroline nodded absently, her hands twisting anxiously. It was a few moments before she spoke again.

"You look very well, Mr. Darcy," she exclaimed. "I mean to say, you *are* well — better. You have healed remarkably, I am sure."

"As I have never before broken my leg, I have no source of reference, but it seems I am recovering tolerably well."

"Of course, you are. When can you return to Town? Would tomorrow be too soon?"

"Tomorrow?" Darcy exclaimed. "Miss Bingley, the physician has requested that I remain here for at least a month complete. I shall certainly not be leaving Herefordshire tomorrow."

"But... oh, but what does a physician know? They are forever overstating the case. I am sure they know nothing of the sort. We have but to ask, and Charles would be happy to transport you to your house in London."

"I am sure you are correct about your brother's willingness to be of service to me, but I shall not go to London."

Caroline's voice rose. "But you must! Your own physician, for example, can better care for you there!"

Darcy was firm. "I thank you for your concern for my health, but for the last time, I am not leaving."

"But if you do not, Charles will stay here and — oh!" Caroline clasped a hand over her mouth and took a breath. In a softer voice, she said, "Mr. Darcy, certainly you have noticed Charles's attentions to Miss Bennet."

"Indeed I have. Bingley has been rather transparent in his interest in Miss Bennet."

"There, you see? He is making a spectacle of himself. If we do not get him away from here soon, it will be too late. He will be forced into a most unsuitable alliance."

Darcy clasped his hands over his midsection, lightly resting on the cat in his lap. "I take it you are speaking of Miss Bennet. You have objections to her?" His voice was flat, without emotion.

"To Jane herself? No. She is a perfectly lovely girl. I say nothing against Jane — but her *family*! Is there a more ridiculous family in all of England? And their connections — or should I say, lack of them! If we do not save Charles, he will do something exceedingly foolish and destroy any chance of his advancing in society!" She spoke with the assurance that Darcy agreed with her.

Darcy suspected that Caroline was more concerned over her own position with the *ton* than her brother's. "You have spoken to him about this?"

Caroline threw up her hands. "I have constantly tried to reason with Charles — we had a row in the carriage after church — but he will not attend to my arguments. He is bewitched by his 'angel!' Can you believe that he told me not an hour ago he cares nothing for society? All of the work and effort we have done on his behalf to make a gentleman of him will be for nothing. The Bingley name will be a laughingstock."

Darcy was not aware of any efforts Caroline had undertaken to promote her brother. To promote herself — that was another story.

She continued. "But you — he will listen to you. He *always* listens to you. Mr. Darcy, you must speak to Charles. Tell him to give up this self-destructive courtship before it is too late."

Darcy weighed the pros and cons of keeping silent. What he was to say would be uncomfortable to more than himself, but Charles was his friend. Darcy's honor and loyalty to those he valued was paramount, even above his natural reserve. Cassandra, as animals can, became aware of his struggles and, disturbed from her rest, leapt off his lap. Darcy sighed and began.

"Miss Bingley, rest assured I will be speaking to Charles." Immediately, Caroline's face lit with a smile, but her good cheer was short-lived. "You are correct that he has been paying extraordinary attention to Miss Bennet. Indeed, I think that he has gone too far to retreat now. He must declare himself and soon."

"What? You mean you will tell Charles to make Miss Bennet an offer?"

Darcy nodded. "At least request a courtship, although that seems redundant, given his actions to date. A *gentleman* can do no less." He hoped his emphasis on the word would be enough to stop Caroline's protests, but he hoped in vain.

"Jane would ruin Charles! An uncle in trade, and another a country attorney. The Bennets go nowhere, entertain no one. And that mother! Can you see Charles introducing that *joke* to London society?"

"I do not see your objections to Miss Bennet," replied Darcy in an attempt to reason with the haughty woman. "Certainly, her connections are not the best. If Miss Bennet were indifferent to Charles, I might have a different opinion, but I believe his affections are returned." In fact, Darcy was convinced that they were. He lowered his chin. "Besides, Miss Bennet *is* a gentleman's daughter. She is a perfectly suitable wife for him."

Darcy expected that Caroline would have some objection to his reasoning, so he was surprised at her sudden loss of color. "What — what was that you said?" she gasped.

Darcy was puzzled. "I said that Miss Bennet is a gentleman's daughter and his equal." A thought occurred to him. "Actually, now that I consider it, she is really a bit above Bingley. A marriage would solidify his standing, I should think and — Miss Bingley! Are you well?"

Darcy saw with alarm that Caroline was swaying on her feet, her face as pale as paper. She grasped the back of a chair while mumbling, "The colonel... that is what the colonel said." She stumbled, causing Darcy to cry out in alarm.

"Good God, what is the matter? Help! Help there!"

Caroline made her way into the chair, not responding to Darcy's entreaties about her well-being. In fascinated apprehension, Darcy watched as the lady's expression changed from shocked incredulity to absolute devastation. Her body shook and her eyes filled with unshed tears. It was as if every dream and expectation Caroline owned had been utterly exploded. Darcy could make no sense of this. Their conversation surely could not have caused such an intense reaction, and Caroline's words earlier seemed to involve Colonel Fitzwilliam, not himself. What the devil was going on?

A moment later, Bingley was in the room, followed by Georgiana, Jane, and the remaining Bennet daughters. Bingley rushed to his sister's side with words of concern, Jane on his heels, doing the same. Georgiana, rather, went to Darcy, and the others watched the scene with varying degrees of curiosity.

Finally, Caroline was successfully entreated to speak by her alarmed brother. She assured all that she was well but felt unequal to the company assembled and begged leave to return to Netherfield. Her request was instantly approved, and her subsequent apology for leaving so abruptly was likewise accepted. Miss Bingley rather slowly rose from the chair, clinging to her brother's strong and steady arm, and made her curtsy to Darcy.

Georgiana moved forward to assist Mr. and Miss Bingley. "I will help you," she said in a relatively calm voice.

Caroline turned abruptly to her. "Dear Georgiana! Such a good friend you are to me!"

Georgiana was taken aback by Caroline's intense look. "It…it is no trouble."

Before Georgiana could move, Caroline's hands shot out to grasp those of Georgiana. In a rather passionate voice, the lady exclaimed, "My dear, *dear* Georgiana you *must* believe I am sincerely attached to you. I *am* your friend, truly I am!"

Georgiana was clearly frightened by the manner in which Caroline assured her of her friendship, and Darcy knew she was of half a mind to flee from a person she supposed to be unhinged. Georgiana was not the only one who held this belief. There was not another person in the room who did not think Caroline had lost her senses.

But with true Darcy courage, Georgiana stood her ground, told Caroline that her declarations were unnecessary, and even squeezed the lady's hands to comfort her. Caroline nodded weakly and then allowed her almost panicked brother to lead her out of the house to their carriage.

Darcy was still flabbergasted at the performance when the ladies returned, all with the same question, although most put it more politely than Miss Lydia.

"Lord, Mr. Darcy! What in the world did you say to Miss Bingley? I think she has gone daft!"

Chapter 14

ONDAY MORNING DAWNED BRIGHT and cold, not surprising for late November. It was too chilly for Elizabeth to walk out before breakfast, so she postponed her ramble. At the table, she learned that more than her own plans for the morning had changed. Kitty was pouting that Mrs. Annesley had cancelled drawing in the rose garden for fear of freezing their subject, Mr. Darcy. As Jane and Georgiana entered the room, Elizabeth realized not all outside activities had been abandoned.

"What a lovely riding habit, Miss Darcy," gushed Mrs. Bennet. "And Jane, you look very smart, indeed! Are you to ride this morning?"

Miss Darcy, well-bred, polite, and still a little reserved, did not laugh at the older woman's folly. Instead she said kindly, "I received a note from Colonel Fitzwilliam last evening. My cousin returned from Town yesterday and has brought my horse. He and Mr. Bingley will call this morning, and we are to have a ride. Jane — that is, Miss Bennet, was invited as well."

"Oh!"

Elizabeth turned at Lydia's disappointed cry. She saw that her youngest sister was not a little jealous, and Elizabeth hoped Lydia would not make a scene. Instead, it was Kitty who complained of losing her drawing companion, and she had to be consoled by Mrs. Annesley and Georgiana. Kitty was mollified with Miss Darcy's assurances that they would sketch together the next day. In the meantime, Kitty would continue her lessons inside. Only a little while passed before it was announced that the gentlemen had arrived. The entire party donned their spencers and bonnets and went outdoors to greet them.

Elizabeth was surprised at Miss Bingley's attendance with the Netherfield party, for she had been told of Caroline's mortifying outburst in Mr. Darcy's room the day before. She was somber and serious, but true to her fashionable nature, the lady's riding habit was of the latest style and exceptionally fine. Miss Bingley would have cut an imposing figure if only her hat were more in proportion to her head.

Also unexpected was that Mr. Bingley had a horse in tow and Colonel Fitzwilliam had two. Elizabeth quickly deduced that Mr. Bingley's extra mount was for Jane's use, but she could not understand why the colonel had brought a pair. Was Georgiana to choose between the two?

Georgiana greeted her cousin sweetly and one of the horses with great affection, entirely ignoring the other animal. Mr. Hill assisted Jane and Georgiana to mount their horses.

"Miss Lydia, how are you this fine morning?" Colonel Fitzwilliam called out.

Elizabeth beheld her sister, standing apart from the others, arms crossed over her chest, obviously sulking. "Very well, I thank you, Colonel."

The colonel leaned over his saddle, a grin on his face. "Hmm, I think the lady is not in the best of spirits, is she, Bingley?"

Mr. Bingley, completed engrossed with Jane's comfort, took a moment to recall himself. "Pardon? Oh, yes. I believe Miss Lydia could use some cheering up."

Colonel Fitzwilliam turned to the other man. "Do you think riding out with us might serve?"

"The very thing!" Bingley said with a laugh. "What say you, Miss Lydia?"

Lydia was astonished. Her eyes popped wide open; her jaw fell to her chest. For once, she was speechless.

"Miss Lydia, do you wish to join us this morning?" asked Colonel Fitzwilliam kindly.

Lydia found her voice. "Do…do you really mean it?"

Caroline narrowed her eyes and pursed her lips. "She is not wearing a riding habit," she observed.

The colonel turned to his companion. "Oh, I do not think that will be an impediment, Miss Bingley. We are in the country, after all. I believe society will forgive us if we are generous." Elizabeth saw something—she was not sure what—in the colonel's look that caused Caroline to color and turn away. Colonel Fitzwilliam turned again to Lydia. "Will you join us, Miss Lydia?"

The girl practically screamed her happy agreement and dashed to the horse's side. Elizabeth knew that Lydia had some partiality for horses, but watching her sister's exhibition caused Elizabeth to understand that she had underestimated Lydia's love of the large imposing beasts. As for herself, she felt no jealousy; the only way someone could convince Elizabeth to ride was to have Mr. Collins chase her, waving a special license.

Lydia was soon seated upon the horse named Miranda, assisted by Hill's strong hands and accompanied by Mrs. Bennet's squeals of delight. Elizabeth was proud to see that Kitty's smile for Lydia's good fortune was devoid of envy. Apparently, her sister was content to stay at home with her art.

It suddenly occurred to Elizabeth that she did not know her younger sisters as well as she ought. She would have expected Kitty to protest most vigorously the attention showed Lydia as she had done so many times in the past, but she did not. And Lydia's excited reaction to the simple offer of a ride was entirely out of proportion to Elizabeth's previous understanding of the girl's character.

To be proven wrong was disconcerting, Elizabeth found. Even Mary was not as Elizabeth thought her. How was it that Elizabeth had no idea of Mary's determination to improve her playing, Kitty's enthusiasm for art, or Lydia's intense love of horses? Had she spent so much time in Jane's company that she had ignored her younger sisters? If so, what kind of sister had she truly been?

Meanwhile, Caroline had made some sort of decision. Instead of ignoring Lydia, she began to assist Colonel Fitzwilliam and Georgiana in showing Lydia the finer points of riding posture. True, her words were more pointed and less kind than those of the colonel or the heiress, but

Lydia was so engrossed in her lessons that she clearly took no offense. In fact, once Lydia was somewhat satisfactorily seated upon Miranda, she was gushing in her praise of Caroline's attire. This pleased the other woman, and Elizabeth saw that the colonel was very amused by it all.

Caroline was aware of Colonel Fitzwilliam's enjoyment and was clearly none too happy. "And what is it you find so amusing, Colonel?" Her voice dripped with sarcasm.

The gentleman only smiled. "Nothing and everything, my dear Miss Bingley. Well, ladies, shall we be off? Bingley and Miss Bennet are a good distance ahead of us."

Elizabeth could see it was so. During the quick riding lesson, Jane and her admirer had allowed their horses to wander off down the lane. The rest of the party set off after them, Lydia's youthful laughter ringing through the leaf-bare trees.

Normally, Elizabeth would have set off on her usual morning stroll about the countryside, but her late realizations had given her pause, and she resolved to spend more time with her younger sisters. She gathered her embroidery and joined Kitty and Mrs. Annesley in Mr. Darcy's room — Elizabeth to finish a screen and they to continue their drawing of Mr. Darcy.

Elizabeth was surprised to see Cassandra resting comfortably in Mr. Darcy's lap. She had not suspected that the gentleman would accept such attention from an animal, even one as even-tempered as the Bennet family cat. Elizabeth grew frustrated with the continuing examples of her mistaken judgment. If these revelations continued, she grumbled to herself, she might begin to doubt the brown of the leaves or the blue of the sky.

Time passed, but Elizabeth accomplished very little on her project. Instead, she was engrossed in studying Kitty. She noted that while Mrs. Annesley would look up from her work to study her subject, Kitty's attention was fixed upon her sketchbook. Elizabeth had drawn a little — a very little, for she lacked the patience to excel at the exercise — but she could not do so without looking at her subject. Surely, Kitty did not possess the ability to memorize her subject at a glance! She did not know what Kitty was about. She could not ask — that was unthinkable — but to wonder was natural and understandable. It was Mr. Darcy who solved the mystery.

"Well, Miss Kitty," he said as he stroked Cassandra lightly, "how fares my commission?"

Kitty blushed. "Very well, sir. I am working on it even now."

"Would it be too much to ask to have a preview?"

Elizabeth was enchanted at the appearance of dimples on Mr. Darcy's face. Goodness, he was handsome!

Kitty bit her lip, and for an instant, Elizabeth thought she might deny the gentleman his request. But she rose and handed her sketchbook over. As Darcy looked upon her work, Kitty said with apparent worry, "It is not finished, you understand. It has been very difficult to sketch without drawing her attention. I have pretended to draw you, you see, and I have to move between the two drawings constantly." Her eyes fell. "It is not very good."

Elizabeth watched as Mr. Darcy's face grew softly serious. "I beg to differ," he said in a low voice, thick with emotion. "I..." He glanced up. Was there a brightness in his eyes? "I am astonished. This is splendid!"

Kitty seemed not to believe her ears. "You *like* it?"

By that time, Mrs. Annesley had joined the two, and she gasped as she looked over Mr. Darcy's shoulder. "Miss Kitty, I must agree with Mr. Darcy. This is very fine work!"

This was too much for Elizabeth, and giving way to her curiosity, she crossed over to see. "May I?" she asked.

Mr. Darcy handed the sketchbook back to Kitty, who gave it to her sister. On the page was an unfinished charcoal portrait of a young lady engrossed in drawing. It was undoubtedly Miss Darcy. Her dress was only suggested and there was no background to speak of, for Kitty had focused on her subject's features — the turn of the chin, the graceful long neck, the curl next to her ear, the way her eyebrows creased ever so slightly when she concentrated. Kitty had captured it all.

"Oh, my," Elizabeth breathed. "Kitty, this is wonderful!"

"Oh, I am ever so glad!" cried the girl. She babbled on: "It will be much better when it is finished, but to know that you like it — (cough) — well, thank you!"

Mr. Darcy had recovered his equability. "I look forward to it."

His face was as Elizabeth expected — cool, unruffled, almost emotionless. Yet, there was a slight earnestness to his statement now that Elizabeth knew to listen for it. How many times had she missed it in the past? She did not know.

To mask her confusion, she mindlessly turned the pages in Kitty's book. Almost by accident, she came upon her own portrait. When, she wondered with astonishment, had *this* been done? She looked up to see Kitty completely red in the face. She gently recovered her sketchbook.

"You were not meant to see that," Kitty admonished her sister slightly.

"Why on earth not?" Elizabeth cried. "You have such a talent; everyone should know!"

"No! (cough)" Kitty was adamant. "Please do not tell anyone. I cannot bear the teasing."

Elizabeth almost asked what she meant by that, when she remembered Lydia's habit of disparaging others who owned talents she did not possess. Elizabeth opened her mouth to tell Kitty that she should not mind, that her skills were such that no one would pay heed to Lydia's silly pronouncements, when the girl herself burst into the room.

Kitty immediately closed her book, but it was unnecessary. Lydia's target was the gentleman in the wheel-chair.

"Mr. Darcy, Colonel Fitzwilliam told me what you did! Thank you, thank you!" She hurled herself at his head, wrapped her arms about his neck, and kissed his cheek. Cassandra scrambled to safety behind a sofa. "Thank you for letting me ride Miranda. She is so beautiful! You are the kindest man in the whole world!"

Mr. Darcy tried to free himself. "I am glad... you are pleased... Miss Lydia." He was unsuccessful. "Would you please release me?"

Lydia heard not a word the man said. "The colonel said that Miranda will remain at Longbourn for as long as you are here! How wonderful! I shall ride her every day, and care for her, and — and I hope you NEVER leave!"

"I UNDERSTAND MISS LYDIA WAS quite appreciative after her ride,"

Colonel Fitzwilliam quipped to Darcy as they shared an after-dinner port in Darcy's parlor. "I hope you enjoyed it."

"It was very embarrassing, if you must know," Darcy admitted. "But I thank you anyway for bringing Miranda — and Georgiana's horse, too."

"No need for all that. You know I can refuse Georgiana nothing. If she must remain here, she should have some entertainment."

"I do not believe Georgiana suffers being away from London, but perhaps you have better intelligence."

"No, no. It is apparent she has made herself quite at home at Longbourn." The colonel took a thoughtful sip of his port. "To be truthful, this sojourn has had a very beneficial effect on her. She is happy and outgoing — just as she was...before."

Yes, thought Darcy, *before Ramsgate*. "The Bennets have been very kind. It is apparent that she benefits from association with cheerful young ladies." His face fell. "I should have known that and allowed her to be in company more, rather than hide her at Pemberley. I have failed her."

Sardonic was the colonel's reply. "Oh, yes. It was very sporting of you to break your leg in order to provide your sister with stimulating companions. You are truly a man without equal." He laughed at Darcy's glare before sobering. "Bingley was quiet tonight."

"Was he? I did not notice."

The colonel eyed his cousin. "Do not play the innocent with me. You two were quartered together for no little time this afternoon. What in the world did you say to him?"

"That must remain between Bingley and me." Actually, Darcy had gently taken his great friend to task for his seeming indecision about Jane Bennet. Darcy learned that Bingley was as enamored as ever but was still uncertain about Miss Bennet's feelings. Darcy swallowed his pride and informed Bingley of his belief in Jane's attachment to him. Bingley was at first ecstatic over the news, but then grew thoughtful. After a bit of wheedling, Darcy discovered that Bingley's mind had turned from *if* to make an offer to Jane to *how*. Darcy suspected that Bingley was planning to make a bit of a fuss out of the business, and that meant a least a week's contemplation, if not longer.

To Darcy, it was all stuff and nonsense. He was a man who thought things through to an exacting extreme, but once a course of action was decided, he did not hesitate for an instant. Should he endeavor to propose marriage to a young lady, he would walk straight up to her and blurt out the first thing that came into his head.

To his cousin, he continued, "It is of little interest to you in any case, I am sure."

"You know," Colonel Fitzwilliam pointed out, "I should take exception to that last statement if I did not know your ways as well as my own. As it is, I shall remember your intentions and not your speech." Darcy, realizing that he had planted his foot in his mouth yet again, tried to apologize, but his cousin would have none of it. "One day, someone will teach you better manners, but it shall not be me."

Darcy brooded. Had not Elizabeth expressed the same misgivings about him? Had he learned nothing?

His cousin continued, "I am certain it had to do with Miss Bennet. Did you give Bingley your leave to marry the girl?"

"Fitz!"

"Ah, you did. Good! Everyone needs to be married and miserable."

"Fitz!"

"Forgive me, but after spending time with my estimable brother and his unspeakable wife, I am quite off the institution altogether. That reminds me." He removed a letter from his coat pocket and handed it over. "This is the reply from Horace. He requires more information about Sally and her family, but he seems predisposed to oblige you."

"Excellent. I shall write the viscount tomorrow."

Colonel Fitzwilliam shook his head. "Saving the world again! When shall you stop? Look what you have done here in little more than a fortnight. Music for Miss Mary, paints for Miss Kitty, horses for that Lydia child, and a husband for Miss Bennet. And you are endeavoring to secure the future of a servant and her family — a servant that is not even your own! You are impossible!"

Darcy did not deign to defend himself.

"Why, the only young lady here to whom you have not given anything is Miss Elizabeth! And she the one I was sure you had fixed your eye upon!" The colonel looked closely at the other man. "Or perhaps you plan to give her much more — say everything you have?"

"Fitzwilliam, I will not discuss Miss Elizabeth with you!"

"You are trying to win her esteem, are you not? Strange, I thought you abhorred gratitude."

"I do!" Darcy cried. "I am not trying to win anyone's gratitude! I have given a few things because…because that is what I want! It makes the ladies happy and Georgiana, too. That is reward enough for me."

"You are the most generous man I know, Darce, but there are times I do not understand you. Never have I seen a person more opposed to accepting thanks. It is quite annoying."

"You should know all about annoying, Fitz, as you are so good at it."

"*Touché.* Annoying the king's enemies has kept me alive these many years. It is a hard habit to break."

"Must you practice on me?"

"Yes. You are too tempting a target, even if you are the best man I know." He raised his glass. "I truly hope you receive everything you deserve." As Darcy sipped, he added, "And Miss Elizabeth."

Darcy nearly choked on his port.

Chapter 15

THE SUCCEEDING DAYS FLOWED in much the same manner as those before. Mr. Bennet spent the bulk of his time ensconced in his book room. Mrs. Bennet supervised the management of the household with Jane's assistance. Mary practiced her instrument and Kitty her art, both in the company of Georgiana and Mrs. Annesley. And when Lydia was not underfoot, she could be found in the stables, attending to Miranda.

Mr. Bingley visited as often as he could manage, which meant every day. He often arrived just after breakfast and seldom left before dinner. He was usually accompanied by his sisters and sometimes by Mr. Hurst, but they always left after tea. Colonel Fitzwilliam was at Longbourn as often as Mr. Bingley, and he spent his time with his cousins.

The cold of the season forced the Longbourn party to remain indoors, except for Lydia's insistence upon riding. As for Mr. Darcy, he was wheeled between his makeshift bedroom in the parlor to the sitting room and dining table. He was not satisfied to be simply a subject for drafting or a passive audience for music. He labored for hours on the reams of correspondence that he had forwarded from London. His capacity for work caught the attention of the household, and even Mr. Bennet remarked on it, although in a rather sarcastic manner that mortified Elizabeth.

The weather curtailed Elizabeth's ramblings, but the reader should know she merely shortened her walks, not eliminated them. When she was not about her chores, she spent more time with Mary and Kitty, taking pains to know them better. She would have done the same with Lydia, but standing for hours in a dirty stable with great, smelly beasts was too much of a sacrifice even for Elizabeth's generous heart.

So occupied was the Longbourn family with their guests that the news of Mr. Wickham's departure for debtors' prison in London received little notice except for Mrs. Bennet's quip of, "Good riddance to bad rubbish! Such a hateful man! Spreading lies about dear Mr. Darcy!"

Fanny Bennet was a creature of extremes. When Mr. Darcy rudely dismissed the Bennet ladies at the Meryton assembly, she judged him the proudest, most disagreeable man in the kingdom. Now that he was a guest in her house and a potential suitor for one of her daughters, the tables were turned. No better man ever lived, she told anyone within earshot. So kind, so refined, so handsome — and rich — surely, he was worth ten thousand a year, if a penny! Mr. Darcy's enemies became hers, and Mr. Wickham was condemned as a scoundrel of the worse sort.

What she would have said about Wickham had she known the true extent of his ill use of the Darcys could only be imagined. Thankfully, for Georgiana's reputation and Darcy's peace of mind, not a hint of Ramsgate ever reached Mrs. Bennet's ears.

A few days later, a break in the weather encouraged Mr. Bingley to invite the Bennet ladies and Georgiana to Netherfield for the day. To be precise, the invitation was issued by Miss Bingley, but no one was deceived as to the real initiator of the offer. Georgiana was loath to leave her brother, but she was convinced by Darcy to go and enjoy herself. So it came to pass that Longbourn was devoid of female inhabitants when an express arrived for Mr. Darcy.

Darcy received the message in his room as Bartholomew shaved him. What Darcy read caused him to start and suffer his second shaving cut in Hertfordshire.

"Oh, sir!" cried his valet, "I must insist you be still, or I cannot guarantee your safety!"

"Never mind, Bartholomew, it was not your fault," Darcy replied as he wiped his chin. "Finish up. I must have words with Mr. Bennet directly."

Darcy's conversation with Mr. Bennet was more immediate than he thought. No sooner had Bartholomew accomplished his task of cleaning the soap from his employer's face than the master of Longbourn came into the room without so much as a knock on the door. Darcy was surprised at the breach of manners, but his indignation turned to astonishment. Mr. Bennet was red-faced as he shook a handful of papers in his upraised hand.

"What can I do for you, sir?" Darcy could see that Mr. Bennet was trying to restrain his temper.

"Mr. Darcy, I am a reasonable man. I consider myself a gentleman, and I know the expectations that come with that office, but this is too much, sir!"

Darcy had been trained from childhood to deal with all sorts of people, from tradesmen to peers. He managed the lives of hundreds between his house in London, his estate of Pemberley, and his manifold investments. An angry person was an unreasonable person, he knew. To accomplish anything, a tense situation must be placated. He calmly sat back in his chair, laced his fingers over his midsection, and spoke in a calm, steady voice. "I do not have the pleasure of understanding you. What is it that upsets you?"

"These! These bills I have just received!"

Darcy's eyes narrowed. "I beg your pardon?"

"You have taken over my household! You treat my servants as your own, you have changed the food served at my table, and you have filled my house with your relations! And I have not said a word, much as I wished. *I*, at least, know my place as a host. You are injured, and I will do right by you even though you hurt yourself by your own thoughtlessness! But now you have gone too far — too far, sir!" He shook the papers at Darcy. "It is one thing to stable your carriage horses while you are in residence, but to expect me to feed and care for your entertainments? You take advantage of me!"

"Entertainments?" said Darcy dangerously. "Do you speak of my sister's horse?"

"Yes, and that other nag, as well!"

"You mean Miranda, the one I provided for *your* daughter's

amusement."

Had Mr. Bennet been more in control of his emotions, he would have taken heed of Darcy's calm, silky tone for the warning it was, but he was too enraged to comprehend that the windy seeds he was sowing were about to reap the whirlwind.

"I do not appreciate your attempts to buy my family's approbation!"

Bartholomew gasped at the insult, but Darcy said nothing. He stared hard at the other man until Mr. Bennet took note of his countenance. Some of the redness in the older man's face faded, and that was when Darcy spoke.

But it was in a voice no one at Longbourn had heard before. It was not the bored tones of a man of quality, which Darcy used when he first entered Hertfordshire, or the more natural and relaxed speech he habitually reserved for family and friends. No, this was the voice of the master of Pemberley, used by a man who could break a yeoman with a word, a banker with a glance, or a barrister with a glare.

His eyes never leaving Mr. Bennet's, he said between his teeth, "Bartholomew, kindly retrieve the paper from Mr. Bennet's steward and hand it to this gentleman."

With a smirk, the valet reached into a satchel and pulled out a single sheet. With a flourish — for Bartholomew was enjoying himself — he presented it to Mr. Bennet, who took it, curiosity and apprehension growing on his face. He waited, but as Darcy said nothing more, only glared, the older man read what he was given.

"What is this?"

"Surely it is self-explanatory," Darcy said drily.

"This is a list of figures. Why do you have it?" Bennet looked up, his anger returning. "Why is my steward giving you details of Longbourn's business?"

"Not all of your business, only that of your stable," said Darcy coldly. "Kindly read aloud the figure at the bottom."

Bennet glanced down. "Seven pounds, six shillings, eight pence."

Darcy continued to glare at Mr. Bennet. "That is the cost of stabling my horses since I came here — all of them, *including* the two additions and the feeding of Colonel Fitzwilliam's horse during his visits, through the day before yesterday."

"You are keeping account of it?"

Darcy did not answer the older man. "Bartholomew, immediately draw up a bank note for my signature. Seven pounds, six and eight, payable to Mr. Thomas Bennet, Esq. of Longbourn."

Mr. Bennet paled. "Mr. Darcy, that is not — "

Darcy shot back, releasing all of his pent-up outrage. "You have questioned my integrity. You have accused me of taking advantage of you. You have leveled great insults against me. How dare you, sir? I am not accustomed to such treatment. I have never cheated anyone — gentleman, merchant, or servant — in my life!" Bartholomew handed Darcy the paper, on which he quickly scrawled his signature. "It was my intention to settle accounts with you upon my departure, but apparently you cannot depend upon my reputation." He gave the bank note back to the valet. "As the physician has ordered that I stay here, leaving is not an option. Therefore, we shall settle all costs thus incurred to date and begin a process of regular payments. Give him the bank note, Bartholomew. Will that satisfy you, sir?"

Mr. Bennet stood white-face and mortified. "I will not take your money. I am not an innkeeper."

"Then you should not act like one. Bartholomew, draft a note for the household expenses."

Mr. Bennet gasped. "You have been receiving figures from Hill, too?"

Darcy was relentless. "Bartholomew, do you have that note?"

The paper appeared before Darcy, who signed it and instructed it be given to Mr. Bennet. Within moments, a chastened Thomas Bennet stood before Fitzwilliam Darcy with two bank notes in one hand and a stack of bills in the other. Had Darcy not been so angry, he might have found the sight somewhat amusing.

"You shame me, sir," Bennet managed.

"You shame yourself, Mr. Bennet."

The older man's lip trembled as he glanced at the notes. "May I sit?"

His anger slackened somewhat, Darcy nodded. Mr. Bennet half-fell into a chair, his face red again, but this time with embarrassment. "I owe you an apology. I have not been as gracious a host as I should. Indeed,

I have not been any proper host to you at all. I have not taken the time to further our acquaintance. I suppose I thought you to be like many other young men from Town, inconsiderate and only interested in their own amusements." He glanced at the notes again. "It seems I was wrong — very wrong, indeed."

"Did my conversation with you about Wickham prove nothing?"

Bennet shrugged. "Only that Wickham was your enemy. I should have given it greater consideration."

Darcy was perplexed. "What have I done to deserve such disapprobation?"

Bennet looked up, disbelief clear on his face. "Mr. Darcy, really! Have you no recollection of your behavior prior to your accident?"

"How dare you question Mr. Darcy!" cried loyal Bartholomew, but Darcy silenced him with a gesture.

"Pray continue, Mr. Bennet."

For the next few minutes, the gentleman cataloged all of Darcy's sins against the people of Hertfordshire — his pride, his reserve, and his selfish disdain of the feelings of others. Darcy's face was placid, but internally, his emotions were roiling. He had heard it all before from the lips of his beloved Elizabeth. While he did not doubt her dislike of his previous behavior, he was shocked that all of Meryton seemed to share her opinion. He began to wonder whether they still felt that way. He also began to think that, while he had improved Elizabeth's opinion — or at least he thought he had — it might be for naught if all her friends thought him an arse.

By the end of his dissertation, Mr. Bennet had recovered some of his old *sang-froid*. "It seems, sir, you show two faces to the world. That you choose to do so must inure you to misunderstandings of your character, I should think."

Darcy was displeased to hear that, but he could not dispute it. Was being more open the price to win Elizabeth? He sighed. "Well, I trust you have a better understanding of my character now, sir."

"These notes — "

"Belong to you." Darcy added with a small smile, "Do with them what you will. If you will allow a change of subject, I have a matter of some importance to discuss with you."

"Indeed?" Bennet frowned.

Darcy reached over for the express he had received. "This involves one of your servants, Sally."

"Sally? What about Sally?"

"Read this and you will see. By the way, we shall need to talk to her mother directly."

Bennet took the message. "It sounds as though you are planning to marry the girl," he quipped.

"Hardly."

IT TOOK ANOTHER TWO HOURS for Sally's mother to be transported to Longbourn and to hold a meeting with her, Sally, Darcy, and Mr. Bennet in that gentleman's book room. It is not the purpose of this work to detail in full the manner by which both maid and mother chose to express their surprise, delight, and acceptance of the offer made to them, save that Sally's mother, in a fit of gratitude, tears streaming down her face, knelt beside Darcy's chair, grasped his hand and kissed it.

"Thank you, thank you, m'lord!" the old woman cried. "You are the saving of us all! God bless you!"

Darcy tried unsuccessfully to retrieve his captured digits. "You are...very welcome. Madam, if you please!" Gentle tugging did not serve, and the woman kissed his hand again.

Finally, Sally, her eyes wet and shining with esteem and awe, was able to disengage her mother from further assault on Darcy's person. "You're as good a man as ever lived, sir," said she, "an' you'll be in our prayers every Sunday, won't he, Mum?"

The old woman was beyond words, so it was left to Sally to assure Darcy and Mr. Bennet that they would be ready to leave for their new home in two days. She thanked the gentlemen again, gave the injured man one last longing look, and guided her nearly hysterical mother out of the book room.

Mr. Bennet was vastly amused by the whole exercise. "I do believe you have won admirers for life, Mr. Darcy! I would be surprised if Sally named her first boy anything other than — what is your Christian name again?"

Darcy scowled at Mr. Bennet. "It was my intention to present this offer to Sally and her mother as a joint effort. I thought we had agreed to that. What possessed you to lay the whole thing at my door?"

Bennet shrugged. "It was merely the truth, my dear sir — *your* cousin, *your* letter-writing, and *your* men helping them pack. I simply provided the deserving poor for your benevolence."

Darcy rolled his eyes. At least he knew where Elizabeth learned impertinent behavior! As it was one of the lady's most endearing characteristics, he should have been more tolerant of jibes from her father, but Darcy found the man annoying. He supposed that teasing from a cranky old man was not as welcome as it was from a beautiful young woman possessing a light and pleasing form, sparkling eyes, and lush lips.

Mr. Bennet continued in a more serious manner. "I trust your cousin is an honorable man."

Darcy did not take offense. "Viscount Fitzwilliam is…eccentric, that is true, but I have known him all my life, and I tell you that he will not mistreat Sally or her family. The viscountess can be demanding, but not out of the common way. If Sally and her family work hard, they will be treated well and their future will be secure. I would not have suggested this if I thought otherwise."

"I am sure you would have not. But to report to London the day after tomorrow? That is abrupt."

Darcy had to agree that it was. "Horace can be impulsive. He thinks about things for a long while to the point of indecisiveness, but once he makes up his mind, he wants everything done yesterday. He and Lady Eugenie leave for Argyle Manor in Derbyshire in a few days, and Horace wishes his new servants to accompany them."

"It was very generous of you to offer your people to help the family pack their belongings."

Darcy did not respond, embarrassed at the praise. Instead, he said, "That reminds me. I must send an express to Darcy House in London to have them brought here by tomorrow, as well as a nurse to replace Sally. May I use your desk?"

"Certainly." Mr. Bennet wheeled Darcy into position and provided a sheet of paper. "While you are writing, I shall have Hill send for a rider."

Darcy bent to his writing. "I shall reimburse you, of course."

"No, you shall not!" Darcy looked up at the now-determined Bennet. "You have done everything to help one of *my* servants, a woman who means nothing to you. I am ashamed to think how much you have done and will do. I have not treated you well, and yet you have been kind and generous to all my family. You are even going to replace one my servants with one of yours at your own expense."

"Mr. Bennet, it is perfectly reasonable that I have a nurse brought here to help me while you look for a replacement for Sally."

"Reasonable for you, perhaps, but how many others would do the same? You teach me my duty." Bennet glanced at the two bank notes lying on the desk. "I know now who the true gentleman is in this room. Give me leave to pay for an express, for God's sake. It is the least I can do."

"As you wish." Darcy returned to his note.

"Why do you do it?"

Darcy glanced up. "I beg your pardon?"

Mr. Bennet's voice was not challenging, but wistful. "Why are you helping Sally? Why have you provided diversions for my daughters? I have a right to know."

Darcy could hardly admit his true motivation. He struggled. "Because I can."

"And this is all the reply which I am to have the honor of expecting? Come, come, sir. There is more to this than your financial circumstances!"

"Mr. Bennet, I assure you — "

"Are you attempting to earn the admiration of my daughters? If so, I must tell you that you have succeeded marvelously. Even Elizabeth, who so hated you before, has fallen under your charms. It then falls to *me* to inquire about your intentions."

"Mr. Bennet, I — " Darcy bit off his next words, returned the pen to the inkwell, and stared out of the window. How to answer? Darcy started carefully. "My intentions in matters to which you allude have always been honorable. Or, I should say, will always be honorable, as I have never … sought an alliance before."

"But you are considering one."

Darcy frowned. "I cannot speak to that as — Forgive me, sir, but this is new to me. I cannot speak as I have not acquired the affections of any young lady."

There was a pause. "It is Elizabeth, is it not?" Bennet's voice was uneven. At Darcy's transparent look, the older man chuckled. "Do not be so shocked that I have discovered your little secret, young man. Even without all you did for her in the matter with Mr. Collins, there is the fact that she is the gem of this house, and you, as a man of discriminating taste, must know her worth. You speak with her as I do, with respect for her wit and intelligence, and not as a besotted youth interested only in her physical charms. You are a man used to the best in everything I daresay, and Elizabeth is the best Hertfordshire can offer. It is logical."

A red-faced Darcy, knowing he had been found out, could only admit, "I consider your daughter as one of the handsomest and most remarkable women of my acquaintance. I suppose I am overdue in requesting permission for a courtship, but I cannot while I am restricted to this wheel-chair. It is just as well; it is only of late that I suspect Miss Elizabeth's opinion of me might be ... positive."

"Might be?" laughed Mr. Bennet. "Well, you will certainly win her gratitude with gestures like helping Sally."

"No!" cried Darcy. "You must not tell her!"

"What? Why on earth not?"

"You must understand. I would not have your daughter accept me out of gratitude."

"What is wrong with gratitude?"

Darcy looked out the window again. "My own excellent parents enjoyed a remarkable marriage. There was totality and equality in esteem, admiration, and affection, each for the other. They were always of one mind. I long for that in my own marriage — one built on the foundation of mutual affection and respect, not on something as transitory as gratitude."

"Good Lord," Bennet breathed. "I always desired that Lizzy marry a gentleman worthy of her, and I am coming to the opinion that you are that man." He bit his lip. "I shall do as you wish, though let me advise you to think better of it. Lizzy is not one to like secrets."

How could Darcy admit to him that he must have her love first? "I will tell her when I deem the time right."

Bennet chuckled. "Oh, my, there will be some pretty scenes in your Pemberley in the future, I can tell! Well, my boy, good luck. If Lizzy accepts a courtship, you have my permission. And I will keep quiet about this little matter."

"Thank you, sir. Your daughter is a very special lady. I would consider it a great honor if she would even consider my suit."

Bennet choked a little. "Yes... well, you have an express to write, and I must acquire a rider if that letter is to get to Town tonight." He opened the door. "Hill! Oh, Hill! A moment, please!"

The housekeeper soon received her orders, and the gentlemen, tasks completed, were enjoying a brandy when the book room door opened. But it was not to announce the arrival of the express rider.

"Mr. Bennet, may I have a word with you, sir?" cried a beaming Charles Bingley. "Oh, my apologies, Darcy, but I must speak to Mr. Bennet instantly on a subject of great importance! One that will forever affect the happiness of me and Miss Bennet!"

Mr. Bennet and Darcy shared a look.

"About time!" they said in unison.

Chapter 16

EARLIER THAT DAY, THE Bennet ladies descended upon Netherfield *en mass* for the first time since Jane's illness, this time accompanied by Miss Darcy and Mrs. Annesley. The Bingley siblings, the Hursts, and Colonel Fitzwilliam received them inside the door, for it was too cold to do so on the porch. While all the visitors were greeted properly, Mr. Bingley's attentions were fixed upon Jane, while Miss Bingley and Mrs. Hurst attempted to monopolize Miss Darcy. Mrs. Bennet, her remaining daughters, and Mrs. Annesley had to make do with Colonel Fitzwilliam's amusing banter.

After a few minutes, Miss Bingley seemed to recall her duties as hostess, and Elizabeth wondered whether it was the result of a pointed remark by the colonel about his mother, the countess. Elizabeth had to restrain her laughter watching Miss Bingley endeavor to keep her composure as Mrs. Bennet droned on about how lovely a house Netherfield was and how all that was required for perfection was the touch of a proper mistress. Her deliberate look at her distracted eldest daughter, deep in conversation with Mr. Bingley, left no doubt as to her meaning. Miss Bingley gritted her teeth and rose, offering the assembled a tour of the house.

Thus was spent the next hour: Caroline expounded upon the beauties and deficiencies of Netherfield with Mrs. Hurst offering her pointed commentary. Strangely, Elizabeth began to have a grudging admiration for the unmarried member of the Superior Sisters. The condescending woman clearly thought herself above her company — except for Georgiana, whom she treated as an equal.

Nevertheless, Elizabeth had to admit that Caroline had elegance; she carried herself well, and her dress was immaculate. The lady knew the history of the house and was honest about its shortcomings. What particularly caught Elizabeth's attention was that Caroline was more erudite than Mrs. Hurst, whose ignorant simpering made even her sister wince. Lastly, Caroline withstood the inane suggestions of Mrs. Bennet to an extraordinary degree. More than once, Elizabeth thought of clasping a hand over her mother's mouth before yet another mortifying statement could be uttered.

Elizabeth was thankful for the surprising participation of Colonel Fitzwilliam, for the gentleman volunteered to accompany the tour rather than flee to the billiards room with Mr. Hurst. The colonel's easy conversation and witty comments defused more than one tense situation, particularly when Caroline's patience was brought to the breaking point by either Mrs. Bennet or Mrs. Hurst. There was no help to be had from Mr. Bingley; he either was engrossed with Jane or chose to ignore the unpleasantness.

A light luncheon was served, followed by performances on the pianoforte. Georgiana only agreed to play after cajoling from the colonel and an offer to turn the pages by Elizabeth. Her performance was flawless and received much praise from those assembled. Mrs. Annesley then proved her abilities. Even Mary acquitted herself with respect. Her flushed cheeks, a result of the first genuine praise she had ever received, touched Elizabeth's heart. Mrs. Hurst played next, and it was then Elizabeth's turn. She performed without major errors and escaped any malicious remarks from Miss Bingley.

It was now time for the hostess to play as Jane, Kitty, and Lydia had never learnt, and Caroline dove into a complicated piece from Mozart. It was lengthy and compelling, and she played it well. Elizabeth listened attentively, and while she was impressed with the lady's skill, she thought something was missing from the performance. There seemed a lack of sensibility, of feeling, from the piece. As Mozart was one of Elizabeth's favorite composers, she knew his work should be performed with great emotion. Caroline apparently chose not to or was incapable of doing so.

So engrossed was she in her analysis of Caroline's performance that Elizabeth did not realize the audience had decreased until Lydia tapped her arm. With a mischievous glint in her eye, her sister gestured to the chairs that had been occupied by Jane and Mr. Bingley. They were now conspicuously empty. Elizabeth's raised eyebrow brought forth a giggle from Lydia.

They were not the only ones to notice the absence of certain members of their party. "I say," remarked Mrs. Hurst, "where is Miss Bennet? Has she taken ill again? And where is Charles?"

Her voice carried over Caroline's music, and the performer stopped abruptly. "What did you say, Louisa?" she asked as her eyes darted to that now-empty part of the room.

All stared at the vacant chairs. Mrs. Bennet, not slow in such matters, grasped the implication of the situation immediately and acted in a manner consistent with her matchmaking character.

"Oh, how wonderful! I am sure there is some good mischief about, but I shall not say more. No, no, not a word from me! These young lovers must have their way. Play on, Miss Bingley, play on! We are not wanted anywhere else, of that you may be certain!"

"No!" exclaimed Caroline as she jumped up from the bench. "We…we should go! Miss Bennet may have met with misfortune, and — "

"Miss Bingley, pray calm yourself." The colonel's voice was gentle. "If your brother is with Miss Bennet, she is in good hands."

"That is no comfort!" cried Mrs. Hurst. "Caroline, we must — "

Just then the door to the music room was thrown open, and Mr. Bingley, face aglow, dashed in. "Congratulate me! Jane has made me the most fortunate man in the world!"

"Oh, Brother, what have you done?" demanded Mrs. Hurst. Meanwhile, Caroline had turned white.

"Louisa, she accepted me! My angel accepted me!"

"Where *is* your angel, Bingley?" asked Colonel Fitzwilliam.

"Eh? Why, right here — what?" Bingley looked about confused until Jane walked in, a picture of blushing contentment. "Oh, my dear! Pray forgive me! I could not wait to share our happiness!"

Jane smiled but said not a word. She moved to Bingley's side and took his arm, her blissful eyes filled with tears of joy.

The room exploded! Shrieks were heard from Mrs. Bennet and her youngest daughters — and Mrs. Hurst too although hers were from a different emotion. Elizabeth dashed to her sister but could not embrace her; the girl's attention was monopolized by her mother. So Elizabeth turned to Bingley and expressed all the love a future brother should have from a new sister.

As she waited her turn with Jane, Elizabeth noticed that, unlike her red-faced sister, Caroline was standing apart from the crowd. She was pale and trembling, and her eyes darted back and forth between the group and Colonel Fitzwilliam. She then closed her eyes, took a great breath, and with the most affected of smiles, approached the happy couple.

"Charles, Jane, I…I wish you joy." Bingley grinned, Jane smiled, and Mrs. Hurst gasped, her protests overridden. "Louisa, Charles has made his choice. We must support him and help Jane with her entrance into society." In her more usual tone of voice, Caroline added, "We will guide her, giving her the full benefit of our experience. She will not embarrass us, I am determined."

Elizabeth was outraged at the backhanded compliment but held her tongue. It would not do to have an argument at such a time. Besides, Jane, who seemed not bothered in the least, was now available for a loving embrace.

"'Tis too much!" Jane said, "by far too much. I do not deserve it. Oh, why is not everybody as happy? Lizzy, why am I thus singled from my family and blessed above them all? If I could but see *you* as happy! If there *were* but such another man for you!" She stopped and whispered. "But there *is*."

"Oh, Jane," said Elizabeth. "Not you too!"

Mr. Bingley soon took a hurried leave of those assembled, declaring he had business at Longbourn. Knowing the gist of that business sent Mrs. Bennet into another fit of elation.

"Oh, my dear, dear Jane, I am so happy; I am sure I shall not get a wink of sleep all night! I knew how it would be! I always said it must be so at last. I was sure you could not be so beautiful for nothing! I remember, as soon as ever I saw him, when Mr. Bingley first came into Hertfordshire, I thought how likely it was that you should come together. Oh, he is the handsomest young man that ever was seen!"

"You hear that, Georgie?" cried Colonel Fitzwilliam. "Your brother and I have been cast out of Mount Olympus and relegated to the condition of mere mortals. How shall I bear the degradation?"

"Oh, Colonel, I meant no slight against you," insisted the chastised matron, "or your excellent cousin." She looked at Elizabeth and continued. "Mr. Darcy is all that is charming and handsome! And you, too, my dear colonel."

Colonel Fitzwilliam grinned. "I thank you for my part, madam."

Caroline was vexed. "Pray refrain from fishing for compliments," she said drily. "It is most unbecoming." The colonel only laughed in return. She then stood, her smile brittle. "My dear Jane, may I tempt you to walk with me? There are many parts of Netherfield that are still unknown to you, and it would be my pleasure to bring them to your attention. As its future mistress, you should become as familiar with the house and the servants as I. The tour will refresh us as well."

Elizabeth did not know whether Caroline's proposal arose from a desire to be of use to her future sister or to be removed from Mrs. Bennet's company. Jane gave no clue as to her opinion of the matter and accepted Caroline's offer. The others were to remain — details of the kitchen could be of no interest to them, they were told — and the two ladies swept out of the room.

Mrs. Bennet, having no other target, engaged Mrs. Hurst in a one-sided conversation, a state of affairs that was accepted with thinly veiled contempt. The other Bennet ladies descended upon Colonel Fitzwilliam. Elizabeth found herself talking with Georgiana and Mrs. Annesley.

"Your sister and Mr. Bingley seem well suited," the heiress said. "I am sure they will be very happy together."

Elizabeth laughed. "Yes. They both are gifted with gentle and pleasing natures. I doubt a cross word will ever arise between them."

Georgiana and Mrs. Annesley shared a look. "I am sure you are right," said the companion. "Not everyone, however, wishes to be paired for life with their mirror image. Some people," another glance at Georgiana, "like to be challenged."

"There is some truth to that. There can be too much compliancy in marriage, I suppose." Elizabeth looked over at her mother. "Respect, I am convinced, is very important."

"Very true," said Mrs. Annesley. "Where there is a greatness of mind, there should also be an appreciation for the same in one's chosen life partner, as well as the modesty of acknowledging that one cannot know everything. A sensible wife can support her husband without offering too much deference. Wise is the man who seeks a clever bride."

"Elizabeth is very clever," Georgiana blurted out. "Do you not think so, Mrs. Annesley?"

"Georgiana! You should not embarrass our friend so," her companion gently admonished.

"She is not embarrassed," said Georgiana innocently as she turned. "Are you, Elizabeth?"

A self-conscious Elizabeth managed, "Of course not."

Without a beat, Georgiana continued. "Mrs. Annesley, would you not say that my brother is a wise man?"

"*Georgiana!*" the other two cried in unison, bringing attention to themselves from the others in the room.

"What was that, dear?" asked Mrs. Bennet. "Is something the matter?"

"No, Mama, nothing." Elizabeth stood up. "I believe it is my turn again at the pianoforte. Georgiana, will you attend me?"

THAT EVENING A CELEBRATORY DINNER was given at Longbourn, and Elizabeth found everyone in high spirits — well, almost everyone. Mrs. Hurst was decidedly morose, and while Caroline was not as rude as her sister, she was uncharacteristically quiet. Colonel Fitzwilliam spent no little time attempting to draw her out but to no avail. He finally abandoned the effort and joined the general conversation.

The party concluded rather early. Mr. Bingley needed to prepare to return to London for business in two days and expected to spend the next day in close consultation with the steward of Netherfield. As it would be a full day, he reluctantly made his adieus, and the Hursts, Colonel Fitzwilliam, and Miss Bingley accompanied him. Mr. Darcy retired to the parlor bedroom, despite the protests from Mrs. Bennet of his abandonment of the ladies.

The young ladies, in fact, were not distressed, for they longed to retreat upstairs and review that delightful day in minute detail. Georgiana was particularly enthusiastic about being included in the conversations to come. With no sisters, she had never enjoyed the close comradeship of ladies her own age and, truth be told, felt the absence exceedingly since her arrival at Longbourn. With envious eyes, she watched the interactions among the Bennet sisters. To be invited to participate in such an intimate discussion met all her dreams of sisterly camaraderie. Jane held court, revealing to the delight of those assembled Mr. Bingley's nervous, stuttering proposal.

"Have you seen Cassandra?" Elizabeth asked Kitty during a lull in the conversation.

"No, but she has been spending a great deal of time with Mr. Darcy."

Lydia smirked. "I think you have a rival for Mr. Darcy's attentions, Lizzy!"

"Stop talking foolishness!" Elizabeth cried, her face beet-red. "Mr. Darcy is a friend — that is all."

"Oh, certainly," was Lydia's retort before she, Kitty, and Georgiana dissolved into giggles. Elizabeth escaped as soon as she could and went directly to the parlor. The door was slightly open, so she knocked as she went in.

"Mr. Darcy, I — "

At that moment, she saw Sally reaching down to hand a glass of port to Mr. Darcy, entirely coatless in his wheel-chair. Her entrance must have startled the maid, for she gasped and lost hold of the glass, spilling its contents over his fine silk shirt.

"Stupid girl!" cried Bartholomew, who had been preparing Mr. Darcy's bed for the night. "Look what you have done!" He dashed to his master's side with towels, mumbling condemnations against the sobbing maid.

"Oh, no, it is my fault," protested Elizabeth. "Do not blame poor Sally."

The two servants tried to sop up the dark red liquid covering Mr. Darcy's shirt, but it was a hopeless task. He was soaked through, the port making his shirt quite transparent. Elizabeth could clearly see that Mr. Darcy was not a man of leisure, at least not in the manner of men like Mr. Hurst. The muscles of his broad chest and strong arms were clearly defined, even with the red hue of the wine, and there seemed to be a small bit of dark hair about the center of his torso.

The sight riveted Elizabeth. "I...I was looking for Cassandra...my cat."

Darcy looked up from the mess as his valet stepped forward to remove the soaked garment. "Miss Elizabeth, please! This is no place for you."

Elizabeth had never felt as flushed before. "Of course. I am so sorry!"

With that, she left the room quickly and returned upstairs. As it was, Cassandra had been visiting Mary's room and was waiting for her. Elizabeth quickly prepared for bed, not saying what had happened downstairs or what she had seen.

But visions of Mr. Darcy in his wet shirt — *and out of it* — haunted her dreams all night.

Darcy awoke early the next morning, no worse for all the hullabaloo of the night before. Once the majority of the port had been soaked up, he had washed and retired. Before Sally left the room, he made certain to assure the girl that she had done him no harm and wished her and her family a good journey to London.

Darcy found he was the first at breakfast. He spent little time there as Mr. Jones was due to inspect his injury. He was on his second cup of coffee when Colonel Fitzwilliam was announced. They retired to the parlor to await the apothecary's arrival.

The gentleman was prompt and immediately began his examination. After much poking and prodding, he judged that the injury was healing much faster than he thought possible.

"You should still remain in your chair, sir," he advised, "but the bone has knit in a very satisfactory manner, and you will soon be on your feet."

"That is welcomed news, sir."

"Indeed. You should know I have put my new knowledge to good use. I used this innovative splint on young Master Baker, who had fallen out of a tree, and his arm shall be as good as new, God willing. What a fortunate thing it was for me to meet Mr. Macmillan!"

"I am glad my cousin was considerate enough to break his leg for you, sir," remarked Colonel Fitzwilliam drily. "All in the name of science, you know."

"Fitz, enough!" Darcy demanded.

Mr. Jones advised that Mr. Darcy should remain at Longbourn until the time set by Mr. Macmillan. The colonel waited until the good man left before speaking again.

"So, you and Georgiana are to remain another fortnight?"

"It appears so, but you are not so imposed. I appreciate your attendance and service, but you must not think that you are obligated to remain. Has Whitehall grown anxious by your absence?"

"Not yet. Things are quiet now, thank the Lord. I consider myself at your and Georgie's disposal."

"I am not sorry to hear it but do own myself surprised. A few days ago you sang a different tune."

"Yes... well, I have found that Hertfordshire holds a certain charm."

IT HAD BEEN A LONG, hectic day, and Elizabeth owned herself tired from all the visiting in the village. Mrs. Bennet had gathered up her brood and marched off to Meryton to crow about her daughter's good fortune as soon as it was fashionable. At least Lady Lucas took it all in stride. Disappointed as the good lady might have been over the Mr. Collins affair, her affection for the eldest Bennet girls fortified her against their mother's bragging. Mrs. Goulding was sweetly insincere, and Mrs. Long was downright hostile. Mrs. Philips declared that she would have Jane and Elizabeth visit longer the next day so that callers could spend time with them — visits to Longbourn being out of the question due to the injured Mr. Darcy residing there.

Elizabeth concluded that it was just as well that she was absent from Longbourn for the majority of the day. Her sleep the night before had been disturbed by the most wanton dreams! She knew she would blush beet-red had she come upon the gentleman at breakfast, and only the exhaustion of her activities gave her the ability to see Mr. Darcy at dinner with any level of modesty. Mr. Darcy himself appeared unharmed by the misadventure of the day before. Still, even attired in a splendid coat of bottle-green and an impeccably tied cravat, Elizabeth's thoughts could barely stray from the fetching aspect of a drenched Darcy in his shirtsleeves. As a result, when it came to conversation with the man, she was tongue-tied, save for the odd innocent comment.

She instead turned her attention to the others, finding soothing refuge in ordinary conversation. Mrs. Bennet was full of advice about Jane's wedding, the bride-to-be accepting it all in her usual stride. Mary and Georgiana spoke of music, while Mrs. Annesley held Kitty spellbound with tales of the great painters of Europe. Colonel Fitzwilliam was in attendance, locked in a discussion of horseflesh with Lydia. Elizabeth was relieved to see her father and Mr. Darcy conversing amiably over matters of field drainage. It pleased her to see that tensions in the house had virtually vanished.

Knowing she and Jane were to be at their Aunt Philips's after breakfast, Elizabeth decided to retire early that evening. Before proceeding upstairs, she went into the kitchen to inform Cook of their plans. Cook thanked Elizabeth for her thoughtfulness but claimed their early departure was no burden as Mr. Darcy often breakfasted soon after sunrise.

The thought of sharing breakfast with Mr. Darcy was an agreeable way to start the day, Elizabeth considered, as she made her way to the back stairs. She should be able to meet the man with composure after a good night's rest. She had only climbed a few steps when her attention was called to a conversation between a downstairs maid and a stable boy.

"Are ya sure about this, Billy?" the girl demanded.

"She ain't here, now, is she? I'm tellin' ya, Mr. Bennet dismissed her."

"And for what? Sally's as hard-workin' a girl as Longbourn's ever seen."

"That may be true, and that may not, but when *the Quality* takes a dislikin' to ya, ya best see to yourself."

"The *Quality*? You mean Miss Bingley?" The maid sniffed. "*She* don't carry no weight around here."

"You say true and no mistake, but I ain't talking about that one. I means th' guest in the parlor."

The maid gasped. "Mr. Darcy?"

"Keep yer voice down," the stable boy advised. "Do ya wanna be next?"

"Why would Mr. Darcy want Sally run off?"

"You didn't hear about last night?"

"I heard about some spilt wine and yellin', but — No, I don't believe it!"

"Believe what ya like, but there's the wine, an' there's Mr. Darcy — an' Sally's gone."

"Maybe she went home sick."

"Lord! Ain't ya got a brain in yer head? Her stuff's cleared out! Look, I know th' Master's not one to run a servant off. Look how long he put up with old Whittaker, that damn thief. He was stealin' him blind, he was, but th' Master wouldn't let him go 'til he retired. No, it was Mr. Darcy that made th' Master dismiss Sally. Ya can depend on that, sure as I'm standin' here."

"Just for spillin' wine?" Elizabeth could hear disbelief in the maid's voice.

"And ruining his shirt. I've heard me some stories about the *Quality*, girl. Makes yer hair stand up on end."

"You've heard a lot o'things at the tavern, Billy, but I'd be careful of givin' any of the fools there any say-so. Mr. Darcy's been nothin' but good an' kind, and I'll not say a word against him."

"I don't think I like what yer sayin'. You sweet on Mr. Darcy?"

"You're daft! He's too high for the likes of me. Besides, if I were, what business is it of yours?"

"Aw, Betsey, ya know I've taken a fancy to ya."

The pair moved off, but Elizabeth remained frozen. She realized she had not seen Sally all day.

No! Stop it! Elizabeth raged to herself. She had been there, and while Mr. Darcy was shocked at the incident, only his valet was angry. He was not. Elizabeth was sure of it. Certainly Mr. Darcy would not make her father dismiss a servant because of a ruined shirt.

Would he?

No! It was impossible! Mr. Darcy had been remarkably kind to her sisters — and to her — since he had been here. Elizabeth knew she had misjudged him. He was firm, but fair — and kind, very kind.

Elizabeth almost went to her father for an explanation but stopped.

It was foolish to confirm what she already knew. Perhaps Sally *was* ill. Elizabeth was sure she would see the girl tomorrow. Moreover, Billy was a known braggart. If he did not cease his tales, Elizabeth was of a mind to speak to her father about him.

Not that Father would do anything. Billy was right about that. No, Father is not a man of action. Not like Mr. Darcy.

Enough of that, Elizabeth Rose Bennet! Time to get to bed!

Chapter 17

JANE AND ELIZABETH WERE invited to return to Meryton the next morning to attend their aunt Mrs. Philips. They enjoyed an early breakfast and set out, walking the well-trod path from Longbourn to the village. They had not seen Mr. Darcy during breakfast, which for Elizabeth's peace of mind was most welcome. She had not slept well again, still disturbed by the overheard conversation between the servants.

The two had gone only a little way before Elizabeth asked her sister whether they might alter their route to pass by the cottage of Sally's family.

"Certainly, if you wish it," replied Jane, "but is not Sally at Longbourn?"

"I did not see her this morning. I fear she might be ill."

"I am sure she is not. Mrs. Hill would have mentioned it. Perhaps she was attending her duties to Mr. Darcy."

"You may be right, but what if someone else — her mother or brother — is ill? Jane, it would ease my mind to see for myself."

"Very well, it shall be as you wish."

They were such a distance from home that neither was aware of the arrival at Longbourn of a coach from London.

DARCY FELT THE ABSENCE OF Sally keenly. Bartholomew had to do the work of two, and they were so behind their time that Darcy had breakfast in his parlor bedroom while his valet struggled to shave him. He had finally finished when Mrs. Hill announced the arrival of a party from Town.

Behind her was a plump, middle-aged woman well-known to Darcy. He had used the nurse before when Georgiana was ill with a cold in London.

"Ah, Mrs. Adams! You made good time. I hope your journey was not too tiresome?"

The nurse curtsied with a smile. "No trouble at all, sir. You have a most delightful carriage. We set off at first light, and here we are. I am grieved, however, to find you in such a state. Are you in much pain, may I ask?"

Darcy briefly explained his injury and the prognosis. By then, Mr. Bennet had made an appearance.

"Sir," said Darcy, "here is the nurse I spoke about, Mrs. Adams. Madam, this is my host, Mr. Bennet."

"Pleased to meet you, Mrs. Adams." He turned to Darcy. "Are you certain I cannot be of use to you?"

"I thank you for your offer, but I shall not presume further on your hospitality. I have secured a room at the Meryton Inn for Mrs. Adams."

"My needs are small, Mr. Bennet. I am sure my room will be sufficient," claimed the nurse. "Pray allow me a moment to freshen up, and I shall be about my work. I have my instructions from Mr. Macmillan, and I will have you back on your feet and returned to London in no time, Mr. Darcy."

"Good," mumbled Bartholomew.

THE LITTLE COTTAGE WAS ON a lane off the main road to Meryton. Elizabeth and Jane had barely started down the path before they beheld two vehicles, a coach and a wagon, in the lane before the little house. The cottage was in a state of upheaval; trunks and boxes were scattered about just outside the door, and strangers were moving things about. The Bennet girls gasped and quickened their steps.

When Elizabeth saw three people enter the carriage, she broke into a full run, disregarding the cries from Jane. She reached the vehicle just as the driver ascended to the box. To her horror, Elizabeth saw a weeping Sally inside.

"Sally — Sally!" she cried. "What is happening? Where are you going?"

Sally struggled with the window and could not lower it until the carriage began to move. She stuck out her tear-lined face. "Oh, Miss Lizzy, good bye! Good bye! God bless you and your family!"

"Sally! Where are you going?"

The noise of the wheels drowned out the young maid's voice. It soon turned onto the main road and out of sight.

"Why are Sally and her family in that carriage? cried Jane as she reached her. "What is happening here?"

Elizabeth took in the chaos of moving with dread. "I fear Sally's family has departed Meryton! But why?" She boldly walked over to one of the workmen in the yard who was carrying a chair. "You there!" she demanded. "What are you doing with that?"

The man, large and unkempt, scowled as he set his burden down. "An' who are ye to be askin'?"

Not intimidated in the least, Elizabeth drew herself up to her full height but reached only to the man's chin. "I am Miss Elizabeth Bennet, and those are the belongings of my servant and her family. You will tell me what you are doing with them."

"Well, ma'am, I'm movin' things out of that there cottage, now ain't I?" he said with a grin, his few teeth fully visible. Meanwhile, two other men began loading the crates onto the wagon.

"Why are you doing that?" Elizabeth pointed down the lane where the carriage had passed. "And where are they going?"

The man smiled again. "Beggin' your pardon, ma'am, but I'm thinkin' that's none o' your concern. An' me master don't pay me for gossiping in th' road, so I'll expect you'll excuse me."

"Your master? And who is your master?"

"I'm thinkin' that's none o' your concern, neither. I've got me papers provin' my authority, but them's for the magistrate, an' he ain't you, beggin' your pardon again." The workman knuckled his hat. "I've got me a wagon to load. Good day to ye, ma'am." And with that, he returned to his labors.

Stunned, Elizabeth stood still in the road. Never in her life had anyone spoken to her that way.

"Oh, Lizzy," cried Jane. "I fear that Sally's family has lost their home."

"I do not understand it. If they were in distress, why would they leave? Surely, Father would have helped."

Jane agreed but sounded less certain. "Or, perhaps, Mr. Darcy — "

In an instant, Elizabeth remembered the overheard discussion from the night before. "Mr. Darcy! Oh Lord, Mr. Darcy! It could not be true, could it?"

"What are you talking about?"

"Oh, I must return to Longbourn as quickly as may be!"

"But Aunt Philips is expecting us."

"Pray make my excuses, Jane. I cannot delay an instant!" With that, Elizabeth dashed down the lane, leaving a confused Jane in her wake.

After she had gone a short distance, Elizabeth slowed to a fast walk, but her mind remained in turmoil. When she first met Mr. Darcy, she was impressed by his arrogance, conceit, and selfish disdain of the feelings of others. Nothing during her stay at Netherfield Park changed her opinion. Mr. Darcy cared for no one but his relations, his close acquaintances, and those of his particular station, she was convinced. Yet, since his accident, for which she still owned a measure of blame, Elizabeth had been forced to revise her condemnation of the gentleman.

True, he still liked to have things his way and had acted in a manner that she considered high-handed, but it was not out of the common way for persons of quality. Mr. Darcy was undoubtedly a devoted brother and faithful friend. Georgiana doted on him, and it was plain that Colonel Fitzwilliam would do anything for the gentleman should his cousin but ask. Bartholomew's fierce defense of any perceived slight to his master spoke of the loyalty Mr. Darcy could inspire in people in service to him. It was obvious that Mr. Darcy also had won the admiration of *Longbourn's* staff — a fact not lost on Elizabeth or her father.

The thought of her father caused Elizabeth to sigh. *His* determined dislike of Mr. Darcy, Elizabeth was now persuaded, was rooted in the recognition of the poor example he made as a gentleman and master in comparison to Mr. Darcy. Mr. Bennet had not been a gracious host, had sulked and complained when he was not mocking, and had expressed little thanks for the service Mr. Darcy had been to the Bennet family.

Mr. Darcy had been uncommonly kind to her sisters. Jane, Mary, Kitty — even Lydia had fallen under his spell. Mrs. Bennet now hung the moon on the man.

As for herself, Elizabeth could not forget Mr. Darcy's valiant defense of her in the face of Mr. Collins's vulgar presumption. The words he used! Only Elizabeth's good sense prevented her romantic heart from running away with her, wishing for things that could never be. She told herself repeatedly that Mr. Darcy was a very good man and would do the same for anyone in a similar predicament.

Which was why Elizabeth now was so distressed. Sally was no longer at Longbourn. Her family had left Meryton, perhaps forever. The only reason Elizabeth could imagine was that Sally had been dismissed from her employment. Why? What had she done?

She spilled wine on Mr. Darcy.

Elizabeth shuddered. She was not an ignorant country miss, no matter what Miss Bingley thought. She had been to Town. She knew some men could be capricious and cruel. She had heard of servants, particularly maids, dismissed from service for not complying with the carnal desires of their employers. It was not out of the question that a member of the *ton* might demand the removal of a clumsy serving woman, even if that gentleman was a guest in someone else's house.

Could Mr. Darcy do such a thing? Would he? *Did he?*

Elizabeth was tortured, and her anxiety increased with every step she took toward Longbourn. She had overcome her first impression of Mr. Darcy, but what if she had been in error? Had it all been an act?

Or perhaps he owned an ungovernable temper. She recalled his words at Netherfield: *"My temper would perhaps be called resentful. My good opinion, once lost, is lost forever."*

Elizabeth shuddered again. She longed to be at Longbourn, to talk to her father — and Mr. Darcy.

Please, God, let me be wrong!

Minutes later, Elizabeth finally crossed the threshold of her family home. However, the first person she spied was not Mrs. Hill, or any other Longbourn servant, but a woman she had never seen before.

Without another thought and in violation of all propriety, Elizabeth blurted out, "Who are you?"

The middle-aged woman, dressed like a servant, took in Elizabeth in a heartbeat. She must have determined that she was a lady in the household, for she completed a quick curtsy and answered, "Good day to you, miss. I am Mrs. Adams."

Elizabeth remembered her manners. "I am Miss Elizabeth Bennet. You are new here. Has my father employed you?"

"No, ma'am. I am in service to Mr. Darcy. I am his nurse."

Elizabeth's heart dropped as all her fears were proven true. Mr. Darcy had shown his true colors. He had a poor, helpless, harmless girl dismissed, endangering her family, just because she ruined a single shirt. Her father would not have turned Sally out; he had not the cruelty. Mr. Darcy must have made him do it.

Elizabeth's anger rose as quickly as her hopes faded. So it had all been a lie. The gifts, the lessons, the kindness — the friendship! Elizabeth had been right in her first assessment: Mr. Darcy was a cold, ruthless man who thought nothing of destroying a destitute and unprotected servant!

I am sure this is the common way in London, but Hertfordshire is not Town! We do things better here, and I will be happy to inform him of that. Mr. High-and-Mighty Darcy! You will not pass this day without knowing my mind on what you have done!

Elizabeth was furious when she barged into the parlor.

"I am defeated, sir! It is utterly ruined!"

Bartholomew held up a silk shirt with a large, pink blotch on it.

Darcy could not hide a smile at his valet's expense. "Bartholomew, I believe you feel far too deeply about the matter."

"But, sir, just look at it! I can do *nothing* with it." The man was truly disgusted. "Fine silk from Chamberlin's of London, and all it is fit for is rags!"

"I can have another shirt made."

Bartholomew continued to complain as though his master had said nothing. "Clumsy girl! She had best mind her steps at Argyle, or the viscountess will have her on the road in no time."

Darcy frowned. He knew his man needed to express his frustration, but this was a bit much. Sally had not intended to spill wine on him, and it was time to put an end to the issue. "Bartholomew, pray desist your — "

Darcy was unable to finish, for in that instant the door was thrown open, and in marched Elizabeth Bennet. Her eyes flew to the garment the valet was still displaying.

"Miss Elizabeth!" Bartholomew cried. "It is ruined!"

Elizabeth's fine eyes, now sparking with anger, turned on Darcy, but *his* attention was still on his valet. "That is enough, man. I am done with shirts and maids. The matter is closed." He turned to Elizabeth. "Miss Elizabeth, good morning. How may — "

"How *could* you?!"

"I beg your pardon?"

Elizabeth began pacing about the room in an agitated manner. "I knew I should not have trusted you! I knew it! From the very beginning — from the first moment, I may almost say — of my acquaintance with you, your manners impressed me with the fullest belief of your arrogance, your conceit, and your selfish disdain of the feelings of others. But even after all your offenses against myself — "

"Offenses?"

"I never dared dream that you could be as cold and unfeeling as to ruin, perhaps forever, the happiness and security of a most devoted servant!"

Mr. Darcy was perplexed and offended. "Miss Elizabeth, I must ask you to explain yourself!"

"Nay, it is *you* who must explain!" By now tears were running down her fair face, and she angrily dashed them away. "Was it for sport? Did it amuse you? You and your gifts and lessons and horses! It was all a trick to win my family's approval. Did you not hold them all in disgust? Have you been laughing at us the whole time?" She began to sob. "And just when I thought... I began to hope... friendship — "

"Miss Elizabeth, please! I do not understand your anger! How have I offended you? Please explain yourself!" He was utterly confused.

"You deserve no explanation! You *know* what you did to Sally and her family, and it merits the severest condemnation!"

Darcy shook his head. "It was not my intention that you should have learned of this, but why the distress, madam? Condemnation for *what*, may I ask?" Darcy's voice rose. "Your father and I have secured Sally a new position. She shall not suffer; indeed, I flatter myself she is better off now than before. I am sorry it displeases you." He had no idea how pompous he sounded.

"Of course, I am displeased! You have persuaded my own father to participate in an injustice! You sent Sally away from the only home she has ever known!"

"She *had* to leave — "

"Because she spilled wine on your precious shirt!"

In a cold voice, Darcy said, "No, so that employment *also* could be found for her mother and brother."

"What did you say?"

Darcy turned to the window. "Positions have been secured for Sally's entire family. Their new employer is a man of good character and will treat them well. They journey to join in service to him." He could not look at Elizabeth for all the world.

"You…you found work for all of Sally's family? Why?" Her voice was low, nearly a whisper.

But Darcy was too angry to note her change of attitude. He answered in a clipped, harsh voice, "You are unhappy about this turn of events, and I shall not further pain you by continuing this conversation. All I shall say is that what was done was done for the best, and I feel not the slightest regret for it." Darcy paused. "Miss Elizabeth, I believe we have said more than we should about this unpleasant situation. You are obviously dissatisfied with the solution that was found for the distress of Sally's family. However, it profits neither of us to continue this discussion. I must beg you to excuse me."

Darcy heard a gasp from the lady, then a sob, and finally her light footsteps as she fled the room, but he continued to sit and stare out the window for some time, refusing to turn. All his hopes and plans were ashes. Elizabeth had not warmed to him as he had hoped. No, she still held him in low regard. What else could explain her jumping to such an unjust conclusion? It did not matter that he was right and she wrong. It would not signify that she might apologize later. The point was she did not trust him, and that had to be rooted in her disinclination. It was foolish to believe any longer that he could change her mind about him.

Elizabeth Bennet would never be his. He could not stay in Hertfordshire a moment longer.

He turned anguished eyes to his thoroughly mortified valet. "Bartholomew, pack my trunks. We leave for London as soon as may be."

Chapter 18

A DISTRAUGHT ELIZABETH DISCOVERED upon leaving the parlor that there was an audience to her confrontation with Mr. Darcy. Not only was Mr. Darcy's nurse without but so were Lydia, Kitty, and Mrs. Bennet. To her horror, Elizabeth also saw Mary, Georgiana, and Mrs. Annesley standing in the doorway of the sitting room across the hall, a piece of music in Mary's limp hand. Elizabeth was convinced that the whole of the household had been witness to her shame.

"What have you done, you foolish child? Why were you shouting at Mr. Darcy? Do you wish to shatter all your chances with him?" She took Elizabeth by the forearm. "Explain yourself, young lady!"

Elizabeth could not say anything for all the world. Instead, she shook off Mrs. Bennet's grasp and fled upstairs as fast as her feet could take her. Only her familiarity with the house prevented her from harm, for her tears had quite blinded her. In a moment, she was in her room, locking her door before her shocked sisters, who had followed. Throwing herself onto her bed, Elizabeth gave over to her injured sensibilities and drenched her pillow with weeping, ignoring the pounding and pleading from the hallway.

Her mind was in anguish. How could she so misconstrue what had happened? How could she have said so many hateful things to Mr. Darcy? Was it true? Had he and her father secured new positions for Sally and all of her family? Why would Mr. Darcy do that? And why was it that she continued to think the worst of him?

The pain in Mr. Darcy's eyes, the coldness of his dismissal! Elizabeth had observed it, and instantly understood — her power was sinking; everything *must* sink under such a proof of insensibility, such an assurance of irrational behavior and insulting speech, of hateful opinions and unjust accusations! Elizabeth felt herself in the deepest disgrace. How Mr. Darcy must hate her! She could neither wonder nor condemn.

Elizabeth's pain was complete. Never had she so honestly felt that she could have loved him as now when all love must be vain. For she knew now that Mr. Darcy was indeed the man to suit her in temperament and talents, that he met her every expectation of marital felicity! And by actions she could only blame on herself, she had unforgivably insulted the man she had secretly grown to adore.

It was in every way horrible!

DARCY SAT MOTIONLESS IN HIS wheel-chair, barely reacting to the chaos about him. Georgiana had come in after Elizabeth fled and fervently pleaded that he change his mind, remain at Longbourn, and talk again with Elizabeth, but he withstood her impassioned entreaties with seeming stoicism. He had patted her hand, said it was, of course, unfortunate, but his mind was made up.

He ordered a concerned Mrs. Annesley to see to Georgiana's packing and an unusually compliant Bartholomew to send a note to Netherfield informing Colonel Fitzwilliam of his new plans. From the hallway, Darcy could hear Mrs. Bennet's nearly hysterical appeals for understanding and forgiveness of her wayward daughter, but he made no response. He only sat and stewed in anguish.

Darcy had labored for weeks to change Elizabeth's opinion of him, but that day's disaster had proved the lady was not to be moved. Oh yes, she could now talk to him in a civil manner when it suited her and even be cordial on occasion, but her heart was forever out of his reach. He could no longer bear to be in her presence if he was never to find happiness with her.

Mr. Bennet came in. "Mr. Darcy, I must speak with you."

Darcy's eyes flicked at the older man before he returned his gaze to the window. "I must ask you to excuse me."

"I know you would prefer it otherwise, but I insist. Will you do me the honor of speaking with me?"

Darcy tried to resist Mr. Bennet's persistence. "Sir, this is neither the time nor the place."

"I disagree. This is exactly the time and place. This concerns my daughter, and I WILL speak with you."

Mr. Bennet's steely tone broke through Darcy's stubbornness. "Very well. Pray excuse us, Bartholomew." The two gentlemen remained silent while the servant vacated the room. Finally, Darcy spoke again. "You seem to have something on your mind, Mr. Bennet. Say what you must, and leave me in peace."

Mr. Bennet took a moment to cross into the room, take a chair, and gaze penetratingly at Darcy. "I do not pretend to understand fully what has occurred here this morning, but I fear there has been great misunderstanding. I would like to do what I can to rectify it."

Darcy would not allow Mr. Bennet to see his pain; he steadfastly refused to meet his gaze. "Did Miss Elizabeth send you?"

"She did not. You are troubled; your bitterness is apparent. I assume you have quarreled with Elizabeth. As her father, I can demand you tell me what this is all about, but I would prefer to discuss it man-to-man, rather than father-to-suitor."

Harsh was Darcy's rejoinder. "I am no one's suitor as your daughter has made abundantly clear."

There was a quick intake of breath. "Ah, Lizzy's temper, is it? Did you insult her again?"

That caught Darcy's attention. "What?" He whirled upon the older man and was astonished to see a smile on his face.

"Forgive me. I disliked speaking to the back of your head." More seriously, Mr. Bennet continued, "Now, I know that Lizzy is upset and has fled upstairs. You are angry, and I heard loud voices. I can only assume a quarrel has taken place. What has happened in my house?"

Darcy could not deny that Mr. Bennet had a right to know. "Miss Elizabeth laid charges against my character — unfounded charges this time. She has made it plain that her opinion of me is so low that she can only assume base motives for the smallest of my actions."

"What in the world brought this on?'

"She accused me of having your former maid, Sally, dismissed and sent away from Meryton because she spilled wine on me."

"Indeed? I wonder how she could have come to that conclusion or even known that Sally was gone. I told Mrs. Bennet about the girl only this morning, and I believe that Lizzy and Jane had already left the house." He sighed. "I am afraid I warned you about Lizzy and secrets." He stopped. "Am I to understand that she has disparaged your character before?"

Darcy realized he had said more than he intended. "I have it on the best authority that she took exception to my comportment when first I came to Hertfordshire. I saw the justice in her appraisal and labored to behave better. I…I thought I had improved in her eyes, but I was mistaken."

"I do not believe it," Mr. Bennet said in a firm voice. "Lizzy is usually a very sensible girl. I have trained her to be so. She can be quick in assessing a person, but she is just and fair. If she is mistaken, she will own it. She has before." He rubbed his chin thoughtfully. "Unless…"

Darcy waited, but Mr. Bennet said nothing more. The gentleman sat, seemingly lost in thought. Darcy could not know what was going through the older man's mind, and the wait for him to continue was extremely vexing. Only Darcy's strong will gave him the patience to wait him out.

Finally, Mr. Bennet's attention reverted to Darcy, and there was a return of the mischievous twinkle he had noted before in Bennet's eyes. "Well, young man, if I read this state of affairs correctly, and there is no reason to think that I have not, I should say you have little to be distressed about."

"I beg your pardon?"

"Of course, that assumes you still wish to court Lizzy. She has not put you off, has she?"

"No!" Darcy exclaimed. "That is to say, my future actions are completely up to her. *My* wishes are unchanged." *For all the good it may do me.*

"Good for you! You will need to be firm of mind if you wish to form an attachment with Lizzy!"

Darcy shook his head. "I thank you for your counsel, but Miss Elizabeth is of a different mind!"

"Oh, I do not think so."

Was this a joke? No, mirth did not seem to be in agreement with Mr. Bennet's mien. "But…but she said — Mr. Bennet, you were not here! She thinks me the worst sort of snob."

"Nonsense! If she did, she would simply dismiss you. She certainly would not confront you."

"I fail to see the difference."

Mr. Bennet sat back in the chair. "Let me tell you something about Elizabeth. I believe you have met my brother and sister in Meryton, Mr. and Mrs. Philips. Lizzy is quite close to them, even though Mrs. Philips is sillier than my wife. About ten years ago, Mr. Philips promised Jane that he and his wife would take her shopping to buy ribbons. Well, the appointed day came, but there was no sign of either one. Jane had just turned twelve and put on a brave face, but ten-year-old Lizzy knew her sister was hurt and disappointed.

"As it turned out, Mr. Philips had simply forgotten his promise. When Lizzy learned that, she became angry. She could not stand to see her sister pained, and she expected better behavior from her relations. Lizzy was hurt for her sister's sake and wanted her uncle to know of it. When next we met, outside of church of all places, Lizzy marched up to her uncle and roundly scolded him for disappointing Jane. Needless to say, Jane got her ribbons in short order."

"I have seen for myself how loyal Miss Elizabeth is to those she cares for," said Darcy. "I speak of her tender care for Miss Bennet when she was ill at Netherfield. But I cannot see why I should be encouraged by this."

"Ah, but allow me to finish. I also have a sister who married a gentleman in Surrey. We do not visit, for Mr. Darlington is a man I cannot respect. Oh, he can be charming when he believes it is in his best interest, but he is in the habit of making promises he cannot or will not keep. I own a temperament which finds diversion in the follies of my neighbors, but I am not amused by gentlemen who refuse to keep their word. His actions have caused great conflict between our houses.

"About the same time as the other incident, before the final break, the Darlingtons were visiting Longbourn and noted that Lizzy had an interest in music. Darlington bragged that he knew great music masters in Town and said if Lizzy would go to London, he would see that they gave her lessons. Well, that was all my little girl needed to hear, and she badgered my Brother Gardiner no end to allow her to visit.

"Mr. Gardiner had just married — to a girl from Derbyshire, as I recall — and they had set up house in Gracechurch Street. Still, Gardiner and his new bride generously allowed Lizzy to visit along with Jane. Every day, Lizzy would sit at the window, waiting for the music masters to call. Of course, no one ever came. Finally, after a month, the girls returned to Longbourn.

"Mrs. Bennet was upset with Mr. Darlington, but Lizzy said nothing. When the Darlingtons visited several months later, Lizzy treated them as though nothing had happened. You see, Lizzy knew her uncle was a braggart and never let on she was disappointed by his inaction. She learned to expect that kind of behavior from him and simply ignored the gentleman in the future."

Mr. Bennet held up a finger. "Mark the variance in her actions, Mr. Darcy. Both times a person had failed to do what they promised, but Lizzy treated them differently. She expected that her Uncle Darlington would act in a thoughtless manner, and she was right. But when her Uncle Philips, whom she holds in some esteem, failed in *his* duty, she acted differently."

Darcy frowned. He thought the man was trying to give him hope, but he could not trust his ears. "I do not understand your meaning."

"You are a clever man, Mr. Darcy," Mr. Bennet chided him gently. "I am sure you see the point I make. Lizzy was upset because she thought you did not meet her expectations of you. Now, why should she be hurt if a man for whom she cared nothing acted in a proud and careless manner, hmm?"

Darcy's heavy heart began to lighten in spite of his caution. "You are saying her anger was due to disillusionment? That she was disappointed in me because she expected better of me?"

Mr. Bennet nodded. "And I say her anger was in proportion to her disappointment, young man."

Darcy made a sound between a cough and a chuckle. "She was *very* angry with me."

"I know. Interesting, is it not?"

"But she was mistaken."

"Yes. I believe she knows that now. Do you not think she is mortified?"

"I cannot say."

"You two are more alike than you think. Would you not be mortified were you in her place?"

Darcy could not stop a small smile. "Utterly."

"And how long would it take for you to overcome your mortification?"

Darcy lost his smile. "I must own I tend to brood. Painful recollections will intrude, which cannot — which *ought* not to be repelled when I have failed in my duty to myself, my family, my people, or my friends. I cannot be easily reconciled to myself."

Mr. Bennet shook his head. "You must learn some of my philosophy. Think only of the past as its remembrance gives you pleasure. Fortunately, Lizzy has learned that well. Perhaps she may teach you."

Darcy looked at Mr. Bennet in amazement. "You will still allow a courtship — after all that has happened today?"

"Mr. Darcy, I have been trying to tell you that Lizzy's actions have proven to me beyond a doubt that she has strong feelings for you. I have also come to the conclusion that you are the best man for *her*. I shall not sit quietly while my favorite's happiness is at risk." Mr. Bennet stood. "I will go to Lizzy and talk to her. All will be well; trust in this. There is no need to leave Longbourn."

Darcy frowned, thinking furiously. He began to hope as he scarcely ever allowed himself to hope before. He saw the older gentleman walking towards the door.

"Mr. Bennet, wait! I must tell you I shall leave Longbourn no matter the result of your conversation with Elizabeth!"

Mr. Bennet turned, astonishment clearly written on his face. "What? I do not understand. Am I under a misapprehension? Do you wish to leave my daughter's company?" In his surprise, he did not mention the familiar manner by which Darcy referred to Elizabeth.

"That is the last thing I wish to do, but I must."

"Why, sir?"

Darcy told him.

THE DOOR TO ELIZABETH'S ROOM flew open, and Lydia marched to her side, followed by Mary and Kitty. "Lizzy," demanded the youngest of her sisters, "just what have you done?"

Elizabeth dashed tears from her eyes. "How did you get in here? I locked the door!"

The young girl held up a key. "Did you not know? All the bedrooms use the same key! I simply used the key from my room. But, enough of this — you will explain why you have quarreled with Mr. Darcy! He is the nicest man in all the world!"

Elizabeth looked grimly at her visitors. "I am surprised my mother is not with you to plead Mr. Darcy's case."

"For shame, Lizzy! Our mother is prostrate in her room, complaining of her nerves," Mary claimed.

Kitty now had her share of the conversation. "That is neither here nor there. Mr. Darcy told Georgiana to arrange to have her trunks packed. He wants to leave. Georgie is in her room now, crying her eyes out!"

"Mr. Darcy is to leave?" Elizabeth shook her head. "But . . . but Mr. Jones said he must remain due to his leg."

Mary pointed outside of the room. "The servants are packing as we speak."

Elizabeth sat up. "We must stop them!"

"Indeed," said Lydia with some passion. "If Mr. Darcy goes away and takes Miranda, I will hate you for the rest of my life!"

"Lydia!" cried Mary. "This is not about your horse!" She turned to Elizabeth. "But my music lessons will end if Georgie and Mrs. Annesley go away."

"And my drawing lessons," added Kitty.

"You must apologize to Mr. Darcy right away!" Lydia commanded.

Mary and Kitty seized Elizabeth's hands. "Come along," said Kitty. "We have time to repair your looks before they finish packing. Hurry!"

"I will get the hair brush!" Lydia dashed to the table.

Elizabeth struggled with her sisters. "Let me go! Let me go!"

"Lizzy, you are being stubborn!" said Mary with some heat. "The Good Book says we must forgive!"

"It also says that children must obey their parents," came a voice from the door. The four girls turned, their quarrel forgotten. "Girls, release your sister. I shall speak to Lizzy — alone." Mr. Bennet was unusually stern.

"But, Father," whined Lydia, "Lizzy must talk to Mr. Darcy as soon as may be, or else he will leave and take Miranda away!"

"It is Mr. Darcy I wish to discuss with Lizzy, so your mind can be at ease, child. You may all go."

"We shall comfort Georgie," cried Kitty as she and Mary ran down the hall to her room.

"I will be in the stables," was Lydia's farewell.

Mr. Bennet turned to his favorite, a gentle expression on his face. "Well, my dear, I fear a muddle has been made, and I hope to clear things up between you and your young man." He closed the door behind him and took a chair near the bed. "Now, pray tell me what has happened."

Elizabeth used a handkerchief. "He is not *my* young man."

"He may disagree with you about that. About what did you quarrel?"

In a halting voice, Elizabeth told her father of her accusations against Mr. Darcy. "I said so many unjust things, and he was so angry! I am sure he wants nothing more to do with me, and I cannot blame him. My sisters tell me he plans to leave Longbourn and risk his health."

"That is so. Mr. Darcy plans to return to London."

"We must stop him! We have not a moment to lose!"

Mr. Bennet took her hand and patted it. "There, there, my dear. Do not distress yourself. We have some time, and Mr. Darcy will not do anything foolish." He looked intently into Elizabeth's eyes. "Why were you so upset over Sally?"

Elizabeth swallowed. Her feelings were in such turmoil she had no opportunity to sort them out herself. She certainly could not speak of them to anyone else, even her beloved father. "I was distressed for her family's sake, knowing her circumstances."

"That is commendable, but they were really not your responsibility. I think there is more to it than that."

"Truly, that is all."

Mr. Bennet smiled, which took the sting out of his next words. "Lizzy, do not try to deceive me. You are a poor actress. If you were only thinking of Sally, you would have come to me. But it is very telling that you did otherwise. I think this had more to do with what you thought were Mr. Darcy's actions, not mine."

"I…I saw Mrs. Adams. I acted without thinking."

"Perhaps, but now I think you deceive yourself."

Elizabeth tried to change the subject. "Why has Sally left your service, sir? Why is her family leaving Meryton?"

"It is not my story to tell. You must talk to others."

"Then Mr. Darcy *was* involved! Will you tell me what he did?"

"I do not speak for Mr. Darcy." His eyes twinkled. "You must ask him yourself."

"I cannot! It is too mortifying!"

"Come, come. Is this my brave Lizzy? Is this the girl who would upbraid her uncle at the age of ten?"

Elizabeth gasped. "Tell me you did not tell that story to Mr. Darcy!"

"I do not say I did, but do not say I did not. Again, you must ask him."

"He cannot want to talk to me. He must despise me."

Mr. Bennet threw up his hands dramatically. "Then he will leave and lose his leg, all because you are embarrassed."

She frowned. "That was a cruel thing to say!"

Mr. Bennet grew serious. "Lizzy, my love, go to him — but only if you really want his good opinion and want him to stay. If he truly means little to you, then remain, and I will say no more about this."

Elizabeth rose slowly from the bed and walked to the door, only stopping as her hand touched the knob. "Are you saying only *I* can prevent his leaving?"

A very serious Mr. Bennet replied, "It seems you have been granted great power, Elizabeth. Use it kindly and wisely."

Elizabeth smiled. "Thank you, Father." And she was gone.

Bartholomew returned to the room and resumed packing, observing his employer as he did so. His master still sat quietly in the wheel-chair, but his demeanor had changed. When once he was angry and dejected, he was now calm, but it was obvious that he was waiting for something—something he was not sure was coming, but hopeful all the same. Bartholomew certainly did not expect Miss Elizabeth to knock on the door.

"Mr. Darcy," said she as she entered, eyes downcast. "I must speak to you. I must apologize. Will you grant me an interview?"

Mr. Darcy looked at her, outwardly expressionless, but projecting a nervous energy. "I am at your disposal, Miss Elizabeth."

Miss Elizabeth looked up, gratefulness apparent on her face. "I thank you, sir." The girl had a blush to her cheek, Bartholomew saw. He was certain it was from her shame for her offenses against his master.

She glanced meaningfully in the valet's direction, and Mr. Darcy noticed it. Bartholomew was certain he was about to be dismissed, and his sensibilities rebelled against it. He did not want Mr. Darcy alone with this harridan again no matter *how* pretty she was.

Instead, Mr. Darcy did something surprising. "The weather is sunny and calm, Miss Elizabeth. I own I would like to enjoy the fresh air of your mother's garden while we have our conversation. Would that suit you, or do you think it too cool for your comfort?"

Miss Elizabeth blinked. "No, it was perfectly comfortable earlier, and I am sure it has warmed since then. I would be happy to accompany you outside." She smiled a little. "You should know I seldom refuse an opportunity to ramble about the countryside, Mr. Darcy."

His master's look had warmed. "I have noted your preference very well, particularly as it coincides with mine."

Miss Elizabeth blushed anew, and even Bartholomew knew that this time it was not from shame. How the valet kept from rolling his eyes he would never know.

"Give me a moment, sir, to fetch my coat."

"I shall await you at the front door, madam." Mr. Darcy returned Miss Elizabeth's smile, and it remained as the young lady left.

Bartholomew groaned as he prepared Mr. Darcy for his interview. He was certain that his master had decided to forgive the young lady, and he was coming to the conclusion that he had other plans for Miss

Elizabeth, as well — permanent plans.

Bartholomew always knew Mr. Darcy had to marry, and he supposed Miss Elizabeth would do, as long as she received more polish. *He* would not have the mistress of Pemberley be an uncultured country miss! As for the lady's other charms, they were quite lost on the valet.

He had no intention of marrying — that was certain! It was too much trouble!

Chapter 19

ELIZABETH WAS SURPRISED WHEN Mr. Darcy requested their conversation be held outside. She was anxious to end their disagreement and prevent his removal from Longbourn, so she did as she was asked and met the gentleman in the front hall. He, too, was dressed for the cold weather, sitting in the wheel-chair, his valet Bartholomew standing beside him. Mr. Darcy explained that the garden might offer them some privacy without violating propriety, and he hoped she was of a mind to agree to his scheme. Elizabeth nodded in understanding, and the party was soon off, stopping only to transfer Mr. Darcy from the wheel-chair, which was quite useless for the rough ground of the garden, to the Bath chair.

The two were soon at the desired spot — a stone bench some small distance from the house but within clear sight of the west-facing windows. The air was cold, but sunny skies and the lack of wind assured comfortable conditions for the two, and once Mr. Darcy made sure that the blanket he insisted Bartholomew bring was offered and accepted by Elizabeth, he dismissed his servant and turned to Elizabeth. He said nothing, however; his countenance indicated that he expected Elizabeth to begin the conversation. Meanwhile, the valet returned to the house with reluctant steps.

This was a sad state of affairs, for Elizabeth had grown shy in the meantime. Her desire to explain herself, so imperative ten minutes earlier, was overthrown by his steady stare. Elizabeth could not look at him for all the world.

Finally Darcy's rich, deep voice broke the silence. "Miss Elizabeth, I believe you wished to speak to me."

Elizabeth took refuge in her wit. "I believe my tongue has caused you great trouble. I am astonished you wish to hear anything I might say."

"I am always happy to hear your voice."

"Even my unkind words of this morning?"

Darcy looked down. "Our conversation was painful, that is true. But even when you suffered from a misapprehension, you always spoke truth to me. That is a rare commodity, one I do not have the pleasure of enjoying as much as I might wish. It is refreshing." He turned to her. "I would rather hear truth from you, madam, even if it pains me, than all the flattering nonsense I experience in London."

Elizabeth looked at him in surprise. "This is too much."

"Nay, not nearly enough." Darcy seemed to catch himself, and his face lost some of the earnest expression he displayed. "Pray, tell me what you wished to speak of inside."

"I have come to learn that there is more to this disagreement over Sally's treatment than I originally considered. Will you answer some questions for me?"

"Of course."

"Sally and her family have left Meryton. Do you know where they have gone?"

"Yes, they traveled to London, to the townhouse of the Fitzwilliams of Matlock."

"And why did they go there?"

"My cousin, the viscount, has taken Sally and her family into his service."

They were to work for Darcy's family? Astonishing! "Why would your cousin take them all in? He does not know Sally."

"My cousin's reasons are known only to him. He is an honorable man, and they will be well-treated."

Elizabeth could not yet voice the question she most wanted to ask, so she tried something else. "I saw men moving their belongings out of their house into a wagon. One of the men said they were working for a gentleman he would not name. Did you hire men to move her family's things, as well?"

Darcy looked away. "If you are asking whether men in my service helped Sally's family relocate, then yes, that is so."

"Someone must have informed the viscount about Sally and her situation. You said this morning that positions had been secured for everyone in her family. It is reasonable to assume that you were the person who brought them to your cousin's attention. Did you do that?"

Darcy did not immediately answer. "I made some small inquiries."

Finally, Elizabeth could bear it no more. "Why? Why would you do that?"

He glanced at her. "It was not because she spilled wine on me."

Elizabeth flushed in humiliation. "Oh! Please do not repeat what I said! I am so ashamed of myself!"

Darcy frowned. "You should not be. It was not an unreasonable conjecture." He forestalled her startled objections. "Miss Elizabeth, I am a man of the world. I know gentlemen — more than I should — who would indeed demand the immediate dismissal of another man's servant for doing far less. It is certainly not in my character to do such a thing, but you would have no cause to know that."

"I should, I should!" Elizabeth returned with some heat. "You have treated the staff here at Longbourn with nothing but generosity and respect, in some cases, better than my family does. I had no reason to doubt you. And now it appears you are the saving of Sally's family. But you have not answered my question. Why did you find a new position for Sally?"

Darcy seemed to struggle for an answer. Finally, he shrugged. "Because it was within my power to do so."

Elizabeth took a moment to absorb the immensity of his short statement. "Then you are a great man. You have my gratitude, and I pray you accept my deepest apology for my unjust accusations."

To Elizabeth's astonishment, pain flashed across Mr. Darcy's face. "Pray, do not say such a thing. If I have been of service to Sally and her family, I was happy to do it. But do not thank me for it."

"Why not? You deserve all the thanks in the world!"

"I did not do it to earn accolades. I do not want anyone's gratitude."

Elizabeth thought about that for a moment. "That is perhaps the silliest thing I have ever heard."

"I — I beg your pardon?"

Elizabeth frowned. "No, I was wrong. That *is* the silliest thing I have ever heard! You do not want anyone's gratitude? That is preposterous! Gratitude is given, not earned. You cannot say whether someone ought to feel thankful or not. It is not in your station or anyone else's to determine what a person *should* feel. I shall be grateful as I choose, and if I think you the most wonderful man in the world, you can have nothing to say about it! You will just have to accept it!"

Elizabeth caught herself. Mortified, she turned to Mr. Darcy, eyes cast down. "Oh, I have done it again! I am ashamed of myself! Mr. Darcy, please excuse me. I should not have put it that way. It was ungracious of me." She glanced at him and, instead of censure, saw what could only be a look of indulgence that sprang from the deepest love.

"That is quite all right, Miss Elizabeth," Mr. Darcy said with a smile.

His smile brought on hers. "But I must insist that you accept my thanks for everything you have done."

"It seems I must accept your gratitude if I wish to keep your good opinion. Very well, I thank you."

Elizabeth continued. "I also should not have spoken as I did to you this morning. Will you accept my apology?"

"If you will accept my apology for my words."

"I was more in the wrong."

Darcy shook his head. "I disagree. I coldly dismissed you when I should have shown more forbearance. As I said, your assumption, while wrong, was not unreasonable. I allowed my temper to get the better of me. I should have acted differently, and I will hold to that, Miss Elizabeth. I shall not be moved."

Elizabeth frowned at his obstinacy. "How can that be? I made such terrible accusations!"

"What did you say I did not deserve? You called me selfish and unfeeling, and I cannot deny it. I have been a selfish being all my life — in practice though not in principle. As a child, I was taught what was *right*, but I was not taught to correct my temper. I was given good principles but left to follow them in pride and conceit. Unfortunately, I was spoilt by my parents, who, though good themselves — my father particularly, all that was benevolent and amiable — allowed, encouraged, almost *taught* me to be selfish and overbearing, to care for none beyond my own family circle, to think meanly of all the rest of the world. Otherwise, I should have been open about my plans and dealings and not thought you were undeserving to know my mind.

"Your father and I spoke, and it was only then that I saw the justice of your words. You were a lady I hoped to please, and yet I would not be honest with you! How should you know me if I did not allow it? Foolish, foolish pride!"

Elizabeth's eyes opened wide. *A lady I hoped to please?*

"But I will be forthright now. I must thank you for all you and your family have done for Georgiana. You have brought her back to the girl she once was."

Elizabeth shook her head at the change of subject. "You...you thank me for Georgiana? Whatever for?"

Darcy colored. "I shall tell you, but I ask you keep this to yourself. I believe Colonel Fitzwilliam has told you something of my family's misfortune at the hand of Mr. Wickham." At Elizabeth's nod, he continued. "Well, we have suffered more mistreatment than you know. Actually, Georgiana has."

"Oh, my goodness! You do not mean — "

"It is not the worst, Miss Elizabeth, but it was bad enough." He quickly told her of a plot between Wickham and Georgiana's former companion, a Mrs. Younge, to facilitate an elopement for Wickham and Georgiana and seize the girl's dowry of thirty thousand pounds. Fortunately, Darcy learned of the scheme before his sister could be taken from her rented house in Ramsgate, and he was able to stop the two malefactors. Elizabeth was horrified.

"You say this happened earlier this year? But Georgiana is so young."

"Her youth must be her excuse for believing herself in love and trusting her adult companion. But she has suffered greatly, mainly from guilt.

Please know I blame her not — others were at fault — but my sister is of a sensitive and trusting nature. Her confidence and self-worth were deeply harmed. It is only by daily intercourse with your family that she has shown improvement. I have my dear Georgie back, and I owe it to the Bennets."

"I will accept your thanks on behalf of my family, but in truth, who could do less for dear Georgiana? If we have been of any help at all, we are happy." Elizabeth then frowned. "But that *rogue*! I admit when I heard that Mr. Wickham was to go to prison for debt, I felt pity for him. But now — gaol is too good for him! He must be severely punished!"

"He will be punished enough. It is exile and Canada for him."

"It is better than he deserves! At this moment, I regret these times. Is there no chance of persuading the Regent to break out the rack in the Tower? At least Wickham will be far away from Georgiana. If we are fortunate, he may be eaten by a bear!"

Darcy laughed. "This is a new side to you, Miss Elizabeth — such a doom for George Wickham!"

Her chin jutted out. "I defend my friends, sir!"

The gentleman sobered. "You have been a better friend to me than I deserve, especially after insulting you so abominably at the assembly in September."

"I admit that my pride was hurt at the — Wait! Your sister's troubles, did they happen shortly before your journey here to Hertfordshire?"

"They occurred not three months before."

"Oh! No wonder you were so reserved! You could not have wished to be in society so soon after that!"

Darcy allowed a small smile. "You know me well. I am never at my best in a ballroom in any case, but my mind was still full of Georgiana's pain. Bingley was badgering me, and I wanted him to leave off. I should not have said such a wicked falsehood."

"Falsehood?"

Darcy's eyes grew dark. "Miss Elizabeth, surely you know that you are exceedingly handsome, and... remarkably tempting."

Elizabeth flushed and modestly looked away. "You should not say such things." Of course, she meant not a word of what she said. No captivated young lady would. And Elizabeth was truly and completely captivated by Mr. Darcy. She longed to hear more expressions of love from him.

However, Darcy drew back and looked towards the house. "Quite right. I apologize, Miss Elizabeth."

Elizabeth was frustrated. First he hinted at admiring her, but when given the chance to expand upon that surprising and delightful condition, he withdrew. Teasing, teasing man! She changed the subject.

"You say that you are not at your best in a ballroom. How is that? Do you not like to dance?"

"Dancing is not a favorite occupation of mine, that is true, but the real reason is that I am ill qualified to recommend myself to strangers. I am very reserved and am only comfortable with those whom I know and know well."

Elizabeth could hardly believe his explanation. "Sir, you are a man of sense and education who has lived in the world. Why do you feel ill at ease around new acquaintances?"

"I certainly have not the talent which some people possess," said Darcy, "of conversing easily with those I have never met before. I cannot catch their tone of conversation or appear interested in their concerns as I often see done."

"That, perhaps, is the case. If you say so, it must be true. However, you seem to be able to overcome this affliction. Look how you have charmed the entire Bennet family!"

Very earnest was his reply. "I did not do it a-purpose, save to — how shall I put it? Take the trouble of practicing. To show I have taken your rebuffs seriously and have tried to improve myself."

"Rebuffs? What do you mean? Our argument was but an hour ago. Your kindness to my family began long before that."

"Oh!" Darcy sighed. "You have found me out. I shall be honest, as I said. I am afraid I overhead you justly berating me several weeks ago."

"When was that? I do not recall — "

"It was in this very garden. You were with Miss Lucas."

Elizabeth gasped. "I am mortified! I recall that unjust conversation."

"You were right."

"No, I was not!" Elizabeth insisted. "I was blind and spiteful! I foolishly held your comments at the assembly against you. I have lately come to understand your character, and I am heartily ashamed of myself. You are not the only one who had their shortcomings pointed out to them. My sisters defended you most strenuously. I know now I jumped to an unjust conclusion about Sally, and I am thankful my family has reproached me for it. Until then, I did not truly know myself." Elizabeth smiled. "Mr. Darcy, when a young lady takes the trouble of apologizing, you should be a gentleman and permit it, if but for form's sake."

"I am a better man for your criticisms."

His compliments were too much for her if he did not mean to act upon them. "Why do you say such things?"

"Were I not in this chair, I would say more."

Elizabeth looked upon him. "I...I cannot understand what you mean."

"Can you not?" he growled as he sat up in the Bath chair. "Elizabeth, I cannot court you from a wheel-chair! I said I would be plain, and plain I will be. I am an invalid, and I will not take advantage of your pity. But once I return, will you allow me a private interview?"

Her joy at his declaration was tempered by one word. "Return?"

"Yes. I am glad we have had this conversation. You cannot know of the depths of my appreciation. It allows me to leave Longbourn, not in the bitterness of spirits I owned this morning, but with a heart lightened by hope." He reached over and took Elizabeth's gloved hands. "Georgiana and I will return to London tomorrow. Too much has been done to alter our plans, but our reasons have changed. It is for the best, after all. In Town, I can be better cared for by Mr. Macmillan. I am determined to be on my own two feet in time for Bingley's wedding."

"But you cannot leave! Your leg—"

"Shall be fine. Your Mr. Jones has declared he has never seen a leg knit itself with more speed. In any case, my cousin and sister shall see to it that I am immobilized with blankets and pillows. The roads are in good condition, my coach is well-sprung, and I should be in my town-house before nightfall without incident." He smiled. "When I return, I shall *not* be in a chair."

Elizabeth smiled in return, her heart racing. "Shall my friend dance with me?"

"I shall probably stumble about the room, but nothing shall prevent me from claiming my set." Darcy's warm look sent the most delightful shivers through Elizabeth's body. "But you have not answered my question."

Elizabeth's mouth was dry. "I should be delighted to speak with you."

Darcy's entire face seemed to glow with happiness. "You do me great honor." He gripped Elizabeth's hands tightly, and she knew he planned to kiss them.

"Mr. Darcy — no!" Elizabeth whispered as she pulled her hands away. Her eyes gestured towards the house. "We are being watched!"

Sure enough, several female faces could be seen looking out the parlor window. Lydia was even waving.

"Can one die of mortification?" cried Elizabeth.

Darcy barked with laughter. "I do think it time we returned indoors. Will you summon Bartholomew?"

Elizabeth got to her feet. "That will not be necessary, sir. I believe we can manage." She went to the rear of the Bath chair.

Darcy was scandalized. "Miss Elizabeth! Do you mean to push me inside? You should not!"

With a mock-serious tone, Elizabeth leaned over his shoulder. "Did we not just have a conversation about allowing a lady her way?"

THE NEXT MORNING THE CARRIAGES were packed, and the Darcys were joined by the party from Netherfield. Mr. Bingley had business in Town; his solicitor's name was mentioned, causing Miss Bennet to blush. His relations decided to accompany him and partake of Christmastide in London, and Colonel Fitzwilliam declared he would help Mr. Darcy and Georgiana. Therefore, Netherfield would be empty until the New Year.

The talk around the table centered on the upcoming nuptials between Mr. Bingley and Jane. Miss Bingley seemed to take pains in conversing amicably with her future sister, an occurrence that had Darcy wondering whether Mr. Bingley had demanded more cordiality from his relations towards his intended.

Darcy paid little attention to his friend. His mind was more agreeably engaged. He had been meditating on the very great pleasure which a pair of fine eyes in the face of a pretty woman can bestow, particularly when she looked upon him with what he hoped was favor. He had let himself believe that Elizabeth was partial to him while her sister was indisposed at Netherfield. Her saucy looks then were as nothing compared to her affectionate glances now. She had called him her friend, and he was determined that when he returned from London, she would call him something much more dear. Bingley would certainly beat him to the altar, but Darcy was encouraged he would not lag far behind.

The time for departure was upon them, and Bartholomew wheeled him outside to the carriages. There were three standing by the front door: The Bingley coach was behind two that bore the Darcy crest. A tearful Georgiana took her leave of her new friends, and Darcy overheard Caroline insisting that Jane journey to London so that they could shop for her *trousseau* in shops apparently approved of by the Sisters Bingley.

Lydia approached him, a glum look on her face. "Goodbye, Mr. Darcy. I am sad you are leaving. Thank you for letting me ride Miranda. You were very kind, and I will miss her — I mean, I will miss you and your sister."

Bingley overhead and interjected, "Oh, I should not worry about that, Miss Lydia. I will be in London for only a few days, and I have your father's permission to stable the horse I have provided for Miss Bennet."

"That is nice of you. I am sure Jane will appreciate it."

Bingley laughed. "But I have not told you the rest! Darcy tells me that Miranda is quite happy here in Mr. Bennet's stable, as she has made friends with my horse, and Darcy has no desire to reclaim her for the next few months."

It took a moment for Lydia to understand fully Mr. Bingley's meaning, but when she did, she squealed and threw her arms around Darcy's neck. "Oh, Mr. Darcy! You *are* the nicest man in all the world!"

Once Darcy extracted himself, to everyone's amusement, he took his leave of the rest of the Bennet family. Mary promised to practice every day, and Mr. Bennet declared that Darcy and his family were always welcome to Longbourn. "But perhaps not on my couch," he added with a twinkle.

Kitty presented him with a portfolio. "Here is your commission, Mr. Darcy. I hope you like it."

"I am sure I shall," Darcy returned.

The girl blushed. "I added something to it," she whispered, her eyes flicking at Elizabeth.

Darcy glanced at the closed package. Part of him wished to open it right away to see if she did enclose her study of Elizabeth along with Georgiana's portrait, as she seemed to hint. But that would never do. He would have to enjoy it in the privacy of his carriage. "I thank you, Miss Kitty."

The girl nervously giggled and gave way to her mother.

"Oh, Mr. Darcy," cried that worthy woman, "we have enjoyed having you and your delightful sister here at Longbourn! I expect it has not been too unpleasant," she looked pointedly at Elizabeth, "as we have attractions not found in even the grandest houses in England! But I suppose you know that! We do look forward to your return and that of Miss Darcy, too. Is that not right, Lizzy?"

Elizabeth turned beet-red, and Darcy felt he should feel sorry for her. But he was enjoying himself too much.

"You are quite right, Mama," the embarrassed girl managed. "Mr. and Miss Darcy are very welcome at Longbourn."

Mrs. Bennet smirked at Darcy. "I know *some* of us will count the minutes until your return for dear Jane's wedding." Darcy almost laughed as Elizabeth covered her face. "You are returning for the event, are you not?"

"That is up to Bingley, madam. I speak for my sister and me when I say it is our earnest hope we should meet again soon."

"Do not worry about Miranda," cried Lydia. "I shall ride her every day!"

"Of course, you shall, my dear," said Mrs. Bennet. "You are a very generous man, Mr. Darcy. So good to my girls. I insist that when you return we have the honor of hosting you and your sister! Is that not right, Mr. Bennet?"

"I have no objection to the notion, my dear" — Mr. Bennet directed a very knowing look towards his second eldest — "but I am of the mind that such a thing might prove to be impractical. Time will tell."

Darcy decided the teasing of Elizabeth had gone far enough. "I thank you for the offer, but I believe my friend Bingley has other plans." He turned to the other man, who was engrossed in making his farewell to his intended. "What say you, Bingley?"

"Hmm?" Bingley looked around, causing general laughter. Caroline openly rolled her eyes. "Oh! Oh, yes! As I hope Darcy will stand up with me, I plan to invite him and his sister to Netherfield at the appointed time. We have plenty of room, and Caroline would be happy to play hostess."

"Of course." At least Miss Bingley did not grit her teeth.

"There," said Darcy to the disappointed matron. "I would not inconvenience you, but I hope to visit Longbourn often while we are here."

"You have an open invitation to come every day!" Mrs. Bennet insisted. "Every day, mind you!"

"I consider myself obligated. Thank you, madam." He turned to Elizabeth. "Farewell, Miss Elizabeth."

"Good journey to you, Mr. Darcy, Miss Darcy, Mrs. Annesley." She looked at Darcy. "I, too, look forward to meeting again." A fit of giggles from her sisters caused her to shut her eyes in embarrassment.

Darcy smiled understandingly. "As do I. Until then." With that, he gave the indication he was ready to be placed in the carriage.

The operation, under the joint supervision of Mr. Jones and Colonel Fitzwilliam, took some doing, as the Darcy footmen took great care with Darcy's injured leg. Once he was well-established in the carriage, his sister and her companion joined him.

"Very well, Darcy," said Colonel Fitzwilliam, now on horseback. "Bartholomew and the nurse are in the second carriage. We are ready to leave. The Bingleys will follow close behind. I shall make certain the driver takes his time and avoids the major ruts in the road."

For his usually jolly cousin to talk so seriously told Darcy that the man was concerned. "I leave things in your capable hands, Cuz." Darcy wished he was on the other side of the coach — he could no longer see the Bennet party, and he wanted one last look at Elizabeth.

It seemed that the lady in question was like-minded, for in the next instant, to his delight, she appeared outside his window, holding a large, ginger-colored creature.

"Mr. Darcy!" cried Elizabeth. "Where are your manners, sir? You would return to London without first taking your leave of Miss Cassandra? She is most put out!"

Darcy smiled. "Ah, an unintended oversight, I assure you. Farewell, gentle friend! Keep your mistress warm." *Until I return.*

The cat meowed and Elizabeth bent down as if to hear what the beast was saying. "Cassandra wishes you Godspeed, quick recovery, and safe return." She looked up, a tender look in her eye. "As do we all."

Darcy said nothing, but he trusted his expression told volumes. It seemed to serve, as Elizabeth blushed prettily and waved as the carriage moved away down the London road. Darcy turned in his seat as much as he could and kept the two in his sight as long as possible.

Chapter 20

IN THE MONTH THAT FOLLOWED, a regular correspondence was established between Longbourn and the Darcy residence in London. Elizabeth missed Darcy intensely—he was now *Fitzwilliam* in the secret reaches of her heart—but propriety forbade any direct communication without a betrothal. Therefore, Georgiana became their willing intermediary. Elizabeth filled her letters with the usual activities an imminent wedding generates—dresses and flowers and breakfast menus—enough to satisfy the curiosity of a young, sisterless girl not yet out. But for Fitzwilliam's sake, she included news of Bingley, of her father's plans for the spring planting, and numerous innuendoes of how completely a particular lady from Hertfordshire desired the company of a certain gentleman from the north.

It was Georgiana's task to relate this information to her brother. After a particularly embarrassing episode from the second letter — some little anecdote about Elizabeth's cat Cassandra purring in Darcy's lap that made no sense to the sister but had turned the brother positively red — it was decided between the Darcy siblings that Georgiana would henceforth just hand Elizabeth's letters to Fitzwilliam for his own perusal.

Georgiana returned letters to her friend, but Darcy could hardly relate his longing for Elizabeth to *her*. No, it was left to Miss Darcy to try to give Elizabeth news of Darcy, using her own powers of observation. Elizabeth had to be satisfied with hearing of her beloved by way of his innocent sister.

To say the least, Darcy was *not* satisfied. He never was a good patient in the past, and coupled with his burning desire to return to Longbourn, his behavior now bordered on the uncivil. Mr. Macmillan bore the brunt of it. The good man withstood the badgering of his employer and would not allow him to try to walk with a cane until Christmas.

Even sweet Georgina felt the sting of his black mood. About a week before Christmas, she skipped into her brother's study, Elizabeth's latest letter in her hand and mischief in her heart.

"Look, brother-mine, a letter from Miss Elizabeth!" She held up the communication.

Darcy, a smile on his face, held out his hand. "Thank you, my dear. Do you not have music lessons soon?"

Georgiana knew Fitzwilliam preferred to read Elizabeth's letters in private. It was her intention to deliver the note, but Elizabeth's witty commentary had apparently ignited the imp in Miss Darcy. She wanted some sport with her brother first. She twirled about, crushing the letter protectively to her breast.

"No! You shall not have this letter! It is improper."

"Georgie," said Darcy wearily, "I am in no mood for this." Indeed, Mr. Macmillan had prescribed exercises to strengthen his leg, weakened by neglect and lack of use, and Georgiana was aware that they hurt like the devil. "Give me Miss Elizabeth's letter, please."

"No! It is mine. You will just have to come and get it," she teased.

"You know I cannot."

"Oh, that is too bad. And it is such an interesting letter, too."

"Georgie…" There was a world of warning in his voice, but Miss Darcy chose not to mark it.

"I shall just sit here and enjoy it again." She sat in a chair on the far side of the room.

He grew sharp. "Georgiana, please."

"Or perhaps I shall take it outside! It is not too cold, is it? What a good idea!"

Darcy snapped. "I am your brother, and you will give me that letter *right now!*"

Needless to say, it took the rest of the day for a contrite Mr. Darcy to apologize fully to his distraught sister.

CHRISTMAS AND BOXING DAY CAME and went, as did the New Year. It was but a few days later that Darcy's butler walked into the study one evening.

"Sir, Colonel Fitzwilliam to see you."

From behind his ornate desk, Darcy granted his cousin permission to enter and carefully stood as the officer bounded into the room. Darcy moved to greet him, a wry smile on his face.

"You are in a good mood, Fitz," Darcy observed as they shook hands.

"I should be," said the colonel, a rather silly expression on his weather-beaten face. "And you? How is your leg?"

"Tolerable. Macmillan has removed the splint, as you see. I manage to hobble about with a cane when it is too painful."

"Good. Georgiana has said you have been rather beastly of late."

Darcy flushed a little. "It is nothing, Fitzwilliam. What brings you here?"

"A drink! I need a drink of your fine brandy, for I bear monumental news!"

Assured that his Fitzwilliam relations were well, Darcy bade his guest sit and soon presented him with a snifter of Cognac. "Well?" said Darcy upon taking a chair opposite his cousin. "Will you tell me this news directly, or shall I have to weasel it out?"

Colonel Fitzwilliam was very smug. "You will never guess."

"Let me see. You have a new horse — that fine chestnut from Knightley."

"No."

"That pointer bitch Willoughby was boasting about? You had your eye on her."

"Come, Darcy, you can do better than that!"

"Truly, Fitz, I am not in a humor for this. Tell me your news or let us drink in silence."

"Congratulate me, for I am to be married!"

Darcy's head jerked up. "Married? To whom? Forgive me, Fitz — allow me to wish you joy, but who is the unfortunate lady?"

"Ha! Miss Caroline Bingley."

Darcy sat back, crossly. "I said I was not in a mood for your jokes." He took in his cousin's expectant expression and raised an eyebrow. "You are in earnest? You have proposed to Miss Bingley?"

"Yes, but officially she has agreed only to a courtship. A mere formality — we have determined we shall be married by year's end. I might yet beat you to the altar unless you have finally proposed to Miss Elizabeth Bennet." He gestured at the drawing of Elizabeth done by Miss Kitty, mounted and hung with obvious care next to the portrait of Georgiana.

Darcy merely blinked. His years of practice in hiding his true feelings served him well now, but Colonel Fitzwilliam was not deceived.

"I know what you are thinking, Darcy, and you are wrong about Caroline." He smiled. "Not that I blame you. Few people know the real Miss Bingley. It is her own doing — those airs she puts on! It is to laugh if one did not feel for her."

"You... you have feelings for her?"

"Of course. Just because I do not moon as you do over your ladylove does not mean I fail to hold Caroline in high regard. We got to know each other quite well in Hertfordshire. It was not so great a burden to keep her away from your sickbed as one might expect. In private, absent from those she means to impress, she is very amicable and amusing."

"Are we speaking of the same Caroline Bingley? Charles Bingley's sister?"

"I am. You only know the public guise she put on — rather poorly, I might observe. Poor girl, always running from her roots in trade without having any proper guidance on how to do it. That ridiculous superiority! One can either despise her or pity her. I chose to show compassion. And do you know what I discovered? A lovely, insecure lady longing to belong to someone. She is terrified of returning to trade, yet she has found entrance into the *ton* difficult. When I found her out, oh how she resisted me! But I was determined; I would not be gainsaid. I wore her down with good humor and patience. She now loves me more than she ever loved you."

"You do realize she wanted to be Mrs. Darcy."

"Wrong, old boy," said the colonel with a smile. "She wanted to be mistress of Pemberley and the acceptance by the First Circles that title would provide her. You just came along with it. Once I was able to get her to see that you were unattainable, it was no hard work to have her understand that the second son of an earl might do as well, especially as he is amusing and has not the abhorrence of society owned by his cousin."

"But you have no fortune."

"True, the loss of the Darcy funds was a blow to her. But I am not exactly poor, and my modest expectations from Father, plus her twenty thousand, should provide a comfortable living in London. London is the key; she longs for parties and dances and society — things I like and you hate. In the heat of summer, we can visit her family in Scarborough and mine in Derbyshire. We will find it very agreeable to have someone else pay the bills a few months out of the year, ha ha!"

"But what of affection?"

Colonel Fitzwilliam shrugged. "We have become good friends. There is affection enough for now, and when the time comes, I am certain we will get along rather better than most — certainly better than my brother and *dear sister.*" He grinned. "The trick is to convince her that passion is *de rigueur* in marriage. I will enjoy teaching her. It should not be too hard. She loathes Mrs. Hurst's marriage, and I have assured her that ours will be quite different." He wagged his eyebrows.

"She accepted your assurances?"

"It was more of experiencing them."

Darcy was shocked. "Fitzwilliam! What have you done? You did not compromise the lady, did you?"

The colonel waved him off with a grin. "Oh, nothing permanent! Just enough of a taste to know what to expect. She enjoyed it, I think. I know I did."

Darcy was not completely assured by his cousin's words. "Then why a courtship? Even a 'small' compromise should lead to an immediate engagement. Are the earl and countess opposed?"

"Of course, they are opposed! They are Fitzwilliams, after all! Father will come around. Caroline is pleasant to behold, and her fortune alone makes her acceptable. Besides, he knows that society expects no better from me, being a second son with no estate. Once Father learns of Caroline's wicked, biting sense of humor, they will get along famously. Mother, on the other hand, will rail for weeks until she gets it out of her system. Then she will magnanimously take the poor girl under her wing and teach her proper Fitzwilliam manners. Between shopping and gossip, the two might become dangerous.

"As for the courtship, it was Caroline's idea. She wants to go through one last Season with me on her arm. That is why we have made no announcement. She wants to show me off and rub her good fortune into the faces of some of her acquaintances. So I must ask you to keep my news to yourself. Only my parents know, besides you. We have not even told Bingley yet. You know he cannot keep a secret."

"Neither can you."

"Very funny. I have received Bingley's official permission to court his sister, and I will talk to him again after the Season."

"Aunt Catherine will be displeased."

"When is Aunt Catherine not displeased? Confounding her is the family sport as you well know."

Darcy wanted to believe his cousin knew what he was about. "Are you certain about this?"

"You do not know Caroline as I do. True, she is vain and dismissive of those beneath her, but so am I to a certain extent. I can tolerate her blemishes, and I certainly have my faults." Colonel Fitzwilliam smiled indulgently. "We get along, Darcy. I make her laugh, and that makes her beautiful. We are friends, and that is no bad basis for a marriage, I think. As for her weaker characteristics, I will guide her to better behavior. All it takes is a gentle, firm hand like the stable master back at Matlock. It is rather like breaking a horse."

"You compare your intended to a horse?"

The colonel laughed. "Not to her face; I am not stupid! But, you must admit there is a certain similarity between horses and wives. Consider that both were made by our Creator for man to ride. Who am I to disparage the Lord?"

Darcy shook his head. His cousin could come up with the strangest ideas! Was it wit or insanity? "You have been spending too much time at your campfires."

Colonel Fitzwilliam grew serious. "That is another thing. Marriage means I can retire from the king's service, and I thank God for it, for I am not ashamed to admit I am weary of soldiering." He turned to the window and looked out into the gathering darkness. "I do not want to spend another cold, wet night around a distant campfire fearing the dawn and wondering whether this will be the battle in which I fall. I long for normalcy — a good house, a soft bed, and an agreeable woman by my side. All my cares behind me."

He took a long drink from his glass. "For fifteen years I have served king and country. It is past time I retired. I have been searching for a way out, for a woman of fortune who was at least tolerable, without success. Until now. I have finally found that fair and formidable lady, and she is Miss Caroline Bingley. We *will* be happy, Cuz. I am determined."

Colonel Fitzwilliam continued to stare out of the study window from his chair, and Darcy watched him closely. He began to suspect there was more mutual affection between his cousin and Miss Bingley than Fitz was willing to let on. Finally, Darcy roused himself, stood again, and extended his hand.

"Then I wish you joy in earnest, Fitz. May you find the peace you have earned."

The colonel leapt to his feet. "Thank you, Darce. I think I shall. Oh, I know Caroline would prefer a title, but joined to the war hero spawn of a titled family is not so bad. I may even wear my red coat on occasion just to delight her."

"Will she be delighted to learn that your name is Algernon?"

The colonel laughed. "Not until the wedding. Must keep some surprises. Then, when it is too late, she will pledge herself for life to Colonel the Hon. Algernon Richard Henry Fitzwilliam. I hope she does not swoon."

Darcy chuckled. "Take care not to cut yourself, and you should be safe."

BY THE BEGINNING OF THE New Year, Elizabeth's feelings were much in common with Mr. Darcy's. December flew by with letters and preparations for the holidays and Jane's wedding. Mr. Bingley's constant visits were always enjoyable even though his presence could not but remind Elizabeth of the gentleman absent. Still, Christmastide was enjoyable as always.

All that changed as the month grew to an end. The weather had turned snowy, curtailing Elizabeth's walks. Worse, Jane left on her trousseau-buying expedition to London. But instead of Elizabeth accompanying her dear sister, she was left behind. Mr. Bennet declared he could not do without her, and Mrs. Bennet selected Lydia as Jane's companion. To the surprise of all, Lydia declined the honor, choosing to stay at Longbourn and attend her dear Miranda. As Mary had no interests in Town, it became Kitty's happy task to accompany her sister. Elizabeth was left to stew in her disappointment.

Her father tried to explain. "I know you would rather be with Jane and the Gardiners. I am sure Mr. Darcy, once he learned you were in London, would brave even Cheapside to visit Gracechurch Street. At least, I am convinced of it. But in any case, I have heard of nothing these six weeks but wedding and balls and dresses and breakfasts. Allow me to be selfish and enjoy some reasonable company. I am certain it will be a pleasure that I will lose sooner than I would like."

Elizabeth could make no answer, both from embarrassment over her father's presumption as well as her resentment of the delay of being in her Fitzwilliam's most agreeable company until Jane's wedding.

She poured her disappointment into her next letter, but upon reading it, she decided it was far too *missish* and tossed it into the fire. The replacement was far more sanguine, but a trained eye could easily see the longing between the words.

Still, Elizabeth was not made for misery. She found employment in her daily practice sessions with Mary and developed a closer relationship with her too. By the time an excited and exhausted Jane returned from Town burdened with purchases, Elizabeth could say she loved Mary almost as much as she loved Jane. It was now Elizabeth's mission to know her younger siblings better, and the month of January passed far more agreeably.

Nevertheless, Elizabeth greeted February with as much anticipation as Jane. The wedding was nigh, and so was Fitzwilliam's return. Only the weather's moderation, allowing Elizabeth to resume her long, meandering walks, prevented the girl from losing what sense she still possessed.

She was on such a walk a week before the joyous event, trying to curb her growing impatience over the Darcys' expected return in the next few days, when she received a great surprise.

Chapter 21

ELIZABETH WAS WALKING ON the London Road, returning from Meryton, when she spied a phaeton, top up, heading in her direction. She knew no one in Hertfordshire who owned such a vehicle, so her curiosity was aroused. Other feelings soon followed as it grew closer, for the little carriage was pulled smartly by a matched team of gray ponies, and the woodwork and brass gleamed in the pale winter sun. Only a rich man could own such a conveyance, and Elizabeth knew a very agreeable rich man was due to visit Hertfordshire presently. Could it be that excellent gentleman was before his time?

It was exactly the case, for the carriage was driven by none other than Mr. Darcy. Within moments, the phaeton had come to a stop right before her. "Miss Elizabeth!" he called out, raising his crop in greeting. For Elizabeth's part, she waved vigorously, a smile spread from ear-to-ear, her heart threatening to burst from her chest.

With anxiety and excitement, Elizabeth watched as Mr. Darcy eased himself down. His leg, now free of splints, was still weak, and Elizabeth feared it would buckle under the strain. She rushed to assist the gentleman, but he waved her off, retrieving a cane which he used to good effect, supporting his tall frame.

"Miss Elizabeth," he greeted her again. "Forgive me for not bowing, but I do not believe that I would recover from the exercise." He said this with such gravity that Elizabeth was unsure whether the man was serious or not. "I see that Cassandra is not with you," he observed.

"No," Elizabeth said, not yet composed enough to speak words of more than one syllable. She wrung her hands, unable to keep them still in her happiness.

"Pity. I believe I was well prepared for her this time." Mr. Darcy indicated the carriage.

Elizabeth, quickly becoming expert in the small alterations of his expression, could see the slight upturn of the corners of his mouth and the twinkling in his dark eyes. He was jesting with her! He stood as tall as he always had, yet there was something different: a relaxation along with nervous excitement.

It was left for Mr. Darcy to carry the conversation. "I hope I find you well."

"Oh! Yes, I am in excellent health! As is all of my family." Elizabeth remembered her manners. "You are very welcome to Longbourn, sir. Your sister — is she well?"

"She is." He smiled. "I must confess I am already acquainted with your family's good health. I am just come from calling on them with Georgiana. She remains there, but Miss Bennet was good enough to mention that you had gone for a walk."

Good, loving, thoughtful Jane! Elizabeth would love her forever! "Yes. I would ask you to join me, but your leg — can you — "

"Mr. Macmillan is very happy with the progress I have made and instructs me to exercise whenever I can. I believe a short walk is not beyond me."

Elizabeth waited nervously while Mr. Darcy secured the team's reins to a branch. The two then moved off at a slow pace, Mr. Darcy's limp quite pronounced. Elizabeth was very aware of his presence. It almost overwhelmed her, in fact. How heartily did she grieve over every saucy speech she had directed towards him. She was satisfied just to remain in his company and share a quiet stroll.

Apparently, Mr. Darcy was of a different mind, for after a few minutes of walking he declared, "Miss Elizabeth, it is well that I find you thus, for I desire some privacy. I must speak to you if you will do me the honor of giving me a few moments of your time. I could not speak before, confined to a chair. But I am not in a chair now, and I can no longer go on in silence!"

This declaration caused Elizabeth to stumble, and Mr. Darcy reached out to steady her. Elizabeth laughingly accepted his gallantry. "It would serve me right to fall on my face after everything I have said and done to you since we met, but I am well." Their progress stopped, she turned to face him. "In fact, I have never been as well as I am this very moment. Please, sir, speak on. I would be happy to hear whatever you have to say."

Carefully balancing himself on his legs, Mr. Darcy took her hands in his, the crook of his cane secured over his arm. "I know I have been an indifferent lover, despite the fact that my preference and affection for you knows no bounds. I have been so engrossed in my own feelings that I have failed to make them clear to you. In my foolishness, I took your wishes for granted, an insufferable presumption on my part. This I vow never to do again. But the only way I can prove this new resolution to you is through my future actions. I will not hide from the world but let it know my intentions — let society see how I love and respect the woman I hope one day to make my wife.

"Miss Elizabeth Bennet, you must allow me to tell you how ardently I admire and love you. I would consider it a great honor if you would permit me to ask your father's permission for a formal courtship." He bit his lip in anticipation.

Elizabeth was silent as she took in the full weight of his words. He loved her, and she knew that she loved him. Her face glowed as a dazzling smile broke out.

"Mr. Fitzwilliam Darcy, I can think of nothing I enjoy more than your company. You may speak to my father, and I will anticipate your calls with every regard."

A whirlwind of emotions danced across Mr. Darcy's face, now more dear to Elizabeth than anything in the world. He brought her hands to his lips and kissed them, not lightly and daintily as young ladies are taught to expect, but with all the passion a man violently in love might express.

"Dearest, loveliest Elizabeth! May I call you Elizabeth?"

Almost choked with love, she could hardly look him in the face. "Yes, you may... Fitzwilliam."

His hands grew tight on hers, and Elizabeth watched as his eyes studied her lips. She could not know how much Fitzwilliam wanted to kiss her; she only knew how much she wantonly wanted him to. But both were creatures of good breeding, so instead, Elizabeth moved to Fitzwilliam's hurt left side, wrapped her arm around his left, and moved as close as she could.

"You would take the place of my cane?" He smiled.

Her eyebrows rose, a sure sign of teasing. "I believe I can serve *tolerably.*"

His bark of laughter brought on hers, and they returned to the carriage in the highest spirits. Ascending into the phaeton caused Elizabeth a bit of anxiety, for Fitzwilliam would not hear of her helping him, and he stubbornly insisted on holding her hand while she climbed into the vehicle. It was a small carriage, built low to the ground, and Elizabeth was relieved to see that her suitor had little difficulty joining her after untying the horses.

Fitzwilliam noticed her distress. "I have been practicing," he admitted. "It would not do for me to be helpless when I so wanted to impress you."

She laughed. "You have mistaken the situation completely! Do you not know that little engages the heart of a young lady more than her favorite needing her assistance? You have missed an opportunity, sir!"

He playfully asked, "Do you need to pity me, Elizabeth?"

She looked at him coyly from under her lashes. "No, sir. I do not pity you — not at all."

Fitzwilliam grinned and expertly guided the carriage down the lane. Elizabeth, seating herself closer to him than propriety allowed, could feel the warmth of his body through her winter clothing. It was a bright, crisp day, made all the more glorious by their understanding, and Elizabeth was in no hurry to return to Longbourn.

Suddenly, remembering Jane's upcoming nuptials revealed an obstacle to their happiness. "Fitzwilliam," she said with more emotion than she intended, "are you not staying at Netherfield?" Told that he was, she cried, "But how will you call on me? Jane and Bingley are off on a six-week tour after the wedding."

Fitzwilliam glanced at her, one eyebrow raised in imitation of her own habit. "You cannot wait six weeks between calls, my dear?"

Elizabeth pursed her lips and narrowed her eyes; she had no idea that raising an eyebrow could be so annoying an expression! "There is a great deal of difference between what one *can* do and what one *wishes* to do! But perhaps your attachment to me is not as great as all that, and six weeks is nothing to you!" The last two months had been excruciating for *her*, and she would not wish to experience it again.

Fitzwilliam seemed very satisfied with himself. "I can assure you that six weeks would seem an eternity without your company. Mr. and Mrs. Bingley's abandonment of Hertfordshire does present certain difficulties." He bent low and whispered, "I suppose that the parlor of Longbourn is unavailable?"

"Fitzwilliam, how shocking! You cannot stay at Longbourn with our understanding!" She smiled. "In any case, while my mother may have no objection — you are quite her favorite now — the same cannot be said of my father. He has grown to like you, but giving up his parlor again is too high a price for him to pay, even for your excellent company!"

Fitzwilliam laughed. "It does not signify, as I do not think my poor back can stand another night on your couch. No, I will just have to make do with a room at the Meryton Inn."

It is strange how the passage of time affects one's understanding of the world. A few months before, Elizabeth Bennet would have been excessively diverted by the idea of the proud and wealthy Mr. Fitzwilliam Darcy, Esq. of Pemberley taking rooms in a small village inn that had seen better days while paying court to a young lady of no note. But now, every fiber of Elizabeth's being rebelled at the notion. Her stalwart, generous, and beloved Fitzwilliam sleeping in a run-down public house, sharing his rough bed with goodness knew what manner of insect or creature? Impossible!

Fortunately, Elizabeth had a solution. "Such a plan may not be necessary. My relations in Town, the Gardiners, have invited me to come to London soon after Jane's wedding."

"Indeed? That is good news." Fitzwilliam grinned. "Georgiana will be so pleased."

Elizabeth, who found being teased not nearly as much fun as teasing, huffed in reply, "I am happy that one member of the Darcy family is pleased!"

Her companion laughed. "Ah, my vain beauty, must you hear the words?"

She crossed her arms over her chest. "Perhaps my vanity needs a bit of reassurance given the rejection it suffered upon out first meeting."

Darcy rolled his eyes. "Will I never live down that stupid pronouncement? Very well." He turned to her. "My beautiful, exceedingly tempting vixen, I am beyond pleased that you will be in Town this spring. Where do they live?"

"Hmm?" Elizabeth caught herself. Lost in his eyes for a time, Elizabeth had to remember to breathe. "I beg your pardon?"

"Your relations — the Gardiners. What is their address?"

Elizabeth realized that Fitzwilliam was ignorant of their being her relations in trade. She nervously licked her lips, fearing his reaction to an address in Cheapside. "My uncle's house is on Gracechurch Street."

He thought for a moment, a pause dreadful to Elizabeth's feelings. "I believe you have mentioned them. They are your mother's family?"

"Yes, my Uncle Gardiner is my mother's brother. He is an exceedingly clever, well-read gentleman," she quickly added. She so wanted Fitzwilliam to like the Gardiners.

He glanced at her. "I think you hold them in some esteem."

"Oh, yes! They, along with Jane, are my favorite people in all the world!"

"Then I shall not be happy until I have made their acquaintance. I assume they will be here for the wedding?"

Elizabeth, thankful for his enthusiasm and embarrassed at her own loss of composure, could only manage a small smile and a nod. The pair continued onward in a companionable silence. By the time the phaeton reached Longbourn, Elizabeth's spirits had recovered enough to be amused by their welcome.

Five young ladies stood huddled on the steps of the house, waving as Fitzwilliam brought the carriage to a stop. He managed to extract himself without incident and helped Elizabeth down. The ladies rushed forward, all talking to Elizabeth at once, while Fitzwilliam handed over the carriage to a stableman. Georgiana greeted Elizabeth with great affection, Jane complained about the cold, Mary spoke of a new piece of music Miss Darcy had acquired, Kitty talked about her new sketches, and Lydia's attention was on Darcy's fine team of horses. Fitzwilliam took the time to accept the personal welcome of each of the Bennet sisters before extending his arm to Elizabeth to escort her into the house.

Most of the others were still preoccupied with their own conversation, but Kitty and Georgiana seemed to take note of how possessively Elizabeth clung to Fitzwilliam's arm. They looked at each other before dissolving into a fit of giggles. The laughing girls' antics caught the attention of the others, and Lydia joined in while Mary and Jane were bewildered.

Elizabeth blushed, but her companion bore the scrutiny with great composure. As they slowly walked to the front door, it was opened by Mrs. Bennet herself. Elizabeth saw that her mother understood everything at a glance, and with an air of pride and triumph, the matron greeted Elizabeth's beloved.

"Mr. Darcy! You are very, *very* welcome to Longbourn!"

THE WEDDING OF CHARLES BINGLEY and Jane Bennet was not unlike any other wedding in England. The bride was blushing and beautiful, the groom was nervous and happy, and the wishes, hopes, confidence, and predictions of the small band of true friends who witnessed the ceremony were answered fully in the perfect happiness of the union. Bingley's sisters expressed their joy in an acceptable fashion although Miss Bingley's congratulations seemed more sincere than Mrs. Hurst's. Indeed, Caroline dropped all her resentment and paid off every arrear of civility to Jane. Unkind observers might have explained this turnabout to that lady's attachment to a certain second son of an earl, and the author leaves it to the imagination of the reader to weigh the correctness of that conjecture.

Within a fortnight of the Bingleys' removal for their wedding trip, Elizabeth arrived at the Gracechurch Street home of the Gardiners. Their welcome was all that was loving and expected. Unexpected was the gift awaiting her — a huge bouquet of flowers. The card simply read, "*Yours, FD,*" but it was enough to send Elizabeth into a fit of excitement.

The gentleman himself called the next day, accompanied by his sister, and if the Gardiners were taken aback by the presence of such august visitors in their house, their good breeding permitted them to face the extraordinary event with composure. The visit was enjoyed by all, but to the greatest degree by the two attached young people, and a dinner invitation was extended the next night at Darcy House.

Thus was spent the Season in Town, with regular intercourse between Gracechurch Street and Park Place. The subject of the Gardiners' plan to visit the Peaks that summer arose, and due to the entreaties of the Darcy siblings, it was settled that the party, which would include Elizabeth, would stay at Mr. Darcy's estate of Pemberley in Derbyshire rather than the nearby village of Lambton.

It might be supposed that Elizabeth had great concern over staying in the home of the man who courted her, but her fears proved to be fleeting. For by the time the Gardiner party arrived at the front door of Pemberley, it was not Miss Darcy's smiling friend who was handed down from the carriage, but Mr. Darcy's glowing affianced intended, sporting a beautiful ruby ring on her finger. Elizabeth could now enjoy the house and its gardens as a delighted lady, assured that Pemberley was fated to become her home.

You, dear reader, are undoubtedly surprised at the speed of these events. But Darcy remembered his family motto — *Fortune Favors the Bold* — and it served him exceedingly well.

HAPPY FOR ALL HER MATERNAL feelings was the day on which Mrs. Bennet got rid of her most deserving daughter. With what delighted pride she afterwards talked of Mrs. Darcy while visiting Mrs. Bingley may only be guessed. The author wished he could say, for the sake of her family, that the accomplishment of her earnest desire in the establishment of so many of her children produced so happy an effect as to make her a sensible, amiable, well-informed woman for the rest of her life, but he cannot. Though, perhaps, it was lucky for her husband, who might not have relished domestic felicity in so unusual a form, that she still was occasionally nervous and invariably silly.

Mr. Bennet missed his second daughter exceedingly. His affection for her drew him more often from home than anything else could do. He delighted in going to Pemberley, especially when he was least expected. In the meantime, he had to make do with the attentions of Cassandra the cat. Apparently, with neither Elizabeth nor Mr. Darcy in residence, Cassandra desired new fellowship and set her mind upon monopolizing Mr. Bennet's time and lap. After recovering from his surprise, for the cat had never before shown the least interest in his company, the master of the house found Longbourn's purring mouser an agreeable reading companion.

The Bingleys remained at Netherfield only a twelvemonth. So near a vicinity to her mother and Meryton relations was not desirable even to his easy temper or her affectionate heart. The darling wish of his sisters was then gratified, and Bingley bought an estate in a neighboring county to Derbyshire where Jane and Elizabeth, in addition to every other source of happiness, were within thirty miles of each other.

Mary was the only daughter who remained at home, and she was necessarily drawn from the pursuit of accomplishments by Mrs. Bennet's being quite unable to sit alone. Mary was obliged to mix more with the world, but she still could moralize over every morning visit and spend the balance of her time at her pianoforte. She would marry a clerk who was much taken with her piety and talent, and she became Meryton's greatest musician and her mother's closest confidant.

Kitty, to her very material advantage, spent the chief of her time with her two elder sisters. In society so superior to that she had generally known, her improvement was great. She rejoiced in her art and was celebrated in Town as Mrs. Darcy's other very accomplished sister, and she would in time marry well and live in London. She and her husband would haunt the exhibit halls and galleries of the great cities of the world.

Lydia spent much time at Pemberley, or rather, Pemberley's stables. She and Georgiana would ride up and down the hills and dales of Derbyshire, until she caught the eye of a visitor who liked both horses and ladies. He was ripe to settle down after undergoing much misfortune in earlier days, and while Lydia was rather silly at times, she was very pretty and sweet, shared her husband's love of horses, and had more of an engaging nature than the gentleman's mother or sister-in-law. Mr.

Bennet and Mr. Darcy had no qualms over Lydia Bennet becoming the future Lady Bertram and mistress of Mansfield Park in neighboring Northamptonshire, and it was hoped by all their friends that Lydia would have as good an influence over the reserved Mrs. Edmund Bertram as the former Fanny Price would have of the high-spirited Mrs. Thomas Bertram.

Georgiana did not begrudge her friend's choice of husband — Thomas Bertram was too outgoing for *her*. Pemberley was now Georgiana's home, and the attachment of Georgiana and Elizabeth was exactly what Darcy had hoped to see. They were able to love each other, even as well as they intended.

Georgiana had the highest opinion in the world of Elizabeth, though at first she often listened with an astonishment bordering on alarm at her lively, sportive manner of talking to her brother. By Elizabeth's instructions, she began to comprehend that a woman may take liberties with her husband which a brother will not always allow in a sister more than ten years younger than himself. Georgiana would eventually marry a reserved and decent viscount, who loved his country estate as much as his new wife, and possessed the additional attraction of living no more than a half-day's journey from Pemberley.

So not only could Elizabeth glory in the love and attention of her beloved Fitzwilliam and enjoy the delight of their children, she had the additional joy of living within easy distance of three of her sisters.

Elizabeth Rose Bennet flourished in her role as Mrs. Fitzwilliam Darcy. Her debut in London caused a sensation, particularly when the newlywed Darcys quit Town before the Season was done to retreat to Pemberley. No member of society was of two minds about Mrs. Darcy; she was dismissed by the envious as a rather pretty, simple country Miss, overwhelmed by the sophistication of the *ton*. Those who observed with unprejudiced eyes praised her as a breath of fresh air in stuffy society and proclaimed the lady lovely, kind, witty, and devoted to her family and friends.

The reason the Darcys spent so little time in London was clear to those who cared to think. In short order, Mr. Darcy's ancestral estate of Pemberley become far more dear to his wife than Longbourn, and like her husband, the lady grew to jealously protect her family's privacy there. The people of nearby Lambton proclaimed that the new Mrs. Darcy was the kindest and most generous of ladies. The Pemberley household quickly grew to love her, and even Bartholomew allowed that his new mistress was more than acceptable, although he still lorded it over the other servants. His employers tolerated the valet with amused fondness.

Thanks to the loving example of his wife, Mr. Darcy became more amiable and approachable, and acquaintances were astonished to see that the man *could* smile, after all. The Bennet family became his in his heart, and he withstood the foibles of his in-laws with great forbearance and charity.

A more unusual change was the chatter about Pemberley that from the private chambers of the house late at night a deep, masculine voice was occasionally heard singing love songs. Neither Mrs. Darcy's maid nor Mr. Darcy's valet would give credence to the gossip. Bartholomew particularly refused even to discuss the possibility of those reports' accuracy.

The more distant members of the Darcy family were soon enchanted by the new mistress of Pemberley. The Gardiners became great favorites of the couple, and the families were often seen in each other's homes in Derbyshire and London. The Fitzwilliams, after a bit of resistance, *generally* accepted Mrs. Darcy into their circle. Generally, the author reports, for Eugenie, Viscountess Fitzwilliam, ever aware of her destiny of becoming the matriarch of the House of Matlock, was a constant source of aggravation with her snide remarks and superior airs. Elizabeth withstood her barbs without injury, and amusingly observed to her dear husband that Eugenie's extraordinary obnoxiousness put the former Miss Bingley's previous behavior to shame.

As for her cousin, the improved Caroline Fitzwilliam, it might be too much to expect for Elizabeth and Caroline to be truly close and dear friends, but to the relief of their husbands, they were very cordial and enjoyed each other's company when family gatherings took place. They were particularly inseparable when the viscountess was at her most annoying. Colonel Fitzwilliam claimed it was because the two ladies formed a unified front before a common enemy. Mrs. Fitzwilliam would rebuke her husband for his impertinence but never openly denied it.

Lady Catherine de Bourgh was extremely indignant at the marriage of her nephew, and as she gave way to all the genuine frankness of her character in her reply to the letter announcing its arrangement, she sent him language so abusive, especially of Elizabeth, that for some time all intercourse between aunt and nephew was at an end. But at length, by Elizabeth's persuasion, Darcy was prevailed upon to overlook the offence and seek a reconciliation, and after a little additional resistance on the part of his aunt, Lady Catherine's resentment gave way, either because of her affection for him or her curiosity to see how his wife conducted herself. She condescended to wait on them at Pemberley in spite of that pollution which its woods had received.

The annual gift of a case of very fine French Cognac for Anne de Bourgh on the occasion of her birthday, acquired through the patronage of Mr. Gardiner, certainly helped matters along between Rosings and Pemberley.

Charlotte Lucas's loss of Mr. Collins was painful only in her fear and her family's worries of her never finding a husband. But due to Miss Lucas's visits to Darcy House in London and some slightly underhanded efforts of Mrs. Darcy, an attachment grew between Charlotte and a brother officer to Colonel Fitzwilliam. True, Northanger Abbey is quite a distance from Hertfordshire, and Captain Tilney might seem a bit wild for Elizabeth's plain friend, but stranger marriages have proven successful, and there was no reason to believe that theirs would be more or less than was expected of such unions of the day.

All in all, the author can report that all lived happily ever after.

Or did they...?

Epilogue

THE MERCHANT SHIP SLOWLY made its way through the gray-blue North Atlantic seas. The winds of March were sharp and cold that mid-day, forcing most of those taking passage to the North American colonies deep below decks. The captain and his crew hurried about at their usual tasks, hardly taking notice of the sole passenger who leaned on the larboard railing, deep in thought. The man was tall, his dark hair whipping in the breeze, his handsome face drawn and grim. His name was George Wickham, late of His Majesty's ——shire militia, and he was sailing to Canada to begin again.

His solitary musings were interrupted by an intruder — a tall, stocky man in black who had just come up from below, his hat pulled down over his head. "May I join you, sir?" he asked Mr. Wickham.

"Stay downwind if you must empty your stomach, if you please," replied he.

"Oh, no, I am not in distress; indeed I have been blessed with a remarkable constitution. It is my custom to take in the fresh air, so beneficial to one's health. I see you share my opinion."

"Actually, the air below was foul." Mr. Wickham looked hard at the man. "Do I know you, sir? You seem familiar."

"My name is Mr. William Collins. And with whom do I have the honor of conversing?"

Mr. Wickham introduced himself. "I remember you now. I met you in a small village in Hertfordshire — Meryton, it was. Yes, it was in the street, not long after I arrived."

Mr. Collins looked at his companion, working his memory. "Yes…I thought you in the militia."

"I thought you a clergyman," Mr. Wickham shot back. "What are you doing here?"

"Sailing for Canada to minister to the heathens."

"A missionary, then." Mr. Wickham narrowed his eyes. "I thought you had a living in Kent from Lady Catherine de Bourgh."

The tall man's face darkened. "I did, I certainly did — but no longer. It was stolen from me!"

"What? It was my understanding that a living was for life."

"I am an innocent victim of circumstance and villainy!" Mr. Collins declared. "I labored unceasingly to minister to the needs of my flock, always taking the advice of my patroness, Lady Catherine de Bourgh — may she rot — into account. My door was open to my parish at all hours. That was my downfall, my good sir. I was too trusting!" He shook his head. "A village girl came, a pretty little thing, seeking spiritual guidance. A young man had made unwelcomed advances, and she feared for her soul. Such tears, such distress! It was my duty to offer comfort in any way I could. She needed and appreciated my attentions, I dare say. No harm was done. I will go to my grave saying that the girl was in a far better humor when she left than when she came."

Mr. Wickham smiled understandingly. "Of course, they usually are. So did her family find out?"

"No, but it seems that the servant provided by my patroness — an evil woman if ever there was one — was under orders to report back to her. Apparently, she made it sound as though I forced myself upon the girl. All rubbish, of course. Indeed, the girl practically threw herself at me! But I was given no chance to defend myself. Lady Catherine — a pox upon her name — summoned me to Rosings a week later to inform me personally that my services were no longer required, that she accepted my resignation, and that I should vacate Hunsford parsonage immediately.

"Of course, I demanded my right to face my accuser as any good Englishman. But my patroness's blasted nephew said that the evidence was undisputable, that he had personally interviewed the girl, and that if I wished to avoid prosecution for assault, I should accept Lady Catherine's generous offer of resignation. I had no choice."

"Nephew?" Mr. Wickham scowled. "Do you mean Darcy?"

"You know the scoundrel, do you?" cried Mr. Collins.

"Unfortunately, I do."

"That devil's spawn was behind it all! In quick order I was commanded to Westminster, for there was an investigation into my ordination. Leading the inquiry was Bishop Darcy, the uncle of the man himself. Was that coincidence? I think not! They accused me of buying my ordination!"

"Did you?"

"Of course, I did! It is done all the time! I had some money my miserly father left me. All those funds gone, and for nothing!" Mr. Collins seethed. "Do you know they sat me in a chair and examined my knowledge of Scripture as if I were a child in Sunday school? It was an insult to my dignity."

"I take it you did not do well."

"Trick questions, all of them! Besides, why should I remember my lessons? Is that not why we have a Bible? This was all a personal vendetta against me by the Darcy family. And do you know why? Because Mr. Darcy wanted the woman I was to marry!"

"Really?" Mr. Wickham was intrigued. "What woman was that?"

"My cousin, Miss Elizabeth Bennet. She was with me the day we met in Meryton."

"Hmm...the lovely blond lady?"

"No, that was her sister, Miss Jane Bennet — now Mrs. Bingley. Miss Elizabeth has brown curly hair and a light and pleasing figure."

"Ah, the one with the fiery eyes! I remember her! Yes, I can see why Darcy wanted her. Too bad, old boy."

"That is not the worst of it," growled Mr. Collins. "At the same time as the investigation into my ordination, Mr. Darcy's lawyers were devising a way to steal Longbourn from me! You see, I was the heir to Miss Elizabeth's family estate. But there was a clause prohibiting immoral conduct in the entail, and Mr. Bennet, assisted by Mr. Darcy's lawyers, was successful in breaking it, using the supposed 'assault' in Hunsford as an example of my so-called 'ethical deficiencies.' I was left with no living and no expectations!

"Therefore, when the bishops in Westminster offered me the choice of suffering defrocking or going on a mission, what real choice had I?"

"So, let me understand you," said Mr. Wickham. "Mr. Darcy managed to steal your living, your inheritance, and your woman."

"That is a fair estimation of the calamity that has befallen me."

Mr. Wickham laughed. "By God, if your story does not sound like mine! It seems you and I are brothers of a sort, for that devil from Derbyshire did the same thing to me!" At Mr. Collins's inquiry, Mr. Wickham related his oft-told tale, which, gentle reader, does not bear repeating here.

"To the devil with Fitzwilliam Darcy!" declared Mr. Collins after Mr. Wickham finished. "But, what are your plans now?"

"Well, I cannot return to England; that is certain. But it matters not. I mean to make my fortune in the New World. And you? Do you still plan to proselytize to the Red Indians?"

"What choice do I have?" Mr. Collins complained. "I cannot eat otherwise. My income is dependent upon the Church."

"Hmm… have you any money?"

Mr. Collins became wary. "A very little. Being a parish priest is not the most lucrative situation in the world. Why do you ask?"

"Ha! I will wager you have more that you say! There is always a little in the poor box, what?"

Mr. Collins could not help but smile. "True. After all, who is a better representative of the 'deserving poor' than I?"

"A man after my own heart!" Mr. Wickham lowered his voice. "My trouble always has been that I had no help. Working by oneself is too hard. But if two clever fellows combined their funds and joined forces —" He waggled his eyebrows.

Mr. Collins smiled. "I begin to comprehend your way of thinking, my dear sir. What do you have in mind?"

Mr. Wickham looked about. "Not here — too many ears. Let us postpone this conversation until we have more privacy. How about a drink, eh? I have a bottle of wine in my trunk. I have been saving it for such an occasion. Let us drink to our partnership!"

Mr. Collins laughed an evil laugh. "Our Lord commands us to enjoy the fruit of the vine, so lead on, George!" He extended his hand.

Mr. Wickham took it. "Billy, I think this is the beginning of a beautiful friendship."

And thus was a notorious fellowship born, ready and willing to reap whatever the New World had to offer.

Oh, Canada!

THE END

About the Author

JACK CALDWELL IS AN AUTHOR, amateur historian, professional economic developer, playwright, and like many Cajuns, a darn good cook. Born and raised in the Bayou County of Louisiana, Jack and his wife, Barbara, are Hurricane Katrina victims who now make the upper Midwest their home.

His nickname — **The Cajun Cheesehead** — came from his devotion to his two favorite NFL teams: the New Orleans Saints and the Green Bay Packers. Always a history buff, Jack found and fell in love with Jane Austen in his twenties, struck by her innate understanding of the human condition. Jack uses his work to share his knowledge of history. Through his characters, he hopes the reader gains a better understanding of what went on before, developing an appreciation for our ancestors' trials and tribulations.

Jack is the author of two Jane Austen-themed books. PEMBERLEY RANCH is a retelling of *Pride & Prejudice* set in Reconstruction Texas. THE THREE COLONELS is a sequel to *Pride & Prejudice* and *Sense & Sensibility*.

When not writing or traveling with Barbara, Jack attempts to play golf. A devout convert to Roman Catholicism, Jack is married with three grown sons.

Jack's blog postings — **The Cajun Cheesehead Chronicles** — appear regularly at **austenauthors.net**.

Other Novels by Jack Caldwell

Available now from Sourcebooks Landmark:
PEMBERLEY RANCH
THE THREE COLONELS — *Jane Austen's Fighting Men*

Coming soon from White Soup Press:
THE COMPANION OF HIS FUTURE LIFE
ROSINGS PARK
THE LAST ADVENTURE OF THE SCARLET PIMPERNEL
PERSUADED TO SAIL

THE CRESCENT CITY SERIES:
THE PLAINS OF CHALMETTE — *a prequel to Crescent City*
BOURBON STREET NIGHTS — *Volume One of Crescent City*
ELYSIAN DREAMS — *Volume Two of Crescent City*
RUIN AND RENEWAL — *Volume Three of Crescent City*

Printed in Great Britain
by Amazon.co.uk, Ltd.,
Marston Gate.